TO KILL A

BLUEBLOOD

A Dak Donahue Novel

STEVE DWIGHT NICHOLS

This book is a work of fiction and the product of the author's imagination. Names, characters, places, events, incidents, business entities, religious entities, and organizations are used fictitiously. Any resemblance to actual places, organizations, business entities, religious entities, incidents, or persons is entirely coincidental.

Books

Murder and the Preacher's Wife

The Sinner's Reckoning

The Good Samaritans

The Last Revelation: The Beginning of the End

The Inception War

Tanger Gold

To Kill a Blueblood

An Angel Never Prays

A Demon Never Prays

Prologue

"The stomach wound is fatal. Your arrogance and pride have killed you. You should have waited for General Redman and his men to arrive and assist with killing me. You now can try and run from us, but the outcome is certain. You have ten minutes tops. Your stomach acid will leak into your belly region and pollute your other organs. You are a standing dead man. I demand you tell me where your master is hiding before you die."

Chapter 1

Veronica tried to force her eyes open. She could smell the unpleasant unfamiliar odor. She tried to remember where she had smelled the fragrance. Her mind was slow to respond and playing tricks on her. She tried to focus and force herself to wake up. She thought back to her childhood and remembered the burlap bag full of old clothing stored in the woodshed. The horrible odor overwhelmed her when she picked the burlap bag up from the ground. The mildew odor instigated by the moisture build up over time and the burlap material never escaped her memory.

The material rubbed against her face when she took a breath. She once again tried to open her eyes a second time. Her eyes lids were too heavy and would not respond. Her brain could not force her eyes open. She felt as if her eyelids were glued shut. She could feel the urgency to wake. Her body felt uncomfortable, full of fear, and dread.

She felt the movement and rocking of her body. She tried to secure another breath, but something was blocking her mouth. She struggled to secure a full breath. She tried to move her right hand to her face, and her wrist was being held and would not move. She tried her left hand and likewise the left wrist would not move. Something was keeping her from moving either hand. She tried to wake up. She tried to force her eyes open. She hated the smell.

She felt the sudden jerk. The fear she felt caused her entire body to shiver with dread as adrenaline surged through her body. Her eyes suddenly opened as fear streamed through her consciousness. The view was dark with something blocking her vision. She pulled hard with both her arms, and neither hand could be brought from behind her to her face to remove the material blocking her vision. Her brain slowly understood her situation. She realized she was tied with both hands behind her back as she struggled to breathe through the burlap bag. Her emotions were running rampant as she tried to focus. Veronica tried to recall her last thought before she lost consciousness. She gasped with fear as she remembered the skinned bodies hanging from the tree limbs at least twenty feet above the ground with their organs and blood in piles below in the weeds. She gasped desperately for another breath of air as she then recalled the monster appearing from behind the rancher's lifeless body with a demonic expression. He was hideous with tattoos, a nose piercing, and eyes cold as the devil's. Her fear spiked as she tried to recall what happened next.

Her entire body froze with fright as she recalled how the monster fought her. She should have won the fight and now she was here restrained in this burlap bag. He had bested her. She now realized the rocking was waves in the ocean, and she was on a boat. What had happened? She tried to move her wrists and legs and could not. Somehow, she had been tied up and placed in this burlap bag. Her mind was slow to respond to her urgent needs. Her entire body was lethargic. She wondered if she had been drugged.

Veronica thought about her options to escape. She tried to recall exactly what happened. Her mind drifted. Would her friends come to rescue her? She then realized her friends were in a rush to cross the mountains and transport King Solman's stolen gold north over a thousand miles to Cliff Tops. Her friends would not miss her for several days.

She remembered Hulk's expression when she said she would return the wagon to the men at the shoreline. He obviously did not agree with her. Dak finally gave the okay and off she rode taking the wagon with her horse in tow. She wanted to see the young man she had just met one last time. She thought about his good looks and how he handled himself. She gasped, then realized he must be one of the four skinned men hanging from the tree.

The noise came from above her. Two men were yelling about changing the sails, so they could head south faster. She recognized their accent to be from the west coast similar to Zenith's. Through the burlap bag, she could tell the light of the day by looking upward through the cabin door. She realized she was in the cabin of a sailboat heading south. She tried to swallow, but her throat was too dry to create saliva. She laid still trying to hear other people. She again tried to move her feet and hands. She then heard someone move from inside the cabin and felt the sudden kick in her low back from the boot and the harsh tone, "Stop moving, or I will gut you like a fish and hang you alive from the stern of this vessel for all to see."

The accent scared her more than the kick to the back. The tone was a harsh deep accent from another part of the world. She then heard footsteps coming down the stairs. She tried to hold her breath and absorb the pain in her back. "We are moving at maximum speed. We should be to port in two days. I assure you my men will do all they can to get you to Southern City safely and fast as possible. Did she wake?"

Veronica thought, "Two days to be in Southern City. They are taking me to King Solman. I will never see my family and friends. How could I have been so stupid? All this over a crush on a man I just met."

The man with the accent reached down and placed her over his shoulder. He was not concerned with being gentle, "Since you seem to be worried about this low life, you can take care of her."

Veronica's breath was knocked out of her as she was thrown across his shoulder. She gasped for her next breath and could feel the bounce where she laid across his shoulder as he ascended five stairs from the cabin to the deck. He dropped her near the mast and cut the string holding the burlap bag closed. He immediately pulled the bag down to her waist and pushed her to her side as he removed the rope around her hands. He quickly tied her wrists to the pole.

Veronica first had to adjust her eyesight to the bright sunlight. She squinted and blinked her eyes several times as she was being tied to the mast of the vessel. She ducked her face to avoid the sun. She then looked at the three men watching her as she was restrained to the pole. They stared at her without moving or saying a word. She glanced down and realized she was nude with only the burlap bag covering her waist and lower extremities.

The monster was not gentle. The ropes cut into her wrists as he secured her tightly to the large main mast in the middle of the sailing vessel. Veronica felt a small amount of relief as she heard him walk back to the cabin door and descend the stairs into the cabin behind her. The older man who appeared to be the captain suddenly was standing by her side. "Here, drink this cool water." He held the container and eased the water into her mouth.

He pulled the cup away and looked at her. "More, please."

He held her chin up and poured the remaining water into her mouth. "Get her some more water and some food." Veronica saw one of the men walk quickly to the back of the ship.

"Who is he?"

"His name is Damon. He appeared at the dock carrying you in the burlap bag. He poured several ears and tongues out of a smaller bag on our deck and exclaimed, if we did not do as he said, our ears and tongues would fit in his bag. We are not fighters. We believe he will kill us if we do not do as he says." The man looked scared as he glanced toward the cabin door.

She rolled her eyes to make eye contact, "He will kill all of you anyway. Damon is a monster. He is a psychopathic killer. Can you help me?" She hesitated to mention that Damon was a Blueblood renegade warrior. If she mentioned he was a Blueblood, they would fear him more than they already did and be reluctant to assist her.

The man looked around and then looked at the other man approaching. As he leaned forward, Veronica noticed the Christian Cross attached to a silver necklace as it slid out from under his shirt. He whispered, "Here is more water and some chicken we ate earlier today. He will kill us if we do not do as he says."

"Is he not a slave trader? Does he not deal in the trade of flesh?"

The captain looked at Veronica and considered the question. "Most of the slave traders are located on the Asian continent. Some of those slave traders choose to sail into Southern City and deal with King Solman. I do not deal in the trade of the flesh. The slave traders I have seen do not kill their cargo. This man is a killer of men, and the trip concerns me that he has ordered us to take you both to Southern City. There is nothing good that happens in Southern City. The city is known as the city of sin. If the slaves are lucky, they are processed and then taken to Merlin to work the fields for the Blueblood people. The unlucky male slaves are forced to work in the chain gangs or fight as soldiers. The women are…." He never finished his sentence. He looked at Veronica with pity and said, "I am truly sorry."

The man took the small piece of cooked chicken from the out-reached hand of the other man and placed the small piece to her lips. He looked at Veronica with a compassionate expression. As he held the chicken for her to eat, she chewed as much food as she could. Her hunger pains and thirst were tormenting her. He gave her additional water and then several additional bites of food. "Do not provide my prisoner with good food," Damon commanded as he approached. "She will die soon."

The captain was short, with sturdy built and strong looking hands, shoulders, and arms. She considered if she could convince the man to fight for her or at least cut her loose. Veronica then remembered Damon, and realized if these men fought him, the fight would be futile. She could tell the men would be no match in a fight with Damon. She remembered how she had fought Damon and lost. She knew in order to kill a renegade Blueblood; she would need several things to go her way. She recalled the glimpse of his one ear when they fought and knew he was a Rogue Blueblood. Only Blueblood people had pointed ears. If the crew saw him without his hood, they would know who he was. Asking the crew to fight for her would be asking them to die.

She now noticed Damon walked with a slight limp on his left leg as he came back out of the cabin, and he looked at the three men. The men stood up and walked backward as Damon approached. "It is not wise to waste good food on a dead person. I am going to cut her into small pieces after I have skinned and fileted her. Her time is short," he snarled and glared at the three men.

She could tell the fourth sailor was manning the rudder as the ship was turning in the ocean waves. She also noticed they were sailing directly into the sun heading south, parallel with the southern part of the continent. She tried to peer over the rail of the ship as the waves rolled the vessel up and down. She could see the outlines of mountains miles away in the far eastern horizon. She now accepted no one was going to help her.

The sun was hot and bright, beaming down on her sitting upright with her arms tied behind her on the deck of the boat. The heat made her uncomfortable, but the constant wind helped make her conditions bearable.

Damon walked closer and with one quick movement of his right hand, he reached down and quickly yanked the burlap bag from under her and pulled the bag over her feet. She stared at him defiantly as she now was nude sitting with her hands tied behind her, in front of the four sailors and Damon. Damon stepped backward close to ten feet and quickly pulled a small knife from his robe and threw the knife with force, sticking the knife in the deck between her knees. His actions and speed with the knife were so fast Veronica had no time to react. She gasped at the knife stuck in the deck so close to her inner thighs. Damon smiled and walked forward then bent down and pulled his knife from the deck and stared into her eyes.

Veronica felt he was looking into her soul as she was so afraid she was paralyzed to move as he stared without blinking. "She is my enemy. She does not deserve to be treated with dignity. She deserves to be treated like an unwanted dog." He pulled his knife from the deck, stood, and carried the burlap bag into the cabin of the boat.

Veronica noticed the limp caused by her kick to his left knee and wondered how his knee had healed itself. She recalled the hard punch to his ribs. He showed no sign of being in pain. She turned to the captain, "How long have I been out?"

The captain could see the fear in Veronica's expression and eyes. "He carried you to the dock three days ago. We believe he gave you a drug to force you to sleep. We have been at sea heading south for two days. We wondered if you would ever gain consciousness. I placed a suture over your right ear and tied your hair together, pushing the cut in your scalp together to stop the bleeding." The captain motioned for the other man to provide her additional food and water. The captain turned to Veronica, "We do not want this kind of trouble. We are traders. We agreed to drop the two of you off in Southern City, and then we will sail back north."

Veronica looked at the captain, "I am also a Christian. We were taught where I am from that most of the Christians in the world were killed in the Transitional Period and very few men or women of Christ were still alive." She stared at the captain, "I am like Daniel as stated in the Holy Bible when King Darius ordered Daniel thrown into the lion's den to be eaten alive. You know what they are going to do to me in Southern City. I will be sold into slavery."

"The prophet Habakkuk requested the help of an angel to provide Daniel food while he was in the pit. You will need to keep your faith just as God's chosen people have done. God took care of the Jewish people because they kept the faith. I am sorry for your troubles. However, your troubles are not our troubles. I have been blessed by our Lord to have survived the Transitional Period with my two sons. I must protect my family. You are right. He will kill all of us if I do not do as he says. My two sons are all I have, and I will not sacrifice them."

Veronica was surprised the captain was aware of the point of apocalyptic literature in the book of Daniel. If the Lord's people keep their faith, the Lord will restore the Jewish people from being slaves, to a self-governing tribe. She knew she could not sentence these men to a certain death asking them to release her. She thought back to the church and the preacher trying to convey the meaning of the books of the Bible to her class growing up. He would often say all the books of the Bible are part of the Bible for a reason and the goal of a Christian is to understand the reason. She also recalled when in need, people turned to their God for help, but the preacher would say we need to always turn to God. Veronica bowed her head and said her silent prayer, "Lord. Please forgive me of my sins. Please watch over these Christian sailors. Please give me the fortitude to do your work and kill this devil named Damon for he will kill again. Amen."

Chapter 2

Dak knew he had pushed the horses and men to the limit.
The horse ride had been brutal ascending the mountains. They
had to walk and lead their horses for miles at a time because
the mountains were so steep and rugged. They blindfolded the
horses in one section on a narrow ledge to prevent the horses
from being able to look down at the five-hundred-foot drop
into a gorge. Hulk had been the first to cross pulling his horse
while holding tightly to the rope around the neck. Each person
causally walked his horse through the peril's areas. If the
animal got spoked while on the ledge, the horse and the gold
would plummet to the bottom of the mountain. The top of the
mountain ranges had very little foliage and were covered in
rock bluffs and steep rock embankments with sporadic patches
of white neve. The escaped Normand sailors looked as if they
could collapse at any moment. The gap in the final mountain
range had been more than a seven-thousand-foot incline with a
rough passage through the patches of neve and underbrush.
They had forged a trail through the mountains by following the
ridge line into the large main mountain range. Hulk checked
the air every thirty minutes for nuclear contamination and tried
to find the easiest path. The mountains had been formed when

the earth had shifted seventeen years prior in the Transition
Period. Looking across the mountains, they could see the
woody areas covered in small trees and thick bushes below the
elevation of five-thousand feet. The climate changed from
warm too cold with high winds as they ascended to the top of
the mountains. Dak wanted to cross the mountains before the
weather plummeted and a large snow fell blocking the passage.

Dak glanced behind him at Trey and Tommy Boy. They
both looked tired. He could see Robin Hood several yards
behind them bringing up the rear of the group as he rode up the
steep incline. He could see the pain in Ronny's eyes as he was
sitting on his horse. Dak yelled, "We camp here."

Hulk heard the command and rode over toward Dak. Hulk
dismounted. He bent over trying to stretch his back and leg
muscles. He was tired, and he knew his horse was about to give
out. Hulk walked over to Dak as he was dismounting. "This is
not a choice spot to camp. We cannot take cover from the
freezing wind." He looked at Dak with a questioning look.
"The temperature will drop below freezing tonight."

Dak turned to his friend. "The horses need rest. If we keep
pushing them any further, we will have to carry this gold on
our backs and leave the horses for dead. We can set the tents
up below the east ridge to block the constant wind. Besides, the
temperature is already below freezing. We have crossed or

went around several small glaziers. Now, let's get a camp set up and find some food. We will need to place blankets over the horses. Everyone will need to seek the shelter of their tents and warm clothing tonight." He looked at the four sailors and Hershel. He knew they were hurting from no rest and the hard trip. Dak then turned and looked at Hulk, "The sailors are not accustomed to this pace. They need to rest. They are not as strong as we are. I must believe the weather will stay clear tonight, and we can descend the mountains tomorrow. I do not want to get stranded with this gold in these mountains."

Hulk started to mention the horses could freeze, and they needed to descend at least below the six thousand feet in elevation but decided against the remark. He looked at Dak knowing he was aware of the risk. He commanded, "Okay, we set the camp here on the east side of the ridge behind these boulders out of the wind."

Tommy Boy rode his horse to Dak's position, "Not one foot further. This horse is about dead carrying me and this gold up this mountain." He dismounted and rubbed the horse as he then removed the bridle and gave his horse a treat.

Trey dismounted. He looked around and noticed the wide area in the trail. "These mountains are tough, and my horse is spent. We need to feed them and allow them to rest. If we push them much more, we will have to kill them. They may not be able to recover from this hard ride."

Zenith had been traveling with the guys for weeks. She had picked up on their sayings. She was a full Blueblood borne in Merlin after the Transitional Period and able to ride longer, eat less, and endure the strenuous physical activity. She stopped the horse and smiled, "That mountain was a ball buster."

Hulk smiled. He knew Zenith heard the guys say that phrase several times over the past few weeks, "Why do you not look tired? Hell, I am tired, Dak is tired, and all the others are broken down."

Trey smiled, "My horse is broken down from carrying my three-hundred-pound ass up this mountain. I am a little tired, but damn, Zenith, you do not look tired at all."

"Zenith is a Blueblood. She does not get tired," announced Dak.

Dak looked at his friends and the other men who had joined them. "We will be going downhill tomorrow. The trip should be easier on the horses. We need to get these bags of gold north to Zenith Point as soon as possible." The four sailors dismounted and laid the gold on the ground. They were too tired to move their aching bodies as they drank some water. Tommy Boy took each of their horses and tied them off and fed them.

Dak noticed his beautiful wife and her smile. Zenith smiled at the name of their home and the fact her home was named after her. "I am homesick, and I miss my two boys."

Hulk looked at Zenith, "You do not have to worry about those two kids. I can promise you they are getting all the attention they need from the people in Cliff Tops. My Mom will love to hold them and spoil them."

Ronny was lying on the frozen ground. Ronny was one of the few men that survived the Transitional Period with a history of sailing vessels. He was taken as a slave by the Normand army and once they realized he was a sailor he was transferred to a ship. The captain of the ship realized his abilities and promoted him to lieutenant. He was later captured by Dak and his men. Ronny had no love for the Normand army and agreed to work for Dak. He looked at Dak, "What is the plan? Me and the boys would like to know what your intentions are. We held up our part of the bargain. We sank the ship and helped you take the Normand gold."

Dak looked at the four sailors. He knew without them they could not have pulled off the heist. He also knew they were not accustomed to riding horses. They had been sailors in the Normand army for the past few years. "You men deserve to be paid for your work. We could not have taken this gold without you. Once we arrive at the bottom of these mountains, we can split up. You will each be very well compensated for your work. However, you might want to stay with us. There are several bandit groups in the area. I left men in charge to try to unite the groups against King Solman. They will face adversity trying to force these groups to trust each other and fight as one army against the common enemy. If they kind out you have gold and were sailors in the Normand army, you will be killed and your gold stolen."

Darnel, the smallest and youngest of the sailors, looked at Dak, "I am having trouble breathing at this altitude."

Zenith announced all of you will need to drink plenty of water. The horses will need to be feed well and drink plenty of water. We can resupply ourselves tomorrow."

Ronny asked, "How much are we going to be paid?"

Dak looked at the men lying on the frozen ground. "Each one of you will get seven pounds of gold coins. That will be enough for each one of you to never have to work. You can go and buy your own town or ship."

Hulk added, "Or your own whore house." He then looked at Zenith and placed his hand over his mouth, "Pardon my French." The group all laughed.

The sailors all looked relieved. Sneedy smiled, "I will take the coins. I am going to buy a ship and enter the shipping business. My ship will carry supplies back and forth along the eastern side of the continent. I do not want to get too close to the Asian continent. That is where all the pirates are located."

Hulk looked at the sailors while smiling, "What do you mean you do not want to get close to pirates? You all are pirates." He held up his bag of gold. The group laughed.

Ronny looked at his men and then at Dak. "Thank you for being fair with us. You seem to be rushed. Do you anticipate having to fight some bandits as we cross the continent?"

Dak looked at the group, "We cannot tell anyone about what we are hauling. If word gets out, every cutthroat within seven-hundred miles will be after us. In addition, I expect King Solman will send spies to locate this gold. Then, he will send an army to retrieve it. There is enough here to buy an army. I would be surprised if he has not already posted reward money for our heads."

Hulk said, "He will have to figure out who stole the gold first before he comes after us. If we start spending this gold, The gold will be traced back to us. Be smart about how each of you spend your share." He looked at Sneedy, "If you buy a ship, you need to make certain the gold cannot be traced back to you. You will need to use a middleman. Dak is right. King Solman will send assassins to kill the pirates that took his gold."

Zenith looked at Dak, "Maybe we should do just the opposite and spend a lot of the gold. Spread the gold out all over the continent. Then, they will not be able to recover it and also, we will not need to worry about them tracing the gold back to us. He will know who took his gold."

Dak looked at Zenith, "We could make friends with the people. We will need them to fight with us. That is exactly what we will do, but first, we need to move north before someone steals the gold from us. Now everyone, we need to eat and sleep. I suspect we will have to fight to keep this gold. We can talk further in the morning but now we need to get warm by a fire." He looked at his friends hoping they would take the hint and start a fire.

***

Hulk sat back and finished eating his dinner. Trey had shot a mountain goat while they ascended the mountains in the thick underbrush on the last ridge line before they reached the steep part of the mountain. He looked over at Dak, "It seems like yesterday growing up. We were concerned who would catch the biggest fish in our tournament, or who could do the most push-ups. Everything we did growing up seems like it was a competition."

Dak looked over at his friend as he was wrapped up in his large fur coat, "Time has flown by these last couple of years. I am now with two sons and two half-sisters who are a few days younger than my boys. I have been in two large battles and killed several men. I have traveled across this continent from one end to the other." He looked over at Tommy Boy and Trey. He then placed his hand on Zenith's shoulder, "I hope we are not making mistakes."

Trey looked at Dak, "Mistakes? What do you mean?"

Robin Hood sat down, "I know I have made some mistakes. I wish I could remember that red head's name with the big boobs back in Homestead." The group laughed.

Zenith was staring into the fire, "Dak, what is on your mind?"

Dak cleared his throat, "Zenith, when we were growing up, we would sometimes listen to the stories about the old ways before the Transition Period. I am not certain the old country, the United States, was the best form of government. The rich got richer and did not pay their share of the tax. I recall Mr. Grant explaining before he passed away the difference between a millionaire and billionaire. There are less than twelve days in a million seconds, and there are eleven-thousand-five-hundred-seventy-five days in a billion seconds which is a little more than thirty-one years, yet the country did not recognize the difference between a millionaire and a billionaire. The billionaires did not pay their share of the taxes.

"The second problem was that only seven-hundred votes mattered, and they were cast by the congress, who established the laws. All the individual votes during the general election did not matter. The federally elected officials, once elected to office, became extremely wealthy being paid by the special interest groups for votes. The special interest groups also funded the election campaign for the congressmen they approved."

Tommy Boy looked at Dak, "So far, your mother, being the queen of our city, has tried to be the best leader. I believe the monarchy is the best form of leadership as long as the king or queen is fair. That has worked best for our tribe. We will support you as the king when the time comes."

Zenith said, "Generally speaking, I do not believe there is a perfect form of government, because at some point, someone is placed in a leadership position either by civil war or dishonesty. The leader will have character flaws. The civil war in my hometown of Merlin did not end well for the righteous and honest citizens. There were those who really tried to do good, and they were all rounded up and killed. The power seems to always follow the wicked."

Hulk spoke, "I recall how Wayne explained in the old world, in the United States, the elected officials were manipulated at first and agreed to certain concessions with the special interest groups. He explained the process was the lure of female prostitutes, male prostitutes, money, stock options, insider trading tips, and land deals. The many benefits were extended to the family members like the kids and then the benefit could not be tracked by the police. One son of a president was paid to be on another countries nuclear program, and the son knew nothing about nuclear power. A daughter of another president purchased a twenty-four-million-dollar home when she was in her early twenties and never worked a day in her life. The elected officials might have agreed at first with the political issue, so why not take a payment. Then, once the official took a payment, they were on the hook. Soon they started voting for the special interest groups and against the political position they campaigned. This went on for decades with the newly elected congress all being enticed by those deep-pocketed groups. If the congressmen voted against the special interest group or groups, they were not reelected because the special interest groups would fund the opposition."

Dak looked into the fire, "The hearts of men are full of sin. Mankind cannot escape the seven cardinal sins no matter how hard we try." He looked at his friends, "We can only do what we as individuals believe is right. I believe in each of you, my friends. We now need to sleep. We have a long day ahead of us." He looked at Ronny and his men, "This might be the coldest night you men have ever faced. The temperature might reach as low as thirty below. You will need to stay undercover in your tents. You will be cold, but you will be okay. We will reach warmer conditions tomorrow."

The group stared into the fire and were contemplating the topic as the wind chill started dropping. The sun had already set in the western horizon.

Chapter 3

Veronica was tired of being tied up. She could not position her body to be comfortable to sleep during the night and during the day, she elected to try to stay awake to observe her surroundings. She might only have one opportunity to escape, and she knew she needed to take the chance. Her muscles were aching from having to sit in the same position. At first, the sailors would glance at her sitting naked on the deck of the boat. She could tell they were sexually interested in her, but after two days, they seemed to accept her being tied below deck at night and tied on the deck in the hot sun during the day. There had not been a cloud in the sky during the voyage. If she moved her legs and her skin rubbed the hot deck, the sting from the heat of touching the deck was noticeable. The captain provided an old rag for her to sit on, and the sailors from time to time would retrieve a bucket of ocean water using a rope from the side of the vessel and carry the cool water to her and pour the bucket of water on her. They also would sneak her drinking water and small amounts of food when Damon walked below deck. She was thankful they helped her. They feared Damon and worried about their arrangement with him. She knew they were asking themselves, "Will Damon kill us when we are done?" There was no doubt in her mind Damon had been genetically enhanced and must have been an expelled psychopathic Blueblood from the pods out of Germany. He always kept his hood on covering his ears. She recalled the conversations with Samuel. Bluebloods like Damon had a master, and Damon did the bidding of his master. She knew to survive the boat ride, she needed to avoid conversation with Damon. She could sense he would cut out her tongue or worse. He seemed to be in constant torment with himself struggling not to kill her and the sailors. Just being in close contact with humans seemed to make him anxious.

When he would sit on the deck of the boat, he would sharpen one of his three knives and sword with the constant hissing sound of the blades being pulled across the flint stone. She could hear the continuous rub of the knife blade as he pulled the blade across his flint stone for hours at a time. He spoke to himself in such a low tone, she could not discern what he was saying. She could hear him constantly mumbling the same rhyme. He also would stand back from the cabin door and practice throwing one of his knives into the door while he repeated the whispering phrase only, he could hear. After he threw his knife for a few minutes, he would then sit still and concentrate on the task of sharpening his blades. She had known an autistic child once, and Damon seemed to have some of the same characteristics. The only difference was that Damon was full of hatred with no ability to have empathy for others and was a psychotic killer. The sound of the continuous rub of the knife blade as he pulled the blade across his flint stone for hours at a time, was tormenting for her to listen. She was aware at any point he could snap and kill her. She had no choices but to listen and pray. The four sailors tried to stay on the other side of the boat and would only whisper so as not to be heard by Damon.

On the third day, Veronica could see the port and heard the young sailor yell in an excited tone to the rest of the sailors that they were close. She could tell the sailors were anxious and happy to make the trip to Southern City, which was located at the most southern point of the continent. After the Transitional Period, the southern point was at the thirty-fifth parallel, located at the halfway point of the old country called Argentina. She had heard them talk during the trip that they had been previously to the Southern City port and had not liked trading with the Normand Army. The captain walked by her and poured the cool ocean water on her. He bent down next to Veronica, "I wish you luck. I hope they provide you mercy. From one Christian to another, I wish we could have helped you. We all prayed for you. You need to be like Job as noted in the Bible and not give up on your situation and never give up on our Lord. I believe the Lord will protect you but that does not mean you will not be tested." Damon walked toward the captain. His two sons looked concerned as they watched their father talking to Veronica. The two sons then walked toward their father and Veronica.

The youngest son asked Damon, "What has she done to be your enemy?"

Damon stopped and looked at the youngest sailor. Veronica sensed Damon was surprised by the question. He hesitated and then looked at the captain and then the young son, "She was born, and that is enough. She also knows information about the rebels which she will tell me once I start the interrogation. Now, do not concern yourselves with her anymore. She acts like she is innocent and knows nothing." He held his knife pointing at her, "She will confess all to me."

Veronica visualized she was going to die in vain. She thought back to Damon leaving the four men hanging in the tree. "I know you are a Blueblood renegade warrior from the old German Country. The mad scientist that created you was also insane." She looked at the deck of the ship. She knew she should not antagonize him, but now she was sitting in the port of Southern City, she hoped for a quick death.

"I will show them how I treat the adversary. I will start by cutting your breast off." He reached down with his knife.

The captain stepped toward her in a panicked tone, "Not on my ship. We had an agreement for us to deliver both of you to Southern City. We will not sit back and watch you mutilate this female."

"I will kill you also. I do not need you."

Veronica knew he would kill the four men. "You need these men to tie the vessel off at the dock. They are good men. They have lived up to their bargain. You should not kill them. King Solman would not want these men killed. He needs traders like these men to bring him and his city supplies." The captain and his youngest son looked at Damon with concerned expressions. The other son and the older man walked closer toward the group ready to fight.

She then heard the older son yell for Damon to move away from her side and put away the knife. The captain hurried to the rear of the boat and took control of the rudder and asked one of the other sailors to adjust the front sails. "Please. We will get you to the dock. We do not need to see any bloodshed." The older son pulled his knife from the inside pocket of his shirt.

Damon looked at the men and considered the situation. He leaned down and slowly cut the rope holding her ankles and then cut the rope holding her hands behind her and the boat mast. He then tied her hands behind her back and placed his knife back into the leather holster. She was pulled to her feet by Damon, and he forced the large burlap bag over her head. "I can assure everyone that you do not know what Solman desires. He will not be gentle like I am. His knives are all dull and cause pain when they cut through bone." He forced her down on her side and pulled the cord tight, tying the bag shut with her inside as he glanced at the two sons and the one ship mate while he talked.

***

Veronica felt the momentum of the boat stop as the deck vibrated when the hull gently collided with the dock. She heard the sailors talking about tying off to the dock. The heat from lying in the sun in the burlap bag while waiting for them to reach the final few hundred yards of the journey had been torture. She was relieved when she felt the bag being lifted as Damon carried her over his shoulder off the boat. She did not dare move or cry out. She was afraid she might die on the deck of the boat from heat exhaustion. Her thirst and hunger tormented her as she tried not to consider her pain.

Damon carried her through the city and up several stairs. During the walk, she could hear people moving out of Damon's path and his heavy breathing. He smelled of sweat and not being cleaned in days. She heard him open a door, and then he dropped her to the floor inside a room. Again, he was not gentle. He cut the rope and pulled the burlap sack off her as she lay motionless on the stone floor suffering from near heat exhaustion. He threw the bag to the floor in the corner of the room, and he quickly cut the rope in the middle restraining her hands from behind her and stood on the rope ends. She tried to pull her hands in front of her but his weight on the rope ends was too much. He then reached down and pulled her left arm up to him and placed a leather cuff around her wrist. He then did the same with her right hand. The cuffs were secured to a chain attached to the hook in the ceiling and ran through an iron peg bolted to the stone wall. She looked down at the floor next to where she had been laying and noticed blood stains on the stone floor where people had been tied and tortured, no doubt, to death.

Damon walked to the wall and pulled the chain tight as she was forced to be lifted off the stone floor hanging by her wrists. At first, the pain was excruciating as the leather cuffs cut into her wrists while she swung back and forth. She clenched her jaws and gritted her teeth and fought off the need to yell in pain. Damon released the chain, and when her feet barely touched the floor, he hooked the chain to the peg on the wall. He smiled at Veronica, making eye contact with a diabolic glare and walked toward her as he pulled his knife. He acted as if he might cut her in the midsection with his curved knife, but instead he kneeled and cut the rope holding her ankles together.

Damon walked behind Veronica and sat down. He pulled his small knife from the hidden holster under his shirt and started sharpening his blade, mumbling to himself. Veronica tried to turn her upper body to look at Damon over her shoulder. She saw him with the blade rubbing over the flint rock sitting in a wooden chair. She noticed all the walls, floor and ceiling were made of concrete and stone. After a few seconds, the large wooden door burst open, and two guards came walking into the room. They stared at Veronica chained to the ceiling. They glanced at Damon. The two guards were big men and appeared to be rough and cruel jailors. The smaller one commanded, "Who is she? What is this about?"

The larger guard then added, "She must go through the clerk and master station before being jailed. Who are you to bring someone into my jailhouse?"

"This is none of your concern." She noticed Damon stopped sharpening his blade. She heard him stand and with a flash of quickness. Damon was standing next to the big guard with his knife positioned at his throat. Damon's smile was demonic, and his jaw was clenched, "Like I said, this is none of your concern. I will cut your head off. You two need to leave and order Solman to come here at once. I demand his presence."

Veronica could see the small amount of blood trickle down the guard's neck under the knife blade and the fear in the guard's eyes. She noticed the demonic look in Damon's expression and thought he was just waiting for a reason to kill the guard. The other guard started to pull his sword in an attempt to protect his partner. Damon looked at the smaller man, "Go ahead and pull that sword, and before your sword is out of the sleeve, his head will hit the floor, and your's will be next." The moment she thought Damon was going to slice his throat, the door opened and in walked another man. This man looked clean, well shaven, with well-manicured hands and a dark suntanned complexion. He stood close to six-feet-four inches and was athletic looking. He walked softly with confidence. He was handsome and rich looking. He waved his right hand and casually announced, "Let him go. You two may leave." Veronica looked at the man and noticed he was not carrying a sword or a knife, but he commands others.

Without hesitating, the one guard started walking toward the door. The other guard did not move as Damon held his knife at his throat and stared into his eyes. The third man noticed Damon had not removed his knife. "Please let my guard go. I do not have time for this." The man then proceeded to walk around in front of Veronica and stared at her nude body. The guard was released, and he quickly headed for the open door while wiping blood from his neck. The third man then slowly completed a circle while looking at Veronica. Damon sat down and started sharpening his knife. The man stood several inches taller than her. She lifted her head and looked at him as he reappeared in front of her. She accepted her doom. She was going to be tortured. There was only one outcome. She prayed in silence for a quick death. She tried to look strong in the face of death.

"Where are you from?" He smiled at her as he stared at her. He then allowed his eyes to scan her entire nude body as she was standing on her toes. He could tell her wrists were in pain from the leather cuffs rubbing against her lower arms.

She could hardly talk. Her throat was dry. She tried to say something, and the words would not come out. He walked over to a bucket of water and dipped a cup into the pail. She noticed that Damon, sitting behind her, had stopped sharpening his knife. The room was quiet and hot. The man walked over to her, gently lifted her chin and poured some water into her mouth. He waited for her to swallow. They made eye contact, and he then poured additional water into her mouth until the cup was empty. "Thank you." She struggled to stand on her toes with her wrist bound above her. She knew she could not stand much longer, but she also knew the pain caused by hanging by her wrist would be unbearable.

"You are welcome." He walked over to the bucket and retrieved another cup of water.

Damon demanded, "No. You will spoil my prisoner. She deserves to be in pain. Pain is a good thing for her."

The man did not hesitate and walked in front of Veronica. He held the cup of water in front of her. "I asked you a question."

Veronica looked him in the eyes. "You know where I am from. The army from this city declared war on my people. I am from Cliff Tops, and we, in turn, declared war on King Solman and his army of death."

"Where is the stolen gold?"

Veronica thought about making up a story, but she knew she was going to be tortured. She knew they already knew the answer. "The gold will be taken to Cliff Tops. The Northern army needs the gold to purchase an army. The gold will be used to wage war against you. They had wished to steal your ship and sink two of your warships, but the hijackers discovered the gold."

The man looked at Damon, "See, I know where she is from, and where the gold is located by asking nicely." He looked back at her.

Damon appeared next to her with his knife sticking with the blade against her left side, under her rib cage. She could feel the sharp blade against her skin. "Since you now know everything, you need to know I will kill her."

"No. I need additional information." The man looked concerned at Damon.

Damon looked through her eyes into her soul. Veronica knew she was going to die. The man reached and grasped Damon's arm that was holding the knife and pulled backward. Damon quickly, with his other hand, produced another knife from his robe and pushed the man backward against the wall with the knife pressing against his throat. "How dare you stop me. How dare you touch me." The door opened and in walked two guards with their swords pulled.

"You know I am in charge. You know what your master would want you to do, and that is to listen to me. We are on the same side, and I outrank you. The master would desire for me to take charge of the prisoner." He held his hand out and waved a signal for his guards to move backward.

In the background a horn blew. The man then said, "That harbor horn alerts the sailors that the boat leaves in twenty minutes. They will not wait on you. You need to be on that merchant ship heading north." Damon lowered his knife. The guards backed up and allowed him to walk out. The man straightened his shirt and walked over to the wall and released the chain holding Veronica from the hook in the ceiling. She immediately fell to the floor. "Take her to be cleaned up, fed, and appropriately clothed and then bring her to my chambers for dinner at 8 p.m." He turned and walked out of the room.

The one guard bent down and released the cuffs and snarled, "Get up and walk, or we will drag you by your hair."

Veronica tried to stand. She placed both feet under her and tried to steady her balance. The guard motioned for her to walk toward the door. She instead walked over to the small table and crammed a small amount of bread in her mouth. She then drank another cup of water. She placed additional bread into her mouth and then drank more water before giving herself time to swallow the bread. Some of the water dripped down her chin onto her belly. The guards watched and then motioned her to the door. She followed one guard, and the second guard fell in behind her. There were four additional guards standing in the hall. The group walked down the interior stairs and out a double door. When she first stepped outside into the sunlight, she noticed the wave of dry heat. She was forced to squint her eyes and place her right hand over her eyes to adjust to the bright sunlight. The city was located at the southern tip of the continent where the climate was hot and dry. There were several men and women who stood back and watched the group pass as they walked on the main street. Veronica was trying to take inventory of her surroundings. She knew at some point she needed to figure out how best to escape when the opportunity presented itself. She noticed everyone was watching the naked woman and the six guards as they walked along the street. They led her to a large building and entered the main floor.

Chapter 4

Dak walked out of the barn, "I just made our first purchase with the gold. I purchased all of you one additional horse and a wagon with a team of horses. We need to buy supplies for our ride north. Hulk, you, Tommy Boy, and Zenith go into the market and stock up on supplies."

Hershel looked at Dak, "I mentioned to Trey that one of us needs to ride back over the mountain and make certain Veronica is okay. I told Trey I would go and check on his sister."

Dak looked at Trey and then at Hershel. Hershel was a slender man, less than six-feet tall. He had been captured at Cliff Tops while working as a soldier for the Normand army. He convinced Dak he hated the Normand empire, and Dak provided him a chance to ride with them. Even though he was fifteen years older, Dak suspected Hershel was attracted to Veronica. Dak could tell the look in his eyes as he would watch Veronica. When Veronica stripped down to her panties and ran through the field to distract the Normand soldiers, he noticed Hershel was aroused. Veronica was very pretty with a curvy figure, and men noticed. She had matured, and while growing up, she observed how the older women in Cliff Tops had dressed and acted. Dak knew she imitated the women of Cliff Tops and learned how to interact with males even though she acted like a tomboy when she was around him and their friends. "Okay, Hershel, you may take a couple pieces of the gold with you in case of emergency. I suspect Veronica is not far behind us. She would ride fast to clear the mountains. You might see her in a couple of hours. We are not going to be waiting. We must keep pushing north."

Hershel knew his horse was tired and hungry after several days of hard riding. All the men would be switching horses and ready to ride north in the morning on the fresh horses. Hershel saddled his newly purchased horse. He filled his two canteens full of water and took some additional bread rolls. "I hope to see you before you make the trip to Zenith Point." He smiled and then added, "We will ride fast and try to catch up with you by tomorrow. I am certain Veronica will stay on our trail. There is no way I will miss her."

He rode off at a fast gallop. Trey looked at Dak, "I should be going to look for my sister, not him."

"I believe Veronica can take care of herself, but I want to make certain she is okay. We did not see anyone in those mountains crossing in either direction. She should be able to catch up with us. Hershel is a good man. He will do his best to help her." He looked at Trey, "If we come under attack, I need you next to me in battle. We are now entering the plains, and we might run into bandits. The men in this area have now learned how to fight with weapons, and some have elected to make a living with a bow and a sword. They learned after our battles with the Normand army a more profitable career. We encouraged them to leave their homes and farms to fight with us. They will now sell their services to the highest bidder as mercenaries. Since the Transitional Period territories like this have no leadership, the survivors have claimed their land, and most will fight to keep their farms and ranches. They do not want to be governed and resent the old world. These people need to set up a sheriff. This territory will need a court system and a leader. Until which time warlords and gangs will rule."

Trey looked at Dak, "Only the strong will survive. I believe everyone who survived the old-world dislikes that way of life. What they need is you. The Normand army will return, and these people need to be united and ready to fight. Dak, you may be the only one they respect." Dak stood watching Hershel riding over the hill heading southwest as he disappeared out of sight and never acknowledged Trey's statement.

***

To Kill a Blueblood

Hershel rode fast for three hours as he followed the dirt road without diverting on shortcuts. When he saw some men driving cattle, he stopped and inquired if they had seen a lone rider. They motioned no, and he rode south for another few hours. He reached the base of the first mountain at dusk and figured he would have seen Veronica on the trail. He thought about how long the trip took him, Dak, and the others to cross the mountains. The ride for Veronica to return the wagon would have been four-to-five hours and then the horse ride back to the west side of the base of the mountain would have been quicker, maybe three hours with a fresh horse and no cargo. Hershel decided to camp at the bottom of the mountain and hope Veronica found him as she was descending the pass in the last ridge of the mountain range. He observed the sun setting behind the mountains located in front of him. He had never considered not meeting up with Veronica on the trail before now. He sat on a log and ate some beef jerky as he now contemplated crossing the mountains.

He noticed as he withdrew his bedroll and unrolled the waterproof layer on the ground how quiet the wooded area had become. He was alone. His horse waved its tail trying to repel a horsefly as he closed his weary eyes. The fatigue caught up with him, and he quickly fell asleep. Hershel woke up six hours later. He needed to pee and noticed the woods were still quiet. He wanted to leave in the dark of night and ascend the mountains. His goal was to reach the highest ridge before nightfall. His sleep had been refreshing, but the long trip was an ongoing challenge. He kept hoping to see Veronica around each curve in the trail as he forced the horse to start up the first mountain range.

He rode up the steep mountain just like he had done on the way across, the first-time following Dak and his band of warriors. He walked and led his horse in the same areas of the steep, dangerous part of the trail. The only sign of riders were the tracks of his group as they had crossed the mountain. He tried to be careful and watch for an ambush as he crossed the smaller mountains heading for the low gap in the larger mountain range. He remembered how Hulk always rode in front of the column and seemed to have a sixth sense on spotting danger and following other travelers' tracks. His anxiety increased as he rode further southwest. He had not considered the danger of riding into a trap when he volunteered. He now reached the final ridge line and knew his horse was tired. He decided to camp at the top of the mountain in the same spot as they had camped coming across a couple days prior. He wanted his horse to be fresh in the morning for the descent down the mountain. He started to wonder if he had missed Veronica. He thought, "She knew the trail. Would she have taken another path? The new growth of the underbrush on the lower elevation is thick and difficult to forge through. Could Veronica have gotten lost?" He knew he should have met her at the bottom of the mountain. He spent additional time looking at the horse tracks to verify if he could discern Veronica's horse tracks. Hershel thought, "She would have ridden through the low gap in the mountain range. I am no tracker, but maybe I missed her tracks." He had watched Hulk study the tracks of horses and knew he could not do what Hulk was able to do. Hulk could tell how fast someone was riding by how far apart the horse tracks were placed in the ground. He could tell the difference in the horses by the horseshoes and which horses were hauling a load of supplies and which one was carrying a rider. He set up his tent and placed a blanket on his horse warmth. He crawled in the tent and thought how nice it would have been if he had met Veronica, and they could have shared the same tent and bedroll to keep warm. He fell asleep curled up in the fetal position trying to stay warm under his fur cover, thinking of holding Veronica tight against his hard body.

He awoke cold and alone. He saddled his horse and descended the gap in the ridge of the mountain. This was the twilight time just as the moon was dropping down behind the horizon in the west and the sun was starting to rise in the east.

The wind and air were bitterly cold at the seven-thousand feet of elevation. He had slept in his seal coat with the fur hood and seal pants and was still cold all night. As he descended the mountain, he started to realize if Veronica had stayed on the trail, he could not have missed her. Dak had made it clear to Veronica the direction and path they would be taking. He started to feel an ominous feeling something was not right. He made the trip to the bottom of the mountains in half the time. He took a break and waited. His horse was tired, and he wanted to remove his cold-weather clothing. The temperature at the bottom of the mountain was in the seventies with blue skies. He was always alert for trouble. He hoped to run into a friendly face to ask them if they had seen Veronica. He also knew he was one man by himself, and if he ran into a group of bandits, he would have no chance. His horse was too tired to flee. He had watched Dak and his friends fight, and no one could fight with a sword and a bow with their abilities. They did not show fear or hesitate to fight in battle. They fought with confidence, were agile, very skilled, powerful, and fast to kill the opponent. He would be surprised if the Bluebloods were better warriors. He waited as he considered trying to travel to the Tanger in a day. Maybe the rancher could tell him the whereabouts of Veronica and maybe allow him to sleep in a bed at his home.

He smiled and shook his head "No" as he craved a bed and a good night's sleep. He had not slept in a bed in weeks.

Hershel took the chance and rode fast on the open trail heading directly toward the spot where they had loaded the wagon. He was surprised he had not seen any other riders. He cautiously rode into the lowland leading to the riverbanks of the inner water way. The river formed in the mountains and flowed slowly to the ocean without a noticeable current, and without an experienced crew, a sailing boat could not move against the current inland. The river was wide and deep as the water flowed toward the ocean.

The riverbank area was flat with few trees and lots of grass and weeds. He could see close to a quarter of a mile before the river turned behind a hill. He noticed there were no boats on the river. He looked toward the ocean as far as he could see along the riverbanks and could not see anyone. The ocean would be another quarter of a mile further west. He held his horse still as he looked around. He knew something was amiss, and he felt as if someone was watching him. He also could tell his horse was tired and hungry. He dismounted and tied the lead rope around the horse's neck and a tree limb. He pulled the bridle off to allow his horse to drink from the river and eat grass in the open field.

Hershel stood and turned a complete circle looking for something or someone. He stretched his stiff back and legs. He noticed the area was isolated and quiet except for the crickets singing in the weeds and tree frogs chirping in the treetops located in the wooded area along the riverbanks. He looked at the large tree close to fifty yards away in the open area and noticed large black vultures lined up and down the tree limbs, with several in the weeds beneath the tree. He could see the black heads pop up above the weeds and then they would disappear. A couple of the big black birds flew to the ground below the tree and disappeared in the high weeds. He studied the large black birds and scanned the area in all directions. He slowly walked toward the tree and noticed even more birds on the ground beneath the tree. He turned to make certain his horse was still eating, and no one was sneaking up behind him. He glanced towards the river and noticed the area was still void of boats. He turned back to the large tree and vultures. The large birds presented an ominous feeling, and he knew the birds represented death. He cautiously approached, glancing in all directions as he walked toward the tree. As he got closer to the birds, he noticed the vultures did not fly away like he expected. They instead held their ground. As he walked within a few feet of the large birds, one large bird jumped in the air and flapped its wings. As it flew, the others started leaving the ground and flew away, and then the ones in the tree followed suit and flew north into the woods. Hershel watched in surprise as the rest of the large birds flew away. He noticed movement in the tree and stared up at the tree limb and saw a ten-foot section of a rope dangling from a large branch. He then noticed another rope and then another. He was surprised to count four partial ropes hanging from large limbs. The ropes had been looped around different limbs, and they appeared to have been cut. His forehead wrinkled as he closed his eyes and concentrated, trying to figure out the riddle. He was perplexed. He first asked, "Why?" Then, how someone was able to climb the tree and place the ropes that high in the tree?" He glanced at the grass in front of him and noticed something red. He walked forward and knelt and realized he was now looking at blood stains and partially eaten guts of a mammal on the grass directly under the tree limb with one of the ropes hanging directly above him. He felt his pulse elevate with the apprehension of his discovery as he knelt next to the ground trying to figure out where the bones were located. He stood and quickly moved to another area with thick blood and a small amount of volume of guts. He looked up and noticed another rope hanging directly above this spot. He quickly ran to a third spot and noticed the same. He realized the ominous feeling was a cruel event, maybe some type of diabolic witchcraft had taken place on this very spot. He had heard rumors of horrible events occurring around the world since the Transitional Period. There was very little government control in the world. Survivors had to fight for the land they claimed, and no one trusted a stranger. His forehead wrinkled again as he realized the truth. He thought to himself, "Damn, something has been hanging in the tree and bled out. No one would do this to an animal. This had to be human bodies hung in the tree with their bellies opened to allow their guts to fall to the ground below. Did four people get hung by the neck and left in the tree without being buried?" He glanced around the area looking for four graves or signs of others.

Hershel was startled when he heard the unmistakable sound of several horses running toward his position. His adrenaline spiked as the noise got louder and closer. He stumbled and fell to his knees as he turned to run. He quickly got to his feet and started to run toward his horse. Hershel glanced over his shoulder and saw men on horses coming down the embankment at a full run and then he noticed men on horses were running toward him at a full run from the direction from where he had come. He glanced over his shoulder a second time as he ran and realized he could not beat them to his horse. He was surrounded. He felt panicked and could feel the fear rush through his body. He at first reached for his sword but realized he did not dare pull his sword. It would be futile to try to fight this many men.

The horses all circled him with the men having their spears and swords pulled. He looked up as the men held their weapons in a threatening manner. Hershel did not recognize any of these men as he spun in a circle looking at the men on horseback. Nothing was said. Finally, the young rancher approached and looked at Hershel. "He is not the one we are after. I do not know you."

"I was with those men and one female that rented your rig." He paused and stared at the young man. He recalled Veronica had mentioned the father was in charge, and the son was good looking.

"The wagon and horses were to be returned. That is why I am here. The young lady you met never returned to us as we cleared the mountains. She said she was going to return your horses and wagon because it was the right thing to do. We used the wagon to reach the base of the mountains. We could not use the wagon to cross the steep trail. Have you seen Veronica?"

The young man's expression showed annoyance as he glanced at his men, "We have not seen the pretty young lady."

Hershel sensed the men were violent, and the young rancher was not telling the truth. No one smiled, and all looked like killers. He stuttered, "Maybe I could talk to your father." He thought maybe the older man would be more hospitable.

The young man looked aggravated. "That will not be possible. My name is Frank Dupont Jr. You will be talking to me. I am the one in charge." The young man spit on the grass at Hershel's feet. "My father was killed and left on the ground next to the tree while four other men were skinned and hung in that tree to be found by the birds. This is all your fault. We never had any trouble until you rebels showed up."

Hershel looked around and considered what he had just heard. "I am truly sorry to hear about your father and your men. Your father, I understand, was a likable person, but I assure you, we did not do this. I am here looking for the young lady. Have any of your men seen her?" Hershel turned and looked at the men.

"We found our rig sitting in the open over next to the hill. We also found a gold coin on the ground near my father's body." He looked aggravated at Hershel, "We found some other items, but no lady."

One of the men brought Hershel's horse over. He held out two gold coins. "He is carrying this gold in his saddle bag. He has a bedroll, a coat with additional warm clothing, and nothing else."

Frank Jr. looked at the gold coins his man was holding. "This is the same type of gold coin we found next to my father. This is Merlin gold." He pulled the one gold coin from his pocket and held the shiny coin, looking at the two coins his man was now holding.

Hershel now looked concerned. "So, she made the trip back here, but you say you never saw her? What could have happened to her?" Hershel now thought they would kill him just like they must have killed Veronica.

"A worker arrived and told me I needed to meet a boat at the north dock. I rode off. My father stayed. My father and these men never returned. We found four of them tied in the tree hanging by their feet. All four in the tree had been gutted, filleted, and skinned. My father had a knife wound in his back that went all the way through his heart and out his chest." The young man looked at one of the other men. "Tie him up and place him on his horse. Bring him to the ranch."

Chapter 5

Hulk slowed his pace and then stopped. He waited for Dak and Zenith to catch up. He looked over at Dak, "We have made great time today. This looks like a good place to camp; we have the creek and the open area. If we keep pushing forward, we might not find a place as nice as this."

Dak looked over at his friend and smiled. He yelled for all to hear, "Let's camp here." He knew everyone wanted a good meal and rest. He could tell the men were tired of riding. They had covered close to one-hundred miles that day and still had a few hours of daylight left. Since they had crossed the mountains, Dak knew the hard part was over. Dak felt the group needed to relax and rest. He smiled to himself as he thought about all of the gold.

Hulk and Tommy Boy started gathering firewood. They had purchased several steaks from the farmer twenty miles prior along the road. The group was surprised when Tommy Boy, while sitting on his horse, had asked the farmer the price of thirty steaks. The farmer had two growing steers, and Hulk flipped the farmer a gold coin and explained he would wait on the steaks and catch up with the rest of the group. When the farmer caught the gold coin, he smiled and said he would have the steaks cut and wrapped in one hour.

They all were looking forward to the meal and resting. The other men knew their chores, and everyone made certain they were complete. Once the fire was burning hot, the steaks were placed over the coals. Trey placed two steaks on the grill for himself and then looked over at Dak, "I thought Veronica and Hershel would have caught up with us. Hershel should have met her at the base of the mountain on the east side."

Zenith smiled, "I believe Veronica liked the young rancher. She might be in love by now." Zenith turned back to cooking the steaks.

Trey looked over at Zenith with a questionable look. "You think my sister is in love?"

Zenith smiled and turned back to the men, "She told me she looked at the rancher like I look at Dak." She held her hand out in front of her and batted her eyes. The group all laughed.

Robin Hood looked puzzled. He was quiet for a moment then said, "You know when I dropped the tree on the Normand battleship that was closing in on you and our stolen gold? I saw something very strange."

Hulk looked over at Robin Hood, "Oh yeah, what did you see?"

Robin Hood knew he fell asleep after smoking three joints and was lucky the tree fell when it did. He awoke and the ship was almost even with him, and he was too intoxicated from the weed to finish the job he was entrusted to do. The tree hit the ship by accident and stopped the large vessel in the small river channel. The plan worked despite his insubordination. "I first watched the tree fall on the ship and then took cover in the woods. I ran toward the tree line and hid in the vines and high weeds. The view was beautiful watching the huge tree hit the large ship, tearing the large sails, and then smashing through the deck into the cabin below. The tree caused total pandemonium on board the ship. The ship leaned on its starboard side caused by my expert cutting of the tree." He used his arms and hands to describe the tree hitting the boat as he talked. "At first, I thought the ship might sink. Men were abandoning the ship and swimming for the shore. I could not tell if the tree pushed the ship into the shallow river bottom or if the tree was so large and heavy it was just holding the ship still in the river. I started to run and then something caught my eye." Robin Hood hesitated.

Tommy Boy looked at Robin Hood, "You are no expert in cutting trees, and you were told to block the small canal with the tree." His voice got louder. "You were told once the ship sailed straight and did not go wide around the island, to cut the ropes and drop the tree. The boat would not have been able to change directions in the wind for hours." They all looked at Robin Hood.

Dak sensed something was not right, "What are you not telling us?"

"I crushed a Normand sea vessel. I think that is something. The ax you provided me needed to be sharpened." He stared at Dak knowing everyone was waiting for him to tell what he saw. "I saw a man walk onto the deck from the aft cabin wearing a robe with a hood. He killed two Normand guards as they tried to stop him as he walked toward their captain. He then walked over to the captain without hesitating, cut the captain's head off with his sword in his right hand while holding a long knife in his left hand. He then killed three additional elite Normand guards without any difficulty. The other Normand sailors feared him and tried to either hide or run from him. He walked to the side of the boat railing and then turned and stared directly at me even though I thought I was well hidden in the vines and trees. The man was covered in tattoos on his face, and what I could see of his upper body. The cape opened in the middle revealing his chest and his hood blew back just enough, so I could see his face. I have never before seen anyone like him. He looked demonic. He started swimming toward the riverbank. I turned and ran to my horse."

Hulk's jaws were clenched with anger and blurted out, "You did not think to tell us about him until now!"

"You should not have ever been that close. Like Tommy Boy said, once the captain of the ship decided to go straight, you should have dropped the tree. The tree was four-hundred yards away. I know what happened. You got too damn high. You should have been long gone, and no one would have seen you. We told you not to get high and smoke that shit." Trey looked furious.

Trey then added, "Tommy Boy and I knew you were going to get high. You were ordered to block the canal with the tree, so the Normand sailors could not advance forward and then they would have had to rent horses on the bank to pull that ship backwards. It would have taken them days to get that ship turned. I bet you just about missed with the tree."

Robin Hood was angry, "But I did not miss. I stopped that sucker dead in the river."

Trey's face was twisted in anger, "And now my sister went back into the area, into an extremely dangerous situation because of you."

"No one said anything about Veronica going back. If you recall, I was riding in front of the group and had no way to know Veronica took the wagon back to the rancher. I never dreamed any one of us was returning. I thought we were heading home, and I was already leading the way climbing the mountains. Hell, I did not know Veronica went back until we stopped to rest at the second ridge thirty miles later. The weed had nothing to do with me and my abilities. The tree hit the damn ship. I took out an entire ship."

Dak looked at his friends and then looked at Robin Hood, "Did he see the direction you were running?"

Robin Hood looked frustrated and cleared his throat, "Yes, I guess he did see me running parallel to the river about ten yards from the riverbank heading northeast."

Everyone was quiet for a few seconds and seemed to be considering what had been said. Zenith asked, "Did you see him do anything special that a normal man could not do?"

Robin Hood looked at Zenith realizing what she was suggesting, "He killed those guards without much effort. The captain of the ship did not try to fight or block the swing which decapitated him. It was like he knew what was going to happen and any action he took would have been futile. The speed with the knife and sword were extraordinary, and he then descended the rope into the river from the boat and started to swim to the shore quicker than a normal man."

Dak looked at Zenith as she announced, "We have attracted the attention of a Rogue Blueblood."

Zenith turned with a worried expression, "The food is done."

The group walked over to the fire, and each picked out a steak. Hulk and Tommy Boy each got two. Zenith looked at Trey. He had not moved. "Are you not going to eat?"

Everyone looked at Trey. Dak said, "Come on and eat. Here, I will give you my steak, and I will get another. After we eat, I will decide if I will go back after Veronica and Hershel. The rest of you guys can push the gold north."

Zenith looked at Dak, "I go where you go. If there is a Rogue Blueblood out there, you do not fight him without me."

Hulk grimaced, "Hershel should find out what happened and report. He has not had enough time to catch us if he crossed the mountains and rode all the way to the ocean. He would have kept going until he met her. We rode close to one-hundred miles today. The best he can do is two days crossing the mountains going west and two days coming back across the mountains."

Trey looked upset, "Veronica is my sister. I will go south and find her. She is my responsibility."

Robin Hood still had steak in his mouth as he also ate some bread, "I think everyone is overreacting. She could have taken another route and by now be further north than we are. Or she could have gone on a date with the rancher's son like Zenith suggested. Veronica can take care of herself. I guarantee you guys she will not be bested by one man or a group of men. She knows how to keep her distance from traps. She knows how to understand danger and avoid being compromised. She is a veteran warrior."

Everyone ate their food in silence. Dak finally said, "Robin Hood is right. Veronica will be okay. We will keep going north and then hope Hershel finds her and updates us in a few days. Now, let's all eat and rest. We will try to reach the main road tomorrow and head to Harpers Ferry Harbor. There could be gangs along the way watching the roads for travelers, so we need to be on alert."

Trey was eating but was annoyed. "The gold is evil." He looked at Dak, "There is no way you would not go back and look for my sister if not for the gold. There is a Rogue Blueblood in the area, and she could not beat a Blueblood." He then looked at Robin Hood.

Dak hesitated. He wanted to diffuse Trey's anger. "The gold has nothing to do with my decision. All of you are treating my orders the same. You want to listen and if the orders suit you, you agree. But, if the orders do not suit you, you do what you like. I am tired of you guys second guessing my orders and not doing as I command." He threw the remaining part of his steak into the fire and walked away from the group into the darkness.

Zenith looked at the others as they finished their food. "I will talk to him. You are his friends. He loves all of you." She looked at Trey, "He loves Veronica. He blames himself for her being missing. Remember, he wanted to sink the Meridian with the gold on board. It was your decision to steal the gold, not his. Remember also, he was shot with arrows while stealing the gold. He could have been killed. We have all taken unnecessary chances over this gold."

***

Zenith removed her clothing and was lying on her stomach on top of her bed roll. The small tent was warm and cozy. Dak was using the candlelight and writing a letter to his mother. He was providing the queen with the instructions of what to do with the gold. As he was writing, he said, "I will give this note to Hulk to give to my mother. You and I will head back and try to locate Veronica." As he looked out of his peripheral vision, he noticed her bring her foot up then slowly lower her lower leg while tightening her calf muscle. His wife was flirting with him. He smiled and placed the note in his saddle bag. He then eased over and straddled her and started rubbing her back.

"That feels so good. Don't forget my legs and ass. After riding all day, they are a little sore."

"How about your foot? Is it not sore also? I bet you are sore all over. Allow me a few minutes to help you feel better."

He smiled as he looked at the backside of his wife and thought about her dark skin and perfectly sculptured body as he rubbed all over her. He reached for her foot and then her lower leg. He whispered, "We need to be quiet. The others need their sleep." He smiled as he spread her legs and lifted her midsection upward and balanced her on her knees. He wanted to take his time as he started thrusting his hips back and forth.

***

"You better get some sleep. You normally sleep all night after our love making." She laid her hand on Dak's chest.

"I am worried about Veronica. Do you really believe she is on a date?"

"No. I do not like what Robin Hood reported. You and I need to go back after her. I did not want to say anything in front of your friends. I believe Robin Hood saw a renegade Blueblood. Someone sent him to guard the gold. I believe there are more renegade warriors than Samuel reported. My Godfather was my trainer. He mentioned to me once, there were a lot of unknowns when talking about the renegade sector. The cult stays hidden, is very hard to locate and even harder to kill. We need to leave at daybreak, and you need to tell Hulk to move the gold north and wait for us at Harpers

Ferry Harbor. We will need to meet up with them, then take the gold and hide it at Cliff Tops. If the gold belongs to the cult, they will come for it. Samuel needs to be made aware of the threat, so he can be prepared. I believe King Solman, General Cuez and maybe a few additional Bluebloods have taken over Southern City. They united the warlords and malcontents who run the entire lower part of the continent. It just takes a few in power to take over by feeding the masses erroneous information."

Dak looked questioning at Zenith. She could tell he was considering something and appeared to be somewhat rejected. He seemed to go quiet when something bothered him.

Zenith smiled and looked at him. She raised her head up from his chest. She realized what was bothering Dak, "I love our two boys. I miss them just as you do. I am a Blueblood warrior and not designed to be a care provider. I am a warrior. Most Blueblood people do not raise their children. The children are cared for by loving caregivers. When we first walked into Merlin, do you recall seeing the Blueblood children playing in the park? If you noticed, each child had a female normal person caregiver who was assigned to the child. This is the same way I was raised."

"That is not how I was raised. I was raised by my mom with help from several families and her adult friends. The community in Cliff Tops raised us."

"The boys will be loved and taught how to be warriors. We will see them in a month, but we need to try to locate Veronica. Her time might be running out."

"Dammit! Tommy Boy is right. Robin Hood was high. He knew what he was told to do. Now, Veronica is missing. I would have never agreed for her to return knowing what I know now. Robin Hood should have mentioned what he observed. My friends do not listen to me. They know there is no punishment for not doing as I command."

"Robin Hood did finally tell us. The rancher and his people also needed to be warned. He made a mistake."

Dak looked at the ceiling of the tent, "It may be too late to warn the rancher. Those men live in a very isolated area. The only way they were visited, was by traders coming by sea and stopping off at their port. If we had not had the radiation detectors, we would not have been able to cross those mountains."

She looked at Dak and rubbed her hand down to his groin. She started to flirt with him and kept rubbing. Dak responded, and Zenith positioned herself on him as she smiled down at him as she straddled his nude body. "I love you." The two smiled at each other as they stared at each other. Zenith started moving her body in rhythm faster and faster with greater intensity.

Chapter 6

Hershel was tired and looked worried. "Why would I come back? There is only one reason and that is to find Veronica. You need to let me go. I am not your enemy."

"The young lady has disappeared," announced Frank Jr.

Hershel looked over from his position in the chair where he was tied. His wrists were hurting from the rope being pulled so tight. He repeated, "You need to let me go. Why tie me up in the first place?"

The rancher looked angrily at Hershel, "You say you're not our enemy, but since you, your friends, and this young lady showed up, I have had to bury four hard working men and my father, whom I dearly loved."

Another man who was older and heavier walked over to Hershel. He slapped Hershel. He then pointed at Hershel, "I am going to kill you. You have brought us nothing but trouble and now my father is dead. That is what I know."

Hershel looked at both men and realized they were brothers. The older brother stuttered when he talked and had trouble pronouncing words. He blinked his eyes as he was trying to concentrate on formulating a sentence. "I had nothing to do with anyone being killed. We had no way of knowing your father and four men would have been killed. If the Cliff Tops group had known or suspected Veronica would have been taken, they would not have allowed her to return the wagon and horses to you. This is not my fault or their fault. You are naive if you think you could stay out of the wars. You will be forced to choose sides." The man hit Hershel a second time but this time he used his fist with power.

The blow caused Hershel's face to turn ninety degrees to the right, and he felt a sudden pain in his neck from the sudden hit. He turned and looked at Frank Jr., "You are blaming the wrong person." He then stared at him as his mind arrived at a revelation, "You know who killed your men and your father!"

Frank Jr. stared back at Hershel. Hershel knew by the stare he was right. These men knew who killed the five men. "You also know who kidnapped Veronica!"

Frank Jr. walked toward Hershel, "All I know is, before you and your friends showed up, my father and four friends were alive. Now they are all dead."

Hershel was tired. His face was red from the hit. "I need to try to find the young lady. That is all I am trying to do. If I do not find her, she will be killed. Her friends will return at some point wanting answers. Most of you men are like me. You survived the Transitional Period, and no one wants to talk about the past. The old world is over as we all knew the world.

This is here and now. You will have to choose sides in the wars to come. I can tell you about King Solman and the Normand Army. I can tell you about the group from Cliff Tops. You will need all your friends. You will need the Cliff Tops' warriors to provide you protection and fight alongside you. Dak is trying to unite the north territory against the Normand invaders. If the Normand army stayed south, we would not have been here. All your property will be owned by King Solman, and you will be killed or turned into slaves. King Solman will need to take over the Tanger Port for his military. He needs the port to transfer men and resources up and down the coast. You believe since the Normand Army has not stopped at the Tanger Port, they do not know about the existence of the port. You would be wrong to believe this. They will come here and take what is yours. That is the Normand way."

The bigger brother balled his right fist to hit Hershel a third time. "Wait! Let me say one more thing." The big man hesitated. "The Normand Army will approach you at first with a treaty which will appear to be very appealing to you. Then, they will break the treaty. When you realize you want to fight back, you will be outnumbered and killed if you resist. They will know your weaknesses and your strengths. They will have your kids and women as hostages. That is their way. Once they make landfall and secure the port with their large numbers of soldiers, you will all be killed. We asked to borrow your wagon and nothing else. They will take your land, horses, wagons, and children."

The man started to hit Hershel. "No." Frank Jr. yelled. "You know nothing of what you speak. There are worse regimes than the Normand Army. The Normand Army will never come here."

Hershel was confused by the statement, but before he could ask what he meant Frank Jr. announced, "Untie him."

Frank Jr. looked at Hershel, "The Normand Army does not frighten our village."

"Who killed your father? Who could be worse?" asked Hershel. Hershel glanced at the faces of the two men. Frank Jr. stood still like he was in thought and never changed his expression or answered the question.

The other seven men and his brother looked at Frank Jr. "What about the master?" asked the older brother. Then he added, "This man caused our father to be killed. Burl, his two brothers, and Little Eddie all are dead."

Frank Jr. took two steps closer. "I said let him go. He did not kill any of our men or our father. If what he is saying is true, then we need all the help we can get. Why else would this man ride into our ranch if he is not telling the truth. I am telling you; he speaks the truth. We need to listen. We have been isolated because of the mountains to the east, the ocean to the west, and the nuclear waste pits to the north and south. We do not know what is going on in the world except what we hear from the traders coming to our port. I said cut him free."

One of the men reached behind Hershel and cut the rope holding his hands. The bigger brother stuttered and hesitated while blinking his eyes and looked at Frank Jr., "I hope you know what you are doing. They might come back and kill all of us."

Hershel noticed the look of fear on the other men's faces and then looked at Frank Jr. inquisitively, "Who might come back? Who is the master he is referring? You never answered my question. Who killed your father and men? Where is Veronica?"

Frank Jr. looked at his men, his brother then at Hershel, "It does not matter. What matters is we need to trust someone, or we all are going to end up dead. I choose to trust this stranger."

Hershel rubbed his wrist. He glanced at the men and made eye contact with Frank Jr. "I speak the truth. I have no reason to lie to you. I do not conspire to take your land or your freedoms. Thank you for trusting a stranger."

Frank Jr. looked at Hershel, "The only items we found which belonged to the young lady were her clothing, the gold coin, her bow, and her sword." He looked at Hershel, "We did not find any of her body parts as we did our friends and my father."

"May I see the items?"

Frank Jr. motioned his head to the man leaning against the wall. He opened the door and reached into the standing cabinet and pulled out the items. He laid them on the table. Hershel picked up the seal skin shirt, jacket, long underwear made of thin silk, and sealskin pants looking for blood. He immediately recognized the items to be Veronica's. He picked up the sword and inspected the grip. He remembered how the grip on her sword was soft leather which she kept wiped down with seal oil. The grip was worn from use. Hershel looked at Frank Jr. and said in an urgent tone, "This is not good. Where would she be taken?" He paused as he looked at Frank Jr., "This young lady was one hell of a warrior. I watched her in combat, and she could take on several men at once and win. You said the Normand army was not your concern, but you and your men fear someone. Someone killed your father and four men. Who took her if it was not the Normand army?"

Frank Jr. stood and walked toward Hershel, "We know a smaller sailing vessel departed shortly after my father and men were killed. The vessel was known to have a four-man crew. The father is the captain, and he has two sons and an older man working as the crew. They are traders from up north. They would take a few of our cows and sheep north from time-to-time to sale. The Port Master in Tanger reported the crew just arrived and immediately departed. The ship was seen sailing south shortly after they docked in our harbor. They normally do not go south. They trade in the city of Merlin and maybe north of Merlin in other ports. They have been to Southern City, but since the revolutionary war in that region, they have elected not to go south. You need to leave immediately. By you being here, represents a danger to our village. That is all I am going to tell you."

"I need supplies and two fresh horses for a trip back across the mountains. I will leave at once."

Chapter 7

Veronica woke by a gentle hand to her shoulder. At first, she was startled and grabbed the wrist of the lady and held her arm tightly. She stared at the lady trying to clear the cobwebs from her mind. She tried to remember where she was, and how she had arrived. The dark-skin lady looked to be in her forties and had a caring smile. "Child, you need to wake. We need to get you ready for dinner."

Veronica's mind was now clear, and she recalled where she was and what had happened to her. She was somewhat frightened waking in a foreign land after being kidnapped. She however allowed the lady to lead her into a large room with a concrete bathtub in the center. The tub was positioned in front of an open window. To her left, she could see the balcony doors were open. "You will need to take a hot bath. I will pour coconut oil in your bath water to help soothe your skin. Then, we will get you ready."

"Ready for what?"

She glanced into the eyes of the lady. She looked worried. "Let us get you washed."

Veronica was led to the tub where the lady removed her robe. She felt the warm water with her right hand and then stepped into the tub. She sat down and at first thought the water was too hot. As her body started to adjust to the temperature, she realized the bath was soothing. She leaned back into the tub and looked over at the lady carrying a bowl and a bar of soap. "What is your name?"

The lady smiled, "They call me Dezie. I am here to assist you." She reached the bowl into the bath water and then gently poured the hot water over Veronica's head. "You have beautiful hair. I will help you wash your hair."

Veronica allowed Dezie to massage her scalp with the shampoo and then wash the shampoo out of her hair. She noticed another maid enter the chambers and say something to Dezie in a foreign dialect she did not understand. Dezie answered the woman, and the woman turned and left. Dezie produced a razor from under her towel. I will need to shave your legs. You do not need any hair on your body other than the beautiful hair on your head. Dezie lifted Veronica's left leg and applied cream and then started shaving her leg.

"Why are you doing this?"

Dezie smiled, "It is my job. I need to have you ready by eight tonight. You will dine with the King."

Veronica pulled her right leg up the side of the tub. Dezie rubbed her leg with the cream and started shaving he Veronica looked at Dezie and noticed how efficient she was with the razor and how thorough she had been washing her hair. "What is going to happen to me?"

Dezie smiled and quickly moved the razor over her shin and her thigh. "Our King will treat you like your husband treats you. Now hold your arms up."

"I have never been married. I have never had a boyfriend."

Dezie looked at her as she lowered her right arm after shaving her underarm. She walked to the other side of the tub and lifted her left arm. She looked at Veronica with concern and whispered, "Child, you need to listen to me. You need to make certain the King is pleased with you. He is a mean King. He will send you to his soldiers in the camps for them to do as they please with you. There, you will receive no mercy." She made eye contact. "Listen to me. You will need to learn how to please the King. There is no returning back from that life after being turned over to the soldiers in the camps. You will not live very long being treated as they treat the slave women."

"I have no training for this." Dezie could see the fear in her eyes.

"Please stand up and sit on the side of the tub. I need to remove the hair around your pelvic area and your upper thighs. I can teach you how to please a king in the ways of the world, but first you must trust me. I was once like you. I have seen young girls and women sent to the soldiers, and they never return." She looked at Veronica. "If you want to live, you must listen to me and do as I say." Dezie applied the cream to her pelvic area and pushed her legs apart. She started gently shaving Veronica. "Men can be manipulated when their sexual desires have been met. The key is to figure out what they desire. Men are different." She looked up into Veronica's eyes, "I will teach you how to survive. It is not going to be easy. If you listen to me and do as I suggest, you will survive. I promise you; I will help you. You will be able to help others at some point. Satisfying a man in bed is a competition between you and the man, and you need to play to win. I once was a Catholic, but I have lost my faith during the Transition Period. I do not wish to mislead you, but you need to thank of the king as Samson and you must be his Delilah."

Chapter 8

Zenith looked up the hill and across the path at Dak. He held his hand up with the palm facing her for her not to move. The hooves from the horse and rider indicated they were fast approaching. Dak could tell the rider was riding dangerously on the steep path. He knew with the steep slope of the elevation, and being covered in rocks, roots, small scrubs, and pine trees; the rider was not being careful. He figured the fast-approaching rider was either being chased or suicidal. Dak looked down the trail toward Zenith and held up three fingers. Each finger represented five seconds. He dropped one finger and then the second finger. He stepped out in the path with his bow pulled tight. He saw the fear in the rider's eyes as he came around the curve in the path and thick pine trees. The rider pulled the bridle backward yelling for the horse to stop. Dak smiled and lowered his bow, "Hershel, you are being very reckless riding down this steep slope at that pace. Who in the hell is chasing you, and where is your horse?"

Hershel smiled and pulled back on the bridle. The horse came to a stop. Hershel jumped off the horse while holding the bridle. He was breathing hard as he glanced at Dak. He then looked down the trail and saw Zenith as she pulled her rope from around the tree. He then looked at Dak.

Dak walked over to him and hugged him, "I am glad to see you."

"Dak, I am glad you stopped me. Otherwise, Zenith was going to kill me with the rope tied across the trail." He smiled as he bent over to get his breath. "I purchased a fresh horse from the rancher."

Zenith smiled, "I was backup in case Dak needed me to stop the rider. Where have you been for the past few days?"

Hershel stood straight and looked at both Dak and Zenith, "I have some very bad news. I rode all the way to the ocean, and I wanted to report back to you as fast as I could. Veronica has been apprehended and taken south. Our best guess is that her destination is Southern City."

"So, she is still alive?" asked Dak.

Hershel looked at Dak with a sad expression, "We do not know if she is alive or not. She was taken by a maniac. The situation is not good. We need to sneak into Southern City and try to gather intel about her."

Zenith looked at Hershel. "Who is your source of these facts?"

"Allow me to drink some water, and I will tell you everything. I am exhausted. I rode another horse through the pass in the mountains and then I let it go. I used the gold to buy this second horse."

Dak and Zenith listen for several minutes as Hershel explains every detail of what he knew.

Zenith looked at Dak, "You know what they will do to her. We need to figure out how we can rescue her. We need to assume she is still alive."

Dak looked perplexed. "Hershel, how certain are you that she was taken south?"

"I believe the men in Tanger. I believe Frank Jr. His father died at the hands of the maniac that took her. We need to go to Southern City. I believe we will find her there. They will need her to locate the stolen gold." He looked concerned, "That is my best guess. The men in the Tanger community fear someone, but they would not tell me who. The maniac that took her must deal in human trade. He will sell her to King Solman." He looked at the ground and then back at Dak. "The men I met do not fear the Normand army. I have no idea who scares them. They all look like men ready for war and look very capable with a bow and a sword, but I know fear when I see fear. They fear evil like I have never seen."

"Southern City will be well guarded. The reports we have received outline more than ten thousand soldiers in that city with thousands more holding other cities and ports up and down the southern part of this continent. We will not be able to enter the city without being detected," exclaimed Zenith.

Hershel looked at Zenith, "You are right. The only way we can enter the city is by sea. We will need a ship. We need to sail into the harbor in Southern City hauling a cargo they covenant. King Solman has too many soldiers for us to sneak through by land. They have too many outposts, and soldiers stationed inland along the highways. I know. I am from that area. The one weakness of Southern City is it is not self-sufficient. They rely on boats sailing into their harbor. Traders sail into the dock daily and leave daily. By sea is the only way."

Zenith looked at Dak, "I know some sailors. They have also been to Southern City. We will need to hire them. They will know how we can gain access to the city."

Chapter 9

Veronica walked behind Dezie followed by two guards as they approached King Solman's chambers. She noticed Dezie seemed to be confident, and intelligent with caring eyes and a loving spirit. Veronica knew she would have to trust someone. Dezie seemed to be trying to assist her and prayed with her. She had never had a pedicure and a manicure. She hated the low-cut silk blouse which was opened in the front exposing her cleavage. On the other hand, she liked the black boots made of soft leather. She thought they were the softest material she had ever felt. She was trying to adjust to the three-inch heels as she walked down the hallway. As they approached the two guards at the end of the hall, Dezie turned to her and waved for the two guards following her to stop and provide her and Veronica privacy. "Child you must be strong. I am sorry, but you need to do as I instructed you to survive. I will be waiting for you back in your chambers. I hope the Gods will be with you." Dezie reached up and rubbed the side of Veronica's face. "You are the prettiest young lady I have ever seen. You are intelligent and confident. Both characteristics can either help you or be your downfall. However, you will need to use them both to survive. I choose to believe you will be okay."

Veronica took a deep breath and looked into Dezie's eyes, "Thank you for your guidance. I am a survivor." Veronica walked with apprehension in her thoughts toward the two guards stationed at the two doors at the end of the hall. The guards were both big men with muscled arms and strong-looking bodies. One had a shiny stainless-steel sword in the sleeve on his left hip and the other one had a large hammer with a four-foot-long handle strapped to his left hip. Both had faceguards on their helmets pulled down covering their faces.

"I am here to dine with the King," Veronica announced.

The guard on the left opened the door and stood to the side as the guard on the right walked through the door. He announced, "Sir, your guest for dinner has arrived."

Veronica walked past the guard holding the door and immediately noticed the lavish room. The foyer led into a large great room with over a twelve-foot vaulted ceiling, all stone walls and a stone floor. The large dining room table was set for two. It appeared to be eight-feet in length made of granite with some dishware located on each end of the table. King Solman approached through a closed doorway. He stared at Veronica and waved his guards out. He walked over to the table and opened a bottle of alcohol and poured himself a glass. "Can I offer you a glass of gin? I acquired a case of Asian Gin from a trader."

Veronica smiled, "Thank you sir, but I do not drink." She looked for weapons. There was a knife on the table next to a fork. She could not discern if King Solman had a hidden knife under his loose-fitting shirt.

He took a sip and considered her response. Then, he clapped his hands and in walked a maid. "We are ready for our meal. Bring the food at once."

The maid announced, "Yes, your majesty." The maid turned and left walking briskly into the kitchen.

King Solman seemed to be rushed with his hand gestures and his movements as he walked toward her, staring at her. Veronica could sense a stirring in him of some type of anticipation. She wondered, "Is he uncomfortable being in the room with me or is he insecure about something else?" She recalled how Dezie had offered her advice to be aware of his actions and anticipate his mood and desires. The instructions for Veronica were to use all her senses.

"Allow me to assist you to be seated." He reached for her hand and led her to the end of the table and pulled the chair out for her. She sat, and he assisted with moving the chair under the table. He leaned over her shoulder and whispered as he gently blew warm air in her ear, "You look exquisite." She now realized the King wanted to be in control. So far, he had seemed to have the afternoon meal planned.

Veronica watched King Solman walk to the end of the table and take his seat. He stared at her. She tried to smile as she glanced at him and then around the room. The door from the kitchen opened and in walked three waiters carrying food and drinks. They all were dressed in white uniforms and very efficient at what they were doing. Veronica looked at the food and could hardly wait to eat. "We are having pork as our main dish, which has been cooking for sixteen hours at a low heat."

The waiter first provided King Solman with his entree and side dishes. Then, the waiters brought the dishes and did the same for Veronica, placing the food on the large silver plate in front of her. King Solman raised his glass and said, "Enjoy. You are here to assist me in the recovery of my stolen gold, but first we will eat."

Veronica did not hesitate and picked up her fork and knife. She immediately cut into the pork and took a bite. The food tasted better than anything she had ever eaten. She took another bite and another bite. She looked up at King Solman as he was watching her eat. He had set his fork down and was drinking his gin. Veronica apologized, "I am sorry for my lack of manners, but I have not eaten a meal in four days." She took another bite with some of the gravy dripping to her chin. "This is the best-tasting food I have ever eaten." She tried to smile with her mouth half full of food.

"I am glad you like our food." She noticed he ate a few additional bites and pushed his dish away as she kept eating. When she finished, he asked, "Would you like seconds?"

"No. I am fine. Thank you for asking."

He clapped his hands; the maid and three waiters came into the room. They retrieved the dishes, and the three waiters left. The maid asked, "King Solman, are there any additional things you require?"

King Solman was staring at Veronica, "Yes there is. However, you are dismissed."

Veronica looked at the maid, "The food and the service were exceptional. Thank you."

The maid looked at Veronica and seemed surprised, "You are welcome."

Veronica wanted to ask why. Why attack her village in Cliff Tops? Southern City and Cliff Tops were at opposite ends of the continent. She also wondered if she could take him in a fair fight. He seemed very confident. She also remembered the coaching by Dezie. She knew she would only have one chance to escape. She had to play this out. She wondered if Delilah had second thoughts as she was a Philistine spy working to coax the Jewish man named Samson out of his secrets. "Thanks for the nice dinner." She smiled.

"I hope you liked the pork and gravy."

"I loved the food. I do not recall ever having a meal that tasted this good." She stood and walked into the center of the room. He carefully watched her. "I understand you would like me to provide you with some adult entertainment." She turned and stared at him. "You know I have never been married or had a boyfriend." She stared at him as their eyes met, he leaned forward and removed his shirt.

He nonchalantly raised his hand and took a drink of his gin. "You are very beautiful. I would like to see you without any clothes. Please make it happen."

Veronica untied the string to remove her long robe and started unhooking the string as it was attached through the hooks on each side of the front of her dress. Once the string was loosened enough, she allowed the robe to fall to the floor. She unbuttoned her blouse and then removed her skirt. She stepped out of the skirt and then removed her blouse and then her underwear. She stepped toward King Solman and placed her left boot in his lap, "Take it off," she demanded. King Solman released the buckle on the side of the boot and then pulled the boot off. Veronica removed her left foot and then placed her right foot in his lap, "Take it off," she demanded. He likewise took the last of her clothing off her.

King Solman looked her in the eyes as he held her foot, rubbing her leg. "I am sorry for the way you were treated in your travels."

Veronica pulled her foot away and stepped closer to King Solman. She straddled him in his sitting position and rubbed her hands through his hair. She kissed him on his forehead and started rubbing his chest. "You are the king. I am your prisoner. You may do what you want with me. However, if you provide me an opportunity to please you, I believe you will keep me in the chambers down the hall."

King Solman held Veronica tight as he stood. He quickly turned her around and sat her on the long dining table. He forced her to lie on her back with her legs spread out to each side. "You are the prettiest female I have ever seen." He started kissing down her neck and lower across her breast. Veronica looked up at the vaulted ceiling and recalled what Dezie had instructed her. Faking her interactions would make the experience with King Solman more enjoyable for him and consequently could lead her to enjoy the love-making. Dezie emphasized and had Veronica to repeat, "A woman should enjoy the interaction as much as the man." She closed her eyes and started to moan and rotate her hips as he kissed lower and lower across her belly.

Chapter 10

Dak was tired from riding fast for several hours. They stopped at the rancher's home where they had stopped the previous time and traded for three horses. The three knew they needed to catch up with Hulk and the others. He also was concerned the sailors were headed further north. He needed to reach Ronny and the three sailors. He hoped they all were still in Harpers Ferry Harbor.

Hershel knew the general area of Southern City, but he had owned a small ranch over one-hundred miles north and had only visited the city three times prior to King Solman arriving and conquering the city. He also went through three weeks of basic training for the army in the city but was not allowed to leave the compound of the basic training facility. Dak knew the city would have changed with the city turning into a military base for the Normand Army. He needed updated intel. His thoughts drifted back and forth between the chances of finding Veronica alive and the perils of the mission.

As they came around the last curve in the trail, he could see the lantern lights of the city. The time was a little before midnight. The three were tired after the hard ride for three days. He looked ahead and could see the silhouettes of posted guards a few hundred yards ahead at the gate on the west entry road. The gate was installed across the small bridge. He slowed his pace. The guards were alerted to their presence as they rode toward them. "We are from Cliff Tops. We seek passage to meet with Vulture."

The front guard seemed nervous, "Who are you?"

"I am Dak Donahue. I need to meet with Vulture." They rode close to the guards. The five guards spread out to prepare to fight. They pulled their swords and two lifted their bows with arrows aimed at Dak.

The front guard walked in front of Dak with the lantern and shifted the lantern to reflect the light in Dak's face. "Hi, General Dak. I am Lonnie. You remember me? I fought next to Little Jimmy at the middle bridge in the battle of Harpers Ferry Harbor. We won that battle." Lonnie smiled with pride.

"I remember you, Lonnie. Little Jimmy spoke highly of you and your courage."

Dak stopped his horse, and Zenith rode up next to him and then Hershel. Lonnie looked at Zenith with her face hidden under her robe's hood. He then looked at Hershel. "You look tired. Your horses are spent."

"We have ridden hard trying to catch up with Hulk and our tribe members heading north. Have you seen them?"

Lonnie looked at the city from his spot high on the plateau, "Everyone has seen them. They are having a great time in our city. They rode into town four days ago and are staying in the motel. Hulk told me to be on the lookout for you. They are expecting you. I will signal the next check point you three are coming." He deemed his lantern and then brighten the lantern and repeated the process three times.

"Then, we must be on our way." The three rode toward the town and the next checkpoint located at the town entrance. They asked for directions to the motel. The guard replied, "You will not have any trouble finding your friends. They are all having a great time, playing cards, drinking and." The guard hesitated as he looked at Zenith, "Well you know what else they might be doing."

Zenith smiled, "I understand there are several pretty young ladies in the city who seek male attention." She then pulled her hood back to reveal her smile.

The guards smiled and the front one replied, "Look for them at the bar at the end of the street. We just got in a shipment of rum smuggled from the port up north on the west coast, near Merlin. The boat made the trip by the Normand ship barricade by swinging further out to sea away from the coast."

Dak smiled, "We need better spears, arrows, and catapults, but rum will do. We will be on our way." The guards laughed.

"As the three rode slowly to the front of the bar, they noticed there was no place to tie their horses. The area was full of horses tied off on the rails. There appeared to be a large group of people inside having a lot of fun. The laughter and cheering could be heard in the street. The three rode to the corral and placed their horses in the fenced area. They took off their saddles and bridles and allowed the horses to rest, eat, and drink the water from the trough. They carried their bedrolls and saddle bags into the bar.

The men at the doorway stepped aside and allowed the three to enter. They stepped across the threshold and glared at the large number of people laughing and drinking. All the tables were full with standing room only at the bar. The bar area and the dining area in the open room were dark with little light provided by the hanging lanterns. As the people inside started to notice the three strangers, quietness fell over the audience. Dak was standing with the hood of his cape over his head and peered into the dark room. He could see Vulture standing behind Trey, who was arm wrestling another man. The group standing and watching appeared to be betting on the outcome. Vulture and others were laughing, drinking, and watching the arm wrestling with a great deal of enthusiasm. He spotted Tommy Boy sitting next to Trey with a large drink in his hand. He was smiling and talking with the people around him. Trey and Vulture noticed the three strangers at the same time. Trey stopped the arm wrestling by slamming the other man's hand down flat on the table and peered directly at the three. He realized Veronica was not with them. Dak pulled back the hood of his cape and then Zenith pulled her hood off. The room was instantly quiet. Dak whispered, "Nothing will quiet a room full of drunks like the entrance of a Blueblood."

Zenith smiled at the remark as she stood next to Dak.

The manager walked over to Dak, "General Dak and Mrs. Zenith, can we assist you with accommodations? Your food and room are on the house." The manager reached for Zenith's hand and bent forward and kissed the back of her hand.

Dak smiled at the gesture but never took his eyes off Trey, "We need two rooms and a hot meal on a clean table."

"Yes, Mr. Dak. At once. Follow me and let me provide you a key to your room, and I will have my employee take your things upstairs. Is there anything else?"

"No. That will do for now."

The manager waved for the people to get up at the large table near the far wall. He then motioned for a waiter to clean the table and the busboy to take their items.

Vulture stood and walked quickly to meet Dak. He hugged him and then hugged Zenith. He shook Hershel's hand. "Have a drink with us."

Dak could smell the alcohol on his breath and walked past Vulture and sat down, followed by Zenith and Hershel. Vulture followed and sat in the empty chair. Dak waited for Trey and Tommy Boy to walk over and have a seat.

"Where is Hulk, Robin Hood and the sailors?"

Tommy Boy understood Dak was concerned about the gold, but he dared not mention the gold. "It's good to see you too," proclaimed Tommy Boy with a smile. "What about saying Hello?"

Tommy Boy waited for someone to say something. He smiled at his three friends. "Hulk and Robin Hood have dates. They are upstairs with girls. The sailors are still in town. Sneedy is upstairs with a girl. The other three left about two hours ago. They are staying in the motel at the end of the street. Everything is being guarded." He drank his drink and looked at Dak with the last remark.

Dak could tell Tommy Boy was high on the alcohol. He frowned, "Who is guarding our stuff? It does not sound like our stuff is being guarded."

Vulture leaned forward with a sincere expression, "I have some men watching your gold over in the stable." Dak noticed Vulture was very drunk. He slurred his words.

Dak felt his anger spike. He did not want Vulture to know about the gold and now he mentioned it inside a bar. When

Dak dropped his horse off at the corral, he had walked by the stable, he had not recalled noticing guards. Zenith reached over and grabbed Dak's right arm. She could tell when he got impatient and angered. His eyes narrowed and his face turned red. Dak glanced at Zenith. He then turned to Tommy Boy, "What rooms are Hulk and Robin Hood renting?"

Tommy Boy announced, "Hulk is in Room 212, and Robin Hood is in 213. They are in the nicest suites at the end of the hall."

Dak stood and clinched his teeth, "At the end of the hall." He walked to the manager. "I need the spare key for rooms 212 and 213."

The manager seemed to hesitate. "Mr. Hulk said he did not want to be disturbed."

Dak's temper flared. He turned and looked at the manager, "Your choice. Either you comply, or I kick down both doors."

The manager looked concerned at the tension in Dak's voice. He pulled a master key from his pocket and handed the key to Dak.

Dak ascended the stairs two at a time and walked down the hall. When he arrived at corner room 212, he used the key, opened the door, and walked into the room. He heard Hulk reply, "Get out. This is my room. Who the hell do you think you are?"

After Dak walked away, Zenith looked at Trey and Tommy Boy, "They may get in a fight. Dak is tired and irritable. He did not talk to me and Hershel the last few hours of the journey." She then looked at Trey, "Dak will update you on your sister."

Dak lit the lantern on the table, "Get her out of here and get your clothes on. What do you think you are doing?"

Hulk heard his friend's voice and the tone. The drinking and lack of sleep started to make him tired. The young lady looked from under Hulk and asked, "Who is he?"

"Dammit, you need to get your clothes on and leave." Hulk rolled off her and got out of bed. He started getting dressed.

The girl complained, "We were not done. We had just gotten started. I wanted to stay with you all night."

Hulk moved to the side of the bed and started looking for his clothes and thought about the two other girls he had bedded earlier in the day. "I am finished. I must work. Sorry sweet thing."

Dak clenched his jaws and walked out of the room and across the hall and opened the door to room 213. He walked in and looked at Robin Hood lying on his back with a dark-skin lady straddling him rotating her hips. "Get your clothes on and get your ass downstairs." Dak turned and walked out.

Robin Hood looked at the young lady, "Duty calls." He then lifted her off him and got dressed and headed for the door.

***

Hershel ate his food and yawned. He very much wanted to stay out of the discussion. He could tell Dak was extremely pissed. Zenith ate her food and would smile at the guys between bites. Dak kept his expression stern as he ate. Hulk looked at his old friend, "Listen to me. Everything is okay with your property. I made certain it is safe."

"Really, who is guarding my property while you two are upstairs getting your dicks wet? Do you know the names of the guards? They could be Normand soldiers for all you four know." He glanced at Tommy Boy and Trey. "We need to meet with our sailing friends tonight and discuss a possible venture." Dak looked around at the crowded bar area. "We need a place where we can talk and not be overheard. I need you four to sober up and get some sleep and be prepared to move out at dawn."

Hulk looked at Dak as he kept eating and then glanced at Zenith and then Hershel. He understood the news was not going to be good about Veronica. "We did not expect you to arrive until tomorrow. We can go to the motel at the end of the street and talk on the enclosed front porch."

Trey looked at Dak, "Where is my sister?"

Dak pushed his empty plate across the table, "She has been kidnapped. We will meet, and I will tell you what we are going to do. But not here."

Chapter 11

Veronica awoke with the sunlight coming through the open window on the east side of the bedroom. She looked around the room and listened. She knew she was alone. She lay still thinking about the prior night. King Solman must have allowed her to sleep in his bed. She considered her evening and wondered if she was going to be sent to the soldiers in tents located in the fields. She felt between her legs, and she was sore to the touch. She stood and walked to the great room and picked up her clothing. She quickly got dressed and carried her boots to the hall door and opened the door. The two guards had their face shields pulled in place over their eyes as they stood in the guard position. "I am ready to return to my chambers." Her two guards led her to her room where she quickly took a bath and got dressed. She laid down on the cover of her bed and fell asleep.

Two hours passed, and she heard the door open and in walked Dezie. She rushed to her bedside. "I was so worried about you. You never returned to your quarters. I waited until after midnight for you to return. I was concerned your stubborn personality took over, and the King ordered you to the soldier tents."

I must have fallen asleep in the King's bed. I woke up this morning and came back to the room. I took a quick bath and fell asleep. I was so tired from my boat trip."

"King Solman's envoy just came to my room. He has requested your company again tonight for dinner," Dezie smiled. "I have never known him to allow someone to stay all night. Maybe that is a good sign that he likes you."

"I did as you instructed. Now I am sore to the touch and sore when I walk."

"You will get used to love-making. The first time is always the hardest. Your body will conform to his. Now, let's get you something to eat and then we will prepare you for tonight."

Veronica spent the afternoon eating and resting. Dezie helped her bathe and shaved her body. She listened to Dezie tell her of her life story, and how she and her two sisters had survived after the Transition Period. She lost her husband and four adult children and six grandchildren during the earth transition. She felt she and her sisters would be okay and then the gangs and warlords started taking over in the southern part of the continent. They moved to Southern City, and her sisters married men in the established government. They all felt safe and then her two sisters died when their husbands were killed in the civil war and the Normand army gained control. No one else in her family or her community survived the slaughter caused by the revolution in Southern City. She further explained the Normand army needed slaves to feed them and attend to their needs. She indicated she was able to find a house-keeping job and later worked in the castle for King Solman.

Veronica listened and felt sadness for all the grief in Dezie's life, but still Dezie was willing to help her. Dezie admitted she had lost her faith with her God. She had impressed Veronica even after all the death, cruel, and inhumane behavior she had witnessed, Dezie still wanted to help others as a person of Christ would have done.

***

Veronica opened the door and noticed the guard was stationed outside with his metal face shield pulled down over his face. He was a medium sized guard, and she remembered his dark brown eyes, clean shaven face, and a boyish smile. He seemed to be quiet by nature. "What is your name?"

The guard hesitated, "My name is Michael Valadez."

"Please pull your mask up." He pulled his mask up and stared straight ahead. "Michael Valadez, where is the other guard? I thought it took two guards to imprison me."

Michael smiled, "I have been assigned to you."

Veronica looked him in the eyes. She could tell he was nervous. She loved his brown eyes, his smile, and facial features. "I like the name Michael. Michael is the name of the archangel who threw Satan out of heaven as Michael was working for our Lord. Are you an angel, Michael Valadez?"

Michael smiled, "I am a humble guard. I am no angel."

Dezie walked behind her, "You do not want to keep King Solman waiting. We need to walk faster."

Michael stepped to the side and motioned to Veronica and Dezie to walk ahead of him. Michael then glanced at Veronica as she passed him in the hallway. He got a smell of her perfume. The rose smell was very addicting. He noticed her outfit was provocative showing off her well sculpted tan legs and her toned body. He noticed she stood with her back straight, her head facing forward with a smile and walked with confidence.

Once they came around the corner, the two King's guards stationed at the double doors opened the doors to allow Veronica entry. Veronica turned to Dezie. "I will see you back in my cell in a couple of hours."

Dezie looked concerned and reached for Veronica's forearm. She whispered, "You must please the King. Remember what I told you. You have an opinionated and stubborn personality. You are also very intelligent. I am worried those characteristics might be your downfall. He will demand total control of you. Please play your part as I taught you." Dezie smiled at Veronica with empathy, "This is a game you are playing. The game is for your life. You must play to win at all costs. I have told you what you must do, and how you must keep the King's attention focused on you."

Veronica turned and walked across the threshold, and the two guards closed the doors. Veronica walked into the great room and noticed the table was set for three. She noticed the candle lights were burning on the table and the smell was a pleasant scent. She had never encountered the fragrance. She felt an ominous feeling about the next few hours. She stood still, trying to figure out why the extra plate. She saw two men talking in the shadows of the evening on the large balcony. They turned and walked through the open doors leading from the porch to the great room. King Solman introduced the younger man. He was well dressed and well groomed. He had soft features, not like a fighter, a warrior, or a construction worker. He was a pretty man. King Solman introduced Brad. "He will be dining with us. I ask you to welcome him."

Brad came over and held Veronica's right hand. He bent forward and kissed the back of her hand while extending the kiss as he held her fingers firmly. He then raised his head up and kept her hand in his and looked at her from the floor to her eyes. He then mentioned how nice it was to meet her. "Our king was just telling me how beautiful you are. We love your long hair with the waves and curls." He reached with his hand and felt her hair. She noticed his white teeth and voice was soft with a higher pitch than most men.

Veronica smiled at Brad and then thanked Brad. "My hand maid spends extra time working with my hair. It is called a perm." She then looked at King Solman with Brad still holding her hand, "May I make a request?"

King Solman smiled and lifted his palms up from his sides and replied, "Yes, you may make a request."

"In order for me to keep this figure that Brad keeps staring at and admiring, I need to be able to exercise and workout. I noticed your guards are all muscular. They must workout at a gym. May I work out in the same gym?"

"Yes, of course. I will instruct your guard, Michael, to escort you to the gym in the morning. You may be allowed to workout. Now we must eat." The King stood and watched Veronica as he was surprised with her one and only request. He also noticed her confidence in herself as she stood with her back straight and seemed to observe her surroundings. He felt a stir inside himself as he watched her.

King Solman clapped his hands and out walked the three waiters and the head waiter. The three took their seats with

King Solman assisting Veronica with her chair. The cook had prepared duck, and the taste was perfect. During the meal, the talk was general in nature. They talked about the weather, the heat, and the swimming hole up north where the Lower River ran to the ocean. Veronica tried to stay focused on the meal and the conversation, but she felt a little uncomfortable with Brad. He did not fit into the personality of King Solman. He seemed more feminine than any of the military men or guards. The meal ended with the three waiters removing the dishes and the head waiter being dismissed by King Solman.

King Solman stood and walked over behind Veronica and pulled her chair out. He took her hand and walked her to the middle of the room where she stood on the rug. He politely asked her if she liked the duck. She of course indicated the duck was magnificent. He then mentioned she and Brad would perform for him. Brad stood and walked over to Veronica and held her tight from behind as King Solman sat in his chair and positioned himself to watch. Veronica knew what was expected of her. Dezie had told her not to be surprised and try to adjust to King Solman's desires. Brad was a nice man who seemed to be forced to be in the chambers of the king the same as her. He acted cautiously with his statements and was overly complimentary of the King during the dinner conversation. The two slowly kissed and then undressed.

After they copulated twice, Brad got dressed and left. Veronica then turned her attention to King Solman. She acted like she was turned on with the King watching her and Brad. The next two hours were filled with very intense love-making. King Solman finally mentioned he was tired. As she was dressing to leave the King's chambers, she thought of Dezie, and wondered if she had known about Brad. Veronica quickly dismissed the thought. The King excused her two hours after Brad left. She opened the door and saw Michael standing in the hall next to the two other guards. She walked toward the three men but did not look at Michael, "I am ready to be escorted back to my cell."

Chapter 12

Dak looked at his friends and his wife. "We will wait for Ronny, Darnell, Sneedy, and Bartholomew." He mentioned all the sailors by name. He knew he needed the help of all four men, and he wanted to make certain he had their names memorized. He wanted to make them feel important. Dak could tell Trey was getting anxious waiting to hear the news about his sister. He sat in his chair focused on the floor and every few seconds, he would nervously glance up and then back at the floor in front of him.

Zenith smiled and looked at the guys. She knew Dak was still frustrated with Hulk and how the guys lived in luxury, and each had been a spend thrift once they had arrived in town. He was also anxious figuring out a mission to locate Veronica. She asked, "Have any of you found a wife while you have been waiting on us here in Harpers Ferry Harbor?"

Robin Hood smiled a little and ducked his head. Tommy Boy said, "There are a lot of single females in the area. Since the wars, several men have been killed. The widows and young ladies are looking for companionship. Of course, some of these females put the whore Becky to shame." He then added, "My big brother and Robin Hood can tell you all about them."

Zenith was a little surprised. Tommy Boy had always been the quiet, best mannered, and the shy one of the group. "So, Tommy Boy, did you find a wife?"

He blushed and the other guys laughed. Zenith noticed Hulk and Robin Hood kept their focus on the floor, both with smirks on their faces. "I would not say I have met Mrs. Tommy Boy Claiborne, but I have met two or three young ladies." The group all laughed.

Zenith exclaimed, "Two or three! What have you been doing?"

Tommy Boy looked at Zenith, "That is nothing compared to those two." He pointed at Robin Hood and Hulk. "Those two have had at least three dates a day since we arrived. That is all they have been doing. They call it Tom Catting around."

Dak knew what his friends had been doing. He wanted to change the conversation. "Here comes Ronny and the other three sailors." Dak remembered when he first met the four men. He thought Darnel lived with fear. He was a skinny man, fast, and with great dexterity. He had survived because, under pressure, he was brave and fought hard. He threw Hulk the life rope when Hulk was not going to be able to clear the deck when they were stealing the gold. The fast action by Darnel saved Hulk's life. Now, he needed these men to sail a ship into

Southern City's Harbor, the most dangerous place on earth for him.

He knew little about each man. Bartholomew was a transplant from another area of the globe and ended up in the south after the Transition Period. He was assigned to Ronny's unit by the Normand command. He was a smart individual that never talked about the past. Everyone assumed he had lost his friends and family during the Transition Period.

Sneedy was a nickname for the fourth sailor. He fit in with Ronny's group. He took orders and was very efficient at being a sailor. He seemed to accept the hardship of life every day and push through the tasks at hand.

Ronny was the leader and had been singled out by the Normand command to lead the group and assist the Normand fleet officers on sailing vessels. Ronny was one of the few men who survived the Transition Period that had active knowledge about sailing ships. He was in his early fifties and seemed easy-going and confident.

The four men walked onto the porch. Ronny looked at the group and then back at Dak. Darnel asked, "You and Zenith arrived and wanted to talk with us. What's up?"

Dak looked at Ronny, "Do you still have your gold, or have you already spent it all on women and drinking like my friends have all done?"

The four sailors looked at Hulk and Robin Hood and smiled. Hulk looked up, "I still have most of my gold."

Robin Hood smiled, "The women are paying me to bed them. I have all my gold coins, plus some. My financial strategy is fairly straight forward." The group laughed.

Zenith shook her head in disbelief and said, "We need to stop talking about your extra-curricular activities and talk about Veronica. I heard all I needed to hear about Tom Catting." She looked at Hulk and Robin Hood and shook her head no.

Dak smiled and thought Zenith was the one who brought the topic up and now she had no desire to hear about the guy's Tom Catting around. He also knew Zenith felt everyone should have a mate and the mating decision should be for life. There was no time or room in a person's life to date several different people.

He looked at Trey, "Your sister may have been taken prisoner to Southern City. This is based on a witness who saw a ship that normally trades with northern tribes, head south around the time she went missing. This is the best information we have." He looked grim, "There were four skinned men left hanging in a tree and the rancher had a large wound from a knife that went through his back and out his chest. Like I said, there was a witness who saw a vessel heading south from

Tanger around the time she arrived and disappeared. We believe she will be taken to Southern City and sold as a slave. We need to come up with a plan to enter Southern City and verify if she is being held by the Normand army."

Trey was now mad, "How did this happen? They will kill her. How do you know she is still alive?" As he talked his voice got louder with concern. He hit the table hard with his fist.

Zenith looked at Trey, "We will try to find out. Hershel knows the area. He has explained we cannot enter the city by land. There are too many soldiers and too many roadblocks. There is no way someone could sneak into that region without being killed. The whole city and southern region are under Marshall Law. King Solman does not trust anyone, and his soldiers are not allowed to fail."

Dak looked at Trey and knew he was upset, "The men of Tanger did not locate her body. They located five bodies and buried them. I personally believe she is in Southern City. This is my fault, and I am going to find Veronica."

Dak looked at Ronny, "We will buy a ship and sail into the harbor. That is the only way for us to enter the city."

Ronny looked at Dak with an instantaneous remark, "You know nothing of the harbor or the Normand fleet. You have never sailed a ship. They will spot you first thing. You cannot fake being a sailor and a trader. You and your men will be discovered."

Dak looked at the floor, "We do not have a choice. Everything you say is correct. You and your men need to teach us as soon as possible how to sail and convince the Normand command we are traders."

Ronny became opinionated and animated as he used both hands as he talked, "We cannot teach you all these things in time. You need an experienced crew if you are going to pull this off. The ocean in that area is hazardous. The wind can change directions overnight. The city is located on the very tip end of the continent where the two oceans meet. The ocean water is the roughest in the world. Plus, you need a cargo they desire. You need to understand not just how to sail, but you would also require fake papers showing your port of origin and the cargo deal sheet." Ronny looked around at the faces of Dak's group and then his crew. He now realized what Dak was needing. "You already know these things. You need me and my crew to sail into Southern City."

Dak looked up from glaring at the floor, "I did not want to ask. I need you and your crew. We need your help. Do you guys want to make some more gold? I know the only way for us to enter the city is by ship. We need to leave at daybreak."

Ronny glanced at his three comrades. He knew he could no longer order them to do anything. They had all earned their freedom. He was also very apprehensive about going to Southern City. All four men hated the Normand army for what they had done to their families and friends. They all were now free and wealthy. Ronny looked back at Dak and then Zenith, "I understand I cannot run from this fight. There will be no place to run if someone does not fight the Normand army. I cannot speak for my comrades, but I am with you. I can get you into Southern City." He looked at Darnel, Bartholomew, and Sneedy.

Darnel looked concerned, "The mission won't be easy, but if someone can come up with a plausible plan, I am in. The fleet run by the Normand navy is not going to allow us to sail into port at Southern City without stopping us. We will need cargo."

Sneedy looked over at Dak, "We need a good plan. Otherwise, you are asking us to commit suicide."

Bartholomew announced, "What is the use of having all this gold if we are all looking over our shoulders for the invading bastards from the south? My people live in a small area on the west coast of the Asian continent, called Israel. The land is the prettiest place on earth, but they are surrounded by Persians who hate them. They will fight, but they cannot defeat the entire Asian population. I was captured by the Normand army when I was trying to negotiate a trade route. Do not make the same mistake I made. You cannot be captured." He looked at Dak.

Zenith asked, "What are you suggesting?"

Ronny exclaimed, "Present them with a cargo that they need, and a possible future trade of the cargo. We can present ourselves as merchants trying to sell a commodity. If the cargo is something they need, they will deal with us. If there are only three or four of us manning the ship, they might not be suspicious. Any more than four will draw their attention. Plus, your accent will be hard to fake."

Tommy Boy asked, "What does the Normand army need from us?"

Dak looked at everyone, "Coal. They need coal."

Bartholomew asked, "Why coal?"

Sneedy gestured, "They need coal to power their steam ships which they might be trying to develop."

Ronny looked surprised, "No one has coal. The entire world is void of coal. After the Transition Period, no one has been able to locate coal. Otherwise, they would be building coal-driven machines."

Hulk looked up for the first time since the meeting started, "We know where there is lots of coal."

Trey looked concerned, "Traveling to Cliff Tops with horses and wagons will take weeks. My sister needs us now."

Dak looked at Trey, "We all love Veronica. It was my decision to allow her to stay behind, and my decision alone. If we can hire Ronny to sail us to Cliff Tops with the gold, we can pick up enough coal in the cargo bay to present the coal to the Normand command. We will tell them we are heading to Israel which is located on the Asian continent." He looked at Bartholomew. "Bartholomew can convince the Normand command of our plan. He speaks the Asian dialect. They will take us to shore, and we will bargain with the Normand command. That is the only way I see we will be allowed to enter the port at Southern City. We will find out if Veronica is being held captive and then come up with a strategy to free her. We might be able to trade them coal for Veronica but first we need to know if she is being held captive. The slave industry is well established in the southern hemisphere."

Tommy Boy looked perplexed, "Ronny just said they are not trying to make engines which need coal. Why coal?"

Dak looked at the others, "They are trying to make gunpowder. They need coal to harness both sulfur and charcoal."

Hulk was the first to say, "We cannot allow them to have coal. Hell, they already have us out numbered with better weapons."

Dak looked at his friend, "We are not going to give them coal. We are going to wave the coal in front of them as bait." He paused, "Ronny, what do you think about the plan?"

Ronny said, "I like the plan to enter the city. They need coal for that large army. They have merchants entering the harbor daily. The mission will be risky, and if we are discovered, we will be killed in a very painful manner. Getting in might be easier than you think, but how would we get out without giving them the coal?"

Zenith said, "While in Merlin, the Blueblood marina security guards discovered a hidden area in the bottom of a trader's vessel. The boat had a fake floor. The smugglers would place contraband items or refugees under the fake floor. The story was told in our training, the floor was installed so precisely a guard could not discern he was standing on the fake floor. The smugglers had a trapdoor dropping down into the sea located next to the keel. We can do the same. We will smuggle some men who specialize in sabotage hidden in the secret compartment on the vessel. We will install a trap door on the bottom side of the ship next to the keel, so they can drop down into the sea. They can sneak out of the ship and then sneak back inside without anyone knowing. They will sabotage the Normand sailing vessels while others of us are checking out the city. No one will be able to chase us once we clear the open water."

Chapter 13

Veronica awoke confused about how this was going to play out. She needed a plan. She also knew she needed allies. Had Dezie known about Brad? He was a gentle, beautiful man, very experienced with knowing the female body and had certain physical attributes that made him desirable for a female lover. He had talked to King Solman as he had kissed her and rubbed oil over her body telling the King how beautiful she was and how she was allowing him to copulate with her as she knew this entertained her King.

Brad was no warrior or a man that fit in with King Solman's inner circle. She wondered if she could really trust Dezie and dismissed Brad as a possible asset to be used. Dezie had somehow been able to survive when others had not and now, she worked and lived in the guarded castle. As she lay in her bed staring at the ceiling, she now realized no one in the castle could be trusted to help her. Dezie would walk by the guards without fear, and she could only have that type of confidence if she worked directly for the King. She would be loyal to her King.

Veronica rolled out of bed and drank some water. She changed clothes and opened the door. Michael had just arrived for the day shift. He seemed surprised to see Veronica so early. "I am going to the gym to workout. You are to accompany me. Now lead the way."

Michael looked at Veronica very carefully and studied her. "Did you not receive King Solman's orders? He said I could work out in the gym."

Michael arrived for the day shift at five A.M. He had not anticipated her to open her door this early in the morning. "Yes, I received the orders. Follow me."

The two walked down three levels of stairs and out the rear door of the castle. They crossed the street and down another set of exterior stairs. They came around a block wall and into an exterior gym with sand on the floor, it had no ceiling, just two ten-foot-high walls and the rear wall from two other buildings. The balcony for spectators extended out from the south side of the rear of the building to the north. Veronica noticed the weights in one section, two punching bags tied up to the balcony floor and an arena for combat competitions taking up one end. The sun was just rising in the sky behind the eastern wall. Veronica knew the temperature would be too hot to workout past nine-thirty A.M. The humidity was low but the dry heat by ten A.M. would be above ninety. "Where does that door lead?"

Michael looked at the wooden door located in the east block wall. "The door leads to the street. There are some merchant stores and the orphanage where the nuns live a few meters south down the street."

She thought about a possible escape route. She glanced at Michael who seemed to be reading her mind. Veronica changed her thoughts to working out and then how she hated acting like she enjoyed being with King Solman. She picked up two dumbbells and started with curls. As she curled the weights, she thought back to the young rancher and his looks and manners. She knew she would never again see him. He had been killed and hung in the tree.

She wanted to work out by herself before anyone else arrived. She wrapped her wrist and knuckles with cotton rags and then she removed her shoes and walked through the sand over to the punching bag and started hitting the bag rapidly with her right fist and then her left fist. She then would balance backward and kick the bag tandemly with both feet. She would use combo kicks and punches. She worked out for thirty minutes straight on the bag. She turned and walked to the wall and the table. She pulled the ladle from the nail attached to the wall and reached into the barrel of water and poured herself a cup of water to drink. She then used the ladle to pour water over her head. She noticed Michael was sitting on a chair in the shade holding his sword, "Do you not want to workout?"

"I am assigned to watch you. It is not allowed. I work out in the dark or late in the afternoon after it cools down."

Veronica placed the ladle on the nail and went to the weights and started doing squats. She could feel the dry heat as the sun started rising in the eastern sky. She heard a group of men approaching as she completed her third set. Two guards and four soldiers turned the corner and saw Veronica finishing up with her last set of squats. "Well, what do we have here?" asked the guard standing in the front. Veronica acted like she did not hear the question and walked back to the punching bag and started her routine of kicking and punching the hanging bag. She had worked up a sweat and the sand from the floor of the workout area was sticking to her feet and legs. Every time she kicked the bag, sand would fly. The men watched her long ponytail with three ties as her hair would swing with the movement of her head with every kick.

The Normand soldier standing next to the prison guards looked over at Michael sitting in the shade, "Who is she? What gives her the right to workout in our gym?"

Michael replied, "King Solman granted her permission to workout. As you can see, I am from the King's Guard and her escort. I am assigned to her watch detail."

The smaller of the guards smiled, "Maybe she would like to do some one-on-one wrestling? I could teach her some moves on the sand floor." The group of four soldiers and two guards laughed. Veronica acted like she did not hear them. She kept the pace and did not slow down with her workout.

The larger guard said, "Maybe she would like two of us at one time?" The group laughed.

Veronica remembered the two guards. They were the two who had entered the cell where she was tied in the nude. After Damon left and King Solman left the dungeon room, they could have provided her some clothing. Instead, they forced her to walk out of the prison and across the street in the nude with the citizens watching her. She remembered the small kids watching her from the windows of their apartments. She also overheard the whispers talking about her over-sized breasts, and what they would do to her sexually.

Veronica turned and announced, "What about a sword challenge? Michael can be the judge who wins. He is a member of the King's Guard, and his integrity should not be in question."

The men looked surprised. The smaller guard said, "I am your man. Let's do this."

Veronica said, "First you must agree to the terms."

The larger of the two guards smiled and asked, "Terms? What terms? We fight until someone gives up." He turned and looked at his friends with his hands out palms up to his sides.

She looked at the men. "You may want to reconsider once you hear my terms. You may be scared."

The smaller man laughed and looked at his friends. "What are your terms?"

"First, we use the training swords. We have three rounds, each round lasting for one minute, and the one with the most hits wins. If one is hit with a kill shot that would be lethal, then the match is over."

The smaller guard smiled, "I am tracking what you are suggesting. Sign me up. I will be first."

"Not so fast. The loser (and she pointed at the smaller guard) will be required to remove all their clothing and walk across the street in the nude to the orphanage and ask the nun for a drink of water. Those are my terms."

The Normand soldier looked at Veronica and then looked at the other men and laughed. "So, you are willing to take off all your clothing in front of us and walk down the street about twenty meters in the nude and knock on the door to the orphanage and ask the nun for a drink of water?"

Veronica stared at him with spite, "I am going to watch your friend take off his clothing and walk down the street to the orphanage and ask for a cup of water." Her face developed a wrinkle across her forehead and her jaws were clinched.

The soldier looked at Sander, "Please tell me you are going to take the challenge." He then whispered, "She is the prettiest female I have seen, and I very much would like to see her naked."

Sander, the smaller of the two guards, walked over to the rack and pulled a sword, "I accept your terms."

Michael stood and was concerned. He knew he was told to watch and protect Veronica. King Solman would not like his concubine injured. His orders were straight forward.

Veronica walked over to the rack and pulled a lighter sword. She then walked over to the fire pit and pulled her sword through the prior days' burned ashes making the blade black. She walked into the ring with the rising sun to her back. She turned to Michael, "You know your integrity is required, and I have the King's ear if you do not tell the truth. He will know."

Michael looked at the guards and soldiers. He then looked at Sander. He walked by Sander and said in a low tone, "Do not injure her. You can beat her, but I am telling you not to injure her. Do you understand?"

Sander looked defiantly at Michael, "What are you going to do if I do hurt her. Hell, getting hurt is part of the competition." He smiled.

"Did you not hear her? She has the ear of our King. If she gets injured, you and I will face the King in this same ring. We will receive no mercy. Do you now understand?"

"Yes. I understand. I will tease her. Now guard boy get out of my way."

Michael felt uneasy about the challenge. He knew he would be held responsible if Veronica was injured. He walked to the table and then looked at Veronica, "Are you certain you want to do this?"

Veronica announced as she stood in the ring facing Sander, "You are holding up the match."

He looked at her with a questionable expression and then said, "Let the game begin." He turned the one-minute hourglass over and set it on the table.

Sander immediately rushed Veronica and swung with great force trying to drive her backward. Veronica easily blocked the first swing and quickly stepped to the side. She positioned her feet squarely beneath her and braced for her pending swing. As she moved to the side, his momentum allowed him to pass her. Sander had anticipated driving her backwards and administering a quick kill shot. He had not anticipated her quickness and placed himself out of position. When she did not move backward, he was too close to her to block the mortally deadly swing to his ribs. Veronica then stepped behind Sander with his momentum going forward, and she changed hands with her sword and swung backhanded, catching him in the back of the neck, knocking him face down into the sand.

Veronica stepped toward Michael, "I declare this match over, and I declare both of my strokes would have been deadly to my challenger."

Michael and the other men watching were all speechless and stood with the feeling of surprise.

Sander had never been more embarrassed in his life. He jumped up, dropped his sword, raised his fist, and rushed toward Veronica. Michael could see the embarrassment in his eyes and his face was flushed. He leapt from his spot and declared, "The winner is the Princess." He stepped between Sander and Veronica.

"No. Her swings were not hard enough to injure a man," declared Sander. He looked at his friends for support.

Michael announced, "When she hit you in the back of the neck, the force knocked you face down onto the sand floor. Look. You got sand on your forehead. If she had been using a combat sword, you would be headless. It is my decision and my decision alone, and I declare the Princess the winner." Michael knew by calling Veronica the princess the men would show her respect and not challenge him on his decision.

Veronica was surprised Michael had now referred to her as the princess twice. She never considered being called a princess.

Sander looked angry. He looked at Bruno, his best friend and work companion. Bruno said, "Sander is right. She did not win. You need to reconsider your decision, guard boy."

"I will not reconsider my position. I announced the winner. She landed not one but two mortal blows in less than ten seconds, and the princess could have landed a third one while he was lying face down on the sand floor." Michael then watched Sander closely making certain he did not rush Veronica. He then announced, "I have no choice but to rule the princess the winner."

Veronica looked at the soldier standing on the end. "Maybe you can allow him to borrow your towel, so he may remove the black ash from his ribs and the back of his neck." Veronica watched, providing the men an opportunity to consider the significance of what she had just mentioned.

The soldier walked toward Sander with his towel extended in his hand. "The Princess has a very good point. You have black all over your side and neck." Bruno, and the four soldiers laughed at their friend's embarrassing predicament.

Veronica looked at Bruno, "Maybe the fight was not fair. Maybe we should have one more competition. We could go double or nothing. You and me. If you win, I will take my clothes off and walk to the orphanage and ask the nun for a glass of water. Your friend will not be required to remove his clothing. However, when I win, you will be required to remove your clothes along with your friend and you two will hold hands as you walk to the orphanage asking the nun for a glass of water. Are you scared of me?" She held her palms up with one hand holding her sword in an inviting gesture with a smile.

Michael smiled at the proposition. He thought, "She has guts." He also knew Bruno was a deadly sword fighter and had killed several men in his occupation, first as a night guard for the city, then as a prison guard. The man was very strong and agile for his size. He always placed in the top of the sword fighting competition tournaments, but he had never won.

Sander announced, "Yes. We will take that challenge. Bruno is the best fighter in the company. Only a few soldiers can beat him."

Bruno looked at his friend and smiled. He considered watching his friend walk down the street nude. How funny it would be. He looked back at Veronica. The lady had a well chiseled female body with tight fitting shorts and shirt. The chance of seeing her again naked was too enticing. "I will accept your terms."

Michael walked over to Veronica, "You have been working out for over one hour in this heat. You have already fought one man. You do not need to do this. You have won. We should leave."

"Those two forced me to walk down the street in the nude in front of children. I have revenge on my side. You need to start the competition." Michael grinned as he looked at Veronica with her sword in her hand and her clinched jaws.

Michael walked out of the pit and watched Bruno pick up a large sword from the rack. His sword was one foot longer than Veronica's, which made it heavier and more dangerous. Michael did not like being the judge. He knew he had to work with the two guards. The four soldiers he had seen walking through the command center with the generals from time to time. He did not know them, but he knew they communicated with high-ranking men in the government. He was assigned protection detail which was the higher rank and a more desirable job than a guard in the jail system or a foot soldier. He knew these six men did not like him being ranked higher and paid more money, but he also knew they had to obey him. He was also aware he would see these men again when he was off duty, and he might have to kill one of them. His concern was not only protecting Veronica but also making certain she did not escape. King Solman had suddenly changed his demeanor and seemed to be happier now that he had met Veronica. He would not want her injured. He was assigned to protect her at all costs. His life depended on it. The consequence of not doing his job could be death.

He raised his hand then dropped his hand signifying the start of the competition. He set the one-minute hourglass down on the table.

Bruno started to rush Veronica as he was facing into the rising sun, but he pulled back at the very last second as she raised her sword. He recalled what happened to Sander. He swung his large sword but kept his distance. Veronica blocked the swing and stepped to the side as both kept the distance. Bruno tried again swinging from the other side. Again, Veronica easily blocked the swing and stepped to the side. She moved easily keeping Bruno squarely in front of her, and she showed no fear as she stepped in front of the fast-moving sword and blocked the blade with her sword.

Michael observed both were playing the round safely with neither overextending. He could tell both were hot caused by the morning sun and heat as they both had blocked and swung their swords several times. He announced, "The first round is over. We have a tie." He stepped into the ring and made certain both would stand down. Both went to the water bucket and drank some water. Bruno looked over at Veronica, "You seem nervous. I cannot wait to see you walking down the street in the nude." He hesitated and then added, "Again."

Veronica responded, "We will see who walks down the street. This will be the last round you have before you must remove your clothing." She walked over to the fire pit and rubbed her sword blade through the ashes to make her blade black with ash.

They both took their positions in the pit. Veronica noticed the sand was starting to warm up as the sun moved across the southern sky. Michael motioned for the start of the battle as he placed the hourglass on the table.

Veronica advanced toward Bruno with four fast swings. He blocked all four swings and then rushed Veronica, bumping her off balance and forcing her to the sand. He saw her fall and advanced toward her with the practice sword ready for a full downward swing. Veronica rolled to the side, and the downward swing missed.

Michael saw her fall and got nervous. The large sword with that much force could kill her.

She still did not have enough time to stand and fight. Bruno forced the battle. He started to swing a second time. Veronica, while on her knees, took a handful of sand and threw it into his eyes. Then she ducked and rolled. He swung where he thought she was and missed. She jumped up on her knees and swung as hard as she could, hitting him in the back of the leg, causing him to fall. She jumped to her feet and pressed the sharp end of the practice sword to his throat. "Do you surrender?" She moved the sword against his throat making a black mark on his neck.

She heard Michael declare the battle over, and that she was the winner. She also heard Sander cuss the now dire situation. The four soldiers were laughing as Bruno stood.

"You bitch, you cheated. I have sand in my eyes." He used his hand to rub the sand from his right eye.

Veronica walked over to the barrel and pulled the ladle from the nail and retrieved a cup of water. She turned and faced the two men. They were both dirty where the sweat had caused the sand to stick to their skin. They also had black ash on them where Veronica's sword had hit them. She reached and started unrolling the rags wrapped around her wrist and knuckles, "You two need to hurry and remove those clothes." She noticed both men were reluctant to remove their items. "I have the ear of your King. You will do as we agreed, or I will ask him to turn you two into geldings as punishment for being dishonest and not living up to your promised commitments. I will be patient no more. Now remove your clothes."

Bruno looked angrily at Veronica, "This isn't over, you bitch."

Veronica placed the ladle into the barrel and poured a second cup of water as she stared at the two men. She then drank her water while peering at the two men.

Sander looked over at Bruno and removed his shorts and shirt. He removed his sandals. Bruno the same. Both men stared at Veronica as she watched and waited for them to remove their briefs. The two slowly removed their briefs and stood naked. "I hope you see what you want," smiled Bruno.

Veronica smiled, "It must be chilly in the air." She smiled as she looked at their private area. "I will see what I want to see when I watch you two hold hands and walk to the orphanage. You must walk down the street and knock on the door of the orphanage and request a drink of water from the nun while holding hands. That is what we agreed on."

Sander looked at his friend, "Let us get this over with." The two men walked to the east wall of the gym and opened the wooden door leading to the street. They stepped outside on the street.

Veronica hurried to the doorway and walked out into the street past them. "Hear ye, hear ye. We have two men who want everyone to watch them as they hold hands and request a cup of water." She whispered, "You need to hold hands." Several town's people watched from shops on both sides of the street as the two men walked to the orphanage and knocked on

136

the door. The nun came to the door and smiled as she noticed the two men standing while holding hands without any clothing. She glanced at the two from their feet to their faces. Bruno looked up the street toward Veronica and Michael as they stood and watched. He then declared, "We each request a cup of water and please hurry."

She agreed to provide them a glass of water. She was older and took her time as she handed each a cup. She smiled again and noticed several other people were watching. Veronica turned to Michael, "I am tired and ready to go back to my cell. I have seen enough."

Michael grinned, "Yes, Princess." He looked at the four soldiers and walked past them following Veronica as they stood with bewildered expressions.

Chapter 14

Ronny looked at Dak and grimaced, "The wind is picking up and the bitter coldness will make our journey more difficult. We need to off-load the gold, and the coal loaded. I do not like being this far north this time of year. We do not want to be caught in an early winter storm. The faster we move south, the better."

Dak nodded his head in agreement as he noticed Ronny had his winter coat pulled tight around his body and the hood snuggly fastened around his head. He knew the four sailors were not acclimated to the cold north. The wind at sea was always blowing, and the swells were always producing droplets of water flying across the bow. The clothing not only had to repel water but also keep the body warm. The sailors tried to limit themselves to the watchout post located on the bow of the boat. The cold wind was bitter to the sailors. They hoped to head south the next day after the one day stop at Cliff Tops.

Dak stood against the rail staring at nothing but waves and the cold ocean. He was thinking how he was dreading talking to his mother, and most of all telling Little Jimmy and Mia their daughter had been captured while on his watch. He was in charge and felt responsible. This entire situation could have been avoided, and with the passing of each day, the chance of locating Veronica alive was decreasing. He recalled his mother telling him being in charge could be painful and making a bad decision could cost you your life and the lives of those around you. He also wanted to see his two sons, but he and his team had to leave as soon as possible. He struggled internally with his frustration having to deal with all the pending issues.

Zenith noticed Dak in deep thought as she stepped out of the cabin into the bitterly cold wind. She knew he worried about the mission. She walked over to him. She was wrapped up in a fur lined coat and was enduring the cold weather. Dak looked at her and said, "You should be below deck."

Zenith tried to smile, "I have been below deck for two days. I need some fresh air. How much longer?"

Ronny looked at Zenith, "We have pulled close to the shoreline and are making a straight line to the dock at Cliff Tops. We should be passing the cliffs located out front of the New York tribe in the next few minutes. Then you will be at Cliff Tops later today."

Dak pulled Zenith in tight against him and held her. "Ronny is concerned we could be hit by a winter storm. We will be home in two to three hours. We will need to load enough coal to make the mission look legit and then head south. I am dreading telling the clan about our mission. We just do not know if Veronica is okay or not. Delores and Wayne will see right through this plan. They will not like my decision. There is a huge risk for all of us, and the reward we seek may not exist. We just do not know the location of Veronica."

Zenith could tell Dak was having second thoughts about finding Veronica. She also knew Dak did not wish to discuss the mission any further. "We need to update your mother on what she will be facing and make certain Samuel understands there are Rogue Bluebloods that we will end up fighting at some point."

***

Dak was conflicted between the opportunity to hold his sons and his dread with meeting the tribe's council. He stepped off the boat and took Zenith by the gloved hand. They went to the lift and hardly said hi to anyone. Once at the top of the cliff, they stepped off the lift and Wayne greeted them. "It is good to see you." Wayne smiled and announced, "I hope your journey was a good one. The kids are in the main house."

Dak and Zenith looked at Wayne. Dak announced, "We need your help."

"Yes, of course. Just name it." Wayne smiled to reflect his welcome attitude, but he could sense something ominous. He glanced down at the boat far below at the dock to see who else departed.

"We have more gold on that ship than we can count. You need to have the men unload the gold and secure it for us. We then need you to load the cargo bay on the aft side with a square of coal. We need to leave at sunrise in the morning. I then need you to take six pieces of gold to Zenith Point and check on our ranch. Pay Juan for running our ranch, and he will pay the hands as needed with the six coins. Tell him we will be home soon." He looked back at Wayne as he turned to walk away, "We also need as many bombs to take out ships as you can provide."

"Where is the rest of your group? Bombs?" He looked confused.

"They are busy modifying another ship we now own." He took two additional steps away from Wayne and made eye contact as he walked backward, "Please, no more questions."

Wayne was caught off guard with the request and the fact Dak and Zenith seemed to have an uninviting manner and then walked off toward the children. He realized Zenith had not made eye contact with him and had not spoken. She normally would smile and be cheerful. Wayne watched them walk

holding hands and considered what Dak had requested. He
went to the blacksmith shop and ordered the two men to help
off-load the boat and for the third man to go load a wagon with
a square of coal. Wayne followed the two men onto the lift and
looked at the ship at the dock as he flipped the lever. The lift
started dropping one foot at a time as the men stood in the cold
wind looking out over the sea.

Wayne walked to the ship and met Ronny, Darnel,
Bartholomew and Sneedy. The men introduced themselves.
Wayne saw the bags of gold as the men were carrying the bags
to the ship deck and then placing them on the dock. Wayne
looked at the gold and was somewhat surprised. He looked at
Ronny, "Where did all this gold come from?" He held his
hands out in disbelief.

Ronny smiled as he sat down a bag of gold on the dock,
"That is a long story. I was concerned about the high waves
and the horrible sailing conditions causing the gold to end up at
the bottom of the ocean. We are so happy we made the trip to
your dock. The gold was headed for King Solman in Southern
City, and we intercepted the ship and gold in transit. Believe
me when I tell you the theft was not easy. The entire story is
unbelievable." Ronny turned to the side to allow Bartholomew
to place a bag on the dock. Wayne then stepped on the deck
and watched Bartholomew walk into the lower cabin.

Wayne said, "I will make arrangements for your crew tonight with a warm room, beds, and plenty to eat."

Sneedy smiled, "A hot meal, warm fire, and a good bed would be gracious and appreciated. Maybe you could throw in some smooth warm rum." Sneedy then set his bag of gold down on the dock and turned to walk back to the cabin.

Wayne said, "I would also like to hear the story of this gold." The men on deck smiled.

Darnel walked by with a bag of gold, "You will not believe the story. Hell, I was there, and I do not believe what happened. I would not be surprised if Dak and his comrades could not walk on water."

Wayne smiled and turned and instructed his two men to start carrying the gold to the lift.

***

Vicky stepped outside her home and saw Zenith and Dak walking in a hurry to see their two kids. The boys were carried outside by Mia and Delores. They each were handed the sons, and they held them and kissed them. Dak announced, "I am holding Denzel. He has the narrow face."

"I have Drake. Mr. Fat cheeks." The wind was chilly, and the day was gray. Zenith then announced, "Let us go inside."

The group stepped inside, and Dak met his two half-sisters. He held all three kids as he sat in a chair. He tried to determine which half-sister was Kindle and which was Kenzie. He sat down with the three, looking from half-sister to half-sister. "Which one are you?" Zenith came over and started guessing. She changed her mind twice and finally Vicky picked up Kenzie.

Vicky then asked, "Where did you find someone to give you a ride in his sailing vessel this time of year? Only Captain J.J. would do something this dangerous."

"Actually, we own the ship. Ronny was a world class yacht's captain before the Transition Period. He escaped from the Normand army with his three comrades." Dak looked at his son and started talking baby talk. He then said, "I asked Wayne to assist with the off-loading of the stolen gold. He then needs help to load a square of coal. We will be leaving at first light."

Vicky could not help but show her surprise. "You are leaving in the morning?"

Dak looked up from the baby talk, "Where is Little Jimmy?"

Mia stepped forward and said, "Let me take Kindle from you." She had a concerned expression.

Delores looked surprised. "Dak, what is it you are not telling us? Why only ask about Little Jimmy?"

"Where are the men? Why is there no one guarding the city? We are at war."

Vicky announced, "A large group took Samuel on a hunting trip, and they were going to swing by Old Thomas's outpost. The hunting trip was to assist in male bonding. We have agreed to post men at the gates along with the New York tribe. We also have set up additional posts on the western front. The villagers from Meadow Bottoms have agreed to assist with those new outposts."

Dak glanced at Mia, "I am glad Little Jimmy is not present to hear my report. I love him, and I will do everything in my power to bring Veronica home."

Mia felt panic. "Where is my daughter?"

"Her disappearance was all my fault." He then looked at Mia, "She has been kidnapped. Our best guess is Veronica is being held in Southern City. Trey, Tommy Boy, Hulk, Robin Hood, Zenith, and I have a plan. Our four new friends are great sailors. We will sail into Southern City and find her, but first we need a square of coal."

Vicky raised her voice, "You need a square of coal?"

Zenith stopped the baby talk as she raised her head, "Dak has been beating himself up over Veronica being kidnapped, but her going missing was not his fault. This would never have occurred if the guys would listen to Dak." She looked back at

145

her son and kept bouncing him and lifting him in her hands. "We also need paperwork showing we are sailors from Israel, the small country located on the Asian continent."

Delores looked with total confusion, "Israel? Why Israel? I want to hear the plan."

Dak looked at his mother ignoring Delores, "After Wayne has some men load a square of coal on the boat, ask him to make us the counterfeit papers. We need identification for my group plus the four men working on our boat. We do not have much time. We leave at daybreak."

Vicky sat her daughter down and let her crawl to a toy. She was now frustrated, "Everyone, please clear the room except for Dak and Zenith."

The group left carrying the four children. Vicky looked at Zenith and then Dak, "How serious is the situation?"

"We believe we ran into a renegade Blueblood in an inlet waterway near the city of Tanger. We now believe there are more Bluebloods from the old German country than we first thought. This one most likely is the apprentice for King Solman but could be working for another cult leader. My first mistake was allowing Hulk to talk me into stealing the gold and not sinking the damn ship. The information from Aquarius was spot-on about the gold shipment. Hulk talked the group into stealing the gold instead of sinking the ship with the gold on board. There is more gold on your dock than you have ever seen. You will need to secure the gold and protect it. Someone will come after it." Dak broke eye contact, "Verónica felt the need to return a borrowed wagon and a team of horses which we used to haul the gold. As she returned the rig to the rancher, she might have been kidnapped. We had already cleared the mountains heading north. A week had passed before I was aware she was missing. Our information leads me to believe she was kidnapped by the renegade Blueblood. We must leave in the morning to beat the cold weather and a possible storm. The sailing vessel we own is not made to travel through fifty-foot swells. We need to do what we can as soon as we can. It has already been more than a month."

Vicky looked worried, "This seems to be a long shot. You could be arrested in Southern City. I do not want you to go. Matter of fact, I am ordering you to stay here. You need to wait for Little Jimmy."

"You will need Little Jimmy here to guard this city, our city, our way of life, and my two boys. King Solman will be coming after his gold at some point. I do not trust the Bluebloods in Merlin." He raised his voice, "You need to be preparing for war."

Zenith looked over at Vicky, "You need to make certain Samuel is ready for the renegade Blueblood warrior. He needs to be prepared. Once we leave, he will be the only one here who could stop a renegade Blueblood warrior."

Dak looked at his mother, "We are leaving in the morning. We have made up our minds. The others are waiting for us to return and pick them up in Harpers Ferry Harbor. I am frustrated with you. While we were down south fighting, you were doing nothing in the war effort. The men have gone camping. Mother, what are you thinking?"

Vicky looked angry and asked, "Why coal? I do not understand. They live in the warm region. Coal is used to generate heat. They do not need heat."

"We need to wave something in front of the Normand army that King Solman is trying to locate. He has advertised he wants coal." Dak hesitated, "We have concluded he is trying to manufacture gunpowder. He must already have nitrate and potassium. Ronny indicated he overheard the navy commanders talking a few years ago about King Solman demanding they locate coal. No one understood why. Then, when we ruled out all possibilities, all that is left is gunpowder.

"We assumed coal was plentiful all over the globe. Now, we understand no one has been able to locate coal since the Transition Period. Evidently, when the earth shifted because of the volcanoes, earthquakes, and the continents reforming, coal was either covered in ocean water or pushed deep under the earth's crust. Cliff Tops is the only territory that can harvest coal. That is why King Solman has attacked and will attack again in the future. Until the Normand Navy intercepted the cargo you sent by Captain J.J. six years ago, no one knew where coal could be located. Captain J.J. traded the coal, and that captain was caught with it and killed by King Solman's men. The coal was traced back to us here at Cliff Tops. He wants our coal, and he ordered General Cuez to take it by force. Now, we need to rest, eat, and love our kids because we leave in the morning."

Vicky looked stern, "King Solman cannot be allowed to have coal. He will refine it and turn it into powdered charcoal. If he has gunpowder, it won't be long before his army kills everyone in their path."

She was frustrated and added, "Let me tell you something. We are preparing for war. We are making Cliff Tops defendable against all armies. We work night and day. Our horse soldiers are ready to ride south down the Continental Trail as soon as the word is given. We have made certain the New York tribe has also accepted the challenge. We up north are ready to fight."

Dak smiled at his mother and then turned and asked Zenith to go bring his kids to him. He looked at his mother, "You need to have some men working on loading the boat with coal and tell Wayne to start working on our fake papers. We must leave tomorrow morning before the storms trap us here for the winter. We need the coal to entice King Solman which might give us time to locate Veronica." He grimaced after he spoke. His mother understood the black rings under his eyes and the frustrated look on his face. The mission was a long shot. She also knew his mind was made up.

***

Vicky watched as Zenith laid her sleeping son down and kissed him on the forehead. She looked at both boys with a compassionate smile. The two women walked out of the upstairs room. "Queen Vicky, I was wondering if there has been any news about my father?"

Vicky turned to Zenith, "We have not received any additional messages or news. Captain J.J. will not travel this far north until next spring."

Zenith looked at Vicky with a worried look, "My father is in the middle of the corruption. I fear it will only be a short time for the security team in Merlin to figure out who the source of the information was about the gold shipment being stolen. They will know by now the Meridian was hijacked while at sea. No one lived to tell the story on how we hijacked the cargo, but the two warships will report the ship sank. We tried to make the hijacking look random, but now we have spent some of the gold. The Merlin Senate will find out soon enough. I fear he will be killed if he does not leave soon." She looked at Vicky with the same worried expression.

Vicky hugged her. "I miss you. I miss Dak and his friends. We all worry about you guys. Tell Dak we are preparing for war. He seemed to think we are on vacation." She looked at Zenith, "I told Aquarius to locate a man I once knew who is in the underground. Aquarius will be protected if he makes contact."

Zenith said, "I met Ivan Chezon. He helped me and Dak escape." Zenith smiled at Vicky, "He smiled when he talked about you. He said there was no one better than you at being a field agent in the espionage business in the old world."

"I also wanted to let you know Dak and I both were shot with arrows as we stole the gold. Dak wanted to sink the ship and the gold. Hulk proclaimed after we were seventy percent through the operation, we should have sunk the ship and sent the gold to the bottom of the ocean. Dak was right, and we did not listen to him. Veronica would not take no for an answer and now she has been kidnapped. Dak tries to do the right thing. He knows you are the Queen, and he loves you."

Vicky looked away with a nostalgic thought about the old days. She considered Ivan as she listened to Zenith. "Ivan is very resourceful. We ran some questionable operations together in the old days. He always came through. I trust him. We will pray for your group and Veronica. As a leader, you are forced to make the best decision you can and go with it. In war, people die."

Zenith was surprised with the matter-of-fact response about war and death. She had never considered the Queen to be accepting the perils of war.

Chapter 15

Veronica was bored as she was slumped over in a chair with her feet placed on the wall. Dezie walked into her chambers and smiled. "How did your exercise session go this morning?" Dezie laid a bag on the table.

"I am tired. I worked out hard for close to two hours. I guess I will sit in the sun on the balcony and rest. I am so bored being imprisoned. I would love to see the city or go for a horse ride in the country. Maybe a walk on the beach would be nice, but staying in here looking at these four walls is not entertaining."

"I brought you some more lotion. The lotion will protect your skin and help keep your skin moist and rich-looking. The air is so dry in this part of the world. You need the lotion. Come out on the balcony, and I will help rub the lotion on your back."

"I do like the view from the balcony. I wish I was a little closer to the ocean and able to see the beach. I like the high view and looking down on the city." She hoped Dezie would suggest a walk to the ocean or a walk through the city. She needed to see how she might escape and by sea was going to be her best opportunity. She glanced at Dezie as they walked out the door to the balcony. She noticed there were no wrinkles, and her face was blemish free. "How old are you?"

"The key to looking young is the lotion. My family and friends all used lotion starting when we were teenagers. I am seventy-six years old."

"My goodness. Please give me the lotion. I thought you were in your forties."

The two were standing on the balcony. Veronica dropped her robe and laid down on her stomach. "Do you have any more secrets you can share with me about men?"

Dezie smiled and started rubbing the lotion on her back and across her nude body to her feet. "I believe you need to understand how fortunate you are to be able to live in this nice chamber and have food delivered to you. I know you exercise a lot here by yourself. I am glad you enjoyed your workout in the gym. My job is to help you look pretty and give you advice. Remember what I told you about men. They are different, and they all have their own vices. You need to learn the deepest desires of a man and then feed the pleasure zone. You must play the game to win, and a woman must also learn to enjoy the encounters."

Veronica said, "The lotion has kept you looking so young. Do not stop rubbing the lotion on me. That feels good. You keep telling me how lucky I am and yet I am imprisoned."

"Honey, you could be sent to the soldiers in the field, and you would not return. Believe me when I speak to you." Dezie rubbed the lotion into her arch, up her legs and then over her butt.

"You have mentioned to me several times about King Solman sending me to the army and forcing me to live as a whore working in their tents. How many females has he sent to the tents?"

Dezie was careful with her answer. She knew the King could be a monster. "I do not know. He has sent several women over the past few years. They no longer please him, and he sends them away."

"What kind of man would do something like that to another human? What type of employee would stand by and allow that reprehensible action to go unchallenged?"

"You ask too many questions. You are very smart and that concerns me. He will not like you asking him questions, but I do not believe the King has the ability to feel empathy for others. Once the King has no use for someone, that person may be forced to be a slave working in the city for another, sold to one of the warlords in the outskirts or worse. I am lucky to work in the castle as I do, and I am trying to help you as much as I can."

They heard the door open and in walked Michael. Dezie kept rubbing the lotion over Veronica's back. Michael walked over to the balcony door and saw Dezie rubbing the lotion on the nude body of Veronica while she was lying on the long bench. He tried to look the other way but became fixated on the view. "The King's personal envoy has delivered the request. You have been summoned by our King to report at once to his office. King Solman demands you hurry."

Veronica rolled over spreading her legs as she sat up with one leg on the right side of the bench and the other foot and leg on the opposite side. She knew Michael, with his face shield pulled down, was watching her even though he was facing the view from the balcony over the city. She intentionally looked at Dezie to provide Michael an opportunity to look at her without anyone noticing. "The King can wait. I need time to have lotion rubbed on my body. Dezie, please help me." Veronica placed her left foot on the bench with her leg extended.

Dezie looked worried. She immediately rubbed the lotion on Veronica's left leg and then her right leg. Dezie glanced at Michael to verify if he was watching.

Michael then said, "Princess, you need to understand our King is very impatient. Our King does not like to wait. He might elect to discipline you for being tardy."

Veronica held her hand out for Dezie to pour some lotion into it. "I understand the definition of impatient. You do not need to repeat yourself."

She took her time and rubbed the lotion on her arms and then her private area while looking at Dezie and allowing Michael the opportunity to observe. "Please Princess, we need to hurry."

Dezie stepped back and noticed Michael was watching through his metal mask which covered his eyes. Dezie could see his eyes fixated and smiled to herself knowing what Veronica was doing. She could tell Michael was powerless to look the other way. She also suspected as Michael first approached the balcony, he would not have been aware Veronica was nude, but once he noticed, he was cataleptic and caught in the trance. She further knew one of the main characteristics to be a King's Guard was the sworn oath to live with honor. The King's Guards were required to follow the rules to the letter, and the guards were required to daily swear to the rules of honor. To become a King's Guard, was of the highest rewards in the kingdom which resulted in the highest pay among the guards, soldiers, and castle employees. The men had to be distinguished in combat but also in character. To be expelled from being a King's Guard was to be forced to live with disgrace. Depending on the circumstance, death by being beaten by the other guards in the King's court room could be the extreme punishment. Dezie realized Veronica was a fast learner on how to gain the attention of a man. She was surprised how fast Veronica had retained her advice about men, and she had allowed Michael the opportunity to observe her as she acted innocent, rubbing the lotion on herself in his presence.

Dezie smiled and stepped forward and placed the robe over Veronica's shoulders, "We must hurry and get you inside and dressed. The King's Guard is correct. You do not need to make the King wait." Dezie looked at Michael, "You need to wait outside in the hall. It would not be appropriate for you to watch the Princess getting dressed."

***

The two started to walk through the dark hallway. "You know Princess, you make this hard on yourself. I am trying to help you."

As they turned the corner in the hall, "If you are trying to help me, why did you not assist by rubbing the lotion on my legs or back?"

He smiled. He knew Verónica was not someone who was accustomed to taking orders. He knew she did not like being held against her will. He also knew she was beautiful, smart, and very good with a sword. "I am scared for you. You are defiant and King Solman does not tolerate defiance. I wish you would listen to what I say." He reached for the door to the stairs, opening the door for her. Veronica stepped across the threshold and kept walking. He again opened the door to the King's office. He whispered, "Be apologetic and not defiant. Please Princess."

Veronica smirked as she looked at Michael as he pulled the door shut behind her as she passed him crossing the threshold. Veronica immediately smiled at King Solman sitting behind his desk. She walked into the center of the room. He immediately told the three commanders, the two-office staff members, and his two King's Guards to clear the room. The men stood from the sitting positions and followed the King's Guards out of the room. Veronica stood still, staring at nothing as she waited. He stood and observed her in her beautiful dress. King Solman took a second to appreciate her standing still with her face level and stern expression as she stared straight in front of her. In a harsh voice he demanded, "What was the meaning of the fighting in the training pit this morning?" He walked forward.

"Your majesty, I was granted the opportunity to work out by you. I worked out for two hours and then returned to my chambers accompanied by Michael, your trusted guard."

"I did not provide you with an opportunity to fight two of my jailers and embarrass them. I understand you forced them to walk down the street to the orphanage in the nude holding hands, and if they did not do as you commanded, you threatened them." His jaws were now clenched, and his voice was harsh, "I understand you told them they would be cut with the loss of their manhood." He stared at her, and she did not flinch. He spoke firmly, "You do not tell my men what to do. You do not select the punishment for my guards."

Veronica was short and to the point, "They challenged me in the combat ring with a sword. They lost the bet. They tried to back out of their commitment. Your prison guards need to live with honor and honor their sworn statement." She turned to look at the king and raised one eyebrow, "I was forced to offer them an additional incentive. As I just said, they tried to back out of the wager." She maintained her rigid posture then turned her gaze back in front staring straight ahead.

"Maybe I should take you down to the pit and challenge you." He slowly walked around her looking at her as she stood stiff with her face looking straight in front of her.

"If that is what you desire, your majesty. I hope you have better footwork than your guards. They are accustomed to punching and butchering people who are in bondage that cannot defend themselves."

He grabbed her by the wrist and spun her abruptly around. He held her tight and looked into her beautiful eyes. "You are special. I grant you that. You will need to report to my chambers at eight tonight."

"Yes, your majesty. I look forward to spending time with you."

"Do not lie to me. I know better." He studied her face for a hint of an expression and then allowed his view of her to drop to her cleavage. He felt the intoxicating effects of her scent.

He released her and stepped toward his desk, "In the daily report from the manager of the maid service, Dezie has indicated you would like to see the country. Maybe I can arrange that for you." Veronica tried to hide her surprise. This might be the opportunity she needed. "But in the meantime, follow me to the court room. You can see that I try to be fair to the citizens. I try to provide for them. I am a loyal king to the people in my realm."

***

When they entered the large room, Veronica was directed to a chair at the front of the court. King Solman sat down on the throne and looked at the standing audience. "Let the court begin."

The court master was an old man with gray hair and was dressed in a robe over gray pants and black boots. He walked out with a stack of papers in his hands. He announced, "First is the dispute between the Sergeant of Little Town and the Bar Owner in Little Town. The allegation by the bar owner initially stated he is overtaxed, but the real allegation as we discovered in the court of Little Town, is the Sergeant of Little Town is taking more money than he is reporting to the City Tax Collector. I have summoned the City Tax Collector as a witness."

The two men walked to the front of the court. King Solman changed his sitting position and leaned forward as he appeared to be more in tune to the trial once stealing tax money was mentioned. He announced, "Proceed."

The bar owner immediately explained his expense of the business and the high tax, and the tax was not fair. He paid more and more each month which was a lot more than the mandated city tax rate. He then added that several soldiers, guards, and naval personnel frequented his bar. He was always gracious to the King's men.

Veronica could tell the bar owner was nervous. After making his allegation of being overtaxed, he tried to win the king over with stressing how he appreciated the soldiers, guards, and naval personnel coming to his establishment. She glanced at King Solman and felt he was trying to show her he was a reasonable fair man. She considered if she was not in attendance and someone complained about paying taxes, he would have the guards punish the person.

The bar owner could sense the King's demeanor changed. He started to add to his story.

King Solman interrupted the bar owner, "Who is your number one group of customers?"

The bar owner now looked nervous, "Your Honor, the large group of soldiers are the number one group. We cater to them. The farmers and other tradespeople leave once they arrive. The soldiers like to fight and break the furniture, but they pay for the damage and broken furniture."

"Who do you think pays the soldiers?"

The bar owner looked scared and knew this was a rhetorical question.

"I pay them to spend money in your bar. You are allowed to run your bar because I said it was okay. The soldiers are a privileged, and you need to treat them as such. Without them, you would be homeless. Now pay your taxes."

King Solman looked mad. He looked at the Sergeant of Little Town, "If I find out you are skimming taxes off the top, I will have your head. I need people like these bar owners to operate their businesses and pay me their taxes."

The Sergeant looked at King Solman, "Sir, we keep records of what we collect from each business. Our records reflect the bar owner's records. We collect the rate the city tax office tells us to collect. I can assure you my men do not steal."

King Solman stared at the Sergeant of Little Town and realized where the extra income from the inflated tax rate was going. He glanced at the court reporter who was recording the testimony of the witnesses to publish the findings for the general population. King Solman mandated the reporting of the trial to motivate the citizens to do what he expected. His final judgements were harsh. He then looked at the bar owner. "Bring me the records. I need to make someone an example of stealing my money." He reviewed the records and laid the paperwork down. "You better not come before my court again, or I will place your head and your men's heads on a stake outside the city park for all to see."

He motioned for the City Tax Collector to come forward. The man was obese and appeared to walk without concern. He stopped in front of King Solman's throne. King Solman motioned for his two guards to come out. "Take this man to the dungeon and remove his head. Place his head on a stake at the entrance gate for all to see. He is the one stealing from the people. He raised the tax rate and kept the increase. Next case." The guards were fast and grabbed the City Tax Collector by the arms. They drug him out the side door with him crying out for help. Both the bar owner and the sergeant looked horrified and turned and quickly walked out the rear double doors located at the back of the court.

The court master walked out and announced, "This case is between two common women, both citizens of Southern City. The disagreement is about which one of the women is the mother of this baby boy."

The two women walked to their positions. King Solman looked at the two women, "Where is the baby?"

"Your Honor, the baby is being housed at the orphanage on orders of the judge in Little Town until which time the case has been resolved. The plaintiff has petitioned the Court of Little Town to appeal the case to your court for you to review. Sister Louise is holding the baby," announced the court clerk.

King Solman motioned for Sister Louise to bring the baby to him. He leaned forward and stared at the child and then at the two women. He could not see a resemblance with either woman. He then looked at the woman on the right. She was a young thin teenager with dark skin. He held his hand out meaning for her to begin. "The baby is mine by birth. I was struggling after the birth with my recovery. I have now recovered, and she took my baby."

King Solman looked at the younger woman, "How many babies have you given birth?"

Your honor, "This is my first."

"Where is the father?"

"Your honor. I work as seamstress, and I was raped by some men one night. Consequently, I became pregnant. I intend to keep my baby. She is paid per child that she houses. She has over twenty kids. I do not want my baby to be raised by a woman who does not love the child."

King Solman looked at the middle-aged, dark skin woman. He knew she was being paid to raise children. The more children, the more the state paid her. He did not like this system, but with the large number of kids homeless and without parents, it somewhat worked. Most of his soldiers came from the orphanages or the state-established situational parents. He had set up training for the kids starting at age eight and by the time they were sixteen, they were soldiers. "Is this your baby?"

"Yes, I gave birth to the baby. Her baby died. It ran a high fever and then died."

Veronica could tell the young girl was the mother. She despised someone taking advantage of the young woman. She thought, "How many other women have lost their kids to the city program instructors." She also knew King Solman was mostly concerned with protecting his established programs. He needed the sergeant collecting high taxes, and the soldiers spending their income in bars who were highly taxed. A high percentage of the soldier's money was circulated back to his account to run the city and expand his army. He also needed people like this lady raising kids and training them to be soldiers. She knew what the King was prepared to do. Veronica announced, "Why do we not place the child on the floor and cut it in half. Each lady can leave the courtroom with half a baby. Then, we will be done with this trivial matter."

King Solman did not tolerate someone in his courtroom speaking out of turn. He was surprised and the entire courtroom full of people looked at Veronica. He announced, "Yes, as long as you swing the sword." He was surprised that Veronica had suggested such a barbaric remedy. He knew she would not kill a child, or had he underestimated her? He smiled at Veronica. He turned to Sister Louise holding the baby. "Place the child on the floor for all to witness."

The lady holding the baby looked in total disbelief and horrified at the thought of cutting the child in half, "But your Majesty? Please provide grace and mercy."

King Solman raised his voice, "I said place the child on the floor in the middle so everyone can bear witness to the court's decision." He glanced at the court reporter who was writing down the testimony of the witnesses.

The lady cried and tried to hide her tears as she laid the child on the concrete floor, making certain the blanket stayed wrapped around the child. He turned to Veronica and motioned for her to proceed. Veronica stood without looking at either lady and walked to Michael and held her hand out for his sword. Michael handed her his sword and whispered, "Do not do this."

Veronica looked Michael in the eyes and took the sword. She walked to the middle of the room and turned to face the audience and the two women. "Which half do you desire?"

The young girl ran past the guard and fell over the child covering the child, "Please kill me and not my baby. Please, I beg you." King Solman looked at the middle-aged woman, and she had not moved or showed any signs of loving the child. He looked back to the floor and watched as the young lady held the child hugging it while crying.

Veronica turned and faced King Solman sitting on his throne, "This is the one true mother. Only a real mother would be willing to sacrifice her life for her child."

The young lady looked up while crying at King Solman, "Please do not kill my baby. I beg mercy for the child."

Veronica walked back to Michael and handed him his sword. She then turned and declared, "We will not be cutting a child in half today. You may take your child and leave. We will try to assist you with payments to raise your child. Southern City needs more mothers like you."

King Solman watched the lady take her child and rush out the back double doors. He motioned for his guard to take the other lady. "Deceit in my court is not tolerated. Twenty lashes to her back. The court has ruled."

Veronica looked at King Solman. She knew she overstepped her bounds by speaking in the courtroom and rendering the final decision on the case. She was concerned about what he might do to her. "I will return to my chambers. I need time to prepare for my eight-P.M. meeting." She turned and walked out with Michael following her.

King Solman smiled to himself and watched her as she left the courtroom. His thoughts, for a couple of seconds, jumped forward thinking about the eight-P.M. meeting, as he considered his sexual desires.

Michael opened the door to her chambers, and the two walked into the suite, "You had no intentions of harming that child. Did you?"

Veronica crossed the foyer and then the great room and opened the door to the balcony. She stood in the breeze and felt the warm wind blow across her body. She then turned and walked to the pitcher of water and poured herself a glass. She studied Michael as she drank her water. "I am tired. I will lie in the sun and tan. I need your assistance with rubbing the lotion on my back. The lotion protects my skin." She walked over to him and smiled and took his hand and led him to the balcony. "The view out here is remarkable. I wish we were closer to the sea to look out over the ocean. Maybe I will be provided an escort to see the countryside. I would very much like to go into the country and see the area on horseback." She had studied the façade of the building under her balcony and one-hundred-foot drop to the street below. There was a balcony over about fifteen-feet to her left side and then another balcony over fifteen additional feet. The castle was not built for luxury. The castle was built for protection against invading armies. She needed a rope to escape to the street. Once out of the large castle, she would need additional assistance to hide in the city. There were too many Kings' Guardsmen and too many soldiers in Southern City for her to escape. She knew at some point the army would be deployed north. She knew her family and friends could not repel such a large, organized war machine. She needed help, and she needed to warn her tribe what was coming.

She turned and stepped behind Michael as he stared at the view of the city below and the ocean in the far horizon. She then removed her dress and then unfastened her sandals as he peered over the balcony toward the sea and the city. She removed her underwear. He turned and froze at the sight of her standing nude in front of him. She was blocking his path to the interior balcony door. He instantly felt despair. He knew if he was seen with Veronica under these conditions, he would be slowly tortured to death over a long period of time in the King's courtroom. He felt his pulse elevate and sweat broke out across his upper lip. "You need to stand to the side and not block my path to that door." He pointed to the doorway.

She moved to the side and got on all fours and then laid down on the mat on the bench. She pulled her long ponytail over to the side of her head. "You need to hurry and rub the lotion on me. I do not have any desires to have cracked, dry skin. I expect you to rub the lotion into my skin thoroughly."

He stepped past her, so he could have a clear path to the exit door. He could not resist, and he turned and looked at her lying on her stomach. He shuddered, "No Princess. I cannot touch you. Not in this manner. I will send for your handmaid."

"I know you reported some of what happened in the workout ring to King Solman. Why did you not tell him the complete true story? Those two were trying to win, and I beat them. You say you live with honor, but you did not tell the truth. This is an order. This is your punishment for not telling King Solman the entire truth. Now rub the lotion on me, or I might have to tell the King you are the one who lied."

"You do not understand. Sander and Bruno reported they let you win. They lied. They reported they were scared the King would kill them if they won. I knew the report needed to be handled very delicately. I told King Solman you won the contest, but the two guards may have been holding back. They are dungeon guards. It would not be good if the King's Dungeon Guards were beaten in a fair sword match by a female."

She raised her left foot and let her foot bend upward and then balanced her foot on the mat. "You mean beaten by a female imprisoned slave. You lied. You know I won with them trying their hardest and now you must be punished. You must remember I have the King's ear."

He glanced at the door and wondered what were the chances of someone opening the door right now. He reluctantly removed his gloves and placed some lotion in his right hand and rubbed the light tan lotion across her upper back with a quick fast motion. He noticed the smell of coconut lotion and the gobbets of lotion on her back. "You need to slow down, use both hands, and rub the lotion into my skin. Now start all over. The next time you will report the truth. You need to be taught there is a consequence to being untruthful."

Michael involuntarily took a deep breath and glanced at the closed door. He looked at her perfectly tan body. He noticed her small waistline and round butt, her athletic legs. "Yes Princess, I will try to do better. Please forgive me of my transgressions."

He slowed down and enjoyed using both hands, "King Solman mentioned he would settle the disagreement and would fight you in the challenge ring. Princess, King Solman can be mean and brutal. He has broken several arms, legs, noses, and ribs in the ring of challenge. He saw my expression. He then asked me if I did not agree with him. I told him he needed not underestimate you with a sword. You took out Sander within a few seconds in round one and you played with Bruno. You did not place the cold ash on your blade until the start of round two. I thought he was going to hit me when I suggested he might want to practice before he challenges you. I very much tried to be honest. Princess, please forgive me." He slowly worked his way to her lower legs and then her feet, rubbing the coconut scented lotion on her feet.

"Princess, I must go at once you do not understand how this effects my judgement." He abruptly jumped up and walked for the exit door and closed the door behind him. Veronica watched him close the door and thought about her options. She needed help to escape. The only two people she talked with were Michael and Dezie, whom she now knew she could not trust. Dezie reported daily everything to the King's Guard and for selfish reasons would not take a chance of losing her job of working in the comfort of the castle. Michael on the other hand, had left items out of his report that could possibly have belittled her in front of the King. She knew she would escape or die trying. Maybe Michael could be manipulated.

Michael hurried, walking down the hall to the indoor privy. He went into the stall and thought about Veronica and how he had touched her. He could not deny his feelings for her. He looked at his hands and noticed the buildup of the lotion. He took himself in his hand and knew he had to release himself. He knew he would need to return to his post before anyone noticed he was not at his station. He rushed himself. Then, he fixed his attire. He wiped the sweat from his forehead and thought about what had just happened. He thought to himself, "I need to stay strong. I must be strong, or I can be manipulated to break orders and the code I swore." He rushed out the bathroom door and returned to his post.

Chapter 16

Trey announced, "This is a little better than our prior voyage. Dammit, that prior voyage about killed me."

Hulk smiled and agreed, "Anything would be better than the prior voyage. Sea sickness is the only disease where a person comes back from the dead." He smiled, "You, Robin Hood, and Tommy Boy looked dead during the prior voyage."

Robin Hood looked angry, "I have told you guys several times. I would not have gotten sick and died if I had not laid down on the cabin floor. Those two who were laying on the only two cots, when the boat rolled on the waves, all their puke flowed down on me. At first, I did not understand how I suddenly was wet and smelled like four-day old dead cats, but when I did finally make the connection, I did not have a choice but to puke my toenails up."

The group laughed. Tommy Boy looked at Robin Hood then added, "Even though I wished I were dead, I still love hearing your description of the boat trip. That was my fault. I should have told you the puke was going to flow downhill. I was dead and could not speak."

Zenith smiled, "We are not close to land this time and maybe the motion sickness is easier on you."

Trey looked surprised, "I still do not like traveling on a ship. I am not meant to be a sailor."

Hulk laughed, "Damn Trey, you complain on horseback and now by boat. You might need to start walking."

"Hell no. I am not made for walking either." The group laughed.

Robin Hood became serious. He looked at Hershel and then Ronny, "So you believe we will sail into the port of Southern City and sail out without problems?"

Dak looked at Robin Hood, "There are going to be problems caused by the Normand army. The city is a fortress. We are not listed on their register of trading vessels. This is going to be dicey. No one leaves or arrives without being searched and questioned. Our main objective is to locate and rescue Veronica. The second objective is to set King Solman and his army back, but the main purpose is to free our friend. I mentioned to Vulture and the men of Harper Ferry's Harbor to be prepared for battle. The war will be coming behind us as we flee north. King Solman will want to attack and conquer the north before the middle tribes unite. He knows if he can keep taking out the small villages along the way and then the larger cities, he will win. He will also not like us entering his city and sabotaging his ships."

Ronny then mentioned, "We have a trap door well-hidden and fake papers. We can smuggle you guys into the harbor without anyone noticing. I like the plan. We are moving twenty-four hours a day at a good speed. We should be arriving in three days. Unless we run into a storm, this should work. They will not be expecting us." He then held his hands out, "The tropical weather could generate a hurricane even this time of year."

Hulk looked fierce, "I hate the Normand soldiers. I will kill all I can of them."

Dak looked at his friend, "I do not hate them. I kill them because it is the right thing to do. I am trying to protect the innocent people and our village."

Hulk looked at Dak, "The sooner you start hating them, the easier the path will be for you to kill them. You need to accept this war, and what we must do."

Zenith looked at the men, "Dak is right. You kill an animal because of a need to eat. You chop down a live tree for a need. You should never kill just to be killing or kill out of hatred."

Dak looked at Hulk, "We must fight these battles and win because it is the right thing to do."

Hulk looked at the ocean and then turned, "I guess I am wired differently than you. When I see what those soldiers do to the innocent people and know what they are trying to do to our tribe, I choose to hate them."

Zenith looked at Hulk, "We were taught not to hate people. The Blueblood army was taught to follow orders, and the Blueblood warriors were genetically designed to be soldiers and be obedient to the Blueblood commanders. I have heard the conditions were so bad outside our city with the warlords and the poor, the good people were forced to turn to crime. They were miserable and when caught, they would accept the consequences The punishment was called suicide by Blueblood sword. There was no easy answer. When the Blueblood army took over the city of Merlin and the Senate, I was still a child. We were told the political restructuring was for the good, but like so many things that happen, the senators became greedy, and greed is a virus that must be controlled." She looked at Dak and friends. "We cannot allow all the bad memories to affect us and keep us from loving. We cannot change the hearts of men. We cannot correct the evil in the world. The world has always been evil. What we can do is love each other and assist the ones we can help. We can fight the wicked and try to protect the innocent. We need to condition ourselves not to hate and that is the best we can offer." She looked at Hulk.

Robin Hood smiled, "I hate that I did not talk to the brunette that works in the hardware store in Harpers Ferry Harbor." The group laughed.

Ronny smiled, "She would be the only female you didn't have a conversation within Harpers Ferry Harbor."

Hulk blurted out, "I am certain she feels blessed not to have talked with you, and I know her father could not have been happier." They all laughed.

Chapter 17

"The ship is flying a Normand flag." He squinted into the binoculars, "The sailing vessel is a warship and headed straight for us," yelled Darnel.

Ronny looked through his binoculars, "What in the hell is a Normand navy vessel doing this far out? The ship has a harpoon mounted on the front extended deck. No doubt the vessel is one of their class B warships with at least thirty-five troops and four harpoons. We cannot outrun them, and with the harpoons, we will not stand a chance. You need to have everyone in the hidden storage. We are going to be boarded. Their protocol will be for them to search the ship." He looked worried and took off his binoculars. "This is not good. We are out of the shipping lanes with no way to defend ourselves. We will be at their mercy."

Dak instructed, "Hulk, you and Tommy Boy set two explosives. You need to be the first in our hidden cargo bay. Hershel you will man the escape door. Robin Hood, you enter and then Trey. I will be in the hidden half closet and signal you two. Zenith you cover up and stay with Bartholomew, Sneedy and Darnel."

Dak looked at Ronny and then Bartholomew, "We need to draw them in close and then sink their ship. They will not be able to warn anyone of our location. We need to stick to our plan and approach Southern City from the southwest, so they will not think we are synchronizing with the north. If this goes sideways, we all fight to the death." Dak looked at Ronny, "You need to stall them and give us a fighting chance."

Ronny shook his head that he understood what Dak had said. Then, he spread his hands out and asked, "Did you not hear me? They will have thirty-five marines on board and four harpoons on their ship. You and your men need to stay hidden. That is the only chance we have. We cannot fight that many trained men."

Ronny then looked at Dak while he was considering Dak's plan. He looked at Zenith and then back at Dak, "Is she as good as they say?"

Dak answered, "You will find out how good she is. She has fought beside me in several battles. She is better with a sword than most of the Bluebloods in Merlin. Zenith, you need to wait on me. Once the cabin is clear, I will open the hatch for Trey, then we will attack."

Zenith gave Dak the expression, "I know." She then looked at Ronny and added, "All these guys are special warriors with enhanced reflexes, strength, and agility. They all are excellent in combat. The thirty-five Normand Marines will not stand a chance."

Hulk looked at Ronny, "There is about to be thirty-five dead marines and one less Normand vessel." He ducked down and hid behind the rail, then followed Dak to the lower cabin.

***

Ronny gave the order to drop the sails. "We need to look passive." Darnel and Sneedy immediately untied the rope and dropped the catch sail. Then, they untied the ropes, and the two main sails dropped. Sneedy reported, "Captain, we are still in the water." Both him and Ronny watched as the Normand war vessel closed in on their position. As they stood and watched the ship move closer, they both could not help but feel uneasy about the larger intimidating ship approaching. They both knew the men on board would be killers, and the chance they would receive mercy was slim.

The Normand warship sailed up next to their sailing ship. The warship had four harpoons, two platforms in the bow and two on the aft aimed at his ship. There were several men with bows loaded with arrows along the warship railing. Ronny yelled at the captain, "We are transporting items for the Country of Israel. Is there a problem?" He waited and then added, "The waves are too high to pull too close and board. My ship will be torn to pieces if it gets pinned under your large vessel." He raised his arms with his palms up trying to convey he was honest and did not present a threat.

The Normand captain was a mean man. He was an alcoholic and when his hidden whiskey ran out, he became very irritable. He constantly lived with a frown and seemed to be bitter with life. He was difficult to work under, and his subordinates feared and hated him. He ruled with anger, and he used the anger to motivate his men to do their tasks. He threatened them with being transferred to be foot soldiers on the northern front where they were required to fight villagers with swords one community at a time as the Normand army moved north. There was no war at sea, and his sailors wanted to avoid being foot soldiers and having to live off the land and kill innocent people. He ignored Ronny, "Hold your fire." He then looked at Ronny, "We will throw you the tow ropes. You will tie your boat to ours, or I will have my men fire multiple harpoons into the side of your ship."

Ronny and Bartholomew caught the ropes and tied off the front and rear of the ship.

The captain looked at the second in command. "Lieutenant, board that ship and report back to me. I want to know who is on that vessel, and what they are hauling. I also want to know why they are so far out at sea." He then grunted in a low voice, "We may kill the crew and sink that ship."

"Yes sir." He motioned for six marines and four sailors to join him. He gave the order to secure the walking platform to the other ship.

As they were entering the hidden cargo hold, Dak told Hulk and Tommy Boy to make certain the charges were turned to blow inward on the large ship. Tommy Boy and Hulk held up the explosives showing the direction the explosives needed to be set.

Trey pulled the hatch door down, and Dak made certain the door panel was in place. Dak whispered they were installing the boardwalk. He then stepped inside the hidden closet and squatted down in front of the backside of the panel as he made certain the panel was in place.

Sneedy whispered, "Dak, the panel looks good from this side. Here they come across the plank. I will go up top." He then walked to the deck and took a seat.

Hulk listened and when Sneedy announced in a whispered voice that the Normand sailors were coming across the plank, he opened the ocean side hatch door located in the bottom of the boat and slipped out into the ocean. He hated tight places, and the fake floor installed in the bottom of their vessel only provided a few inches for him to crawl. Tommy Boy also hated the hidden cargo bay both men were having trouble breathing in such a restricted area. Tommy Boy was fighting the effects of claustrophobia. He was happy to follow Hulk into the warm water. The two men swam to the front of the large ship while under water. They proceeded down the starboard side of the Normand vessel. Hulk motioned for Tommy Boy to install his explosive device in that spot. He mouthed, "I will wave to you when I am in position."

Tommy Boy held onto the side of the large boat. He glanced up every few seconds along the seaward side making certain no one was looking over the rail and could spot him. The crew of the warship had been focused on the ship tied off and being boarded on the portside. He looked down the length of the warship and saw Hulk raise his hand. Both men went under water and attached the explosive devices. They set the timers for ten minutes. They both surfaced and gave the thumbs up sign to each other and headed back to their ship.

Once on board, the lieutenant ordered one marine to check the cabin. He ordered the other marines to search the crew. Darnel, Sneedy and Bartholomew stood, and all three men were searched quickly and then forced back to their knees. The guard looked at Zenith as she stood. He judged her to be a teenage boy and not a threat. She was wearing baggy clothes and had her hair hidden under a large brim hat and pulled under her large baggy shirt. He looked at the small person that stood less than five-feet four inches tall and appeared to be scared and shy. The guard did not see a sword or weapon and signaled to the lieutenant the person was not carrying a weapon. The Lieutenant walked up to Ronny and pushed him backward. "What are you hauling?"

Ronny developed a frown, "Coal. We are scheduled to deliver the cargo to Israel in three weeks. Our manifest is hanging next to the wheel."

The lieutenant ordered the sailor to bring him the paperwork. He smiled as he read the word coal. "Where are you sailing from?"

Ronny knew the manifest outlined they had departed from Vermal. The city located on the northeast coastline of the Asian Continent. "We are scared of the pirates along the coastline of the Asian continent. The trip is safer to sail around the continent and pass Southern City."

Dak waited in his hidden spot in the closet. His legs were aching as he was in a squat position with his back pressed against the back wall. The build-out had worked but was tight. He could see through the small hole which was covered with a picture as he watches the stairs of the cabin. He could see the Normand marine walk-in front of him as the man passed into the cabin.

Zenith sat down after being confronted by the marine. She had watched as the three other sailors were searched. She observed the Normand marines how they appeared confident in their numbers and superior training. She determined her next move, and which to kill first. She sat and waited in the middle of the deck along with Sneedy, Bartholomew, and Darnel.

Trey, Robinhood, and Hershel were hidden under the floor in the hidden cargo bay. The men had worked night and day to install the false floor while Dak and Zenith had sailed to Cliff Tops in the other sailing vessel. Two trap doors were added to the bottom of the boat. The trap door leading into the ocean prevented anyone seeing them exit the ship underwater. The buoyancy of the vessel would not allow water to enter and flood the lower level. The key to the installation of the trap door was the door had to be installed in a flat area in the very bottom of the boat with a six-inch drop into the ocean. This provided enough air pressure to hold the ocean water from entering the bottom of the vessel.

Dak waited as three minutes had passed. His legs were aching as he needed to shift his weight. He knew he could not take a chance on making a noise. He could hear the soldier going through the personal items of the crew. No doubt he was looking for items with value to steal.

The guys hidden in the cargo bay were being forced to lie flat and very still. If water entered the boat, they would be forced to lay in ocean water. Dak knew they would be miserable lying on their backs in the bay. Hershel had to wait for Hulk and Tommy Boy to return, so the two men could enter the ship. Hulk and Tommy Boy could only hold their breath for a minute under water. The door had to be opened quickly while one at a time entered.

Dak knew that as soon as the marine walked out of the cabin, he would open the trap door for Trey. He saw the marine pass in front of him as he stared through the peephole. He heard the marine ascend the steps leading to the deck and then announced, "All clear." Dak glanced at his watch. Six minutes had now passed. He was not certain how far from the cabin door the guard was standing.

Trey and Robin Hood could hear the Normand soldier as he stepped on the wood floor inches directly above them. They knew if they made a sound they would be discovered. Hershel was lying next to the trap door hoping Tommy Boy or Hulk did not knock on the door while the Normand guard was searching the cabin. He held his breath and prayed in silence.

Five of the Normand men were standing guard over Ronny, his three crew members and Zenith. The lieutenant was more concerned with the cargo. When Ronny mentioned coal, he was excited. He ordered two of his men to open the large cargo door and to drop down into the bay to verify coal was being hauled. Once the first sailor pitched a piece of coal through the cargo door with the coal landing on the deck, the lieutenant seemed to relax. The lieutenant held the coal for the captain to see. "They are hauling a square of coal."

The captain smiled for the first time in a long time at the sight of the black coal. He knew he had just gotten lucky. King Solman rewarded men who produced results, and he had just located coal. King Solman had placed a reward for coal to be delivered to him in Southern City. "Kill all the sailors except the captain, bring the coal to the aft storage and then sink their vessel. Bring the captain to me."

Ronny yelled, "This is a small amount of coal. If you kill my employees, you will not find out where the coal mine is located. You will see no more coal. Your king will want more." The soldiers pulled their swords and stood still.

Zenith edged the throwing knife from under the sleeve on her left arm. She played her moves over in her head. The guard to her side watching Sneedy would be the easiest to kill and then she could reach his sword. She then would take out the two guards standing behind Bartholomew and Darnel. She knew she needed to be patient. Ronny then yelled, "We can deliver future cargo loads of coal to King Solman, but first we must be allowed to deliver this load to the country of Israel. They would not like the news their coal was stolen by the Normand Army. If any of my crew is harmed, the future deal is off."

The captain hesitated and looked at Ronny standing on his boat with his hands placed together pleading for the lives of his crew. He saw his five guards standing over the four prisoners. They had their swords out ready to administer death by sword as soon as he issued the order.

The captain and his crew suddenly felt their boat shake, and they heard some type of explosion. Every one of the Normand sailors looked perplexed. Zenith did not hesitate. She pivoted and threw the throwing knife six feet with the blade sinking all the way to the hilt in the marine's chest. She rolled and came up grabbing his sword before he fell backwards dead. The other four guards were looking at their ship in confusion, trying to figure out what had just happened. They heard an explosion, and maybe two. They noticed a vibration in their ship, but they could not figure out what had happened. Zenith swung her sword, killing the next guard. Ronny's men did as they were told. They ran for cover with Sneedy closing the access door to the coal and locking the two sailors in the cargo bay.

The sailors misjudged the smaller crew member. They had not realized the smallest one was a Blueblood warrior. Zenith killed the third guard who was slow to realize he needed to raise his sword to block her blade. Her sword cut into his left rib cage which caused him to fall to the deck bleeding. The marine on the deck of the Normand vessel fired his arrow. Zenith blocked the arrow and then rolled toward the fourth Normand man.

Dak held his breath and opened the hidden closet panel once the marine ascended the four steps leading to the deck. He looked up the stairs to the deck and could see the backs of two soldiers. He eased over to the trap door while trying to be quiet. He immediately opened the trap door in the floor. The soldier had stepped right across the panel and had not noticed the gap for the trap door. He looked down into Trey's eyes. Trey was lying on his back in about an inch of water. His movements were very limited in the small, confined area. Dak could not help but smile at his large friend, "What is up with you?"

He whispered, "Get me the hell out of here." Trey tried to sit up and then Dak helped him crawl out. Dak said, "I need to help Zenith. We are at the nine-minute mark. Make certain everyone crawls out of that death trap. You know what you and Robin Hood must do." He walked to the edge of the cabin door and watched the backside of the two army guards stationed on his vessel.

He heard the two explosions and smiled as he ran up the stairs to the deck.

Dak saw two marines standing with their back to him. They were preparing to fight Zenith who had dropped three of the standing guards. These two soldiers were better trained, in full combat armor, and better equipped to fight with swords. They had been stationed on the Normand ship to provide protection for the captain against any possible mutiny at sea. They were both hard core Normand soldiers, sanctioned party members as noted by the two red arm bands around their left biceps. Dak eased up the stairs and struck the first one in the unprotected back portion on the thigh. The soldier fell limply on the deck. The other soldier heard him yelp and turned and saw his comrade fall and turned to fight Dak. Dak swung his two swords simultaneously forcing the soldier to retreat. Dak hit the man in his armor which protected him from being cut, but the impact still could be felt. Dak hit him hard in the helmet knocking his head sideways. The man lowered his sword, and Dak rammed his second sword through the man's face mask, killing him.

Trey rolled out and then Robin Hood crawled over to the trap door. Trey picked his friend up through the access door.

Robin Hood said, "I thought I was going to die in that wet coffin. He reached for the closet door and pulled his bow and headed for the deck. Trey stuck his head back into the hidden compartment.

Hershel was lying on his back in the water. "I heard the knock." Hershel turned as far as he could on his side and flipped the handle for the ocean side door to open. He immediately crawled toward Trey.

Tommy Boy's head appeared through the opening and struggled to pull his head through the trap door to take a breath. He knew he had to hurry. Hulk would need to do the same. He could only hold his breath so long. Tommy Boy placed his hands on the ceiling part of the fake floor and pulled himself upward and out of the ocean. Once Tommy Boy crawled through the entry point, he laid on his back in a couple inches of water. He had difficulty turning his large frame around inside the restricted area. He knew he had to close the door to keep additional water from entering the access hole. With the vessel rising and rolling in the waves, the access hole would leak water inside the boat floor. He knew he must close the access door and wait on Hulk to knock and then crawl to the interior access panel. He was afraid the boat would sink with him trapped in the hidden space. Each time the trap door to the ocean was opened, additional water would enter the bottom of the boat.

He thought about opening the access door and crawling through the access into the cabin above. He started to panic while lying in the water and waiting to hear Hulk's signal by knocking on the ocean side access door. At some point if the ocean access door was left open, the vessel would sink. The system was designed to work in smooth waters. He saw Hershel crawling through the light coming from the cabin. Hershel was on his back as he pulled himself through the access panel to the cabin. Tommy Boy could hardly breathe. The water level had risen more than three inches and was getting deeper by the minute. His impulses were telling him to exit now. He knew he had to wait on his brother who was hiding under the bow of their ship waiting to swim underwater to the trap door. He heard the knock on the trap door. He quickly reached the door handle with his left hand and pushed the lever, pulling the door ajar. Hulk pushed upward taking a deep breath as he was about out of air. Tommy Boy said, "Listen to me big brother. The water level is getting too deep in this chamber. You need to crawl out on your back using your hands to pull yourself on the ceiling until you close the hatch. You will not be able to turn over if you come out on your stomach, and you will be underwater. Crawling back into the ship is more difficult than exiting. I am going to crawl out. You need to close the hatch behind you and hurry. I will wait for you at the interior access panel. If you do not close the access door quickly, the boat will sink. Now hurry."

Hulk motioned his head he understood.

The first Normand marine knew he would be killed if he laid on the deck. He knew his hamstring was severed by the sword and his right leg was not going to function. He also knew two additional men had run out of the cabin carrying weapons. The pain in his leg had started to dissipate, but he could not consider the pain. He looked around and started to crawl for cover. He headed for the stairway leading into the lower cabin. He was gritting his teeth with each pull of his arms as he dragged his injured leg behind him. He could feel the sweat running down his face and back as he feared for his life. He looked around and saw his comrade was lying next to the rail killed by Dak. Then, he glanced toward the main section of the deck and noticed the lieutenant was dead and five other Normand men were lying dead or wounded on the ship's deck. He looked behind him at the streak of blood draining from his leg on the boat deck as he moved toward the cabin door. He cussed his captain for not firing the harpoons into the ship and sinking the boat. He whispered, "We have been ambushed by these rebel scum." He made the distance to the stairs, and he tried to brace himself on the palm of his hands. He hastily went down the first step and then his left hand slipped on the second step causing him to tumble down the stairs headfirst. He landed hard, bumping into someone at the bottom of the stairs. He laid flat across the floor on the access door causing the door to close. He instinctively reached for his knife as he saw a man on the floor of the cabin trying to stand, leaning over as he stood under the low ceiling. The man proceeded to walk closer. He knew he needed to act dead. His only chance was to allow the man to get within striking distance and wait for his comrades to advance from his ship and kill these rebels.

***

Hulk took two additional breaths and started pulling himself up through the narrow access trap door. Tommy Boy crawled through the water while on his back to the access panel leading into the cabin. The panel slammed shut over him as he reached the trap door. He heard someone fall on the panel blocking the access from above. He was stuck. He could not see Hulk in the darkness of the hidden space, but he could hear him breathing heavily as he was trying to crawl through the small trap door. He knew Hulk, like himself, would have trouble turning and pulling himself through on his back. He started to be claustrophobic, and he fought the panic feeling. The area was totally dark with no light coming down from the cabin access. He pushed upward on the panel, and the door would not open. He heard someone fighting above him. He thought he heard Hershel grunt and then he felt a liquid substance dripping down through the cracks in the access panel. There was not enough space for him to push upward with force. His arms were pinned to his sides and the water level kept rising and lowering with the boat pitching in the ocean waves. He tried again and again but could not push up the access panel hard enough to force the panel open. He placed his forehead against the panel above him and tried to push upward using his head and his neck muscles. He realized the panel must have been blocked from above. Someone was holding the panel shut.

Hulk cleared the trap door and turned his body enough to reach the floor panel. He was in complete darkness as he turned the panel and position the panel back in place. He took a deep breath of relief after he closed the access panel to the ocean. He placed his hand over the panel and tried to make certain the panel was not leaking and in place. The panel would go under water as the boat shifted in the waves. He could feel the water level had increased to close to six inches. He knew he needed to be quiet, but he could not see. "Brother, what is going on?"

Tommy Boy offered, "The access door is blocked. I cannot open access hatch. We are stuck." His panic increased as the water level would cover his face as the boat rocked up and down in the waves. His body would go under water when the boat shifted in the waves. The two men thought of the options, with both considering going back out the ocean access door, but they would not be able to close the door and the boat would sink. They could feel the motion of the boat in the ocean waves and could tell the boat was starting to move forward. The panic feeling had reached the maximum level for both men. Hulk said, "Brother, I am stuck. The access panel is now under water. I cannot reach the ocean access door, and if I could open the panel and we crawl out, we would be left at sea. The back of the boat is now under water. Do you understand, the door is under water? You need to open that damn hatch, or we are going to drown."

"The hatch is shut and must have something blocking it. I have tried. I cannot push upward. There isn't enough damn room."

***

Hershel saw the wounded man and the blood on his leg and pool of blood on the floor. The man positioned his face tilted downward and was not moving. He reached for the soldier, as the man moved his head upward and now was facing Hershel. Hershel instantly realized his mistake, but he was over extended as he saw the knife. The man pulled a knife hidden from under his jacket, cutting Hershel deep in the side. He thought the blade pierced his lung. Hershel felt the nauseating feeling through his whole body as he knew the knife blade had extended deep into his side. He noticed his vision was blurred as he fell backward looking at the blade of the knife seeing his blood dripping to the floor. He landed on his side and noticed blood on his hands. As his vision refocused, he looked at the knife and the soldier and realized the soldier was lying on the access hatch. The man had an evil, angry expression. Hershel knew he had to save the two men trapped below in the confined space.

Both he and the Normand marine were injured. Hershel stood and jumped on the soldier reaching for the hand holding the knife. He grabbed the blade holding the knife away from him. He grunted and forced his weight on top of the soldier. The men fought with Hershel trying to hit the soldier. His right fist landed on the helmet of the soldier pushing the mask to the side blocking the soldier's view. The soldier's armor protected him but now his helmet was ajar, and he could not see out of his visor in the mask. Hershel realized the man was not moving and was injured. He reached for the man's injured leg and clawed at the wound with all his strength. The pain shot through the body of the soldier. Hershel yanked his hand and bit down on his fingers holding the knife while trying to squeeze the wounded leg. He grunted and growled at his attempt to win the fight. He was determined, knowing the men were trapped underneath him. He pulled the knife from the man's hand and turned to face the soldier. He pulled his other hand from the wounded leg and pushed the right hand of the soldier out of the way. He then shoved the knife through the eye hole of the helmet as he lowered his body weight on top of the other man and fell over him.

The soldier was dead, and Hershel was straining to keep his vision in focus. He was covered in sweat, and he felt nauseated. He was having trouble breathing. He knew he had to open the trap door. He struggled to pull the heavy soldier off the access hatch. There was not enough room to push him to the side. He hurried and with all his strength, he pushed the man over the stairs. He then pulled the access panel upward. He fell over on his side and felt the blood pouring out. His breathing was restricted, and he struggled for his next breath. His mind flashbacked to his childhood before the Transitional Period, and his parents playing soccer with him in the yard. He then stared with open eyes as he took his last breath.

Tommy Boy immediately tried to pull himself out of the hidden compartment. He twisted back and forth trying to rise. He knew Hulk would die soon if he did not move over. The dead guard was still blocking the area in the room for him to crawl out. He pushed the dead man upward over the first step. He finally pulled himself clear. He stood and picked the dead guard up and pushed him over the top of Hershel. He laid down and looked into the cargo area. "Hurry."

Hulk's face appeared in the frame of the trap door. He was close to being underwater. Tommy Boy reached his shoulders and pulled him to the access panel. Hulk lifted his head up and took two deep breaths. He then pulled his arms through, then his upper torso through the access panel. Tommy Boy pulled his older brother's mid-section through the access panel. Hulk turned to his side and rolled out. "Get me the hell out of that wet coffin." Both men sat on the floor out of breath. Both looked over and noticed Hershel was not moving. Tommy Boy stayed low on his knees and moved toward Hershel. He pulled Hershel up right and noticed he had been bleeding from his mouth and side. Tommy Boy reached for his wrist and checked his pulse. He then opened his shirt and looked at the lethal knife wound. He sadly reached and closed Hershel's eyes and placed Hershel in a sitting position. He looked at Hulk and motioned his head no. "Did you secure the panel to the ocean? The area is full of water."

Hulk motioned his head up and down, "I closed the panel. I could not see in the darkness. I believe the panel was secure correctly. The latches seem to work." He then looked at his brother, "Another few seconds, and I would not be alive."

Tommy Boy was saddened, "Hershel saved our lives with his last breath." The two brothers stared at each other and then glanced at the dead Normand marine.

***

Robin Hood loaded his bow as he proceeded up the stairs. He saw the archers lined up on the other ship firing at Dak and Zenith. Dak picked up a shield and was using the shield as cover as he ran to the aft part of the ship and cut the rope where the Normand boat had tied onto their ship. The archers had chased Dak along their ship's railing firing arrow after arrow.

Robin Hood did not hesitate. He fired upward at the first archer he saw. The archer in the middle was hit in the center part of his chest. He reloaded the second arrow and hit the next archer. He then jumped behind the ship's mast dodging arrows. He knew he could not hit all the archers in time. The plan was to cut their vessel free and drift away. The Normand ship could pull their smaller ship under as it sank. He peered around the mast as he pulled his third arrow and saw the captain yell to abandon their ship.

The captain had crossed to the starboard side and saw the hole caused by Hulk's explosive devices. He then ran to portside as the ship started to sink at an angle with the portside sinking. The captain repeated his command to abandon the ship. "Do not allow them to cut the ropes."

Robin Hood could only see his head. His shoulders and lower body were hidden below the railing. Robin Hood, at forty yards, could hit a stationary hickory nut or a bird flying with an arrow. He adjusted for the waves and fired his arrow traveling an inch over the Normand vessel railing hitting the captain in the temple. The man fell dead on the deck of the ship. Without the leader, the Normand sailors started trying to survive the sinking ship. They panicked and ran to the small rowboats located on the starboard side. They must have been aware there were not enough rowboats to carry the entire crew. They fought for seats in the two rowboats which were untied and released. The other four row boats were tied to the portside and when the boat rolled and started sinking, the four additional rowboats could not be reached.

Dak ran toward Robin Hood with the shield trying to block arrows. We need to cut the other rope. You need to provide cover fire for Trey and Zenith at the bow. Robin Hood jumped up and ran bent over to the front of the boat. He squared himself and fired three quick arrows hitting three archers. Trey was holding a shield which had several different arrows sticking to the face of the wooden shield. Zenith was blocking arrows trying to provide herself a chance to cut the rope.

Dak met the Normand sailors running across the boardwalk. He killed the first one with his sword. He blocked the arrow from the second one with the shield and then rammed him in the neck with his shield. The sailor fell into the ocean between the two ships.

Robin Hood fired another arrow hitting the archer as he was about to release his arrow. Zenith swung with full force downward cutting the rope and then rolled over dodging multiple arrows and ran behind Trey and his shield. The two boats started to drift apart with the walking plank falling into the ocean.

One of the soldiers, desperate to survive, jumped into the seat of the rear harpoon. He aimed and released the harpoon. The shot hit the mainsail post and stuck. Robin Hood loaded another arrow and fired, striking the man in the center chest.

Trey ran to the end of the harpoon and cut the rope. The end of the rope fell into the ocean as the boats drifted further apart.

Ronny and his men waited. He was watching the elevated pads housing the harpoons and was thankful when the Normand men abandoned their posts. He knew while watching their ship sink, that was the only chance the Normand sailors had to stop them. Ronny waited until the boats were close to thirty feet apart before he ordered them to raise the sails. Sneedy and Darnel tried to go unnoticed and ran from behind the front cargo bay and first raised the catch sail. Their boat tilted close to forty degrees as the boat turned and picked up speed. Ronny ran to the wheel and turned the rudder. Raise the middle sail. Bartholomew pulled the quick release and started turning the winch as the sail rose. Once the sail was raised, the distance between the two ships increased and positioned them out of the range of the rear mounted harpoons.

The Normand sailors were trying to release the small rescue boats which were now under water. They panicked and were preparing to abandon the ship. The men were swimming toward the two rowboats from the sinking ship. The sailors in the rowboats would use the oars to hit them and beat them away. The ship turned to the side and then sank in less than a minute. The men stuck on the ship had realized the opportunity to jump over to the smaller vessel had passed as the smaller vessel drifted over five meters away and then raised the sails and pulled over one-hundred meters apart. They had also lost the opportunity to be on the two rescue rowboats that were dropped into the ocean. They stood on the sinking ship rails, mast, and top of the cabin and realized they were going to die as the boat sank.

Ronny ordered, "Raise all the sails."

Hulk and Tommy Boy walked out of the cabin in their wet clothes with Tommy Boy covered in Hershel's blood and looked around at the dead men. They noticed the Normand ship was sinking as they watched the flag go under water.

Bartholomew looked at Dak, "We have two prisoners." He motioned his head to the cargo bay.

"We need to get them away from the coal. Bring them up. We also can use these men's uniforms. Dump the bodies over the side," ordered Dak.

Hulk walked further from the cabin and announced, "We've got some bad news. Hershel did not make it."

Tommy Boy added, "He died a hero. He saved me and Hulk. As he was dying, he killed the marine and opened the hatch. He deserves a hero's burial."

Dak looked at Hulk, "I am sorry he is dead. He turned out to be a good friend, but dammit, he was our guide once we landed in Southern City. We will need another guide." He then looked at the cargo bay, "Unless they can be of use."

Trey walked to the access doors to the cargo panel. He motioned for Robin Hood to open the doors. He yelled, "You two need to come out."

Dak and Hulk both walked to the area next to the doors. The first Normand sailor peaked out of the opening. Hulk said, "Come on out."

The man hesitated and climbed out. Trey pushed him to his knees and searched him for weapons. The second man also hesitated and slowly laid his sword on the deck and then climbed out. Hulk searched him and yanked his shirt off pulling a hidden knife. He then pushed him to the railing and tied his hands. The sailor turned and looked at the crew, "Where is my ship?" He was confused. The other sailor on his knees was startled and tried to look around in all directions.

Robin Hood announced, "There are two rowboats about four hundred yards behind us. The rest of the crew and the Normand ship are headed for the bottom of the ocean."

Dak walked over to the Normand marine and, "Your ship and all your comrades sunk and are dead except for the men we spared in two rowboats. Those two rowboats might make the journey to land in a few weeks."

"There is no way. How did the ship sink that fast? Where are they?" He looked bewildered.

Dak motioned for the two men to look around on the deck at the dead sailors. "They are dead." Dak knew they might have some useful information. He wanted to start asking broad-type questions and not specific about Veronica. "What does the Normand army do with prisoners?"

The man against the rail looked around and then at the sailor on his knees in front of Trey. As the boat shifted in the waves and the side of the ship lifted, the man abruptly jumped up and ran across the deck and jumped headfirst over the rail into the ocean.

Dak watched him leap from his vessel. He turned to Trey, "I might have over-thought my questioning technique. Hold him in place." Trey reached down and grabbed the sailor's shirt. Hulk and Robin Hood walked to the rail and saw the sailor trying to tread water with his tied hands behind his back. Robin Hood waved goodbye to the man and yelled sayonara ass-hole. Hulk turned to Dak and shook his head no.

Ronny asked, "Are we going to go back and get him?"

Dak looked at Ronny, "He made his decision."

Ronny replied, "That is what I thought. Sneedy, turn the forward sail twenty degrees."

Dak turned back to the man on his knees, "I will make a deal with you. You might live if you answer my questions."

The sailor looked at Dak. "What kind of deal?"

"We will allow you to be placed in a lifeboat with some water and food, but you must answer our questions." The man looked questioning at Dak. He noticed the other sailors had now pulled all the sails tight and the boat was moving south, fast across the water.

"I do not believe you. Who are you? Where are you from?"

"Do you really have a choice? Who we are and where we are from are no concern of yours. Since I am in charge, and we are close to one-hundred miles from shore, I will be asking the questions." Dak then held up his hand with his index finger in the air. "Choice one: we will allow you to jump overboard with your hands tied behind you like your friend just did." He held up two fingers. "Choice two: we will throw you overboard if you do not answer our questions." He held up three fingers "Choice three: we will set you in a lifeboat as I described after you answer all our questions and hope you can paddle the lifeboat to the shipping lanes along the coastline and be rescued."

Robin Hood started taking the uniforms off the sailors. Tommy Boy carried Hershel up the steps from the cabin and placed him on the deck. He walked back to the cabin and then carried the dead soldier to the deck and started pulling his uniform off. Sneedy and Darnel started helping with the uniforms.

The sailor noticed all his comrades were dead. He looked at the lieutenant lying dead from two different cuts to his torso. "I like option three, but I do not trust you."

Dak smiled at the man, "I do not trust you either. Your comrades were going to kill my friends and my wife."

"Your wife?"

Zenith walked over next to Dak and pulled her hood back revealing her pointed ears and blond hair.

"She is a damn Blueblood?" He stared at Zenith in disbelief and then asked, "Your wife is a Blueblood Warrior? What type of questions?"

"Yes, she is, and she is very specialized at killing men in war. Are there any more Normand ships in our path?"

"No."

"What was your ship doing this far out from land?"

"Our captain made that decision. He was a hard man. I really do not know. Our orders were to patrol the east coast up to Harpers Ferry Harbor. We were returning down the coast when he, ordered us out to sea on a whim. We were completing recon for a possible assault on the northern army at Harpers Ferry Harbor and also, we were part of the naval blockade preventing merchant ships from delivering supplies to the rebels."

"When were you to report to Southern City?"

"If we did not see an army in training, we could stay out for months. We were to intercept merchant ships going to port in Harpers Ferry Harbor taking them supplies. There are three other ships working in conjunction with each other to block off the port. If we saw the buildup of an army, we were to report back to our home port with the information. The north army appears to have dissipated with some men still at Harpers Ferry Harbor. We had nothing new to report."

Dak glanced at the others. Zenith walked over next to Trey. She asked the sailor, "Have you never met a Blueblood? You seem surprised."

The sailor looked at Dak and then back at Zenith, "I have never met a Blueblood. I have always understood they were all up north in the city of Merlin."

Dak smiled, "That is not true. There are several in Southern City. There was one in Harpers Ferry Harbor until he had his head removed. Did you not know General Cuez and King Solman both are Bluebloods?"

The sailor motioned his head no. Dak asked, "If we were going to locate a prisoner taken by the Normand army, where would we look?"

The man seemed to think and then he announced, "Most are turned into slaves or soldiers. If they trust the slave, they might place them on a ship. If they do not trust the prisoner, they place them on the front lines of the northern front. If you kill fifty villagers, you can move up so to speak and transfer to the back lines or a special unit to carry out classified missions. Sometimes, you can take a job in logistics or become a sailor. However, a large number of captured soldiers are killed."

Zenith looked at him, "Is that what you did? You killed fifty innocent people?"

"No, I have never killed anyone. I started out as a sailor. The man that jumped overboard was transferred from the front line. He said he had killed seventy-seven people. I was fortunate. My father knew someone, and I was placed in the navy from the start. I grew up in Southern City."

Dak noticed the man was small with glasses. He did not appear to have a demeanor full of hate, or a man who kill others. Dak asked, "What if the prisoner was eighteen and a very pretty female? Where would she be?"

"Normally, they are used by the ranking officers as concubines. Sometimes they are slaves, but they do not have as much value as a male slave. A female could be anywhere inside Southern City. I understand they are sometimes transported to Merlin and sold to the rich."

Trey asked, "Have you heard of a certain young lady that arrived close to one month ago?"

"I have been at sea for fifty-nine of the past sixty-three days. I cannot help you. Why are you so interested in this female?"

Trey looked at the man. "She is my sister."

The sailor looked perplexed, "All of you risked your lives for this one female? Your mission is to enter Southern City just to find your sister? Do you not understand how dangerous that will be? The city is on alert and ready for battle. The commanders are judged by results. They will be on the lookout for you. You need to turn around and go home. You will not find her." He shook his head in disbelief.

Chapter 18

Veronica looked in the mirror at the reflection of her nude body. She smiled, and for the first time in her life, she felt satisfied with herself. She thought, "I am happy with my body. All the attention I receive from the soldiers, guards, and men in general, I must be pretty. All those men take time to check me out daily from head to foot." She stood and turned to the side and looked at herself from a side view of her reflection. She turned backward to the mirror and looked at her calf muscles and her body from the rear view. She smiled to herself. She then thought about what Dezie had told her about men. She thought, "Dezie must have lived somewhat of an exciting life. How else would she have known such things?" Veronica looked at her smile, then thought, "I just do not trust Dezie. If I plan to escape, and she finds out, she will report me to the Castle Guard. She is not an option for help, but maybe Michael will help. I must have someone I can trust, and I must escape."

***

"King Solman will be back late this afternoon."

Veronica turned to face the view out across the city. "Dezie, where has the King been for five days?"

Dezie looked concerned, "I do not know where he has been. You know what I know. He rode out with two of his top generals five days ago with many soldiers, all of which are part of his honor guard. We received a message from the scout a few minutes ago." She hesitated, "Our King will want to see you. We need to prepare you. I had a special dress made for you. He will like the dress. He has mentioned he likes your hair long and wavy with you wearing a dress. I will put a perm in your hair. He also likes your nails colored red."

Veronica kept gazing over the city as she stood on her balcony. She felt the heat from the fading sun. She was still tired from her early morning workout. Additional soldiers and guards started showing up and working out with her. She noticed the attitude of the men had changed. They were more tolerant of her presence. They would not complain about pulling heavier weights off the squad rack when for her turn or act inappropriately. She tried to fit in with them. She would bring them leftover food from the kitchen that was brought to her to eat the previous night. She would teach the men how to move and anticipate what the other person would do in a competition. She was careful not to reveal too much knowledge. She had recalled what Billy Ray, her instructor, always stressed. The element of surprise and allowing the competition to underestimate you was the best weapon in a fight against a superior challenger. The guards and soldiers started competing amongst themselves and the loser would walk down the street in the nude. She had witnessed several dozen naked men make the walk. She also knew her guard Michael was always present to make certain she was not harmed. He reported to his boss any unusual comradery between her and the men. The direct order from King Solman to Michael was to not allow her to build a rapport with any of the men. She was not certain if his decision was made because of security to not allow her the opportunity to escape or jealousy.

She smiled as she thought about the women of Southern City, and how they would line up outside the guard gate on the street to watch a nude guard or soldier walk to ask the nun for a glass of water. The nude men would obtain names and addresses of the females for future dates.

"Do you not know where he goes, and who he meets?"

Dezie folded the laundry and looked at her suspiciously and shook her head no. She then glanced at Veronica as Veronica turned to walk back into the great room, "No, I do not know who he meets, or where they meet. He has these meetings about every four months. That is all I know."

Veronica walked into the middle of the room, "They are preparing for an assault north. Did you hear anything about the army moving north? You must know more."

"I do not know when the army will move out. I do know our King does not like living in the wilderness. He prefers the maid service, the nice comforts of his palace, and his encounters with you. The only time he leaves the castle is for those meetings."

"You know soldiers and you know women who sleep with soldiers. The soldiers talk. You must know something about when the army will move out, and where he goes."

Dezie smiled, "You need to try on the new black dress, and you need to listen to me. I can help you. You ask too many questions with regards to our King. King Solman will not like you asking questions about him, and where he goes. Please remember that when you are with him."

Chapter 19

The messenger arrived at her door. Michael recognized the King's personal envoy as he approached. He announced, "The King has arrived, and I have a message for Lady Veronica." Michael opened the door. The messenger entered and was direct and to the point, "The King has demanded to see you now. You are to follow me to the war room. The handmaid has also been summoned. You two must come at once. I will wait in the hall for both of you." They both watched as the skinny small man turned and walked to the hall as Michael closed the door behind him.

Dezie looked worried. "Why would our King need to see me? I understand he has not seen you in six days and his male hormones have built up in his body. He I understand will crave you, but why me?"

Michael looked at Dezie, "I do not know. You two will leave at once with me."

Veronica considered the question and statement by Dezie and became a little concerned, "Would the King send both of them to the army in the tents?"

***

To Kill a Blueblood

Veronica walked behind Michael as he followed the envoy.
Dezie followed her. No one said a word as they walked
through the halls and down the interior stairs. Veronica could
tell Dezie was worried. The look on her face when the envoy
announced she was to accompany Veronica inside the King's
war room was one of surprise and worry. The rumor was the
war room was the location where King Solman punished his
commands who did not perform as he desired. Veronica
noticed as she turned the corner in the hall Dezie rubbed her
hands together in a fidgety manner. She was fearful. Veronica
and Dezie were ushered into the room and Michael remained
outside with the two King's Guards. They were announced and
the envoy stood to the side.

King Solman walked from behind his table which outlined a
map of the continent, and her homeland located in the territory
north. Veronica walked toward the table and glanced at the
map. She noticed the map was incomplete. The map did not
reveal the lay of the land north of the Midnight hole leading
into and beyond the New York tribe. The map did have the
Eastern cliffs along Cliff Tops' mountain range and the
mountain range along the coast of the New York tribe territory.
The map did not outline the nuclear waste pits to the west of
Cliff Tops or the New York Tribe. The map also did not reveal

the large gorge that separated the New York tribe and the Cliff Tops Territory. She glanced over the map as quickly as possible not to draw attention to herself looking at the world map. She did notice the map revealed the glaciers north of her tribe but did not reveal the rough terrain of the glaciers and frozen tundra north of the jet stream and her tribe. She quickly scanned the map in the southern section looking for the symbols of troop movements and signs of when they might be deployed north. The other Asian Continent also appeared to be incomplete.

King Solman walked to the front of the room and announced, "You and I will be married later today. The ceremony will be in the garden with a few privileged citizens. Several distinguished people are in town for the mandatory meeting and then I will address our city for a speech in two days." Veronica was beyond surprised. King Solman turned to Dezie and the envoy, "You need to make certain the ceremony is set up, and the appropriate citizens are invited." He turned to Dezie, "You need to make certain the Queen to be is prepared. That is all. You may leave. I have meetings to attend." He turned and walked back to the map.

***

To Kill a Blueblood

Veronica sat at the dressing table. She knew the hour was fast approaching. She thought about how exciting it might be to be a queen. She would have room service and a hand maid for the rest of her life. She then thought how she had been locked in her chambers, and she really did not know King Solman. She knew to fear him but not his aspirations and dreams in life. She thought, "Would I move in with him?" She stared into the mirror without seeing her reflection. Her mind registered, "He would require her to produce his children while she continued to be his slave. He knows nothing of my dreams and aspirations." She considered how he had to be always in control and not just of her but the entire environment. She could see the fear in the eyes of the waiters and his assistants. He was a cruel man. The thought scared Veronica.

As Dezie stood behind Veronica she noticed the concerned expression in the reflection of the mirror and pulled Veronica's hair up and placed the long hair in a bun. "You will be the prettiest bride ever in Southern City." Veronica awoke from the daydream and looked in the mirror at her lipstick-covered lips and the makeup on her cheeks. She thought, "I am confident in myself. I will get through this. I must survive. I just do not like getting married to a man I despise and being forced to conceive his children." She then thought back to her childhood and how Queen Vicky taught her and her friends about the Holy Bible. "Maybe he will be a good husband. People can change." She remembered hearing the story of the self-proclaimed Apostle Paul, and how he hunted Christians and either killed them or turned them over to others to be persecuted. Paul then accepted Christ, died in prison for Christianity, and was known to be one of the most important apostles for Christ. She started feeling a little apprehensive considering her wedding scheduled for later in the day. She wondered what would happen if she said no to the wedding. She then realized no was not an option. She also reaffirmed in her thoughts, King Solman was not going to change. Unlike most people who tried to evolve and better themselves, he thought of himself as perfection. He was an egotistical and psychotic man designed in a laboratory. He would never change for the better.

Dezie must have been able to sense Veronica's thoughts. She was standing behind her looking into her eyes in the reflection from the mirror as she finished with her hair and then touched up her makeup. "You are the prettiest lady in all the land. You will be a great wife to our King."

Veronica glanced at the mirror into Dezie's eyes, "Why would he want to marry me? He doesn't love me, nor do I love him. I am his prisoner. I am forced to stay in this chamber except for the occasional horse ride with the King Guard or the workouts in the gym with the male soldiers and guards. You are the only female I am allowed to have conversations."

"In my opinion and based on what I have observed, there are two reasons for a man getting married. First, a man decides he is ready to get married either to have children or companionship, or second, he falls in love with the woman so much he cannot live without her. Our King wants to have a male son."

She looked at Veronica's face for the reaction. For selfish reasons, Dezie wanted Veronica to be wed to the King. She knew as Veronica's status improved; her life could improve. She would be named the Queen's handmaid, which would place her as the manager over the Queen's other maids and maybe even the King's maid services and butler service. She knew being a manager, she would no longer be required to work. She would instruct others to complete the fruitless manual labor. She was tired of endless workdays.

The other handmaid walked into the room carrying a white dress with a long train. The two women talked in a foreign language. Veronica assumed the conversation was about the dress since the handmaid held up the dress and then commented about it. She then laid the dress across the table and unrolled the long train of the dress. She looked at Veronica, "Do you like it? The dress is very pretty."

Veronica stood and walked to the dress and felt the silk material. "The dress really is beautiful. It is so long."

Dezie walked over to the dress and picked up the train, "This part is the train. The longer the train, the wealthier and higher status the couple. Your train will be longer than all others in the city." Veronica was surprised with the beautiful dress, and how fast they were able to provide her such a glamorous wedding dress so fast. The wedding ceremony was a couple of hours from starting.

Veronica remarked, "I love my dress. Thanks to both of you. My dress takes my breath away."

Dezie announced, "The dress and your wedding will be the talk of Southern City. You will be a great queen for the people. It is an honor to serve you. You will be asked to model the dress for our citizens in the future. Who knows, maybe we can store the dress for your daughters."

***

Veronica walked into the gallery and noticed the high priest, the court director, and close to one-hundred people. She noticed three generals and a few other military men. They all were with their wives. She noticed everyone was dressed in uniforms or expensive looking attire. One by one the wives walked over to Veronica and introduced themselves. They all commented on how pretty she was and the beautiful dress. Then, King Solman's personal manager walked into the gallery and announced, "We need to start the ceremony. Please, everyone walk to the garden." The envoy immediately directed Veronica to the center of the garden located behind the podium and then motioned for the High Priest. He then pointed for King Solman to stand facing Veronica. She knew the High Priest was not a Christian but would refer to Gods. The only Christians in the city were the few nuns and the one priest. Very few people in Southern City openly embraced Christianity. The people of the city were not allowed to seek out religion but were forced to obey the laws set forth by her husband to be.

The ceremony was over as fast as it began. The High Priest wrapped the rope around their wrists and pulled their hands together to symbolize the bonds of matrimony. She listened to the High Priest and tried to make eye contact with her husband. He was standing three feet beside her staring at the floor. The wedding was completed in less than a minute with the High Priest announcing the couple was now man and wife. She stood in disbelief as the King whispered, she looked stunning. He pulled her veil up and kissed her on the lips for all to see. He then turned and led her to the opening of the garden to the main city street. They posed for the guests of the wedding as they both smiled and waved. She heard the King tell the envoy; he had a meeting which started in thirty minutes. The envoy turned to Veronica, "You must hurry and change. Our King will introduce you to the citizens after his speech in two days. He insisted on the wedding now while all his generals and landowners are in town for the meetings. Some people have traveled a great distance for the mandatory meetings. He has scheduled a speech to address his intentions after the completion of the landowner's meetings." He turned to leave and announced, "We are on a tight schedule. Our King is not a patient man. One more thing." He opened his notepad. "You are to have a five-man squad of guards assigned to protect you. At least one will go everywhere you go. You will be advised of additional orders they have in securing your safety. I will select the group of five."

Veronica thought about guards in general. She knew Michael was honest and believed a man's character and oath were most important. She had tried to seduce him, and he stood strong as an oak. She knew she wanted guards loyal to her with high standards and morals. She knew she could not trust the assistant to the King. "I want Michael Valadez as my Chief Guard, and he may select the other four guards. You will not select my guards."

The envoy was stern, "I will pick the five guards."

Veronica cut him off, "I am the Queen, and I will be named the Queen of the Normand Army and Southern City for all to know. You will not tell me what to do. I will tell you what to do. I have told you who my Chief Guard will be, and he will select the other four guards. I am not discussing this further."

Veronica walked to her chambers with Dezie carrying the train of her dress. Michael stopped and opened the door. Dezie could sense Veronica was not happy with the way the ceremony was conducted. Dezie smiled as she carried the dress train across the door threshold, "Princess, I would suggest you remove the dress. We will store it for you to model for the entire city to see in weeks to come. The King will announce you as his bride and our queen at the end of his speech in two days. He is in a hurry to meet with his command staff after the meeting with the district landowners. He is meeting with each district landowner individually which is taking more time."

Veronica thought, "He is extorting the wealth from the warlords and ranchers from his realm. His gold shipment was stolen and now he is forced to raise money for his army. The landowners have no choice but to provide him what he is requesting."

Chapter 20

Veronica walked down the hall with Michael following her. "Princess, you look very pretty in the black dress. Your wedding was beautiful, and your wedding dress was very pretty." He paused and she smiled as she walked, "The King's envoy came to me and indicated I have been selected the chief of your security detail. I selected four guards to assist me. The four men and I provided our oath to King Solman a few minutes ago. We will guard you and die for you, if necessary. It is a great honor to be your chief security guard. I will be honest, loyal, and not let you down. None of my men will disappoint you."

She turned in the hall and faced Michael, "Thank you for noticing my dresses. Does this mean you have to do whatever I tell you?" She stepped close to him, invading his space while facing him in the hall.

He looked both ways in the hall to make certain they were alone. He held his ground and did not move backwards. He felt his body start to change to the welcome stimulus of the beautiful female, he then smiled, "No, Princess. I will guard you and protect you with my life. I am also required to follow the procedures as set forth with my oath. I will set the schedule for the other four guards. We will work as a unit to provide your security. I report to General Redman daily. I am also responsible for you not running away, so please keep that in mind."

"Congratulations on your promotion. I am no longer a declared Princess. I believe you to be the first person to start calling me a princess, however, I am now your Queen. I wish I was still a Princess. I believe life would have been so much simpler." She raised her eyebrow and smiled. She quickly turned and walked around the corner toward the double doors and the two guards at the King's door in their red capes. The guards opened the door for her and announced that the Queen had arrived.

Michael whispered as Veronica stepped across the door threshold, "You are defiant as always. Please do not be so bold with our King."

Vernonia walked into the King's chamber with the guard closing the door behind her. She noticed the table was set for three as she walked from the foyer into the great room. She thought, "This is her wedding night, why would there be three for dinner?" She noticed Brad and King Solman smoking cigars on the balcony. She had noticed Brad at the wedding, standing in his black suit near the back of the garden talking with another well-dressed man. Vernonia walked to the doorway and asked, "What is the topic between you men standing on the balcony on my wedding night?" She smiled and noticed both men looked at her. She leaned against the rail and allowed her left leg to stick forward showing off her leg. She could tell King Solman liked her new black dress with the split up her thigh all the way to her waist. She turned around in the dress and smiled at Brad and playfully asked. "Brad, how do you like my new black dress?"

Brad smiled and complimented her. "You look stunning in both white and black." She could sense something was not kosher with King Solman's mood. He seemed angry ever since he had returned from his out-of-town meeting. She hoped his mood would soften since he had concluded his personal meeting with the landowners. Her wedding night had arrived.

After some small talk, the three walked into the dining area of the great room. King Solman clapped his hands as they sat down for the meal. Out walked the head waiter and the three waiters. They placed the main course, fried duck, in front of each of them. The older waiter dropped a fork and the sound of the fork hitting the polished concrete floor was noticeable. Veronica noticed movement from across the table as the King stood and grabbed the waiter by the neck and pushed him backward. He then slapped the waiter and pushed him toward the door. Veronica had not witnessed the display of hatred and anger from her husband until now. She was scared what the King might do to the older man. She stood and walked over to the fork and picked the fork up. She then walked past the King and handed the fork to the waiter. "You may leave." The waiter turned and hurriedly walked through the doorway into the kitchen.

Veronica turned and walked to her seat. She looked at the King and suggested, "May we enjoy our meal?" Her husband walked to his seat and sat down and then staired at Veronica as she ate. She noticed he finally started eating and then proceeded to join in with the conversation with her and Brad. Veronica watched and noticed how pretty of a man Brad appeared to be in his black suit and white shirt. He had high cheekbones, long dark hair, dark tan skin, and a pretty smile. He was naturally good looking. During the small talk when he was describing a shirt and how well it fit, Brad came across to Veronica as being less masculine than she realized when she met him on the one prior occasion. Veronica started to understand what her husband had arranged with Brad. She started to feel the anticipation within her body knowing what she and Brad would be doing in a few minutes. She also noticed Brad seemed nerves with his gestures and his conversation. She wondered if he was scared of the King after

watching the King slap the waiter, or was he always this
insecure.

After the meal, the head waiter and the other waiter removed
all the dishes. The older waiter never reappeared. The waiters
left the King's chambers in a hurry with no miscues. King
Solman walked over and sat down in his large, cushioned
chair. Veronica was aware of what was going to happen next.
She recalled Dezie explaining King Solman, and how she
needed to cater to his vices. She could sense the anticipation
with the King during the meal, and she also was aware of how
her own body was reacting to the pending love-making. Brad
on cue walked up behind her and rubbed her shoulders. He
unbuttoned the dress and allowed the clothing to drop to the
floor. Veronica smiled at King Solman. She raised her right
foot placing the boot in his lap and ordered, "Take my boot
off." The King smiled and unbuckled and removed her boot.
She placed the other foot in his lap, "Take it off." King Solman
removed the second boot while Brad rubbed her shoulders and
kissed her neck. "Your wife is perfectly pretty. She has the
small waist." Brad placed his hands around her waist and held
her tight. "See I can in circle her waist with my hands. She has
athletic looking legs and pretty feet. Her breast are perfectly
formed." He rubbed his hands over her breast as he stood
behind her. She turned and started taking Brad's clothes off.

She could sense his lack of being energized. The two laid on
the large rug on the floor and made love. Veronica did her part
and acted like she was having a special experience. She finally
whispered into Brad's ear, "Are you homosexual?" She already
knew the answer. Veronica also knew being gay was not
allowed in Southern City. The homosexual men were killed if
they were lucky. The unlucky men were taken to the soldiers in
the tents to be raped and then killed. Dezie explained the
treatment was cruel and the soldiers were ordered to punish the
gay men by raping them until death occurred. Veronica looked
into his eyes, and she could see the fear and the dread. "I will
protect your secret. Allow me to handle the situation. She
rolled him over on his back and started kissing down his body.
She told King Solman what a good-looking man Brad was and
how lucky she was to have such a wonderful King. How
special her wedding night was. She glanced at the King and
noticed he had been rubbing himself. He seemed to enjoy the
show. She kissed Brad down to his feet and then back up his
body. He laid with his eyes closed and finally responded. She
straddled him and moved her hips faster and faster. She knew
what Dezie had told her about acting during sex. She played
her role and after the climax, she stood, with Brad quickly
getting dressed and leaving. He whispered thank you to
Veronica as he kissed her on the neck and exited the King's

chambers. She could sense his fear of his sexual preference being discovered and his insecurity of not being able to perform for the King.

After he walked out the door, Veronica secured a deep breath and turned to the King. She stepped across his lap and sat facing him. She told him how excited she was with him watching her and Brad. "You watching really turns me on." She started kissing down his chest, pulling his shirt over his head. "Matter of fact, you can put me in any position you wish. I am yours."

He carried her to his bed and forced her on her stomach and tied her wrists over her head to the headboard. He was not gentle. He then tied both her ankles wide apart to the two opposite bedposts. He tied the gag around her head and forced the rag into her mouth. He pulled her tight and whispered in her ear, "The time has come for me to punish you and teach you who is in charge. I am your king, and I will teach you to be my obedient wife."

Veronica immediately tried to hide her surprise. She tried to play along. The gag was pushed deep into her throat and was uncomfortable. He pulled the leather belt from his waist and struck her several times with force across her lower back and thighs. He then picked her up mid-section and slid his body in behind hers. He slapped her cheek from behind and then as her head turned, he hit her other cheek with his fist. He placed his hands around her neck and started applying pressure. At first, she yelped and then she bit down on the gag and tried not to cry from the pain.

***

Veronica pulled her hood over her head and tried to hide her face from Michael as she exited the King's quarters. The King's guard on the left noticed her red cheek, and he smiled. He knew his king. She walked past Michael and tried not to reveal the pain with each step. "Princess, please slow down." They walked around the corner in the hall out of sight of the King's guards. She placed a hand on the wall to balance herself. "What is the problem?"

Veronica turned to face Michael. He was surprised with the large bruise on her neck and her red cheek. Her lower lip was swelled and split. He realized she had been hit. "What did he do to you?" He noticed the rope burns on her wrist and the dried blood in her left nostril.

"I do not know if I can walk. I am not going to survive much longer. I will never allow him to treat me like that again. I would rather be dead." Michael picked her up and carried her to her chambers. He opened the door and sat her gently down in a chair.

She stared at the floor, "I am going to take a bath and then sleep. Please leave me alone."

"Do you want me to send for your handmaid?"

Veronica looked at Michael and said in a harsh voice, "No, I do not want any visitors." Michael turned and walked out. She removed her clothes and looked at the bruising on her body in her mirror. She memorized her condition. She never wanted to forget what had happened to her. Her breasts were sore and hurting. She had dried blood in her nose. She noticed her lip was swollen. She limped to the tub and sat down in the warm water. She looked at the rope burns on both of her ankles.

She thought about what had happened on her wedding night. She considered the advice Dezie provided her on how best to entertain the King. She had done as suggested and acted frisky and aroused like she loved to be with Brad. She thought about Brad and him being homosexual. She knew he lived in fear every day of being discovered. He was forced to perform with a female in front of the King. Now, she was in the tub hurting and sore from being mistreated. She knew if she had fought him, she would have never left the King's chambers alive. He would be difficult to kill and had too many guards to be able to flee. She thought about her options. She thought about the concerned look on Michael's face. Veronica closed her eyes and prayed for mercy. She then considered jumping off the balcony to her death. She could only act so long. At some point being asked to act like a person enjoys something that they do not is devastating to a person's psyche. The king was mean and seemed to enjoy beating her. He had to be in control at all times. As she was sitting in the tub of water, she realized she would be beaten and raped again in the future that was who her husband was as a man. If she fought back now after the wedding, she would be killed by orders of the King. She knew she needed help, or she would die.

Chapter 21

The sailboat pulled into the mouth of the wide harbor in the morning hour of ten. The vessel was moving fast toward the dock with the swift wind blowing from the west. Ronny looked at his watch and noted the time. He felt an ominous feeling in his gut as he looked at the large warship sailing parallel to them with four large harpoons aimed at their deck. The ship escorted them into the bay and further to the dock located at the Southern City Port. Ronny yelled to the men on the dock, "Tie us off." He turned and noticed two other warships had entered the bay and were dropping anchor. The crew from both warships were watching. He tried to act cheerful and present himself as a captain who had arrived where he was meant to be, but he and his crew could not help but noticed the large number of soldiers. As he looked beyond the dock, he could see soldiers walking the streets and guards positioned on the dock and the intersections of the streets of the city.

The commander walked to the dock. He announced in a commanding voice, "I am Lieutenant Springer. I do not have your ship on my list as a trading vessel. You need to state your business."

Ronny tried to smile. He could not help but be nervous. He felt the insecurity of the mission and started to question if the plan would work. There appeared a column of soldiers, all carrying bows and swords next to Lieutenant Springer. If the hidden cargo bay was discovered, they would all be decapitated or worse. The Normand command would normally order men to be tortured for rebellion. A fast death was rare. The hidden comrades in the bottom of the sailing vessel had to lie still and go unnoticed. "We are traders." He raised his hands showing his palms in a gesture of goodwill. "We have something King Solman desires."

Lieutenant Springer walked by his thirty archers all holding their bows aiming at the four men on board. He closed his notebook with the manifest of the trading ships. "What do you have to trade?"

"We have the good stuff. We have coal."

"Hold your positions." All the archers dropped their bows to their sides. Lieutenant Springer smiled. He knew King Solman had sent out inquiries along both the east and west coasts trying to locate coal. The rumor in the captain's circle was King Solman had sent traders to the continent of Asia looking for coal with no positive results. He had heard rumors about a territory up north, but General Cuez had kept the location a secret from the other generals to gain favor with King Solman.

The secret of the location of the coal died with General Cuez unless King Solman was already aware of the coal location. "Bring me a piece of the coal."

Ronny walked to the rear cargo bay and pulled the door open. He dropped to his knees and reached downward inside the cargo bay and picked up a black piece of coal the size of a softball. He turned, "Is this black enough for you?"

Lieutenant Springer's smile grew. He motioned for Ronny to step off the vessel and ordered his men to inspect the ship. Three men set the ramp between the vessel and the dock. His sergeant and two of his men walked across the boardwalk and peered down at the coal. Another soldier walked down into the cabin. He stood on the hidden trap door with his body bent over due to the low ceiling but did not discern the small line in the wood where the trap door could be opened. He checked the bunk beds, the bathroom, and the kitchen. He walked in front of the hidden closet. He bent down on one knee and closely examined the trim and felt along the edge with his finger. He hesitated as he studied the trim and the buildout of the area. He then pulled the board, and the door opened as he peered into the empty closet.

Bartholomew was standing on the deck peering downward into the cabin and watched the search. He was nervous. He knew the men could not exit the access panel into the cabin and be prepared to fight if they were discovered. He had watched them practicing crawling out of the trap door, and the process was a struggle for everyone except for the small frame of Zenith. She was flexible enough to bend her legs and then step up. She would then stand, but even Zenith was an easy target and vulnerable while exiting the hidden cargo bay. The guard walked up the stairs as Bartholomew looked at Ronny with a look of relief. Ronny knew his three men were scared as they were all surrounded with men holding shields, swords and spears. Ronny walked across the boardwalk to meet the Lieutenant.

Lieutenant ordered, "Unload the coal."

Ronny stood next to the lieutenant, "Lieutenant Springer, should we not discuss the terms of the trade before you off-load our coal?"

Lieutenant Springer looked at Ronny, trying to understand why he would ask such a stupid question. "We are the Normand army. We will be seizing the coal. If we pay you anything for the coal remains to be seen."

Ronny smiled, "This is a small load, one square. There is a lot more coal, but you need to understand you will not steal our coal. We will not tell you where the coal came from, and without us, there are no more boat loads of coal. You need to take me to King Solman. I will deal only with the King."

Ronny knew he was either going to see the king or be killed standing where he was. He had rehearsed the line for two days. He hoped the Normand Lieutenant bought his speech. He only had to convince the one leader. The other soldiers were taught to take orders or end up in jail. There was also the threat of forcing the Normand men to the front lines of the pending assault north where they would kill or be killed while living in the wilderness moving north.

***

As he and Bartholomew walked along the street of Southern City, Ronny noticed the large contingency of soldiers. Lieutenant Springer and four soldiers led the way with ten additional soldiers following, walking in twos. Some of the other soldiers stationed in the city were training, and some were partying. The pubs lined both sides of the street and were full of soldiers as Ronny looked up and down the streets. He was led into a large building with guards stationed at the double doors. They turned left into a large room with huge windows and a high cathedral style ceiling. Ronny could see King Solman sitting in the high back chair in the middle of the great room. He also noticed ten guards standing in a row on the left and ten on the right. They had walked through a hall leading to this room with six additional guards stationed at the entrance. He then noticed six guards wearing red robes standing in a half circle around King Solman. Ronny and Bartholomew approached slowly as the fourteen soldiers from the dock and Lieutenant Springer stopped. Two Guards in red robes approached and stopped Ronny and Bartholomew when they were twenty feet in front of the stairs leading upward to the chair of King Solman. Lieutenant Springer announced from behind them, "We have before us Captain Davy, and his associate Isaac from the city of Israel. I have their paperwork showing they are traders from the Asian Continent. They claim they would like to trade with Southern City. They are hauling a square of coal."

King Solman looked at the two men. "Bring me their paperwork." One of the guards walked to the Lieutenant and retrieved the documents. He took the information to King Solman. "Why did you come into my harbor?" He glanced at the paperwork.

Ronny was nervous with the King inspecting the fake documents. He knew Dak's tribe had tried to copy the stamp of two of the Asian ports. The fake stamp was close but not perfect with the color and the design. He noticed Bartholomew had a look of fear in his eyes. Ronny wanted the King to look away from the paperwork and look at him. He smiled and stepped forward. The large guard held the metal spear with the large blade on the end with both hands and used the middle part of the spear to push Ronny backward. Ronny understood he was not to approach King Solman. He held his hands out with a gesture of friendship. "We would very much like to open a trading route with Southern City. We are ambitious to trade coal for gold." He held his palms up a second time as a gesture for friendship. "This is no way to treat a business partner." He glanced at the big guard and then back at King Solman, "Why else would we sail into your harbor if we did not intend to be partners with you?"

King Solman looked at Bartholomew's paperwork and then looked at Ronny. "I will decide if you will trade with us. I will want to know who you are first. Do you speak the dialect of the religious zealots, and the Persians located on the Asian Continent?"

Ronny announced, "I do not, but my business partner does speak the Persian language." He motioned at Bartholomew.

In the Asian dialect, Bartholomew said, "Thank you for meeting with us. We look forward to being business partners."

"I want to know the location of the source of this coal."

Ronny was nervous, "Your majesty. The coal comes from the Asian Continent. I have not been told the exact source location. Our contact in Israel is very cautious. There is great turmoil in that part of the world. We suspect the middleman living in Israel is mining the coal outside their territory under the zealots' noses."

"So, this coal did not come from Cliff Tops?"

Ronny was surprised the King knew Cliff Tops had coal in the mountain regions. "No. This coal is from the Asian continent. I would tell you the exact location if I knew the location, but our contact will not agree to reveal the location of the mine. He fears for his life."

King Solman looked at the two men, "Then, we agree. You will bring me five squares of coal in thirty days. I will pay you two Merlin gold coins. I will give you four copper coins for the square of gold. I have ruled. I will also send with you an associate to meet your contact in Israel."

Ronny knew the four copper coins would not begin to cover the cost of the voyage, however, the two Merlin gold coins for five squares was fair. The Merlin gold was pure gold and not mixed with copper. He asked, "An associate?"

"Yes. You will remain here in my city as my guest until my associate arrives in four days."

Ronny suspected the associate would be the Rogue Blueblood. He felt the urgent need to leave Southern City. "Your Excellency, I would like to make a request."

King Solman stared at the two men. The King did not negotiate with traders. He snarled, "You do not like my terms? Please tell me you like the terms. Do not upset me."

Ronny could feel the anger in his voice. "Your Excellency. The trade terms are fair. I look forward to meeting your associate."

King Solman felt surprised. "What is it you now request?"

"Your Excellency. For me and my men to travel to Israel and load the coal and sail back to your harbor, I would need a concession. I need to be able to sail the shortest distance. You have placed many ships around the east coast blocking passage. I cannot sail around the blockade and be back here in thirty days. The trip will take me six months. I would be forced to sail seven hundred miles out of the way and not take the direct passage north, up the coastline and through the Bering Straits which would be safer and faster. My intentions are then to sail east straight across the Atlantic Ocean with the winds to my back. By doing this shorter route, I could also avoid sailing west and running into possible Asian pirates. Could you grant me a Document of Safe Passage?"

Chapter 22

One by one, Dak and his men along with Zenith, dropped through the hidden trap door to the warm waters of the bay. Dak would have wanted to wait until nightfall, but he and his men could not hide in the hidden compartment any longer. The area was too small and uncomfortable. The Normand Guards on the deck of his ship were relaxed and sitting at the gangway under a temporary awning. Sneedy opened the access door and gave the okay to proceed. He then crawled into the access panel and closed the trap door to the ocean as Trey was the last to exit. Sneedy then hurriedly crawled out of the hidden area, closed the trap door, and walked to the deck. He mentioned to the guard he had used the bathroom. He then proceeded to sit down in the shade of the mast. He looked at his partner, Darnel, and motioned everything was working as planned.

The six swam underwater, one at a time carrying their bags with weapons and dry clothing. They came up under the dock, and then proceeded to swim from one pier support to the next under the dock watching through the wooden decking cracks as the soldiers walked back and forth three feet above them. The guard house with a gate was located in the middle of the pier.

Dak pushed off with his legs from one pier to another while holding his dry bag. Zenith had done the same. Hulk and Tommy Boy both proceeded at the same time. One of the guards had moved to the side of the pier directly above Tommy Boy. Tommy Boy froze in place. Hulk motioned for him to push his dry bag to him and then for him to swim under water toward Dak and Zenith. The dry bag had trapped air pocket and buoyant. Tommy Boy pushed his bag toward his brother Hulk.

Hulk tried to reach the bag as the current caught the bag and floated the bag toward the edge of the dock. Dak held his finger to his lips for all to be silent as the group watched the bag float toward the edge of the dock. Hulk looked up at the soldier standing four feet above him and waited. Robin Hood motion to hulk and then threw a knife from under the other side of the dock and hit the ship hull tied off to the pier. The soldier turned and walked to the other side of the pier as Hulk reached the floating bag and pulled the bag under the pier.

They all, carefully, one at a time, swam under the gate area. When they arrived at an abandoned boat which was under repairs and tied perpendicular to the dock, they climbed aboard the boat and walked into the cabin two at a time and then hurriedly changed into dry clothes. Trey and Tommy Boy picked up a bucket and some paint brushes as they exited the dock to appear like they were repairmen. Hulk and Robin

To Kill a Blueblood

Hood dressed in the sailor's uniforms they had confiscated from the battle three days prior. Dak dressed in the clothing of one of the dead marines, and Zenith dressed in baggy thin cotton pants and a shirt to blend in with the other working women of the city. Dak looked at his friends, "Veronica would do this for us. If Hershel was correct with the directions, I should be able to locate the building. I hope our hideout has not been torn down. Hershel said the walls are bowed outward and some of the roof has fallen. The roof system was built on six-foot spaced rafters and the span of the rafter system could not support the weight of the roof. His platoon was going to repair the roof, but they discovered the building needed to be torn down. This mission is going to be risky. Keep your heads about you. Try to go unnoticed."

Hulk smiled, "The one sailor we released confirmed the building's location. I like the way you tricked him into providing you with the needed details of the location. When Hershel was training to be a soldier, he stayed down the street from the building in the army barracks. The sailor did confirm the location of the barracks when you mentioned the soldiers that were in training stayed down the street from the abandoned building. The man then confirmed the abandoned building was still standing and scheduled to be torn down in a few months."

Robin Hood looked at his friends, "We all hope Dak tricked him, or else we are in for a rude awakening." He then smiled, "How did you like my knife trick under the pier?"

***

They spread out and hurriedly walked to the alley between the backroads. Dak tried to recall what Hershel had said about the route to locate the deserted building. They could hide in part of the second floor of the storage building. They all were apprehensive about being in the large city surrounded by thousands of Normand soldiers. Dak hesitated at the split in the city street trying to guess the correct direction. Zenith and Hulk walked next to him. "One wrong move, and we will be captured," stated Dak. He glanced at his other friends as Trey and Tommy Boy were walking on the opposite side of the street, and Robin Hood was walking slowly fifteen yards behind them.

He turned and walked to the road on the right and walked past the pub and west along the street that paralleled the shoreline. He turned north along another street where the workers of the city lived. The area was trashy with a few older people out on the sidewalk talking. His group was spread out close to fifty feet as they walked along the city streets. Dak then led the group west to the factory building. The group followed Dak, and he ascended the old wooden stairs on the back of the building. Once he made it to the top, he forced the door with the door jamb busting into pieces. Hulk walked up the stairs and immediately walked to the front and looked out the dirty window overlooking the street. He turned to Dak, "So far so good. If it rains, we will get wet." Both men looked at the hole in the roof.

Dak looked at his friends, "We need to spread out in pairs and complete a recon mission. Hulk, you and Robin Hood visit a pub. A pub might be the best place to find out information. Trey, you and Tommy Boy visit the stables and verify if we can purchase horses and also if any travelers matching Veronica's description arrived. Zenith and I will try the local restaurant to verify if anyone has information. Report back here in two hours."

Tommy Boy walked to the window next to Hulk and looked down at the street below. He could see the length of the alley leading to the main street. "There are hundreds of soldiers and city guards all over the city. I do not like this."

Hulk looked concerned, "No one likes this. Make certain you stay calm and do what Dak tells you. Two men together will not suggest a threat. Remember, do not look a soldier in the eyes and keep moving. Also, remember who you are.

Remember each other's fake names. Dak, Robin Hood and I are military men. Zenith should be able to fit in as Dak's girl. You two are traders from Israel visiting this beautiful city. You have your paperwork to prove your identity. They will not make a request to the Port Master to verify if you checked in through the security gate at the dock."

"We hope not," mentioned Trey as he looked concerned with the dire situation of the mission. "Thanks, you guys, for trying to help my sister."

Dak looked at his friends and announced, "She would do the same for any one of us."

***

Dak and Zenith walked into a restaurant and sat down in a corner booth. Zenith ran her hand over her hood and made certain her thin hood and cape were pulled tight and covering her head. She glanced around at the tables and noticed the customers were mostly well-dressed men, and there was no one else in the restaurant with a hood on a cape pulled tight around their face. When the waitress came to their table, they ordered stew and water. Zenith noticed the waitress glancing at both she and Dak, looking at their attire as they ordered. The waitress as she was waiting wiped her forehead and looked to be hot with a red face. When the waitress returned with the drink and food, Dak smiled, "We are looking for a friend." He described Veronica.

The waitress looked around nervously. She glanced at the shirt and noticed the stain under the right arm on the side and the sewing of the material where the shirt had been cut. The stains had been washed and the material was faded on the right side. The waitress noticed when Dak extended his right arm the uniform sleeve extended short on his wrist. "Where are you from?"

Zenith smiled, "We are from a city north of here called St. Pete. My family and I are in the shipping industry. He was recruited as a foot soldier two years prior. He has been in several battles up north."

The waitress knew she was lying. No wife of a foot soldier would be in a nice restaurant dressed as Zenith and no army officer would be walking around in Southern City in a damaged uniform. She glanced down at the tabletop, "Your uniform does not fit you and the hole in the jacket appears to be caused by a sword. The Normand Lieutenant that was issued that uniform is now dead and you took his clothes. You need to be careful. Your accent might cause concern with the soldiers. I do not know your friend. You might check the dancing clubs. Most single women end up working for the corrupt city police or in one of the many clubs. The young women are forced to sell their bodies to the soldiers. You two need to leave. You do not want to be caught by the officials of our city. They are all corrupt." She glanced at Zenith's pretty face. "You need to be careful. They will arrest both of you."

"Why would they arrest us? I am a soldier."

The waitress looked nervous as she glanced around. She said in a voice so others could hear, "Is there anything else I can bring you?" She then whispered, "If anyone is caught helping an outsider, they will be arrested. They will be taken as slaves the same as the outsiders. A good slave is worth four gold coins. It is obvious you two do not fit in. The repaired tear in the side of the shirt was done by a sword and would have killed the person wearing your uniform. Your two stories are not plausible. You are asking me to help two strangers and risk my freedom and maybe my life."

Dak reached for the waitress's arm and gritted his teeth, "Please. She is my sister. I need to find her."

The waitress looked at Dak, "You may go two blocks along the street toward the waterfront. There is a store that sells uniforms to the military men. I know the manager. Ask for Mr. Musier. When was the last time you saw your sister?"

Dak looked around trying to discern if anyone could hear the conversation and if he could trust the waitress. "I will pay you gold for information. She was on another ship that came to port one and half months ago. She was kidnapped by a slave trader."

Zenith added, "We really need help. Can you help us?"

Zenith and Dak turned their heads when four soldiers walked by their table. The waitress noticed Dak and Zenith's actions of both turning their heads away from the soldiers. She recognized they were trying to hide. "I am trying to help you. I am telling you to run away. Meet me in the alley out back." The waitress used the opportunity to walk to another table. The two ate their food as Dak thought she seemed scared of the soldiers as they passed. The waitress then walked over to the table with the four soldiers. They appeared to high-ranking officers in the Normand Army with nicely pressed uniforms. The one with the mustache and glasses stared at Zenith and Dak as he sat down and then placed an order with the waitress.

Zenith kept her eyes facing the table and pulled her hood tight as she finished her food. She glanced toward the table with the four soldiers and saw the one commander point in their direction while talking with the waitress. "We need to leave now. They are onto us," Zenith whispered.

Dak left a copper coin on the table and hurriedly followed Zenith out the door. The army officer in glasses watched the young couple stand and hastily walk out to the congested sidewalk. Dak and Zenith immediately turned and walked twenty feet on the street away from the view of the restaurant window and then doubled back and down the alley next to the restaurant. Dak then noticed the waitress headed towards them out the rear door and to them in the alley. She reached and handed him a note and acted like she was giving him his change. She whispered, "They are always watching. You will be followed. You two need to stay hidden until night and then leave this city. You do not understand. They take what they desire. Your sister might be better off dead. There is no mercy." She looked with concern into Dak's eyes, "However, there is one young lady I understand being held in the castle. You can see her in the courtyard late this afternoon. She will be attending a speech of our King. Remember the name Mr. Musier."

Dak handed her a gold coin. "It is Merlin gold." The waitress smiled, turned, and walked back into the restaurant. She acted like everything was normal. She knew the one commander was watching her as she walked back through the restaurant. She went into the back and told the cook she was sick, then she fled out the back door. She hoped she had enough gold to smuggle herself, her brother, and sister out of Southern City by sea.

Dak pulled Zenith's hand and glanced behind him as they walked swiftly along the sidewalk in the busy part of the city. There were vendors with booths along the street with crowds of people walking in both directions. As they turned a corner, Dak said, "This is the store. Let us duck in here. We might have a tail."

Zenith walked into the store and looked at the row of clothes. Most were uniforms for soldiers or naval personnel, "If we are going to a speech this afternoon, we need to change clothes." She raised her eyebrows when she looked at Dak, who was watching the front door and street full of mostly soldiers walking in both directions.

Dak turned and looked at all the uniforms in the long rows. He smiled, "Yes, we do need to fit in better."

The male employee walked over. "You will need a large. What is your rank and division?"

Dak looked at the man, "Are Mr. Musier?"

"Yes of course,"

Dak noticed he was from another part of the world. Dak assumed he must have ended up in Southern City like so many other people who had survived the Transitional Period. Dak smiled at the young man, "We were told to ask for you by the waitress down the street. I am a newly promoted lieutenant in the fifth division. I need a suit for the presidential speech."

Mr. Musier looked at the damaged soldier uniform with the tear in the shirt. The man smiled at Zenith, "It is a male only speech. Wives are not allowed, and it is called the king's speech, not the presidential speech."

Zenith smiled back at the employee, "Of course. I was here to help him be better fitted. His old uniform never really fit him. I would like him to be noticed and enhance his appearance. What do you suggest?"

***

Hulk and Robin Hood walked into a drinking establishment with adult entertainment. They sat down at the stage at the end and watched the almost nude dark skin woman as she walked out from the stage door and danced. Some of the soldiers and sailors started yelling for her to keep dancing and remove all her clothing. Hulk ordered a beer for himself and Robin Hood. The two men sat quietly and talked between themselves and watched the parade of women walk out from the back door and dance. They drank four additional beers. The place started to fill with more sailors. The singer was loud, and the customers were drinking and yelling at the woman on the stage. On the fifth visit, Hulk asked the waitress if she or any of the dancers knew of a certain young lady. He described Veronica. The waitress looked concerned and replied, "No love, I do not know of her. No one that fits her description works here."

Robin Hood grabbed her arm, "We will pay for information. She was coming to visit my friend." He looked directly at her, and then added, "She vanished into thin air."

The waitress realized these two men were not trying to locate this girl for romantic reasons. The reason was more personal. She looked at Robin Hood and then back at Hulk, "I will see what I can do. Is she your sister?"

Robin Hood was stern with his reply, "Something like that." The waitress walked into the dressing room in the back. Hulk and Robin Hood saw her return to the bar and then take drinks to some drunk sailors in the far corner. The waitress was old and dirty. She did not care about her appearance. Hulk figured she tried to be unattractive by wearing loose fitting capri pants that hung to the knee and a tee shirt that hung past her waist. Hulk thought she did not desire for the drunken military men to bother her. He then thought most of the dancers were either overweight or too skinny. Their bodies had the appearance of being abused. Most had crooked teeth or were missing teeth. He felt sorry for the abuse these women received from the male clientele. Listening to the men yell vulgar remarks at the women as they danced was no enjoyment for Hulk and Robin Hood.

The next female came out and danced. It was her first-time dancing. Robin Hood noticed she was an upgrade over the other dancers. She smiled at Hulk and then at Robin Hood. She stood in front of them and danced while she removed her clothing. She bent down and whispered, "I have some information, but it will cost you. The waitress told me you were looking for a sister." She smiled. Robin Hood pulled the large gold coin out of his shirt pocket and held the gold coin for her to see. The dancer's eyes lit up as she saw the Merlin gold coin. She whispered, "Go out the back door to the alley, and wait on me." She stood and then kept dancing, walking back and forth on the stage doing her best to entertain the customers. Most of the men were loud, drunk, and a few were rushing the stage as she walked back and forth as she was by far the prettiest dancer.

Hulk said, "I do not trust her, but what choice do we have. Be ready to fight and leave in a hurry."

Robin Hood could not resist, "I trust her. She looks nothing like that whore Becky." He then acted like he was perplexed. "Where did you meet Becky?"

"Kiss my ass. She was from New Foundland." Robin Hood laughed as he exited the back door with the memory of Hulk being forced to walk around back on the exterior of the bar half

To Kill a Blueblood

naked with his hands tied being pushed by two men with swords after Becky, the whore, set him up.

They both walked out back and stood facing the wall of the building as they urinated. They both watched the area and tried to figure out which direction the trap might be coming. Hulk looked at Robin Hood, "We can escape down the alley and then through the building on the left. We need to split up with one of us standing guard."

Robin Hood looked concerned. "I do not like this setup any more than you." They both heard the door open, and the pretty black dancer appeared. Robin Hood announced, "I will meet with her. You stay back in case I need back up."

Robin Hood walked over to the lady. He noticed she looked mid-twenties, and she was wearing a white robe and sandals. The contrast in her beautiful dark skin and the white robe was pleasing to the eyes. "Why are you helping us?"

She glanced at Hulk standing fifteen feet down the alley, "Us dancers stick together. I might know the girl you are trying to locate. The information will cost you." She looked at the pocket where she saw Robin Hood place the gold coin.

"I have Merlin gold coin worth one-hundred times the coins you are accustomed to receiving, but the information needs to be solid and substantiated."

"How the hell can I substantiate anything. Do not waste my time." She looked mad.

"Tell me something special about the girl I seek." Robin Hood pulled the gold coin and held it up for her to see. "This gold coin is one-hundred percent gold. If you want the coin, you got to earn it."

She glared at the gold coin and fixated on it. The door opened and a large man looked in the direction of the dancer. Robin Hood placed the coin back in his pocket and turned toward Hulk. "Bernard, everything is okay. I am talking to a date." He looked at Robin Hood who glanced over his shoulder at Bernard. Bernard closed the door and went back inside.

"Does your friend know how to fight with a sword?"

"Yes, she can beat most men. She can fight with a sword. She is exceptionally pretty."

"The girl I have heard of is the talk of the city. She first beat two prison guards in a competition sword fight. They lost a bet and were forced to walk down the street in the nude. Now, we females wait outside the practice pit every morning to watch other soldiers and guards walk down the street in the nude."

Robin Hood knew that had to be Veronica. "Tell me more of this girl. Where is she? Where is this fighting pit?"

"Give me the gold."

To Kill a Blueblood

Hulk saw three soldiers head their way from the street located to the side of the building. He recognized them from inside the bar. They had been sitting next to the window at the door. He walked toward Robin Hood. "Heads up. Watch her closely." Hulk motioned his head toward the three men walking toward them. Hulk walked past the two and stopped near the wall of the building in the path of the three men.

Her expression changed, "Why are you so concerned about the soldiers?"

Robin Hood knew she was aware of the location of Veronica, but he now felt an ominous feeling this dancer was about to shake them down for additional gold. He noticed the three soldiers were smoking cigarettes and laughing as they approached. The dancer seemed to hesitate as the soldiers moved closer. "They are taking a shortcut."

Robin Hood pulled his knife as he moved in intimately close and held the blade against the dancer's side, "I will gut you if you make a mistake with these three soldiers. I suspect your man Bernard and perhaps you have sent them. You are stalling. If you think you can rob us, you are mistaken. I do not like that look in your eyes. You tell me what I want to know. I will give you the one gold coin, and you live. That is your deal. That is the only deal you need to consider." He held the knife hidden under her robe against her side. While holding her right wrist

264

tight pushed against the wall, he stood close like he was trying to obtain a romantic favor. "I will gut you in this dirty alley, you will bleed out here, and this will be the place you die." The dancer shifted and moved her left arm to her side. Robin Hood reached her wrist and held the arm firmly pressing against her side. He clenched his teeth, "I know you have a knife hidden under your robe strapped to your leg. Now, do not say a word." She looked scared as she tried to get her left hand free from his forcible grip. The three soldiers were now ten meters away. Hulk acted like he was lighting a cigarette and kept his head tilted down. He was watching the men out of his peripheral vision.

The black men slowed down. "What do we have here?" The middle one exclaimed. "I believe we have a business deal going down with two sailors and our friend, Candy." The other two soldiers laughed.

The soldier standing nearest to Hulk said, "We want to be part of the deal, and we want to be first. The sailors will pay our tribute."

Hulk walked toward the soldiers, "No deal. We are just talking to the young lady. You need to keep going."

The largest soldier looked at his two friends, "I do not think these water boys want us around while they do their business. I bet while they are at sea for months at a time, they do each other." The three men laughed.

Hulk placed his hand on his sword handle and then unlatched the band holding the sword in the sleeve. The soldiers smiled with the one in the middle saying, "Matter of fact after we do her, we will do you two." He pulled his sword.

Robin Hood held her tight by the arm and spun her in front of him and pulled the knife strapped to her upper thigh. He clenched his teeth, "I told you not to move." He pushed the blade in his left hand against her throat causing a slight amount of blood to trickle down her neck. He held his knife in his right hand inside her now opened robe pressed against her side.

The lady looked scared. Robinhood whispered, "You set us up."

Hulk pulled his sword and stepped quickly forward killing the soldier closest to him with a hard swing into his side. The man fell against the adjacent building and then slid down the wall to the gravel driveway.

The middle guard seemed surprised that Hulk had attacked first. He saw his friend being killed and pressed the attack. The other soldier pulled his sword and also headed toward Hulk. Hulk moved to the side, so he would be engaged with one soldier at a time. He blocked the swing of the middle guard and then stepped forward toward the guard and stuck his knife into the soldier's chest. He pushed the dying soldier to the side and then blocked the swing of the third soldier.

The third soldier seemed to sober up as he noticed his two comrades were now dead and the killer was fast approaching him. He tried to remember his sword training. He swung his sword which Hulk blocked. He stepped forward with his knife in his left hand and tried to ram the knife blade into Hulk's stomach. Hulk blocked the left arm and the blade and pushed his arm out wide. Hulk stepped forward and headbutted the soldier. The soldier's eyes rolled back into his head as he blacked out. Hulk rammed his sword through the man's heart.

Hulk announced as he stepped toward Candy with his sword dripping with blood, "Your story will be that the three men were drunk and wanted to rob two sailors. We do not have an issue with you." Then he added, "Or do we?" He walked two additional steps toward Candy. Candy closed her eyes and seemed to accept she would die. Hulk looked at Robin Hood, "You need to hurry. Bernard will be back with more men."

Robin Hood tossed her knife to the ground and then reached with his left hand and turned her head sideways toward him as he stood behind her. He looked in her eyes and shook her, "Candy, What will it be? I spill your guts out here in this dirty alley, or I give you this Merlin gold coin?"

"Your friend killed those three soldiers in less than a couple of seconds. You two are not sailors. Sailors would have run away from those three men. Who are you?" She glanced at the three dead soldiers. Robin Hood realized she knew the men and squeezed her tighter in his grip.

"I am sorry for their loss, that is not why we are here. We had no choice. You have a choice. Who we are is none of your concern. Your story will be-those three men were drunk and got into a fight with two sailors. Candy, I know a pretty girl like you knows the guards and soldiers in this city. You need to make certain you tell them what I tell you. That is your story for the authorities. Stop stalling and tell me what I need to know."

"The girl you are looking for is in the palace."

Robin Hood clenched his teeth, "What is she doing in the palace?"

"I do not know what she is doing there. I understand she is being kept in the palace. Her room is located on the top floor. Her balcony is overlooking the ocean and the east part of the city. There is no way to get to her. The palace is well guarded. That is all I know."

He pulled his knife down and released her. "Here is your gold. If you keep your mouth shut and do not tell anyone about us, we will not come back. If you tell anyone about who we were asking about, we will kill you. That is the deal?" She shook her head yes and placed the gold coin in her underwear.

"Hit me."

Robin Hood looked at Candy. "I said hit me. You must hit me."

Robin Hood understood she was scared. "I do not wish to harm you."

"You two need to leave. They will question me. You need to hit me hard, or they will kill me."

Robin Hood struck her in the left cheek with his fist with force knocking Candy to the ground. Hulk and Robin Hood ran down the alley.

***

Trey and Tommy Boy walked two blocks toward the stables. Trey looked at the sidewalk and whispered under his breath, "It is hard to blend in when just about all the men are wearing a uniform and most appear to be drunk."

Tommy Boy looked ahead of them along the street, "We need to cross the street and then head down the alley and find a back entrance to the stables. There appear to be guards at the front entrance."

Trey glanced about one-hundred yards ahead and could see four men, "Those men are not drunk, and they are not soldiers. They must be guards. Follow me." The two crossed and hid behind a horse-pulled buggy and then crossed behind two mules pulling a wagon. Trey whispered, "We need to act nonchalant and be cool. There are four guards watching us and walking toward us. One of them just pointed our way. We need to clear this street and run down that alley before they get too close. If they look closely at our attire, they will know a sailor working on a merchant ship would never wear leather fur-lined boots."

The two men walked bent over and once the mules and wagon were even with the alley, they continued crossing the street and ducked into the alley. The guards could no longer see them as they walked behind the buggy and then the wagon. Once they entered the alley, they were out of sight of the fast-approaching guards. The two ran close to one-hundred feet and turned left around the building and up another alley. They crossed the wooden corral fence and entered the barn from the backdoor.

The four guards stood on the street looking down the alley and ahead of them on the street trying to discern where the two large men went. One of the guards asked an elderly lady, and she shook her head no. They were perplexed how the two men could have disappeared.

Trey and Tommy Boy approached the young boy in one of the front stables as he was shoveling the floor of the empty stable room. The stable boy looked surprised when Trey and Tommy Boy appeared in the back of the stables. With a smile, Trey announced, "We know who the hardest working man in the city is."

The boy turned and stopped shoveling, seeing the two large men both smiling at him. Trey then asked about Veronica. "Maybe you could help us and of course we will pay you." The boy smiled. "We are looking for a pretty young lady who appeared in your city about forty-five days ago. She came by boat from up north along the west coast from the city of Tanger."

"You mean the Princess?" He seemed excited to tell them he knew her. "She is really nice and gives me food from the palace. They are leftovers, but they are good. She rides with the King's Guard from time to time. She is very pretty. She hugged me and told me I needed to wash my dirty face." Denco walked out of the stable with a shovel full and poured the contents into the old wheelbarrow.

Trey looked surprised and glanced at Tommy Boy and then asked, "Princess? Where does the Princess stay?"

The boy looked small for his age and unkept from not washing regularly. His hands were covered in dirt, and the ends of his fingernails were black from not cleaning. His face was dirty, and his teeth were brown. Working in the dusty stables and mud from the horse stalls had permanently stained his work clothing. He seemed to be hard-working and friendly. A man came out of the office in front of the stables, "Denco, what are you doing? I need you to shovel out that stable." The man then looked at Trey and Tommy Boy, "Who are you? If you want to buy a horse, we have none for sale. The Army owns all the horses." He hesitated, "You should know this." The man looked suspiciously at the two men. "What do you want in my stables?"

Trey smiled, "We were trying to get out of the busy streets and saw this young man in here working hard. We are not looking to buy a horse, but we thought about renting a horse to ride in the country. We are sailors from Israel and desire to see the countryside. We were listening to Denco tell us about the Princess who rides with the King's Guard. When is she scheduled to ride next?"

The man started to relax. He seemed proud that the Princess rode his horse. "Yes, she rides the horse owned by the King's Guard. One of the King's assistants will come by about one hour prior to her arriving and have us prepare her horse and one for the King's Guard. I understand she is a very good equestrian. She also is a good sword fighter." He smiled.

Trey glanced at Tommy Boy and asked, "So she does not come by on a certain time?"

"No. She rides randomly. We never know for certain."

Tommy Boy asked, "Why would you say that she is good with a sword?"

"The story is she beat two prison guards in a sword competition, and the loser had to walk down the street in the nude. It must have been quite a show seeing two nude men on our streets. However, you believe what you want to believe." He shrugged his shoulders.

Trey and Tommy Boy both laughed and tried to build a rapport with the man and Denco. "Yes, two naked men on your street would be a show. So, you do not believe the story?"

Denco announced, "He does not believe a female could beat two of the King's Guards."

The man looked at Denco. "They were prison guards." The man looked at Tommy Boy and Trey, "It makes for a good story. It is just a story. A tall tale." He motioned with hands and smiled.

"Where does your Princess come from?" asked Tommy Boy.

Denco could not wait to tell them she stayed in the King's palace on the top floor. "We do not know where she came from. We can see her looking down from her balcony located on the southeast corner of the castle from time to time. The next time she comes to ride, I will ask her where she is from."

The man looked at Trey and Tommy Boy, "I would not suggest you go riding in the country. There are many soldiers, and they might arrest you." He waved his hand in a friendly gesture, "It would not be safe for you. The landowners in the outer realm are nothing but warlords with a gang of bandits working for them." He glanced around to see if anyone else was in the area. "The warlords, soldiers, and guards can be ruthless to outsiders. I would suggest you walk back to the Port Authority and stay close to your ship. My brother-in-law works at the dock. They normally do not allow the sailors to leave the dock area. The city is on lock down." He looked inquisitively at the two men, "Where did you say you were from?"

Trey announced, "We will head back to the dock. We checked in with the Marina Authority. Our captain is meeting with the King discussing future terms of a trade. You two have a nice day." He flipped Denco a copper coin and watched him catch it. They turned and walked out the back of the stables.

***

The two men had not talked as they walked at a fast pace along the sidewalks and street, watching out for city guards as they proceeded to the rendezvous location. Trey and Tommy Boy walked into the empty room. "I hope they hurry. That must be Veronica. We now know where she is staying," announced Tommy Boy.

Trey looked concerned, "We might have to watch the stables and meet her there. I hope the lady the stable boy was referring to living in the castle is Veronica. He described her perfectly. I must believe she is still alive. We need to get her and leave." Trey was fidgeting and rubbing his hands together. Tommy Boy knew Trey was playing the what if game and concerned why his sister would be held as a prisoner in the castle.

"I am not going to lie to you. This is going to be tough. It sounds like there are a lot of guards. We must find Veronica. We need to leave before we are discovered." Trey looked out the dirty second story window. He pulled his sword when he saw Hulk and Robin Hood running toward them down the alley and turning on the street. They were dodging people on the congested sidewalk as they ran. They ran down the alley which led to the rear of the old building and ascended the stairs and into the room. Hulk was somewhat out of breath and announced, "We know where she is located. This place is not safe for us. It is just a matter of time before someone turns us in for a reward. Dak and Zenith need to hurry."

Robin Hood ran into the room and picked up his bow and satchel of arrows. He then walked over next to Trey, stood to the side of the window, and peered out to the street below. "It is not like them to be late. We need a backup plan and a more secure location." He kept watching the sidewalk for a possible squad of soldiers coming their way.

Trey said, "You should be trying to blend in. No one else is running down the street. Every damn person out there was watching you two."

Trey looked at Robin Hood and observed he appeared to be anxious as he was hiding behind the wall and peering out the window to the street below holding his bow. He then looked at Hulk and saw blood stains on his pant leg. "Did you two run into trouble?"

Hulk looked at Trey looking at his leg with blood on his pants. Hulk then nonchalantly said, "I had to off three soldiers in an alley behind a bar." He held his hands out to his side as if to say it was no big deal.

Wrinkles appeared on Trey's forehead, "Dammit. This entire city will go on lock down. They will be looking for us. Why did you kill three soldiers?"

Hulk looked pissed, "We had no choice. We should be okay. The witnesses will tell the police the killing was a fight with a couple of sailors, and the three army soldiers lost. The sailors ran away. I assure you it was either them or us."

"We hope Ronny was able to convince King Solman on the coal for gold deal. He needs to have the boat ready," announced Trey. Trey seemed more anxious with learning the three soldiers were killed. "I am worried about my sister." He hit his hand on the table as he turned to look at Hulk. His expression was one of apprehension. "Was there no way you could have avoided killing three soldiers? They will be on the lookout for us. This is going to be an almost impossible mission. We all agreed we needed to be in stealth mode. We cannot afford to make mistakes. Can you two not go one hour without killing someone?"

Robin Hood announced, "Here they come. They are carrying bags. They look like they have been shopping." He turned to Trey, "Hulk had no choice. Besides, there are three less Normand soldiers." Trey turned and watched out the window to verify if Dak and Zenith were being followed.

Dak and Zenith walked into the room. Dak threw the bag of clothes to Robin Hood. You and I are going to a political speech. We need to leave in thirty minutes. Zenith will be waiting for us on the east side of the palace."

Hulk announced, "We know where Veronica is staying. She is in the castle on the top floor."

Zenith glanced at Hulk and replied, "Finding the location of Veronica is not the problem. Everyone in the city knows where she is located. She is the talk of the town. We believe we might have an opportunity to contact her outside the castle walls." She looked at Dak and Robin Hood, "You two need to hurry and get dressed. While you two are listening to the King's speech, I will scout out the exterior of the palace. We will need to hurry and leave tonight. Ronny needs to be ready for a fast departure."

Trey announced, "We might have additional problems. Hulk killed three soldiers in an alley behind the bar."

Hulk looked at Dak, "I had no choice. The city guards will be looking for two sailors fleeing the scene. We are not sailors. We are traders from Israel. We have changed clothes and thrown the uniforms in the trash. There are no witnesses." Robin Hood glanced at Hulk thinking about the dancer. He knew he needed to keep his mouth shut.

Dak added, "The guards will all stay close to the King working in his protection detail. They might not start looking for the two missing sailors until tomorrow. We should be gone by then. The King is not going to cancel his speech tonight over three soldiers, who were killed in an alley. We were told

Veronica should be at the speech. King Solman arrived two nights ago from a trip and now his speech starts tonight at eight. We believe he will reveal his plans and strategy for his kingdom, and when they will attack the North. Robin Hood and I will try to make contact with Veronica." He pulled his shirt over his head and dropped his pants. Robin Hood watched and then did the same. Both men hurried getting dressed. Zenith assisted them with their jackets, ties, cuffs, and making certain they were dressed properly. Dak kissed Zenith and said, "You follow us and keep your hood tight around your pretty little ears." She smiled.

Dak looked at his friends, "The news is better than I thought possible, but we must hurry. I have a feeling something bad is about to happen. We need to rescue Veronica and leave tonight. The city is full of soldiers who appear to be on leave and ready to celebrate. We will try to blend in with the soldiers."

Hulk looked perplexed, "How are we going to pull this off tonight?"

"Tommy Boy, I need you to update Ronny on our plan. You will need to set the charges and timers and have them ready. We leave at three tonight. Anyone not on the boat gets left behind." He looked at his friends, "Every one of us needs to be on the boat headed out of the harbor. Hulk, you, Trey, and

To Kill a Blueblood

Tommy Boy will place the explosives for the three-A.M. party.
You need to take out the three large warships and the cruiser.
The cruiser has greater speed capabilities than our vessel." He
paused as he pulled his jacket on and figured Hulk was about
to say something. Instead, Hulk seemed to like the plan. Dak
added, "Zenith will carry mine and Robin Hood's change of
clothes. We will become traders from Asia after we leave the
speech. Zenith and I will ascend the north façade of the castle
and then cross over the rooftop and drop down to Veronica's
balcony on the east elevation. We will enter Veronica's
chambers from her balcony. Robin Hood will rotate his
position to the east side and guard our retreat from the
building. The three of us will then meet Robin Hood on the
street below. We will see you guys on board. As the four
Normand ships blow up, we will sail south right by them." He
used his right hand to illustrate a straight line. "Once we are
three miles from land, we will turn north and go home. Mission
accomplished."

Hulk looked at Dak, "It sounds like you are making this plan
up as you talk with us."

"I am making this up as I go. We need to hurry. This is too
dangerous being in this city. The citizens all appear to be
scared. They do what they are told. This plan has several
moving parts, and I do not believe any part will be easy. What

I do know is that we need to leave this city. Zenith and I were followed from the restaurant. We lost the tail. The waitress provided us with a stern warning. None of us are safe in Southern City. All of us must leave tonight." He kissed Zenith and looked at Robin Hood, "We need to leave now."

Hulk looked at Dak, "What about King Solman? You will be right there."

Dak looked at the group, "We will be lucky to get Veronica." Dak walked to the door and held the door open for Robin Hood and Zenith.

Chapter 23

Tommy Boy pulled from the pile next to the pig trough a stem of bamboo as he walked toward the waterfront. He broke the bamboo in half as he kept his pace and made certain the bamboo was hollow as he peered through the shaft toward the light of a street lantern. He kept his head tilted down as he walked but also was cognitive of the soldiers and possible on duty city guards. He followed the direction provided by Dak as he walked behind the old home built on piers located on the shoreline. The ocean tide was out, and the area was starting to begin dark as the sun had set and there was no one in sight. He could hear the loud ruckus of the men and women drinking and having fun at the Port Bar two blocks east from the dilapidated home. The home was built after the Transitional Period and had survived the revolution which had occurred close to ten years prior. Like most buildings and homes built in that period, the structures were built of inferior materials and would not hold up in the large windstorms which frequent the area. Tommy Boy did not hesitate. He walked in the mud of the harbor until he made it to the water and entered the water from the edge of the home and used the bamboo as a snorkel as he swam from the shoreline into the darkness of the harbor. He crossed in front of the Port Bar out of sight of the people on the balcony. He reached the same boat tied off under repairs on the dock. Then, he retraced his prior steps by floating under the pier. He was relieved for the darkness of night and cloud cover as he pushed from one pillar to another under the dock as he moved further toward Ronny and his boat. Once in the middle of the dock, he could smell the Normand Guards as they sat in the chairs at the gate under the lanterns halfway from the land and the end of the dock. The guards were eating fish and throwing the bones over the rail into the water. He was careful as he approached the guards floating three feet under them listening to them talk as they ate. Two of the guards stood and urinated from the side of the wooden pier into the inland bay as he held to the cross support connected to the pier. He was careful to avoid the ambient light of the lanterns tied to the light poles near the guard station and the gate. He could see the guards through the cracks in the planks of the wooden dock as he eased from pillar to pillar heading further out the dock.

After the thirty-minute process of moving under the dock unnoticed, Tommy Boy peered out at the ocean from behind the dock pillar. He saw the two Normand guards sitting at the boardwalk leading to his boat. He saw Darnel sleeping as he was leaning against the mast. He then saw Sneedy walk from the cabin over to Darnel under the ambient light of the lantern.

He pulled the dry match from his concealed pocket and removed it from the dry plastic. He struck the match and waved the match in the darkness. At first the two men did not react. Then, he noticed Darnel respond as if he saw the flash of light. Darnel woke Sneedy, "You need to open the trap door. We just received the signal." Darnel whispered.

Darnel walked toward the boardwalk and the two guards stationed at the access from the dock to the boat. Tommy Boy knew Darnel was distracting the guards, and he swam to the rear of his boat. He thought of the location of the access door from his location as he headed to the rear hull. He took a deep breath and went under water heading for the trap door. He felt of the keel and knew the door would be to his right. He reached and knocked on the door panel.

Sneedy walked unnoticed back into the cabin and hurriedly pulled up the interior panel and gently laid the panel to the side. He noticed a small amount of water on the floor of the cargo bay. He then removed his shirt and pants and crawled into the hidden cargo space and waited. Once he heard the knock, he opened the ocean access panel and placed the panel to the side. He watched as Tommy Boy's head emerged from beneath the boat. He whispered, "You need to hurry and be quiet. There are two guards stationed on the deck."

Tommy Boy whispered, "Tell captain Ronny we leave at three A.M. on the dot." Sneedy then turned and crawled to the other access panel and pulled himself into the cabin. He quickly replaced the cover over the opening and got dressed.

Chapter 24

Veronica walked toward the stairs as Michael was following her, "My Queen, I am to escort you to the balcony seat. I will be stationed against the wall behind you at the exit door." Veronica listened but kept walking. She was concerned about having to meet the King after the speech. She had not seen him in two days since he beat and raped her on their wedding night. She also suspected the large army and navy were about to be deployed north. The long-waited period to attack the north and conquer all the villages, small cities, and communities had finally arrived. The people of the north would not unite and fight the Normand invaders. The Northern tribes did not trust each other, and no one wanted to believe the Normand army would return.

Michael stepped in front of Veronica and opened the door to the stairs leading to the balcony. She walked across the threshold and up the stairs. She could feel her legs ache as she stepped up on each stair. She had worked out twice as hard earlier at dawn. She had completed every exercise twice the number of her normal workouts. She knew she wanted to be prepared, and she wanted to go down fighting. The King would be requesting her soon. She took her seat in the front row of the balcony. As she pulled her turtleneck up tight to hide the bruising on her neck, she noticed the large number of men walking to the outside area in front of the castle. Most of the men were in uniforms. She saw the large contingent of guards all carrying their shields and right hands resting on the handle of their swords as they made their appearance. She knew this was a show of strength, and the King wanted everyone to know he was in charge. Veronica saw group after group of men walking from different streets and along the sidewalks to the open area. She then noticed three generals enter the front near the stage from the side castle door. She recognized them from her wedding ceremony. They each took a seat up front facing the audience. She noticed several men were looking at her as she was one of the few females that were present. King Solman had not allowed the announcement of their wedding to be public although the rumor of him taking a wife had spread throughout the kingdom. She had mixed emotions with the anticipation of the announcement tonight. She glanced down at the large number of soldiers standing in the middle of the area waiting for the speech. They all seemed to be anxious for the command for war.

As she sat at the rail of her balcony, she peered downward and scanned the hundreds of people standing. The men in uniforms were still walking into the rear area and the side walkways were crowded as the city streetlights were starting to be lit. The sun was setting and the heat from the day was dissipating. At first, she thought her eyes were playing tricks on her. She saw a man in a gray lieutenant's uniform leaning against the wall close to one hundred yards away as he was standing opposite of her on the lower level. He looked like Dak. She stared at the man. He stared back with a smirk of a smile on his face. He removed his cap and flashed two fingers meaning two o'clock tonight. He pointed to the tower the same way he would when they were growing up when he pointed to the large cliff overlooking the ocean back at Cliff Tops. He would signal from the ocean jetty to she and their friends at the top of the cliff that the area was clear to jump. She waved her right hand and then gasped in her breath and placed her right hand to her chin. Dak turned and walked down the street as he made his way through the crowd. He was one of the few people to leave before the speech started. She then noticed Robin Hood fell in behind Dak as they both walked away from the area. She said to herself, "They came for me."

She turned and glanced at Michael to see if he noticed the man sending her signals. She realized Michael could not see Dak from the rear wall of the balcony. She then thought about Michael. He would be killed by the King's Guard if she fled. She also knew Dak would kill Michael if he was in the way.

She knew Michael loved her. He would tell her about his dreams when they rode the horses through the flat lands and along the beaches. She in turn had told him about her parents and her city, Cliff Tops. She had reluctantly shared a part of herself with him knowing they could never be anything but a queen and her guard.

Before the Transitional Period, he had been a soccer player in a country in the South American region at age nine. He loved soccer. He had talked little about his family. Veronica knew he was like every other person still alive older than twenty. They had all suffered, lost friends, and lost loved ones. The world conditions had turned brutal, and the condition to survive had been unmerciful in some parts of the world. She now realized how fortunate she and her friends had been. They had been raised in the secluded city of Cliff Tops away from the brutal conditions of the world and wars between the clans of people. The clans of people were slow to unite and create cities working together to make a better life for the survivors. Instead, the clans fought over the limited resources and in order to survive the strong killed the weak.

While riding along the beach, she and Michael had discovered the river and the cool water with the beautiful waterfalls north along the ocean. There were two small waterfalls and then one larger. The river then flowed into the ocean. The view from the hill was magnificent.

She remembered she walked her horse to the riverbank down the steep bank allowing the horse to drink from the river. Michael had advised her not to descend the steep embankment because of the danger, but he had followed and also led his horse to the sandy area. She went swimming, but he had refused to swim with her. She knew she needed someone's help to escape, and she tried to persuade Michael by seducing him. He never crossed the line. He was the perfect guard. He worked for honor and was consumed with pride in his job. Veronica respected him for being of high moral character and dedicated to his sworn oath. She then realized Michael was with her a great deal more than the other four guards. They were expected to rotate ever six hours with two escorting her to the workout arena and horse rides, but Michael was always present. He was the captain of her detail. He could order another to work those hours. As she sat in her balcony seat, she now had come to terms with Michael and excepted he loved her that would be the only reason he was on duty with her so much more than the other guards.

She snapped out of her thoughts when she noticed one of the generals step forward. She knew he would be introducing King Solman.

King Solman was introduced as the sole King of Southern City and the southern part of the region. He was dressed in gold-looking material and armor with a gold sword. Everyone stood and clapped except her. She stayed seated and watched from her balcony seat. She could not deny his good looks, charisma, and the ability to lead others. He started his speech by announcing he was going to unite the entire continent under his leadership. He announced Southern City, would be the capital, and all the citizens would prosper. The land and the resources of the north would be under their control. Veronica listened to the thirty-minute speech and considered how the northern communities, villages, and cities would all fall to his armies. She thought about how the elders in her tribe in Cliff Tops would sometimes talk about spies and information being transferred in the old world. The importance of leverage and knowledge when dealing with the governments in the past. Her tribe had no leverage and no way to defend themselves against this large army, and the people of Southern City loved to hear how they were going to prosperous and all be rich under his leadership. The King did not mention all the innocent lives of the northern people that would be killed, and the brutal conditions placed on the refugees when they were forced off their land. In his speech Veronica noticed he feed the greed of his citizens and the ambitions of his army. The people desired to be wealthy, and the soldiers wanted the glory that came with butchering the armies of the north. He pointed to a squad of soldiers and had them stand and received the recognition for being great warriors and killing several hundred people of the north. The people all stood and clapped.

Toward the end of the speech, King Solman changed the subject and explained every king needs a queen and heirs. He pointed to Veronica and declared she was his queen and would produce him several heirs. The entire audience looked at her and all stood and clapped at the announcement that the two had been married two days prior. She waved and smiled to the standing audience.

King Solman ended the speech by promising the audience the wealth of the north would be theirs. He described the people of the north to be uneducated, uncivilized, and easy to conquer. He guaranteed the audience wealth beyond their dreams, and his armies would conquer the north. The audience was standing and all cheering for him as he declared himself their supreme leader. "Under my leadership, our army will make all you rich beyond your dreams. People of Southern City need to support our soldiers, and all of you, I promise, will share in the wealth."

***

Veronica did not want to go back to her room. She started to hate being locked up and now she was going to be forced to be married to a man she did not love. A man who would lead the armies north and kill the people of her village, her friends, and her family. She also now knew what he could do to her. She wanted to talk to Dak. She needed Dak to understand King Solman's plans. She wanted to walk around in the city and think. She also knew Michael would have his orders to escort her back to her room where he would stand guard outside in the hallway. In her thoughts, the notion of Michael and how he would be treated if she fled came rushing into her mental images, "He would be tortured to death if she escaped." She stood from her balcony seat overlooking the exterior auditorium. Most of the guests had already disappeared as they walked away from the open area into the streets and alleys. She turned and walked toward Michael and the rear double doors as she thought about how King Solman had now unveiled his intent to start the war campaign north. He was not specific where he was going to initially attack, but he was clear he was going to conquer the entire continent and all of Southern City would prosper under his leadership.

She ascended the four stairs to where Michael was standing. "We will take the long way back to my cell. I would like to see the city."

Michael hesitated knowing he had his orders to take her to the King's chambers. He considered if the extra thirty minutes of walking in the city would go unnoticed by the King. He was also concerned if the Queen would be noticed even with her hood pulled tight. His other concern was that the soldiers were going to be intoxicated, and the city would be wild with fights and disorderly men. The streets would not be safe for her or any unescorted female. When the army was told they would be deployed for battle and the Navy was told they would be deployed two days after the army, some of the men would be celebrating, and others would be drinking their worries away. Both groups would be getting drunk and fighting. The sailors were required to report to their vessels one day prior to departure. The sailors hated being at sea for weeks without seeing land or female companions. Michael knew the soldiers and the navy personnel would fight. There were always fights after the soldiers and navy personnel were provided a couple days off and drinking was the priority. The men were prideful about their placement in the army versus the navy. The City Guards and the King's Guards would be on patrol breaking up fights and arresting the drunk soldiers and sailors.

Michael looked at Veronica, "My Queen, this night in the city might not be safe for you to walk the city streets. There will be men celebrating and others drinking their sorrows away. There are not enough King's Guards to police the entire city."

"I want to walk the city streets. You are my guard. No one will dare come after me with you as my protector." She pulled her hood over her head, "Now follow me." He smiled at her joke about him defending her, and she was safe with him watching her. He rushed behind her as she descended the stairs and walked swiftly through the crowd of soldiers standing outside the double doors onto the sidewalk. She walked fast dodging the men lining the sidewalks and narrow streets. She was halfway down the sidewalk heading toward the ocean when Michael finally reached her left arm and spun her around, "You need to slow down. What is the meaning of this?"

"I thought you could keep up." She looked him in the eyes and then took two small steps toward him. By invading his space while standing on the sidewalk for all to see, he felt awkward. He backed up providing space as a soldier walked behind him and bumped him from the rear. The street was full of people walking in both directions. She turned and pulled her arm free, breaking loose of his grip. Two army personnel

walked between Michael and Veronica forcing Michael to
hesitate to follow. She walked into the establishment.

Michael was caught off guard and tried to stop her. He knew
what this establishment was, and the Queen was not allowed in
such a place where only men were allowed to visit with
working women.

Veronica ran up the stairs and through the doorway by the
four sailors who were arguing with two soldiers. Veronica
heard the big soldier say with a stern threat, "I will beat the
living shit out of you."

The man working for the brothel who was stationed at the
front door was watching the men square off, and knew they
were about to fight. The employee walked between the two
sides and explained if they fought, they could not enter.
Michael was pushed backward as the men started pushing each
other and then had to dodge another soldier walking toward the
conflict. The crowd on the street and the sidewalk started to
push forward, wanting to watch a fight. Michael knew he did
not have time to fight or stop the fight. He knew he had to
catch Veronica and remove her from the whore house.

Veronica walked through the foyer of the brothel and
noticed the naked female dancing for the sailors at one table
and then two other naked female dancers on two small tables
for two groups of soldiers. She noticed one dancer had on heels

and the other dancer was barefooted. She glanced back at the stage and noticed the naked female dancer was bending over for the men customers on both sides of the large stage. Then, the dancer started pulling her bra between her legs back and forth as she danced in front of three sailors. Veronica looked forward as she walked further into the large room at the hallway directly ahead of her and saw a man going into a room holding the hand of a working woman. Both the man and the whore were smiling as the man was pushing his body up against the female as he held her hand and stood behind her.

Michael ran around the soldiers and by the sailors. He ran through the door and across the foyer into the open large room. He tried to reach for her wrist, and she pulled away walking quickly into the hallway past two men talking to a half-naked woman. She heard them ask how much for both of them at one time. She noticed the female smiled and licked her lips. Michael heard a drunk man he had just passed say loudly, "What is a King's Guard doing in here?" He frantically tried to catch Veronica. He knew she needed to be protected from this type of establishment, and her presence had to be kept a secret. He reached her in the hall by grabbing her elbow and forcibly spun her around. He proceeded to hold her tight with both hands on both her arms and pushed her back against the wall of the hall, "My Queen, you should not be in here. You are innocent. You do not understand what this place is. Now follow me." He tried to leave.

She interrupted him and pulled back against his momentum to leave, "Why should I not be here? You stated I am pretty, did you not? You said you like my dress. Do you not believe these men will like me?"

He glanced around both ways in the hallway and was somewhat caught off guard by her response. He looked concerned as he stared into her eyes as she once again stepped closer to him moving into his personal space. He could feel her rub against him. "This is where men pay women for sexual favors. We need to leave. This is no place for you. Matter of fact, I need to get you out before someone recognizes you." He involuntarily swallowed.

Veronica interrupted him. "This is the perfect place for us. How much will you pay me to bed you? Surely you have been here before. I have heard the soldiers and guards refer to this place while we are working out as the best whore house in the city. You can have me in one of these rooms." She stared into his eyes as she rubbed against him with her body weight pushing into him forcing him into the opposite wall.

He looked around trying to discern if anyone was watching. He knew this was not a place for a King's Guard to be in his guard uniform. Someone would notice and report him to

General Redman. "No, we need to leave." He forcibly pushed her backward against the opposite wall and then tried to pull her toward the door. Two drunk sailors walked by them standing in the hall. Michael had to press against Veronica as the men passed in the narrow hallway. Michael was trying to shield Veronica from the two men blocking their view of her. Veronica stood on her toes and peered into his eyes. "I can feel your body pressed against my body. I know you would like to take me in the room. I am a whore, and this is a whore house."

Michael felt drops of sweat appear on his forehead. He was uncomfortable. He looked at her, "No one must recognize you being in here. Please follow me. I need to get you back to your chambers. The King will want to see his Queen tonight." She noticed his clench jaws as he stared into her eyes.

"You mean my prison cell? But first would you not want to have me? I won't charge you much. How about a week's wage?"

"My Queen, you toy with me. Come on. Please."

She held her position and changed her tone to one of concern, 'I was never a princess, and I am no queen. I am just like these women working here. I lay on my back with a man I do not love, the same as they. I have provided the King nothing of value about myself. I have not made myself vulnerable to him and shared my dreams and my desires as he has not done so with me. There is no chance we are in love."

Michael held her tight. They could hear the cheers of the male audience as another dancer walked on the stage and started removing her clothing as she danced. A blond woman came out of one of the rooms holding the hand of a soldier. She smiled at Michael as the two passed Michael, pushing Michael into Veronica. Veronica looked him in the eyes the entire time with Michael pressing her arms above her head against the wall holding her still. "I can feel your body pressing against me. I know what you desire. Let me tell you about my desires. I have desires to be with a man that loves me and not be with one that I am forced against my will. That is my desire before I die, to be with a man that cherishes me. Our King cannot feel empathy for anyone. He will never be able to love another. He wants total control of me. He enjoys raping and beating women." She pulled her left arm free and her hood off and her collar back to reveal her neck and the bruising. She looked him in the eyes. "See this bruising. He just about killed me. Maybe I should take to the stage. Maybe those men in the audience would covet me. After all, who would desire my life?"

"My Queen, it is an honor to guard you. My personal feelings for you cannot get in my way of my job and responsibility. My responsibility is to watch you and protect

Steve Dwight Nichols

you. I have taken an oath to protect you and die for you if required. My oath is all I have as a man to offer. Without my oath, what kind of man would I really be? Please do not make this difficult for me." He reached out, pulling her dress upward around her neck and her hood tight around her face.

She pulled her other arm free and turned to walk through the open area toward the stage heading to the front exit. The male customers saw her walking from the back hallway. The one sailor stepped in her path blocking her from leaving. As she tried to go right, he went the same direction. As she tried to go left, he went that direction forcing her to stop. The man was drunk, and his friends were also intoxicated. He blocked Veronica's path to the door. She looked from under her hood into his eyes. "I want to see you on the stage with nothing on and then me and my friends want to take you in the backroom and fuck you."

She replied, "So you crave me?" She then smiled.

"Yes. You are a whore, and we will pay." Before the man could finish his sentence, he fell to the floor.

Michael tried to step around Veronica and move the drunken sailor out of the path to the door. Before he could reach the man, Veronica kicked the man in the crotch with her right knee. The man doubled over, coughed, and then slowly fell over on the floor into the fetal position. Veronica stepped across him and walked to the exit door. The man's friends tried to fight Michael as Michael tried to keep up with Veronica. He ran out the door behind Veronica with the drunken sailors trying to catch him. Veronica started running, weaving in and out of the crowd as she escaped the sailors following her with Michael in close pursuit. After three city blocks, she turned down an alley and stopped fifty feet next to the brick wall of the building. She laughed, "I believed we escaped." She smiled, "I knew you would protect me. They stopped chasing us. They must be aware of your oath and fear the consequences of your ability to protect me."

Michael looked behind him and smiled at the last comment. "You certainly know how to start a fight. That poor sailor will not be having sex tonight and for that matter, he might not be having sex for several nights."

"I was worried they might beat you up. I thought you needed some help keeping me safe." She reached down and unfastened the boot on her left foot. "These boots are made for looks and not running. She removed the other boot and the two started walking to the opposite end of the alley. "I guess I am ready to go back to my prison cell. Thanks for showing me the city. You might be the most honorable man I have ever met. You certainly believe in your job responsibilities. I respect that in you. One day some lady will be lucky to your wife." The two walked next to one another to the end of the alley and then crossed the street down the sidewalk two blocks to the rear castle doorway.

The castle guards saw Veronica walking to the door barefoot carrying her boots with Michael by her side. The guards recognized the two and allowed them to pass. Michael opened the door for her as she approached her chambers. When she walked into her room, she noticed Dezie standing by the window. Michael closed the door behind her and positioned himself in the hall.

"The King demands to see you at once. You are late."

Veronica had not seen Dezie since before her last visit with the King two days prior. She dropped her boots on the floor and turned to Dezie, "Why?" Dezie looked perplexed. "Why not tell me he was going to beat me?" She pulled her high collar down showing her two-day old bruising. She held up her wrists and pulled her sleeves up showing the healing rope burns. "You knew he was a monster and what he was capable of and yet you did not warn me. Matter of fact, you instructed me how to perform with Brad in front of your King. You told me to act frisky. You knew."

"I did what I thought was best for you. I am sorry he hurt you. We all know our King can be a cruel man."

Veronica interrupted her and in a direct tone, "You did what was best for you. He almost killed me by choking me from behind. He did things to me for the purpose of hurting me. How many other females has he done this to?" She watched Dezie who stood still and did not answer. "I am going to see the King tonight. I am going to tell him I desire another handmaid. I want someone that I can trust. You could serve better working in the tents with the soldiers. They do not care about your age, and based on what you have taught me, you should be very popular, acting frisky for the soldiers."

"Please no. You do not understand. I will serve you better." Dezie had tears in her eyes. "The King is a mean man. He will not show me mercy. At your request, I would be sent to the tents. I beg you for forgiveness. Please be gracious and show me mercy. I swear to you, I will serve you better." She bowed her head and cried.

***

Veronica was announced by the King's Guard as she entered the King's chambers. She noticed his empty dishes on the table and her unused dishes. He had already eaten dinner. He walked in from his balcony carrying a drink. "Your speech was very convincing. You are a natural leader. The soldiers are ready to rally behind you. Your citizens love you and are also ready to fight for you and support your troops. You will no doubt crush your enemies."

He looked at her with a smile on his face, "You are such a liar." He smiled at her as both looked at each other. "You certainly are a beautiful woman. You will produce me several heirs. However, you know what concerns me about you?" Veronica looked him in the eyes and then glanced away to the balcony door. She knew the question was a rhetorical question. "You are very smart. Your ability to outsmart others concerns me. You are also very confident in yourself. You may be too confident."

"I have these bruises that have not healed. My younger handmaid suggested I wear long sleeves to cover my wrist from the rope burns and the high neck dress to cover the bruising around my neck. I do not wish to be placed in bondage and beaten. I do not wish for you to use your baton on me. I do not wish to be beaten, bitten, pinched, and forcibly sodomized." She stared at him.

"You are my property. I will do with you as I please. The sooner you learn this, the better." He stared back at her. "I must teach you and all my servants how our relationship works."

"I am here to please you that much is true." She glanced at the view from the open door to the balcony and thought about jumping to her death. She did not wish to appear melancholy in front of King Solman. She had stated her thoughts and now was a time to move forward.

King Solman walked over to her and held her tight. He kissed her on the forehead. "You are my property. You will do as I command." He applied pressure on her shoulders forcing her to her knees in front of him. She understood what he was forcing her to do. She unbuckled his pants and pulled his pants down and took him. When he was finished, she thanked him for allowing her to service him. She walked to the balcony, "May I make one request?"

He pulled his pants up and fastened them, "What is your one request?"

"My guard, Michael, has worked twenty-eight days and some nights without time off. The other four guards all are scheduled off tonight. Michael has missed parties with friends. Can you ask General Redman to replace him tonight with another guard?"

Chapter 25

Michael was surprised when Bruno and the King's Envoy appeared in the hallway where he was standing. The Envoy announced as he approached, "The King has summoned you two guards to his office at the Queen's request."

One of the King's Guard opened the door for Veronica, Michael, Bruno, and the Envoy. The group walked into the King's quarters followed by his two guards. Michael glanced at Veronica as she walked to the balcony. She showed no sign of acknowledging him as he and Bruno both stood in the King's Chambers waiting for the order from the King.

Veronica knew Michael did not like Bruno. Michael had not selected Bruno to work with him as one of her personal guards. Bruno had more experience as a soldier and as a guard than Viking and Pretty Boy. He took the decision personally and cussed Michael off duty at a bar. The two had to be separated by other off-duty guards before they fought.

She turned and was staring at the view from the balcony with her back to the men inside the chambers. The King's two guards stood on both sides of Michael and Bruno. "Bruno will be replacing your watch." He looked at Michael and hesitated, "He will be watching my Queen tonight."

Michael could not hold back his surprise. He looked at Veronica to see if she had said something about the prior events in the city. "Your Excellency, may I ask why?"

King Solman never had the patience to be asked questions. He looked at Michael, "You have been replaced tonight. Your service has been commendable. I have spoken to General Redman. He has ordered your replacement. Now go and have a night on the town with the other four guards." King Solman turned to his guards to say he wanted to be left alone.

Veronica then turned and walked into the room from the balcony and announced to Bruno, "I am ready to return to my chambers."

The envoy stayed behind in the office as the four guards and Veronica walked out the door. The two King's Guards both took their positions in the hallway. Michael tried to make eye contact, but Veronica looked the other way. She followed Bruno with Michael following her. After they passed the corner in the hallway out of sight of the two King's Guards, he reached for Veronica's wrist. He pulled her to a stop. Bruno heard the two behind him in the hallway and turned. Bruno was surprised with Michael's actions of touching the Queen. He turned to look at Michael holding her wrist. Veronica pulled her wrist free from his grasp. "This guard will keep me locked up tonight. You need to go and have fun for once in your life.

You need to go back to the whore house and meet that blonde you kept eyeing and take her into the back room for some fun." She turned and walked by Bruno toward her chambers. Bruno looked confused at Michael. He wondered about her comment about a whore. He knew the Queen was not allowed to go into the city.

Michael saw the look in Bruno's eyes. He immediately turned and walked to the stairs and out the door. He went straight to the guard house and removed his uniform. He sat naked on the bench looking in the mirror confused about Veronica and his own feelings. He loved the fact that she was not always obedient. He also liked the way she showed empathy for the town's people and provided extra food from her chambers. She ordered more than she was going to eat and then she would take the extra to the stable boy and even the guards and soldiers who came and worked out with her early in the morning. Most of all, he loved her beautiful body, her hair, her complexion, and her overall physical appearance. She walked with confidence and her entire personality was one of self-assurance. The memory of her sitting nude on her balcony was an enchanting moment forever etched into his memory. He thought of her before he fell asleep, and the first thought when he awoke was of her. Her physical appearance was the perfect match for the female body type he was attracted. He could not date another female for thinking of Veronica. He heard someone walk into the guard room. The other guards were always changing clothes and going out on the town after their shift was over. He knew he had eighteen hours before he was required to report for his next shift. He reached for his clothes and headed for the small pub on one of the back streets. He figured he would be left alone to drink, eat, and console his frustrations.

Chapter 26

Dak changed clothes quickly while Zenith watched for guards. He threw the lieutenant's uniform into the pile of trash. He turned and looked up at the north façade of the building. He knew once he climbed the first twenty feet, he had ledges and a good path similar to the cliffs at Cliff Tops. The bottom wall of the castle was smooth concrete. Once he climbed to the second-floor balcony, he could reach the next balcony and then the block stone with ledges made for natural gripping points all the way to the roof of the building. He wrapped the rope around his shoulder and kissed Zenith. She was clothed in all black with a hood pulled over her head and face. Zenith said, "There is no moon light, and the street is clear. The guards are stationed at the front and rear entrances. The city guards are all over the city trying to keep peace in the city with the soldiers all getting drunk. We have a little more than one hour to climb this sucker and get Veronica and return to the boat."

Dak looked at his beautiful wife, "Not to mention to kill any Normand soldiers that get in our way."

Zenith wondered why Dak mentioned killing Normand soldiers. He had not mentioned assassinating King Solman. They were going to be so close. It was not like Dak to miss the opportunity which is so obvious with the King being in the castle. "Do you think we have any chance to take out King Solman? Could we be that lucky?" She looked at Dak trying to pick up his reaction to her question.

He rolled his eyes at Zenith, "Our mission is to spring Veronica. We will see about taking out King Solman. We have no back up. He will be more difficult to reach than General Cuez. We had a plan with General Cuez. We will be pushed for time. I know one thing; we need to reach the apex of this sucker before the rain sets in. I do not want to be halfway up, and it starts raining. It would be too dangerous to scale in the rain. The stone would be too slippery."

Zenith stood on her toes and kissed Dak on the cheek. She heard another rumble of thunder in the distance and noticed the wind had increased. She also realized Dak had considered taking out King Solman, but he had not mentioned the assassination to her.

Robin Hood ran around the corner and saw the kiss, "It is clear, or do you two need privacy?"

Dak smiled and Zenith said, "We are good. You need to make certain the exit route is clear. We will be in a hurry the next time you see both of us." She then looked at Dak, "No one is staying behind."

Robin Hood held his bow in front of him, "I will be prepared to take out the guards on the street. Let's get this done. I do not like this city. There are too many flies, and it is too damn hot with all this dry heat. It is going to rain, but I hope the rain will hold off."

Robin Hood felt anxious to locate Veronica. He had blamed himself for her being kidnapped, and that he had not initially mentioned to the others he had observed a possible Rogue Blueblood kill the captain of the ship and then swim ashore. He should have known of the grave risk presented by the Rogue Blueblood. He thought the group could outrun him across the mountains with the stolen gold and a head start. He had quickly loaded the three bags of gold on his horse from the wagon and rode ahead of the others to scout the trail over the mountain. When he waited for the others at the top of the first high ridge, he was devastated when he was told Veronica had returned the horses and wagon to the rancher. He never considered Veronica would return the wagon and team of horses. He had thought maybe the Blueblood without a horse would not follow them, and he regretted smoking the pot, getting high. He knew Trey and Tommy Boy were right. He had failed to complete his simple task and then Veronica was taken.

Dak announced, "Here I go." He ran across the street, up the wall two steps and then leapt to the ledge of the fifteen-foot-high balcony stretching his hands upward to reach the floor of the balcony. He pulled himself up and then stood on the rail and jumped, pulling himself upward to the next balcony. He tried to hurry as he reached the third balcony and dropped the rope for Zenith. She held herself in place as Dak lifted her to the third balcony. She pulled herself over the railing. "We've got two more balconies to go."

Zenith whispered, "I can climb from here. We need to hurry. I noticed the thunder and lightning getting closer. This might be a tropical storm blowing in from the west."

Chapter 27

Hulk looked at Tommy Boy and Trey. "I know you guys know which way to aim the charges but humor me."

Both held up the explosives and turned them, so the blast would blow inward. "We have one and half hours to set these four explosives and get back to the hatch. Trey, you and Tommy Boy keep your heads down while you are swimming in the channel. You need to stay in the shadows. Set the explosives and swim back under the dock and wait. We do not want any screw ups. Trey, you set yours on the battleship on dock one. Tommy Boy, you swim under the dock and set yours on the battleship tied off behind us. I will swim across the harbor and set my two explosives on the battleship and the cruiser. I will leave one hour before you."

Trey looked at Tommy Boy and then Hulk, "We've got this. This warm water is so much easier to swim in than the cold ass jetty back home. Remember how cold the ocean water was during the summer?"

Hulk smiled, "Our parents wanted all of us to know how to swim. I believe dad liked teaching us."

Trey said, "We set the explosives and then we leave. The question is, do Dak, Zenith, and Robin Hood understand what they must do? I do not desire to leave any of my friends in this damn town."

Hulk undressed and put on his seal skin clothing. "We will pave the way for all of us to go home. You two need to get ready. After I leave, make certain Sneedy is ready to man the access door. We will knock on the seaward side of the boat when we return. Tommy Boy, you can wait for Trey to return, and you two can stay hidden under the dock. But you need to be clear and enter the access doorway one after the other before I arrive. You will need to stay hidden from the two guards."

Tommy Boy started changing clothes, "Hell, this is easy compared to what they must accomplish. There are at least ten moving parts to Dak's plan. Our part is pretty straightforward. We set the explosives, hide, and wait."

Hulk looked at his brother and friend, "We must get this right. If we destroy three of their large warships and the cruiser, we have set them back a year. Plus, we should not have anyone following us out of the harbor."

Tommy Boy announced, "Ronny indicated the coal was moved to the cruiser. The Normand Lieutenant gave him four small copper coins for a square of coal."

"Damn, that is nothing. Does the Normand Army not understand how difficult the task is to dig coal from under the ground? Hell, the risk of life under the ground and being buried alive is not worth four small copper coins. Plus, the hassle of transporting the coal over a thousand miles by sea," announced Trey.

Tommy Boy added, "Ronny acted like it was a great deal. He was scared for his life. He said they were going to torture him to find the location of the coal. He finally convinced them he did not know. There is a middleman. The middleman knows. He promised the lieutenant he would bring them more coal."

Hulk smiled, "They understand. We need to blow the cruiser up with it catching on fire. We need that coal to burn. Do you know if the coal is stored in the front or rear of the cruiser?"

Tommy Boy looked at his brother, "They stored the coal in the aft storage. Once the coal was removed from our ship, the guards all relaxed. They sit at the gate, talked, played cards, and take turns sleeping."

Hulk announced, "I will set the explosion to blow inward on the aft of the cruiser. I will set the charge to blow right into the coal worth four copper coins." The three men changed clothes and entered the hidden access under the floor.

***

Hulk whispered after they had waited in the bottom hidden area for two hours. "You two stink. I am leaving." He opened the access door and crawled through headfirst. He went under water and headed for a hiding spot under the seaward side of the bow.

Tommy Boy reached over and closed the ocean access door. "Damn, I did not wish to say anything, but he really smelled," he whispered. Trey smiled and thought about how they all needed to bathe.

Tommy Boy and Trey waited for another hour for Sneedy to sneak past the two guards and enter the cabin. He opened the access panel in the bottom of the boat and peered inside the hidden compartment. Trey gave Sneedy the thumbs up as Tommy Boy opened the ocean access panel and crawled headfirst into the ocean. Trey followed Tommy Boy, and Sneedy crawled into the hidden department and closed the access panel to the ocean. He quickly crawled back to the interior access panel and crawled out, closing the panel on the floor as he heard one of the guards walking toward him. He jumped into the kitchen compartment and then walked toward the guard who was peering downward into the cabin using the light from his lantern. "I was looking for a snack." He smiled at the guard holding a piece of dried beef.

Chapter 28

Veronica laid down and tried to rest. At one A.M., she pulled the cover back and quietly changed into her black riding clothes. She walked to the balcony and looked out to sea. When the lightning struck far in the western sky, she could see the silhouettes of warships tied to three docks and other ships also tied off to the docks. A massive storm was approaching. The night was dark with no moon-just clouds and thunder heard in the distance. The wind was blowing from the west pushing the cloud cover and storm toward Southern City. She took a deep breath and prayed the large storm would hold off until her escape was complete. She thought of the bruising on her neck and the bite marks caused by her husband. She knew now she had to escape. Her husband would be demanding her presence in his chambers this coming evening. She walked to her door and listened. She could hear Bruno lightly snoring, as she hoped he would be, sitting in the hall. She knew he was working a double shift and was tired. She hoped he would sleep until morning.

Dak carefully stood on the rail and jumped upward reaching the roof's edge. He pulled himself over the rake of the roof on the west elevation into the valley of the roof, holding himself in position with his hands braced on one slope and his feet braced on the other slope. He dropped Zenith ten feet of the rope, and she placed the enclosed loop around her. Dak laid back into the valley of the roof placing his legs and feet on the opposite slopes of the roof and lifted Zenith up. "We need to scale the steep pitch of the roof, up the valley and slide down the east side to the chimney." He glanced down at Robin Hood hiding in the shadows of the stairway across the road at one-hundred feet below. He waved for Robin Hood to move to the east elevation and wait on them. He turned and crawled up the valley of the roof and then reached for Zenith's hand at the apex. He pulled Zenith by the hand next to him as he straddled the ridgeline of the roof. Dak crossed the apex of the roof of the building and slid down to the eave behind the chimney. He motioned for Zenith to ease down next to him. A large streak of lightning reached across the sky and hit something on the other side of town. They looked down the side of the elevation to Veronica's balcony.

Zenith said, "It is going to start raining any moment. I am not certain if I am more concerned with the rain and being on the roof of this building or being struck by lightning."

Dak did not waste time. "I will loop the rope around the chimney. If it starts raining, we will not be able to stay on this slick roof. Hold on to both ends of our rope. You can pull the rope free once we are on the balcony." He then turned his face to look into Zenith's eyes. "I might never have an opportunity like this again. I need to finish King Solman while I am here."

Zenith looked at Dak and clenched her jaws, "We will not be able to make the boat and sail Veronica to safety. Why have we not discussed this?" Zenith was now aggravated. She now knew Dak was always planning to assassinate the King without her.

"You two will leave with Robin Hood. I will catch up with you on the dock."

Zenith grabbed Dak by the wrist and was still clenching her jaws, "I am not leaving you. Veronica can leave with Robin Hood." He looped the rope around the chimney and without looking at Zenith he slid down the rope to the balcony and landed softly.

Zenith stared at him as he landed on the concrete balcony and was so mad she was frozen in place.

Veronica saw the silhouette of a man land on her balcony with multiple weapons attached to his body. She opened the door and hugged Dak. Dak said, "I am so sorry. This was all my fault." He hugged her. "Are you ready? Your time to meet Robin Hood on the street is running out. We have a ship in the harbor and a major storm blowing in from the west. We must hurry."

Veronica jerked her head around. She heard someone running down the hall toward her door. She heard Bruno ask someone, "What are you doing? You are without a uniform." Veronica ran to the door and tried to listen. The voices got quiet. Dak stepped forward and pointed for Veronica to stand in the shadow of the room. Dak pulled both his swords and took a position in front of the door.

Chapter 29

Michael stayed true to his mission. He ate several pieces of chicken and drank eight mugs of beer. He felt intoxicated as he sat still thinking about Veronica and nothing else. He thought about seeing her naked lying on her bench with her handmaid applying the lotion to her back and then she stood. The memory was etched deep into his mind. He also thought back to his oath, and how Veronica had selected him to oversee her guards. Now he was relieved of his night watch by King Solman and replaced with Bruno, a guard he despised. He knew the request had to come from Veronica. When the females in the bar tried to talk to him, he asked them to leave him alone. He was aggravated and his temper was on edge. He thought, "Why would she want him replaced?" He walked outside and leaned against the wall and urinated. He could see the castle where she was staying and her balcony high above. He had scored good on all his reviews, and he finally made King's Guard four years prior and now was working inside the castle. To guard King Solman was the highest honor among the guards. To guard his Queen was the second highest honor. The guards lived by a strict code and were very prideful of being a King's Guard. The higher the rank of a guard, the better the assignment, benefits, and the better the pay. Now the queen was being watched by Bruno, the jail guard, who he despised. Bruno had hoped to be picked to guard the queen and move out of the jail. When Michael had elected four other guards with less experience, and they did not place as well in the sword fighting tournaments, Bruno was angered and vengeful and wanted to fight Michael.

He walked toward the castle as he could hear the thunder in the distance. He watched as the lightning struck in the western sky and the large castle would illuminate each time lightning lit across the night sky. Then, he heard the thunder again in the distance. He remembered when he was a child, he was told to count slowly by one starting with the sight of lightning and stop counting when the thunder struck, that number would reveal the minutes that would pass before the rain to arrive. He guessed he had a few minutes to make his walk to his small apartment before he got wet from rain. He counted to fifteen and was watching the castle roof system as he walked on the dark sidewalk. He stumbled as the alcohol effected his ability to look upward and walk on the brick sidewalk. He also elected to stay clear of the busy areas where the main bars and strip clubs were located. The street and sidewalk he was walking on was almost vacant. He could see someone ahead of him run across the street.

At first, he could not believe his eyes. The large streak of lightning hit in the sky above the city. He wondered, "Am I that drunk?" He thought he saw someone scaling down from the apex of the castle roof to the Queen's balcony. He stood in shock. Then, without hesitating he ran the three blocks along the sidewalk and through the dungeon door. The guards were stationed on the front and rear exit and on each level. No one was aware of the secret dungeon entry way except the castle guards. He ran to the stairway and ascended the stairs two at a time up to the fifth floor. He could feel the muscles in his thighs burning as he cleared the last step. He ran down the hallway trying to breathe. He could see Bruno sitting in the hall. Bruno seemed to come awake and watched him approach.

Bruno frantically tried to place his gloves on without fastening them to his wrist protectors. He did not have time to fasten his throat protector. He knew he was not allowed to sleep, but he was too tired, and the uniform was too tight and hot for him to be comfortable. "What are you doing? You are without a uniform."

Michael commanded as he approached Bruno "Open the door."

Bruno looked at the sweat on his face and pulled his sword as he approached him, "You are drunk, out of uniform, and off duty."

Michael was breathing heavily and sweating, "The Queen is in danger. Open the door."

Bruno looked at Michael and considered the request. He then unlocked the door, and Michael went running inside. He looked toward her bed and saw the empty bed. He saw a figure of a man and ran toward him. The man stepped to the side and pushed him headfirst hard against the wall. Michael was able to place his hands ahead of him to protect his head from the collision with the wall and the small table with the burning candle. He fell to the floor with the table folding into pieces on the floor. The candle burned out and the wax poured onto the floor.

Bruno followed into the room with his sword pulled. He swung hard right to left. His sword was blocked and then he felt his throat itch. At first, Bruno was confused about what had happened. He noticed blood on his left hand coming from his neck. He could not secure a breath to his lungs, and he gasped for air as he struggled to breathe.

Dak blocked Bruno's sword with the sword in his left hand and lifted his unfastened throat protector with his sword blade in his right hand as he slid the blade under the loose-fitting metal guard hanging in front of the neck. Dak then pushed the sword handle with the smaller blade and slashed deep into Bruno's throat. Bruno hesitated and then fell face down to the floor gasping for air, bleeding from his neck. He rolled over on his back holding his neck thrashing back and forth then died.

Veronica ran to Michael and told him, "No". She helped him up. Michael stood and started to pull his sword. He knew he had to protect her. He tried to push her to the side. She pushed him back and held her position. She held his forearm preventing him from pulling his sword. She then turned her back to Michael while holding his shirt, "Do not kill him."

Michael stood and noticed Veronica was standing in front of him with her back to him facing the would-be assassin. "I said do not kill him."

Michael watched the man holding two Sai Swords and noticed the adversary was tall and muscular with the look of a warrior. The man stood still and looked confident in his abilities. Michael glanced at Bruno lying dead on the floor and realized this man was no normal warrior.

Michael noticed the man seemed to relax as he stared at him. Veronica turned around, "Michael, you are not supposed to be on duty. Bruno would have discovered I was missing."

Michael was confused about the man in her room and the effects of the alcohol affecting his judgment. "My Queen, I will die for you. Now step to the side."

Veronica turned and stepped closer to Michael. She was now inches away from him looking him in the eyes, "Do not pull your sword. He will kill you if you do. He killed Bruno, and he can kill you."

"My Queen, I will kill him. I am the King's Guard. This is why we train daily."

She hugged him, "No, Michael, he killed General Cuez. General Cuez was a Blueblood the same as King Solman. This man would kill you with little effort. Please put your sword away. I am not going to allow him to kill you."

Michael stepped backward and was surprised, "King Solman is a Blueblood?"

Veronica announced, "He is a Blueblood. He was engineered to be a tyrant and the only way to defeat him is kill him."

Michael took his eyes off Dak and looked into Veronica's eyes, "That is treason to say something like that. Why my Queen?"

Zenith walked across the threshold from the balcony with her sword in her right hand. Veronica noticed her and was surprised, "What is she doing here?" Veronica realized as she asked the question. Their mission was not just too free her, but also kill King Solman.

Dak did not take his eyes off Michael. He was prepared to kill Michael at a moment's notice. Dak did not understand why Veronica would turn her back on the guard and then face him.

Dak now was confused with Veronica protecting this guard. Dak glanced at Veronica and announced, "She is my back up. She will make certain you make it out of here. I am going to finish this tonight."

Zenith pulled her black hood back revealing her blond hair and pointed ears. Michael noticed she was a Blueblood female and was surprised a Blueblood had entered from the balcony.

Veronica announced, "No, you cannot. It would be a one-way mission. I assure you of this. You will end up dying in vain. He is not the one you seek. Dak, we need to leave." Veronica turned to Michael, "Did anyone see you come to my chambers?"

Michael looked perplexed as he looked at the three other people. He noticed Veronica was in all black clothing and had her riding clothes on. She had planned her escape. He thought for a second, "No one alive saw me. I came into the castle through the hidden passage." He glanced at the dead body of Bruno.

"Then, you need to leave and go someplace where there are a lot of witnesses. Michael, thank you for helping me. I will leave with my friends."

Michael looked at Veronica, understanding this man and the woman were here to help her. He knew he loved Veronica. He was conflicted with his job, and the love he felt for her. He also knew she would die if she stayed. The King would have her killed when he discovered she had planned to escape. There would be no mercy.

Zenith could see the love in his expression for Veronica. Zenith then announced, "We must go. We are running out of time." She looked at Dak. "You will be leaving with us. This mission is over."

Dak kept his swords pulled and never took his eyes off Michael. Veronica could see the hurt in Michael's eyes. She knew he loved her. Veronica ordered, "Michael, you must leave and do as I say. I cannot remain here as a prisoner, and you know this. You know I will die an ugly death if I remain."

"But my Queen." He never finished the statement. He looked into her teary eyes. He turned and ran out the door and down the hall.

Zenith announced, "Follow me. We must go. This city is about to be on full alert." She walked to the balcony and crossed the railing and waited for Veronica. Veronica followed and grabbed the rope and slid down to the third balcony. Dak went and turned the key left in the lock by Bruno. He then stood in the hall and broke the key off in the lock as he stepped inside the room and closed the door. He turned and saw Zenith standing on the balcony waiting on him. He made eye contact and approached Zenith. "I will follow you." He then watched her land on the lower balcony below. He slid down the rope and then pulled the rope from around the roof chimney and down to them. Dak had not wanted to leave a rope as evidence. He knew the rope would reveal how Veronica had escaped. "Taking the rope with us might buy us additional time. The guards will first search the castle for you." Veronica nodded her head she understood. They needed to buy time and make the trip to the sailing vessel. He wrapped the rope around the rail and pulled the middle of the rope to the rail.

As he was the last to land on the sidewalk, he felt the rain drops driven by the wind. Robin Hood looked at his watch as he was waiting on Dak, "Follow me. We have thirty minutes to make the trip to the boat. There are soldiers watching on the main street. We will go by way of the back alleys."

Zenith looked at Dak, "You made the correct decision. Veronica was right." Dak was noncommittal as he glanced at his wife. He also understood she was mad at him for not telling her of his plans to assassinate King Solman.

Robin Hood started running through a dark alley. Dak pulled the rope down and threw the rope into a trash pile and followed the two women and Robin Hood. They cleared the four blocks in the inner city and made the trip to the shoreline. Robin Hood held his hand up for the other three to halt and stay still. Dak eased up to Robin Hood's spot behind the light post. Robin

Hood whispered, "We need to wait until the guards clear the pub. Those guards must have been summoned to the pub. There must have been a huge fight with the drunken customers of the bar. There are over twenty horses belonging to the City Guard unit tied off out front."

Dak noticed Zenith and Veronica walk up next to them while staying in the night shadows. He whispered, "We cannot afford to wait. There may be an alarm go off from the castle. Plus, we are running out of time." He looked at Veronica with concern.

Zenith spoke up, "Michael will do as Veronica instructed him. He will not sound the alarm." She looked at Veronica with the understanding Michael loved her. Veronica stood still, impatiently waiting to run to the ship.

Robin Hood glanced over his shoulder, "Who is Michael, and why did Dak not kill him?"

Veronica glanced at the back of Robin Hood and then at Zenith. She shook her head and grimaced. While staring at the guards ahead, Robin Hood whispered, "They are pulling up in a wagon to cart off the drunk men who must have been fighting and now arrested. They might be blocking the dock for hours. I do not know of another route."

Dak looked at Robin Hood and then at the wagon with the bars around the horse-pulled trailer. "We have twenty-one minutes. We must get past the guards on the dock. We have no choice. We will try to walk past them."

Zenith then turned to Dak, "This party goes live in twenty-minutes. We must get on that boat. That is our only ride out of here."

Robin Hood looked at Dak, "I very much want to make the boat. I do not want to stay."

Dak looked at Veronica, "You need to hide your face. Keep your hood pulled over you. The rain may be a blessing. We will walk past them. Robin Hood, you go first. One man walking by himself in the rain might not spark concern. If they stop you and you need assistance, we will attack. Remember, you are from the trader's ship. Act like you belong here. Veronica, you and Zenith go a minute later. Lead the way, Robin Hood."

Zenith asked, "What about the guards at the gate halfway out the dock?"

"We do not have time to swim past them. We will need to take them out. We need to hurry. We need to be in the middle of the harbor when the party starts," announced Dak.

Robin Hood carried his bow over his shoulder and had his hood pulled down. He acted as if he was trying to stay dry from the wind-driven rain with his face tilted down looking at the brick covered road. As he approached the dockside bar, he could see several men standing in the rain. The guards were loading what appeared to be drunken sailors and soldiers who were injured from fighting. Some were walking and some were being carried. The horse pulled wagon was parked across from the bar and was blocking the walkway and the street. Robin Hood walked through the dark shadows on the opposite sidewalk and kept his head down. He could feel the guard posted outside the bar staring at him as he walked. One of the guards watched him but dismissed the lonely stranger.

Dak turned to Zenith, "You and Veronica go next. Keep your head down and try to avoid eye contact. I will watch to see if you need help. Here Veronica, you take my second sword."

Dak moved and watched from his hidden spot at the entrance to another building. He checked his watch. "Damn this is going to be close." He saw one of the guards notice the two walking toward the bar. The time was close to three hours after midnight in the wind-driven rainstorm. Two women would not be out walking at this time of the night in this weather and not in a city with Marshall Law strictly enforced by these guards. Dak reached down and removed the strap on his sword. He eased up to a parked wagon trying to stay in the shadows, hidden from the light given off by the gas streetlight.

He stayed focused on Zenith and Veronica as they approached the guards and the mayhem in the street.

Dak saw the guard approach the two. He started walking toward them in the shadow of the building. He knew he had no choice.

The guard walked in front of the two and announced, "Where are you two going this time of night in this weather?" He looked at them as they kept walking past him.

He turned as they moved past him, and this time he commanded, "Stop right there." This caught the attention of the five guards standing under the canopy next to the road and the three other guards forcing three restrained soldiers to the horse driven wagon.

The guard turned his back on Dak and followed Zenith and Veronica demanding them to stop. Zenith and Veronica turned and looked at the guard. Zenith announced, "We are headed to the dock. We are nurses to help the wounded."

The guard looked confused. "What injured men?" Dak walked further ahead in the shadows near the building. When the guard confronted the two, Dak used the opportunity to run and catch the guard from behind. The guard heard someone approaching him from behind and tried to turn, but Dak cut the left hamstring of his leg. The guard grunted and instantly fell to the street reaching for his injured leg.

Robin Hood carefully walked back retracing his steps toward the bar in the shadows and now stood twenty-two feet away from the guard. He aligned his arrow and shot the guard closest to him through the lower back under the metal protected back plate. The guard fell face first into the road. The sharp arrow pierced his spinal column preventing the guard from lifting his arms and hands to prevent the face plant. Robin Hood loaded a second arrow and hit the next guard in the temple. The arrow pierced the earhole of the helmet, killing the guard instantly.

The other guards all froze with the excitement of someone in the darkness killing two of their comrades. Zenith had not hesitated. She took out the two guards ushering the two prisoners. She hit one in the side of the helmet forcing him to turn his body. She then cut the back of his thigh severing the hamstring. The second guard released his hold on the prisoner and swung his sword left to right. Zenith easily blocked the sword and used her forward motion to cut his hand off. Her sword connected between the wrist plate and the protective glove. The guard dropped his sword with his sword hand falling to the street. He limped to the standing sign of the bar and dock entrance and fell into the sign caused by the shock of losing his right hand.

Veronica ran past the entrance to the bar as the guards inside the bar had now been alerted to a ruckus going on in the street. Zenith quickly followed Veronica as the two ran past Robin Hood who had his bow up looking for another target.

Dak ran to the horse pulled wagon and could see ten men sitting in the rain with blood running down their faces and over their bodies. He knew some had been beaten by the guards and others had not fared so well in the bar fight. Some men appeared to be knocked out with missing teeth and open head wounds. He swung his sword which was a decoy. He knew the guard would block the swing. He pulled his knife with his left hand and ran the knife through the eye hole of the guard's helmet. The guard fell dead. Dak turned to the trailer, "We are here to save you. King Solman has ordered you men to be executed tomorrow in front of the city as an example. He wants to show what happens to men who cause trouble. He reached and pulled the key from the guard's waistband and opened the trailer. "You men need to fight these guards or die."

The men that were able to fight jumped out and picked up the now injured guards' swords or the dead guards' swords and killed the wounded guards and then fought the guards as they ran out of the bar.

The other injured men crawled out of the trailer and ran with the assistance of each other into the darkness of the city.

Dak ran past Robin Hood as he was protecting the retreat. Robin Hood observed the guard commander coming out of the bar and giving orders. Robin Hood kept his aim and as the lieutenant cleared the sidewalk and took his first step into the street, he released his arrow. The lieutenant was a big man with a bald head. He had pulled his helmet up to assist in seeing through the darkness and the wind driven rain. The arrow pierced through the right side of his head and drove through his skull with the arrow sticking close to twelve inches out of the opposite side of his temple. Robin Hood turned and followed Dak and the two females along the wooden dock.

Veronica and Zenith quickly approached the gate located on the dock. The four guards could hear the commotion, but the visibility was hindered by the weather and darkness. The squad leader stood as he could make out the silhouettes of two people running toward his position. He stepped out from under the carport shed roof into the rain. He commanded, "Stop. What is going on?"

Veronica replied as they kept running, "We are being chased by some men. Please open the gate and protect us."

Zenith added, "The guards are fighting the drunk soldiers. There are two men chasing us. The guards need your help. They are outnumbered. Please open the gate and allow us through."

338

The squad commander looked past them and saw Dak and Robin Hood running toward them. With the rain he could not discern who they were. He removed his helmet to assist him in seeing as he studied the two females. The squad leader was surprised to hear the voices of two women at this hour of the night, "Open the gate. Allow them through."

Veronica stepped through the gate and then Zenith. The squad leader was watching Dak and Robin Hood approach, "Close the gate." He commanded while looking at the two men running toward him, "You need to stop. State your business."

As the guard reached for the lever to close the gate, Zenith pulled her sword from under her cape. She clenched her teeth as she swung downward, cutting his hand off. Her second swing cut him deep across the front of the neck. She spun and cut a deep gash in the back of the head of the squad leader. Veronica saw the guards without their helmets from the dugout watching and one started to stand. Her sword cut him across his face, killing him instantly. The fourth guard stumbled as he jumped for the door to the opposite side of the dock. He quickly opened the door of the office at the gate and stepped to the far side of the dock. As he pulled his sword, Robin Hood's arrow nicked the wire fence as the arrow traveled by the fence hitting the guard in the side of the head. He fell dead, over the side rail, into the ocean below.

Dak and Robin Hood ran through the gate with Zenith locking the gate behind them. Dak wiped the face of the wet watch and held it under the lantern and still could barely make out the time on his watch. "We have five minutes."

The four walked in tandem toward their boat. The two boat guards stood and commanded, "Who goes there?"

Dak announced, "The guards allowed us through on orders of King Solman."

As the guard was considering what Dak had said, Hulk quietly walked out of the cabin followed by Trey. Hulk snuck up behind the guard and hit him with force in the helmet with a hammer, knocking him out. The other guard rotated to the side and tried to pull his sword. Trey picked up the smaller man and body slammed him headfirst into the deck of the sailing vessel. The force of the impact broke his neck.

Hulk looked at his four friends fast approaching. "Look what the cat dragged in. We waited as long as we could."

Trey stood and watched as Veronica approached him. He hugged her. "Damn, it is good to see you, big sister."

Hulk looked at Dak and Zenith, "We need to leave. Ronny is scared of this weather. The bombs are all set. We have minutes before they blow."

Dak saw Ronny and the three sailors emerge out of the cabin. Ronny looked concerned, "Not the best weather for sailing." He commanded, "Untie us, push us off and lift the main sail. Hustle. We have four minutes."

Darnel ran to the aft rope to release it, and Sneedy ran to the other rope and released it. Bartholomew raised the main sail. Robin Hood pulled the gangway across and then let it fall into the ocean as the boat eased away from the dock. Ronny looked worried as the wind caught the sail. They rapidly started to pull away from the dock.

Hulk looked at Tommy Boy, "Help me with these two." Tommy Boy picked up the one guard with the broken neck and dropped him gently overboard. Hulk picked up the man he knocked out and did the same.

Veronica hugged Trey, "I did not believe I would ever see you again. I love you, little brother."

"All of us were here for you. I am sorry you were captured."

Veronica broke off the hug and wiped the tears from her eyes. She went and hugged Zenith and then Robin Hood. Robin Hood whispered, "I am truly sorry if I caused you to be captured."

She whispered back, "It was not your fault." She turned and wiped the tears of joy from her cheek and hugged Hulk and Tommy Boy. When she turned to face Dak, she noticed his smile, "This is surreal seeing you here with us."

They hugged. Veronica whispered, "Thanks. I love you," She stepped backward and rubbed the tears of joy from her cheek.

"Yes, my Queen, it is so good to see you." He hugged her again and then declared, "Did you guys know she is a Queen?"

Ronny yelled some commands to his sailors to adjust the sail and raise the second sail. He looked at the group, "We got two minutes if everything goes as planned. This is not going to be easy. You need to brace yourselves for one hell of a ride. Better tie yourself off to the deck. We need to stay in front of this storm and move out of its path."

The group stood on the deck and held to the railing and mast as they turned to watch the rainstorm. Trey looked at Tommy Boy and Robin Hood, "We are in for some shit now."

The ocean water was noticeably rougher as they headed out of the bay area. As they cut through the wind-driven waves, they heard guards running toward them on the dock. The sailing vessel picked up speed heading toward the open sea and away from the dock. The guards were yelling for them to return.

The large warship first rocked and then the group saw a flash from under the water line as the ship rolled over and started to sink. The second warship blew at the front and the group heard the loud explosion. They could see a small fire as it started to tilt over toward the dock as the hull sunk into the bay water. Screams in the night could be heard from men trying to abandon the ships. The third large warship responded as the first one. It rocked and then the underwater flash of the bomb took out over ten feet of the exterior wood framing. The soldiers in the bunks near the explosion were killed instantly.

The alarms in the city were now blaring, and Ronny could see the large cruiser raising the sails as it quickly approached with the intention of intercepting them before they made it to the open water. He also saw sailors loading the harpoon, aiming in their direction. He heard the voice from the megaphone come over the water, "This is the only warning you will receive. You are ordered to drop your sails."

The cruiser on cue rocked and then there was a flash from the explosion. The men manning the tarpon were lifted off the deck and flew over the boat railing into the ocean from the recoil of the blast. As they sailed past the sinking cruiser, they could hear the scream of dying men and the mayhem of men realizing their ship was sinking.

Zenith announced, "We need to get you out of those wet clothes." She and Veronica walked below deck. The men held tight to the railing and stayed on deck giving them privacy. The vessel started to roll up and down in the twenty-foot-high swells.

Dak and Hulk walked over to Ronny as they both had trouble with their balance with the rocking of the vessel in the violent rainstorm. They both held on to the rail and then the mast and then back to the rail before making it to the wheelhouse. Ronny had strapped his harness to the wooden frame holding the wheel and was standing behind the wheel with both hands trying to steer the vessel. They could see the veins in Ronny's arms and hands as he was straining to turn the wheel. Ronny announced, "You better hold on. This is not going to be easy. This might be a typhoon traveling about ten miles-per-hour. We need to head north as fast as we can to try and beat the eye of the storm coming from the southwest direction. This is far from over. This boat will not survive swells greater than thirty-five feet." He looked at Dak with concern.

Dak now understood the worry in Ronny's voice, "You need to get us the hell out of here. I agree head north and do not spare the horses."

Ronny gave the order to raise the catch sail. He knew this was risky in these winds, but he did not have any other plan to deal with the fast-approaching storm. Without the stars to navigate he could only guess the correct direction. The compass could not be held still in the rough ocean water and the needle was moving too radically to tell the true reading.

Ronny swore to himself as they headed out to sea in the dark of night.

The lantern light provided dim light in the cabin as the lantern swung back and forth with the movement of the ship. At first, Zenith could not distinguish why Veronica's appearance had changed. Once she removed her cape and pulled her hair back in a ponytail, Zenith noticed Veronica was more attractive. Zenith then noticed her manicured nails. She looked back into Veronica's face and realized Veronica was wearing makeup. Her eyes had shadow, and her cheeks appeared rosier. The skin on her face looked perfect with no blemishes and no dry skin. She was wearing lipstick. Zenith looked at her friend as she laid her cape off to the side and then started to remove her wet boots. "You have on make up?"

Zenith could tell Veronica seemed to think about something before she answered, "Yes, I have on makeup." She smiled at Zenith.

Zenith hugged Veronica and held her tight. "The guys and I really love you."

Veronica returned the hug. She was somewhat taken back by the gesture. Zenith had never shown affection for anyone but Dak and her two sons. She was a Blueblood warrior designed biologically to be a warrior, and hugging people was not something she was known to do. The boat started thrashing back and forth in the waves and the two broke off the hug.

The two looked at the cabin floor and noticed an inch of water. "Are we going to make it?"

Zenith smiled, "We always make it. When you want to talk, I would like to hear about this guy named Michael. He was very good looking and said he would die for you."

Veronica looked at Zenith with sad eyes, "There is nothing to tell. I do not want to talk about what I have been through. I did what I needed to survive. The memory of my home, family, and most of all my friends, prevented me from jumping over the balcony to my death." She looked at Zenith, "The Normand Army is brutal. I do not believe they can be stopped unless we cut the head from the snake. That is the only chance we have to win. I will need to update Dak on what I know, but I am not certain what their weaknesses are on the battlefield. They have overwhelming numbers, better training than our farm boys up north, better technology, and way more resources."

Zenith looked at her and thought how she changed the conversation from what happened to her personally to the pending war. "We will keep trying to win the battles and maybe we can win the war." The two reached for the wall to hold their position as the lantern wobbled back and forth. The boat was rocking more and more as time passed.

Chapter 30

General Redman looked at his captain, "What do you mean there is an uprising at The Port Bar? You know to send additional squads of guards to handle the situation." The General rubbed the sleep from his eyes. He looked irritated as he sat up in bed and looked at the floor of his bedroom.

The captain stuttered. He could tell General Redman was frustrated. He knew waking the general at 2:55 A.M. could be a career decision. The general had a reputation for wanting to be kept in the loop, but he also demanded his captains make decisions and handle the small issues. General Redman was the general of the guard details, and he tried to keep the soldiers and sailors out of the jails. He knew King Solman wanted his soldiers to be warriors, and there was an allowance made for the soldiers and navy personnel. His captains understood the need to process the soldiers and sailors through the jail system and return them to their squad commanders for punishment. General Redman understood the mandates of his King.

He frowned, "Captain, we discussed this issue. We knew the men were going to fight and some were going to get injured with the news they were going to be marching north." He looked at the captain, "How bad could the fighting be?" He was afraid several of the soldiers were going to be taken to the brig. He clenched his teeth, "Captain, that is why most of our guards are on duty."

The captain knew he needed to be stern. He was conflicted with waking the General. He had questioned the runner from The Port Bar. Several guards had been killed. An unknown man had shot the lieutenant in the head, killing him. "Sir. The lieutenant of the squad was killed with an arrow through his head along with eight guards under his command, and all four guards stationed on the pier are dead. We have not located the two guards stationed on the trader's vessel from Israel which left during the storm."

General Redman appeared to be surprised, "You mean I have twelve guards that have been killed, the lieutenant over the night watch, and two more guards missing?"

"Yes Sir. Sir, we discovered the arrow which killed the lieutenant and two guards in front of The Port Bar and the one guard on the pier, which we pulled him from the surf, were all killed with special arrows made with a razor-sharp arrowheads and leather weighed balance strips to help guide the flight of the arrows. We have never seen arrows like this."

"We need to close the city down and call out the reserves." He quickly started getting dressed as he thought his guards had never been killed in working the shifts since he had been appointed the general over the guards two years prior. His policy had always been in all situations to send an overwhelming number of guards and crush the lawbreaking citizens. The guards were all required to train several hours a week, and the guards had a reputation for being brutal in dealing with the common people. "Also, direct the guards from the central garrison and both the north and west division headquarters. Close the city down. No one is allowed on the streets. I need answers before dawn."

"Yes Sir." The captain turned to allow the general some privacy as he got dressed and both men reacted with shock when they heard the first blast. Both men knew immediately the blast was not thunder. The General looked with panic at the captain, "What in the hell was that blast? Sound the alarms. We must be under attack."

Chapter 31

The generals and five advisors were ushered into the war room. They all sat around the large table and apprehensively waited. They heard the double doors being opened by the guards. In walked King Solman with his steel sword on his side. He looked angry. All the men stood when the King walked into the room and then sat. All were concerned with his mood and the fact that he was wearing his steel sword and not his nice ceremonious gold-handled sword. The steel sword represented death. The rumor was the King did not want to get blood on his gold-handled sword. In addition, normally if the King was in a bad mood, the King would kill someone to prove his point. Failure was not acceptable, and someone would be held to blame. King Solman positioned himself at the end of the table. He looked at the Naval General and in a commanding voice yelled, "What happened?"

The general stood, "Your majesty. We lost three warships and a cruiser. We are still counting the dead. We know seventy-two men died in the blast. We pulled two hundred sailors from the water. Another three hundred swam to land."

"How did this happen?"

"Sir, we suspect sabotage. There has been no enemy identified."

The King looked surprised, "Sabotage?"

"Sir, we have other boats in the harbor. The captains on each boat have reported they did not see an enemy vessel. The lookouts on the boats were all interviewed. They reported they saw no one."

"Are you telling me someone did this to my navy, and you have no clue who is behind this terrorist act?"

"Sir, we have not ruled out anything. The investigating is still underway, but sir, the initial report indicates your ships were sunk by explosives with timers were attached to their hulls. We first wanted to save the men and protect the rest of the fleet. We had ordered all vessels to be secured in our harbor to protect them from the storm."

"Is there anyone else that has information?" King Solman stood and walked behind the right side of the table. "Now is the time to speak."

General Redman was reluctant to speak. He was surprised the other general had not reported what he knew. "Your majesty. I lost fourteen guards on the night watch, and the lieutenant of the night watch was shot in the head with an arrow while he was standing in the road in front of The Port Bar. Eight guards were killed by three or maybe four unknown persons in the street in front of The Port Bar. The four guards stationed on the pier were killed, and the two guards stationed on the trader's vessel were found a few minutes ago in the surf near the beach front. The trader's vessel from Israel carrying the coal was reported to have sailed out of the harbor during the explosions. The coal had been transported to the cruiser, and that ship was sunk with the coal burning as it went under. We discovered the arrows used to kill the three guards and the lieutenant were arrows crafted by someone else." He looked at King Solman, "As you know arrows are made with different components from around the world." He laid three arrows on the table. General Rivers in charge of the army noticed the precision crafted arrows and picked up one of the arrows and inspected the arrow as he listened.

General Redmen further explained, "The tips of the arrows are razor sharp and were made with steal, so the arrows could penetrate the metal breast plates of our armor. We also noted there was extra time spent to make the shafts perfectly straight. The steal tips were installed with a fine twine made from seal leather. Sir, we suspect foreigners have attacked us. We interviewed an injured sailor who was beat up inside The Port Bar. He testified an unknown man killed one of my guards standing at the jailor's wagon. The unknown man then unlocked the wagon and told the arrested men to run or fight.

He then mentioned as an example you had ordered the men to be executed at daybreak for fighting."

He yelled, "I made no such order. Who was this man?"

"Sir, the rain and darkness prevented a clear view of him. His accent was an accent of a northern warrior. We have been unable to find out his identity, but we also had another witness state that, at first, a man with a bow and a sword walked by the bar headed to the pier. The man had his head down, and he was covered in hood and cape. Then, two other individuals followed him and were stopped by one of my guards. Then, a fourth man approached the guard in the street and cut his hamstring. He knew where to strike. The unprotected back of the leg. He then killed the guard at the prisoner trailer and released the men. Sir, we have not lost a man in two years and in one night I lost fifteen men. We believe we were attacked by outsiders from the North. Sir, my men were very good at fighting. They had undergone extensive training. Whoever killed them, Sir, was very well trained and knew our weaknesses."

The door opened and in walked a captain of the guard squad assigned to the castle. He walked over to General Redman and bent down and whispered in General Redman's ear.

General Redman looked angry and stood, "The Queen is missing. She has disappeared. The guard assigned to her was found in her chambers with his throat cut. The guards are searching the castle for her and trying to establish where she might be." He turned to King Solman, "I can assure you Sir, we will find the Queen."

King Solman balled his fist up and hit the table. The vibration caused two drinks to turn over and spill. He yelled, "I want my Queen located and brought to me. I want to talk with the sailors who saw the trader's vessel sail out of port. I want the guards and men at The Port Bar brought to the courtroom for me to interview." He still had his fist balled up. His face was red with anger as he looked at General Redman, "Where is the Queen's chief guard, Michael? I want to see him and her handmaiden at once in this chamber."

"Michael, Sir, is off duty. We will summon him at once." General Redman turned and walked swiftly out the doors. Once he cleared the view of the King's Guards posted at the double doors, he wiped the sweat from his forehead. He felt the relief of leaving the room. He then walked into his office and ordered Michael to be summoned to his office immediately.

***

The six guards arrived at Michael's door, and they waited for the captain to walk in front. He walked next to the last guard in the small hallway and ordered, "Open the door."

The guard carrying the large steel bar walked in front of the door and rammed the steel rod into the door near the knob forcing the lock to burst through the door jam. The first two guards rushed into Michael's small one-bedroom apartment. He had not awoken or moved while lying face down in his bed. The other guards rushed through the apartment and cleared the two other rooms.

The captain walked into the bedroom and saw Michael lying face down in his bed with a slight snore and a dead sleep. He walked into the small kitchen and picked up a pot of two-day old coffee. He walked over Michael and poured the contents on his head.

Michael's body jerked from the liquid pouring over his head. He tried to understand what happened. First, he was outraged that someone had woken him. He then saw the three guards and the captain of the guard standing in his bedroom. The captain ordered, "Get him out of bed. He needs to be taken to General Redman."

The two guards each lifted Michael by his under arms and stood him up. Michael could not understand what was happening and had difficulty balancing himself. The two guards carried his upper body with his feet dragging behind him out the broken door. Michael jerked his arms free from the two guards and started walking on his own once he was in the hall.

General Redman saw Michael being pushed by the guards as he stood outside the double doors to his office. Michael walked into the guard office, and General Redman spoke, "I hope you can answer the King's questions, or you will be executed. You need to remember your oath when conversing with your King. You smell and look despicable. You do not have time to clean up. You need to follow me."

The General turned to his guard, "You need to summon the Queen's handmaid at once and escort her to the King's office. I can only hope she appears better than the Queen's Guard."

Michael seemed surprised and announced, "King?"

"Yes. You have been summoned to the King's office. Now follow me."

General Redmon thought as he and Michael and the other guards walked toward King Solman's office, "Michael might be the scapegoat and not me." He relaxed as he pondered the situation.

They walked into the foyer of King Solman's office. The King's Guard on the right looked at Michael, "What is the meaning of your appearance? You smell like puke and alcohol.

You are disgusting. I cannot allow you to meet our King looking like this. Where are your pants and boots?"

The guard turned to General Redman. The general announced, "This is the man King Solman has requested to see immediately. This is the way we found him. Now open the door."

One of the guards opened the double doors and announced General Redman. The guards pushed Michael through the door, and he fell as he crossed the threshold and slid on the concrete floor.

King Solman stood and walked toward Michael. General Redman said, "This man is a disgrace. He will pay for his appearance. His inebriated appearance is not acceptable as a Castle Guard. I will deal with his indiscretions once you have completed your inquiry."

King Solman held up his hand for General Redman to be quiet. He stepped from behind his desk, "Leave us." General Redman walked out the double doors followed by the two King's Guards. Michael pulled himself to his hands and knees and then stood. King Solman watched Michael and understood he was still intoxicated. His hair was a mess, and his white shirt was half unbuttoned in the front. "Where is my Queen?"

Michael replied, "I assume sir she is in her chambers. You granted me a two-day pass."

"You appear to have gotten drunk. You look and smell disgraceful."

Michael looked at King Solman, "Yes Sir. I overindulged during my time off from work with my drinking. The Queen ordered me to have a good time."

King Solman walked over to Michael and punched him in the gut with his fist. Michael, not expecting the punch, doubled over out of breath and fell to the concrete floor. He puked his guts out. "The Queen is missing."

Michael tried to breathe and then coughed. "Maybe Sir, she went on a ride with her guard, Bruno, or she is working out in the guard workout arena."

He yelled, "The guard was found in her chambers with his throat cut. She is missing. I find it coincidental that she went missing after requesting you be granted a two-day pass." He kicked Michael in the side.

He coughed, "She might have thought it would be easier to slip past an inexperienced guard. She would not have slipped past me."

There was a knock on his double doors. "Enter."

The King's Guard opened the door and announced, "The handmaid has arrived."

Dezie entered. She noticed Michael on the floor in the fetal position. She could tell he was still breathing. "Leave us." The guard closed the door.

The King had his sword pulled and walked over to Dezie and made a circle around her. She stood firm but could not help but fear for her life. She tried to hold her shaking hands still. She knew King Solman had never shown mercy to anyone. "You two were the last two to see my Queen. I find it difficult to believe one of you or both did not know she was planning to escape. She would have needed help." He looked at both with a frown on his face. "You will tell me everything, or I will have you taken to the dungeon where my guards will force you to talk."

Dezie looked at Michael on the floor lying next to his puke. He rolled over on his back, and she could tell he was intoxicated. She had heard a man running in the hall close to two thirty A.M. last night, and she had suspected the unknow man was Michael. She thought she heard him command for the Queen's chamber door to be open. The guard on duty had replied the man was drunk. A few minutes later the door had opened, and she heard a man run out of the Queen's chamber and past her door. She knew if she mentioned this, Michael would be killed. "Your Excellency. I discovered her door would not open this morning, and there was no guard posted as normal outside her door. I first suspected the guard might have been summoned by the Queen to come inside her chambers. She was scheduled to work out in the guard arena. She normally likes to eat a small breakfast before she works out. I do not know her whereabouts." She looked at King Solman, "I swear this to you."

The King looked at her with his temper flaring. "I do not believe either one of you. She had to have help." He then said "The traders must have done this. She has left by sea."

Michael grunted, "I will go look for her. They would head north. I will find the men that kidnapped her and kill them. I will bring her back to you."

King Solman looked at Michael and thought about what he had just said. She could have been kidnapped. Dezie turned to King Solman, "Your Majesty. There is one thing that I might add." The King looked at Dezie, "The Queen is with child."

Michael sat up on the floor and looked determined. He was tired and hung over. He knew he was going to die, but he had never considered Veronica was pregnant. She would have been desperate to escape.

The King demanded, "How do you know this?"

"Sir. I am the handmaid for the Queen. I would notice if she was running late with her bleeding. She would have been scared for her child. She had indicated the Bluebloods in

Merlin would kill any child born with a Blueblood male and a normal female. The Bluebloods have outlawed that type of breeding. They will try to keep the perfect genetic imprint." She hesitated, "She asked me if you were a Blueblood. She suspected the man that knocked her out in Tanger and brought her to you was a Blueblood." She hesitated, "Sir, she would protect her child with her life."

He flashed back to his court when Veronica proved the young girl was the mother of the baby when she jumped on the infant and begged for the child's life. "You are dismissed." Dezie turned and walked out the door, closing the door behind her.

King Solman knew Damon was a malcontent Blueblood, and Veronica could have figured out Damon was a Blueblood. The master had trouble controlling him. He enjoyed torturing people. He then killed them once he became bored with the process.

He was surprised to hear that Veronica knew he was a Blueblood. No one knew he had his ears surgically altered to appear normal. He thought his secret was safe. All the slaves he had raped had all been killed and none had given birth. He looked at Michael, "Do you know where she would go?"

"Sir, you indicated she might have left by sea. They would dock at Harpers Ferry Harbor and then ride horses one thousand miles north to a small place called Zenith Point and then further north to Cliff Tops. The winter is coming, and the weather would be too cold and would prevent them going further north in a sailing vessel. She has indicated there are very few locations for a vessel to dock and men make it ashore once they pass Harpers Ferry Harbor. There are over one thousand miles of cliffs along the shoreline."

Michael turned to face the King, "Sir, did you grant the captain of the trader's vessel the Document of Safe Passage?"

King Solman looked at Michael. He knew the Document of Safe Passage with his seal would allow the boat to sail anywhere in the world which included sailing by his naval blockade set up around Harpers Ferry Harbor and further north along the east coast. "I did grant them the Document." He then thought back to the meeting, and how the captain had requested the Document of Safe Passage and must have tricked him.

"I will need a squad of trained men that I can trust and one tracker who has been in that region. We will need to be able to blend in with the locals. We will need to slip into Harpers Ferry Harbor and slip out. If we hurry, we might catch them still in the city. Sir, if she is pregnant, she will not be able to travel as fast. We should be able to catch up to her, but we must leave today."

King Solman noticed how Michael's demeanor had changed. He no longer seemed drunk and was concentrating on the mission parameters. He seemed to be personally driven to locate Veronica and bring her to him. "You need to clean up. You will report back to me in three hours. The squad will dress in plain clothes and ride north. I will get our best soldiers. You will find the Queen and bring her back to Southern City unharmed. I also want the heads of that crew delivered to me. The reward is two Merlin gold pieces per head. Now get your ass up and get prepared. You will leave in a few hours."

Michael looked at King Solman as he now was standing straight and proper, "It is my honor. I swore to protect Veronica when she was a Princess. Now, she is your Queen, Sir, I will not stop until I locate her. It is my duty and personal challenge to protect your Queen and die for her if required. I apologize for my behavior last night. I swear to you, I will not allow my drinking to affect my future missions."

Chapter 32

Hulk looked at Dak, "It has rained on us for three days. I am glad to see dry land. Mercy, it is a pretty sight." Dak smiled at his friend.

Hulk then added, "I could not imagine being a professional sailor and living like this on the ocean."

Dak nodded his head, "Smooth water could make all the difference. As Wayne would say, Mary, sweet mother of Jesus, the sight of land is beautiful."

Hulk smiled, "I miss home." He looked at the wheelhouse and saw Ronny talking to his sailing partners, "Those guys are tired. They have been awake most of this trip. They deserve their gold on this mission. They got us through the storm and by the blockade."

Veronica and Zenith both walked out of the cabin onto the deck. The waves had calmed down, and the boat was not rising up and down near as much as in the prior two days. The two women pulled their robes off and enjoyed the sun. Dak said, "Speak of pretty sights." He smiled at his wife, "It is good to see you two out of the cabin."

Hulk said, "Now we know what the phrase means, the calm after the storm." He smiled.

Veronica looked at her brother. He appeared to have grown a couple of inches and was stronger looking. All the guys appeared to be more physically mature. Tommy Boy appeared to have changed the most, finally growing out of his baby face, and the body fat had turned to solid muscle. He was an inch shorter than Trey but looked stronger. Both men weighed over three-hundred and twenty pounds and stood over six-feet-seven. Tommy Boy was bigger than his older brother Hulk. Hulk and Dak both appeared to be stronger, but not taller. She thought even Robin Hood had matured in his shoulders and looked more muscular. All the guys seemed more mature now and appeared to have more confidence.

Zenith announced as she glanced at Trey, Sneedy, Tommy Boy and Robin Hood playing cards, "I am over the sea voyage. I am going to take a bath and clean up as soon as I find a room. This has been an ugly past three days."

Veronica looked at Dak as she walked next to him, "Thanks for coming after me. You know you should have left me in Southern City. There is a lot that has happened."

Hulk was shocked by the comment, "We risked our lives for you. Hell, Hershel died on this trip for you."

Veronica looked at Hulk and said in a soft voice, "I do not mean to be ungrateful. You should have left me in Southern

City. I could have been a better asset where I was than here with you."

Zenith also walked closer to the group, "You could also have been killed. We are at war with the Normand army. King Solman is unpredictable and cannot be trusted. We need you with us. You are part of us."

Dak looked at Veronica, "It was my fault. I am sorry. I should not have allowed you to go back by yourself to the ocean with the wagon. That decision has haunted me ever since I discovered you were missing."

The four card players had all gathered around the group as the boat headed for the dock in Harpers Ferry Harbor. Veronica looked at Dak, "It was not anyone's fault I was taken prisoner." She looked at Dak and then Robin Hood. "If anyone else would have gone with me, they would have been killed by Damon." She looked over the rail of the boat at the landing and approaching dock. "You do not understand: King Solman is not in charge. I know there is a cult of renegade Bluebloods well hidden in that region. The master is anonymous. We need to find the master and kill him." She turned to Dak and Zenith, "We will need the help of the Blueblood empire in Merlin. Damon held his knife to King Solman's throat and threatened him. He then walked out of the castle and sailed north along the west coast. King Solman referred to the master when talking with Damon while the knife was held to his throat. There is another in charge."

Zenith asked, "Could the master be Senator Dale in Merlin?"

Veronica looked at Zenith, "I do not believe he is the leader. King Solman rides with a company of soldiers and his generals to a meeting. I believe the cult leader is within a two-day ride from Southern City. He does this four times a year. Unless Senator Dale has left Merlin, he would not be the cult leader. It is a four-or five-day trip by boat from Merlin, and by land, the trip would be at least two weeks to travel inland to avoid the nuclear waste pits."

Dak thought about Senator Dale, and how he wanted to kill him. He was corrupt. He also knew Zenith was in constant fear for her father, Aquarius. He had volunteered to return to Merlin and work as a spy. Zenith had told Dak, at some point her father would be discovered and killed. Dak looked at the dock, "Now we will land and prepare for the war coming our way."

Veronica turned to Dak, "You cannot stop the army from the south. I have seen them. They are too well trained for our farmers and part-time soldiers."

Hulk announced, "We pushed them out of Harpers Ferry Harbor."

Veronica was fast to respond, "General Cuez was withholding information from King Solman. This time they will be better prepared. I should have stayed in Southern City."

Trey shook his head, "No, big Sister, you should not have stayed in Southern City. Mom is worried to death about you. Fortunately, dad was out hunting when the news about you being kidnapped was mentioned in Cliff Tops. Otherwise, he would have insisted on coming after you, and he would have been killed. The older men in our clan cannot do what we can."

She smiled at her brother, "You know I love you guys. Thank you for risking your lives for me. You do not understand their strength in numbers and the training with their soldiers. I could have perhaps got additional information on the cult leader if I stayed behind. That is who we need to target."

Veronica turned to Dak, "I do not wish to see my friends be killed. If Damon was on this deck right now, he would kill who he desired. You do not understand. He is that good. Killing King Solman is not going to make a difference. He is a puppet leader. He will stay inside his castle because that is what he desires. He does not like the discomforts of the wilderness. His generals are very good at planning and strategy. King Solman will allow them to fight the war. We cannot win."

Robin Hood looked at Veronica and then at the others and announced, "See how things worked out. If you had not been kidnapped, we would not have known about the renegade Blueblood master."

Tommy Boy smiled and looked at Robin Hood, "Yeah Robin Hood. How is your guilt meter running these days? You never allow a crisis to go to waste."

Dak announced, "We will fight to the bitter end. The kidnapping was my fault. I was in charge and should have known better than to agree to allow you to return the rig with the horses." He took Zenith's hand, and they walked toward the back of the boat to talk with Ronny and the three other sailors. Veronica walked to the front of the boat with Trey and Robin Hood walked to the cabin.

Hulk was leaning over the rail. Tommy Boy walked up next to him, "Hey older brother, what do you think about what Veronica said?"

"I believe Veronica has been through a lot; that is what I believe."

The sailing vessel was within two-hundred feet from the dock and moving forward. Tommy Boy leaned over the rail and looked at the motels behind the dock at the women on the roof side porch and balconies. "Older brother. Once we land, why don't we run down the dock and go fuck one of those whores?"

Hulk smiled and replied, "Why don't we walk down the dock, younger brother, and then fuck all of them?"

Chapter 33

Michael was relieved to be leading the squad. He knew the mission was going to be dangerous entering enemy territory. General Redman was leading the way as they walked along the hall to the courtyard. He was trying to prepare Michael for the trip. "General Rivers has reported more and more of his spies have been caught, and once caught, they are decapitated and then their bodies burned. His recon units have been finding their remains along the front lines for the past six months. If you are caught, you will be killed." General Redman led him to the yard and announced to Michael, "The men standing in front of you are some of our best soldiers."

Michael looked at the one-hundred-twenty men. "Sir, am I in charge of the squad and the leader of this expedition?"

General Redman was careful, "Yes. King Solman has made that clear."

Michael announced, "I will address these men." The general took a step back and motioned for Michael to start. "Between two-thirty A.M. and two-fifty A.M. last night, a group of rebels entered Queen Veronica's chambers and kidnapped her and killed the King's Guard assigned to protect her. They killed over seventy of our sailors and several city guards. They fled by sea. We believe they will dock at Harpers Ferry Harbor and then head north on horseback. I have been appointed by King Solman to lead a group of warriors to locate our Queen, kill the men who kidnapped her and bring her back unharmed. There is a reward of two Merlin gold coins for the head of each of the people responsible." He paused and walked in front of the men. "Since we are going to be relying on stealth, I elect to take a five-man crew."

General Redman looked surprised. Michael turned to the General. "I will take the four guards whom I know and trust and Bebo, the scout, who has experience in fighting in that area."

General Redman looked at Michael, "You can take additional men. You need to consider what you are up against."

"General, I believe for us to be successful, we need to sneak into their camp and sneak out. We cannot do this with one-hundred men. I will take a five-man squad."

***

Michael looked at the map. He was trying to study the roads and the rivers. His four friends walked over to him along with Bebo. Michael looked up from the map and spoke to the men, "General Redman indicated this is the path the last two recon teams traveled. The recon team waited for the lone scout to return, but he never returned." He pointed to the northern front lines of the Normand Army and then traced the path. "One week later another scout left from this point. He also never returned. Neither man has come back. The General Staff assumes they have been captured, decapitated, and burned. Two bodies were found by our patrols here in the valley at the Plains of Jellico. They were disfigured so badly; the men could not be identified. General Rivers needs information on the rebel scum, and he keeps ordering spies north. They have lost twenty-two spies in the last three months. Our mission is going to be dangerous." He pointed to the spot on the map. "I am trying to figure out a new entry point. If we are apprehended, we will be killed."

Bebo stepped forward, "Sir, I was part of the retreat when we were driven out of the Midnight Hole. We were told we were a disgrace for retreating. As we passed Harpers Ferry Harbor, I heard one of the sergeants suggest they needed to station lookouts along the ridge line here." He pointed to the ridge north of Harpers Ferry Harbor located near the ocean. "The sergeant was stationed to guard the dock. We never sent a squad to protect that hill. I saw the sergeant in the bar in Southern City a few months ago. He said he got out by ship during the battle of Harpers Ferry Harbor. He said the enemy used the viewing point from that ridge to scout us. They could see the ocean, the harbor, and the city along with the valley north from that point."

Michael looked at the map, "They may not expect anyone north of their location. Their entire army should be facing south. We would need a ship to drop us off at night and pick us up. I will make the request to our King. Going by sea would place us one day behind them. The storm has passed, and we should have clear sailing."

Chapter 34

Veronica walked to the command tent. The two guards standing at the entryway stepped aside. She entered through the tent door and noticed that the talking among the occupants ceased. The sides of the large tent were open to allow the breeze to blow through. Dak was standing over the table in the middle with Hulk, Vulture, Trey, and several other men. Robin Hood and Tommy Boy were standing to the side drinking coffee. Zenith was standing opposite Dak looking down at the table and the map of the large extended battlefield and front lines. The mood was one of concern. Dak looked up when Veronica walked toward them. Dak wanted to be nice to his old friend. He knew she had been through a great deal of emotional and physical pain being captured and held prisoner. Veronica requested of him and the others she had no desire to talk about her four months behind the enemy lines being held as a prisoner. He respected her wishes.

Dak pointed so Veronica could see, "We assume the Normand Army will attack from three areas. Our plan is to fight and fall back to the bridges: here and here. We will burn the bridges as we cross them. We will fight them as they try to cross the rivers. The rivers make for a natural barrier. Our goal is to make the pursuit north for the Normand army a difficult one while minimizing our losses and maximizing their losses."

Veronica noticed Dak was animated while he talked about the battle. She knew he must have spent several days thinking and planning for the upcoming attack. His strategy was well thought out and his men seemed to like the plan. She looked at Dak and pointed to the map. "What if they cross here and proceed east along the north side of the river? They will have all your men cut off from retreat across the Waldo Bridge, and the men will be captured. The same with the other three areas. The battle line is over one-thousand miles wide. There are too many places for them to spearhead an attack along the front. You do not have enough soldiers to fight that type of battle and win."

The men looked at Veronica. No one else had been able to question Dak's plans. Dak designed a plan and then he ordered his captains to carry out the goals. Trey told Veronica, Dak had become impatient in dealing with people. She could tell the stress of the war was troubling him. However, Dak smiled, "Our plan is to make the assault difficult for them to advance, but we want them to advance. We will fight them all the way north to the village here." He pointed to the village, Beech Grove Village, close to two-hundred miles south of the Midnight Hole. "Here we will retreat no more. We will use the river and the mountains to our advantage. We will block them from advancing. Then, we will sail south from Cliff Tops and attack their supply lines coming north from Southern City. By cutting off their supply lines we will destroy their ability to reinforce their army and then their spirit to fight. We will be supplied food and supplies by the underground network, and their army will not have access to the needed food and supplies. Most of their army are southern men used to the dry heat of the south. They will not be prepared for the winter. We will force the Normand army to surrender in the cold bitter winter, or we will kill every last one of them." He stared at Veronica and watched her.

Zenith also watched Veronica. She noticed the change in her mannerism. She seemed more confident in herself. She thought before she spoke. Her wardrobe was more carefully planned, and her looks were more appealing. The make-up made a difference. Zenith thought, "She looks prettier, more mature, and she walks and handles herself with confidence. She knew the men noticed."

Veronica asked, "I assume my father will lead the Cliff Tops army and be waiting for your army to retreat to Beech Grove Village and establish a new frontline."

Dak looked at Veronica, "Yes, that is our plan."

"What about the spy network from the Normand army? You assume they will blindly walk into your trap." asked Veronica.

Dak looked at Vulture. Vulture appeared aggravated. Dak knew he did not like a female reviewing the plan. He also knew Zenith and Veronica both were exceptional warriors, but he still did not like females being part of the meeting. "We have caught their spies, and we have dealt with them. I can assure you, Little Lady, their spies are not making the trip through our lines."

Veronica looked at Vulture. She knew the comment 'Little Lady' was a derogatory statement with him trying to spark an emotional outburst. She also understood after the battle of Harpers Ferry Harbor that some of Vulture's men were Midlanders who had crossed over from their territory near New Foundland and agreed to fight with Vulture. Those men were brutal and fierce warriors. She also knew Dak had to be aware of those soldiers from the Midlanders territory. He needed all the fierce soldiers he could find. "I would hope you are securing the spies to work out a future trade, our prisoners for their prisoners."

Vulture stared back, "There will be no trade. The way we must deal with the Normand spies is through execution. We take their burned bodies without their heads to the front lines and leave them for their patrols to find. We are sending them a message. They will be killed if they come across the southern front into our warzone."

Veronica looked at Dak, "You allow this type of treatment of the prisoners? This treatment should be outlawed."

Dak looked at Veronica and studied her. He remembered his mother always saying when he was growing up, "Always put yourself in the other person's shoes before you judge them."

Dak did not want to discuss this issue in front of the men. He announced, "This meeting is adjourned. Everyone is dismissed."

The men all walked out of the tent. Dak could tell Vulture was upset. He seemed to stay upset, but Dak also knew he needed him. He was a leader, and his men did as he commanded. The group fighting under him were brutally efficient at killing Normand soldiers.

Dak walked over to Veronica, "Do you still think we have no chance?"

Veronica smiled at Dak, "You are a natural leader. Your plan will provide the north with a chance to win this battle. What the men need is hope. Hope will provide them the needed courage to fight. Growing up with you, I always knew you would be a great leader."

Dak looked at Veronica, "You seemed to have changed."

"I have seen the Normand Army's conviction for war. I do not believe the next battles will be that easy. Dak, have you considered they might assault your army from other places? The front lines are spread over a thousand miles. You had better not underestimate them. I do not believe they are going to fall into your trap. Do you recall how we landed here and watched them from this ridge?" She pointed to the hill where they first watched the Normand army and spied on them.

He never took his eyes off Veronica. He was trying to figure out how much she had changed. The way she handled herself, the way she moved, her outfits enhanced the appearance of her curved figured, and the tone of her voice had all changed. "I do recall."

"I would suggest you need to make certain that area is secure. I would also suggest you need to keep your eye on Merlin and the Blueblood army. There is a rogue cult of Bluebloods hidden somewhere within a two-day ride of Southern City. There are several unknowns." She turned and smiled at Zenith and walked out.

Zenith looked at Dak, "If she is correct, we need to have our army mobile and ready to adjust. We cannot afford for a division of our army to be trapped and captured. You need to have Vulture secure that ridge line. I personally do not like

Vulture. He is a mean man. His anger has turned to hatred, and he thrives on being cruel. His men are killers."

She looked at Dak. Zenith then pointed to the Homestead located two-hundred miles north of Harpers Ferry Harbor. "We need to watch that area. If I was the Normand commanders, I would attack us from the ocean north of our location. I would try to win this war quickly with an all-out attack from several locations. Homestead has a small access river between the large ocean cliffs. If they land at Homestead and spearhead a battle line north of us, they will cut us off, and we will not be able to retreat north along the coastline. The two armies from the north, the Cliff Tops, and the New York army, will not be able to respond fast enough. You know that is what we would do to them. Why have you not considered this?"

Dak looked frustrated as he leaned over the table, "I have considered this and a lot more, but we do not have enough soldiers to send north to secure that beachfront."

Zenith looked at Dak, "You are in charge. You are going to have to force those ranchers and farmers to fight with us. They cannot avoid the war or choose to stay neutral. You will need to send some men there and force them into joining the army. They must create a militia and defend that beach front. Otherwise, I am afraid we will be crushed by the superior army."

He turned and his face was red as he glared at Zenith. He clenched his jaws, "Do you not realize I know this? I can only fight with what I have."

"You are going to have to learn to delegate and then realize you are not the only one fighting this war." She turned and walked out of the tent. He threw the pointer across the room out of anger. He then glanced at the map and thought about the Normand army using the ocean to travel north of the Harpers Ferry Harbor with a regiment of soldiers. "Zenith was right, Homestead would be the logical place to attack the beach and the inlet. He was going to have to take responsibility for drafting more men to fight. The city of Homestead would need to be defended." He grimaced at the thought. They would be trapped with the main Normand army coming north. He then thought about Zenith being upset with him for not revealing his plan to assassinate King Solman without her. She would not allow him to touch her of a night, and she had turned a cold shoulder to him. He was now frustrated with himself for raising his voice to her. He had just made their relationship worse.

Chapter 35

Cruise jumped off the small rowboat and pulled the tow rope to the shoreline. The four other men jumped off and then Michael. The temperature was seasonally warm with a half-moon producing just enough light for the men to see where they needed to walk. Bebo peered through the thick woods and brush looking for signs of the enemy. Pretty Boy and Cruise carried the rowboat inland close to twenty feet into the weeds and hid it under the brush. Viking cut a pine limb from a small tree and smoothed away their tracks in the sand. The men formed around Michael. Michael looked at his watch, 2:30 a.m. He pointed to the ridge of the mountain and ordered, "Bebo, lead the way."

The six men walked through the weeds, honeysuckle vines, and small trees staying close to ten feet apart. They made the trip across the thick-covered field and into the edge of the woods. They listened for sound. Michael held his hand out for the men to sit tight and thought, "This is too quiet." He pointed to Bebo and then his ear. Bebo then shook his head no, meaning no sounds. There were no animals moving in the woods. In the distance he could hear a limb rubbing against another tree when the wind blew. He considered his options and then pointed for Bebo to lead the way up the steep incline of the hill.

The woods were not as thick as most. Most of the trees were pine trees close to seventeen years old which had started growing after the Transitional Period. The trees were spaced about four feet apart. The ground was covered in pine needles and easy to walk on and not be heard. As they approached the ridge line, the trees had thinned, and small bushes and small trees became thick. The forest foliage became more difficult to forge through. Bebo crawled to within ten feet of the ridge line. He looked behind him and saw Michael and the other four men carefully approaching-walking bent over in tandem, close to ten feet apart. All were carrying their weapons in the ready position. He waited for Michael and then the others to catch up. Michael looked over the ridge top at the thick underbrush and noticed a trail running along the ridge. He whispered, "Go ahead. We will find a place to hide on the ridge. We need to be well hidden before the sun rises." He looked at his watch. The time was four A.M.

Bebo stood and walked into the open area and then forward twenty feet along the ridge. Michael and the other men walked into the open area at the top of the ridge and rested. The squad was surprised to hear someone speak, "Look what we have here." Suddenly, they were surrounded by close to twenty well-armed men all holding bows with arrows, swords, and spears."

Bebo pulled his sword and was shot three times by three different men. The arrows all hit his torso. He fell dead. Michael could see in the moonlight they were surrounded and had no choice but to surrender. He looked in all four directions. He could hear men talking from the coastline area at the bottom of the hill. He looked at Bebo lying dead and knew they could not run or win a fight with this many men. He ordered, "Lay down your weapons." His squad complied. He could see the fear in their eyes as they looked to him for direction. He felt an ominous sick feeling come over him as he accepted, for the first time in his life, he was going to die.

The sergeant in charge was a big man with a full dark beard. He had a nasty reputation for being cruel. "Search them." Four soldiers came forward and took their swords and personal items. They then searched Michael and his men and forced them to lie face down on the ground. The large sergeant walked closer to the group, "You five present me with a little problem. We normally leave your burnt, headless bodies on the front lines, so your comrades may locate the Normand spies. We want them to know what happens to spies. The closest front lines are over fifty miles south. We will have to carry your dead asses fifty miles if we kill you here."

Michael spoke, "We are not spies."

The sergeant urgently walked and stood over Michael, "Well excuse me. We want your comrades to see what happens to Normand soldiers we capture. You do know that your soldiers killed my two brothers, mother, and uncle while you bastards advanced north last year. If you lie to me, I will enjoy torturing you for hours before I kill you."

Michael said, "We are not soldiers of the Normand army." The sergeant kicked Michael in the ribs. Michael knew his ribs might be broken. The pain was acute and knocked the breath out of him. He balled up into the fetal position.

The Sergeant clenched his teeth, "Do not lie to me. What the hell do you think we are-stupid? You just happen to be crawling around at four A.M. in the morning after you rowed a small boat to our shore. You were dropped off at sea by a Normand battleship." He looked at his men with his palms raised. His men laughed. "You then got out of the boat and hid the damn thing in the underbrush and walked up this mountain hiding as you walked." He kicked Michael a second time in the back. "What were you doing? Coming here for a picnic?" The men holding the weapons all laughed.

Hector knew they were going to die. He thought they might have one chance. "We are part of the Queen's Guard. We are sworn to protect our Queen."

The sergeant walked over to Hector and kicked him in the head. Hector started bleeding from his forehead. Michael groaned, "We request to be seen by the Queen."

The soldiers looked confused. The sergeant glanced at his men, "The Queen? Who in the hell is the Queen? Are you men lost?" He smiled at the five men lying on the ground. He walked over to Viking and kicked him in the face. "We are going to kill you. Tie them and make them walk down the hill, so we do not have to carry their dead asses."

Michael said, "The Queen would not want her guards injured. We have sworn to protect her."

The sergeant started to walk over to Michael and kick him again. The soldier standing over the men with his sword at Pretty Boy's back asked, "Are they talking about Veronica?"

The sergeant kicked Cruise and Pretty Boy hard in the sides. "I work for Vulture. I do not work for those split tails." He then walked by each man lying on the ground and kicked them again. He then ordered, "Take them to the holding cell."

"Should we not tell General Dak and maybe Veronica? She might have some information on these five men. Sir, think about it. What would these six men be doing out here?"

The sergeant smiled, "I guess you can tell Veronica. There is no reason to bother telling General Dak. Our commander, Captain Vulture, has made our mission clear, we are to kill all

387

the spies and leave them for the Normand soldiers to find. Now force those men to carry their dead comrade down the mountain and place them in a holding cell."

Chapter 36

Veronica did not sleep well. She knew her body was changing. She suspected she would be a mother in seven-and-half months. As she laid in bed, she heard someone walking down the hall of the hotel. She noticed the footsteps stop outside her door. Her mind immediately flashed back to the evil face of Damon and him holding his knife to her breast while she was in restraints on the boat sailing to Southern City. She thought the area was well guarded with the men instructed to be on the lookout for Normand spies. She also realized the guards would be no match for Damon. She pulled the covers back and reached for the sword next to her bed and stood ready to fight with her back against the interior wall next to the door. She felt relieved when she heard the knock on her door. She laid down her sword and lit the candle sitting on the nightstand. She opened the door with her left hand while holding the sword behind the open door in her right hand. The hallway was well illuminated with the lights of the hall. The messenger looked like a boy of about fourteen. He scanned Veronica standing in the doorway wearing only her thin white short cotton gown and bare feet. Veronica noticed the young soldier's glare, and how his eyes slowly roamed over her body.

The army was taking all males they could locate, and age did not matter. She noticed the young man seemed nervous and would not look her in the eyes. He looked like he was a new recruit right off the farm. He wore old looking boots stained in dirt and mud with his shirt sleeves rolled up to his biceps. His upper face was white from being protected by a hat from the sun while his neck and arms were tan. His hair was stringy, long, and unwashed. He only had facial hair on his chin and a mustache with no hair on his jaws or neck. He hesitated and at first did not speak. She held her position and waited. "Mrs. Veronica. Mrs. Veronica, I am here. I am here to report to you five spies have been apprehended by the night watch on the ridge north of our city. They are scheduled to be executed at daybreak."

Veronica looked at the young man and was somewhat amused. He stated the sentence like he had been rehearsing the lines for a few minutes. He had repeated himself at the beginning, not hesitated in the middle of the two sentences, and at the end of the two sentences he took a deep breath. He appeared to be nervous as he dropped his hat on the floor. As he reached down for the hat with his hand, she noticed his eyes were not looking at the hat but were focused on her lower legs and bare feet. She was amused that he had been sent to tell her the news, and he had trouble formulating his thoughts into a correct sentence. As he stood holding his hat, she tried to make eye contact. She felt the urgent need to reach the young man's chin and lift his face upward so his eyes could focus on her eyes and not elsewhere. She restrained herself from embarrassing the teenager and asked, "Why wake me up at this time of the morning with the news of five spies?"

He stuttered and was nervous. He lifted his eyes to look her in the face, "The leader first denied being a spy. He also claimed they were not soldiers."

Veronica felt confused, "Are they Normand men? Who are the men?"

"They were seen departing a Normand vessel at sea and sneaking ashore. As soon as Captain Vulture awakes, he will have them executed and the bodies taken to the front line. I was ordered to provide you this report by the sergeant of the night watch. They say they are not spies or soldiers but are the Queen's Guard."

Veronica urgently commanded, "Go and tell the sergeant of the guard not to harm them. I am on my way." She closed the door and pulled her pants, boots, and shirt on. She fastened her sword and knife around her waist. She wrapped her hair in a ponytail. She opened her door and then knocked firmly on her brother's door. Trey opened his door with sleepy eyes.

Veronica announced, "I need your help. Vulture is about to execute my guards, and I am going to stop him."

Veronica turned and walked along the hall and down the stairs. Trey stepped back into his room and got dressed. He was confused about why he was being asked by his sister to go to the jail for "her guards". As he was walking by Dak and Zenith's room, he knocked on the door. Dak came to the door a few seconds later. "There is trouble at the jail. You might want to follow me over. Veronica is going to confront Vulture over the treatment of the captured guards. I must support sis."

Trey walked down the hall and down the stairs. Dak stood in his underwear looking down the hall as his friend turned the corner and disappeared down the stairway. He was mad he had been awakened by something to do with prisoners. He knocked on Hulk's door. Hulk came to the door and kept the door closed as much as he could by standing in the doorway, so Dak could not see the two females in his bed. Dak knew what Hulk was doing, "Trey woke me. He said Veronica is on her way to the jail. Somehow, she was informed Vulture is going to execute some men. Do you mind going over there and checking it out? You need to meet Trey at the jail." Hulk looked frustrated. Dak then said, "I was up late with Zenith last night, and you were able to get a full night's sleep. I figured one of us should go."

"Yeah, I will go," replied Hulk.

Hulk closed his door and Dak walked back into his room smiling at the fact Hulk was hiding the ladies in his room. He lifted the covers and saw his wife's nude body lying face down. Although he was aware she was upset at him for not discussing his plans to assassinate King Solman, his smile grew with anticipation. He felt his sexual desires become activated as he studied her nude body. He quickly removed his shorts. He thought, "At some point she would forgive me." He crawled next to Zenith's nude body and rubbed against her. She whispered without opening her eyes, "Please tell me the war has not started. I need a couple additional hours of sleep. What is going on? Who was that at our door?"

He softly rubbed down her back and legs with his right hand. He then rolled his nude body on top of hers as he became fully energized with his body positioned on hers. He whispered in her ear, "Trey was heading to the jail to meet Veronica. Someone told Veronica some Normand spies or guards were captured last night and are going to be executed. She went over to the jail to confront Vulture." He rubbed his hand over her shoulder and placed both his hands on top of her hands above her head and then kissed her ear and then her upper back.

Zenith suddenly rolled out from under Dak, jumped out of bed and started getting dressed. Dak looked confused, "Where are you going? I thought you needed two additional hours of sleep."

Zenith put her pants on and sat on the bed and put her boots on. "That is not what you were thinking as you rubbed my ass. I told Veronica I would help her if she ever needed my help. That is what friends do for one another. I am going to help my friend." She jumped up from the bed and grabbed her belt with her sword. She turned to look at Dak staring at her while he was lying in bed with a confused expression. Zenith reached for her bow and case of arrows, "There is going to be trouble. You may go back to sleep and avoid this if you like." Zenith turned and ran out the door and down the stairs. Dak laid in bed on his back and looked at the ceiling. He was frustrated and then punched the mattress with the back of his hand, "Dammit to double hell. When is she going to forgive me?" He slowly got up and dressed.

***

Vulture preferred waking early in the morning before sunrise. His routine in life was to eat a simple breakfast, walk a mile for exercise, and enjoy the morning daybreak. He enjoyed the solitude of an early morning walk. He walked from his room in the command building to the breakfast area where he ate an egg. Then, he walked to the war room. His assistant approached him. "Sir, there were six spies caught by the night watch on the north hill overlooking the city. One spy was killed. The other five are being held in the jail. Here is the report from the night watch commander."

Vulture looked at the report and read the first sentence. He then dropped his vision to the last sentence at the bottom of the page as he said, "Go to the barracks and awake the new trainees. Have them meet me at the jail." The assistant turned and ran toward the barracks.

As Vulture walked toward the jail, he considered the upcoming war. His men were ready for the battle. They had fought admirably in two prior battles. He knew most of them were prepared for the Normand attack. An experienced soldier was worth two maybe three inexperienced soldiers and most of his men were all killers. He had a few new men, but the ones that had traveled with him from New Foundland would not back down in a sword fight. The New Foundland Tribe was located west of a nuclear waste area, and on the east side of the nuclear waste area was the Midlander territory. Some of the men and women from each tribe had married and the two groups had worked out a peaceful existence. There was a path around the nuclear waste pit and the two groups had learn to live as neighbors. Some of the Midlander warriors had agreed to fight with Vulture and his men against the Normand army. The Midlander warriors were all killers and very efficient in battle. Dak and Vulture had talked about the Midlanders. They were very conservative in their beliefs and would not accept anyone or any ideals in conjunction with the old world that existed prior to the Transitional Period. The Midlander people blamed the people of old earth for the destruction of the modern world. Dak had been concerned if he could trust the Midlander warriors, but he soon realized he had no choice. He needed every warrior he could get, and these men worked for Vulture.

As Vulture approached the jail, he heard the horse riders' approach from behind him. He knew the new soldiers were young and needed experience. He watched them pass him and then tie off their horses to the corral fence as he approached the jail yard. The sergeant of the jail walked out the door. Vulture approached him, "I understand you encountered six spies last night on the ridge and killed one of them."

The sergeant glanced at Vulture with a nod and a smile. Vulture said, "Good work. Well, I guess we need to get to it. Bring them out here. We have a lot to do today. We must hurry and move the execution along." Vulture turned to the trainees and commanded, "Your training today will assist you in becoming a soldier. You must learn how to kill to be a soldier.

That is what soldiers do, kill their enemy." He looked at the ten soldiers. He noticed they all were teenagers. They had passed the ten-day training course using swords and spears. Vulture knew these men were not ready for battle, but the army had no choice. These men needed time to grow and mature. They needed to be stronger and practice a great deal more with weapons. Two of the soldiers were fourteen. The Normand army was preparing to attack with a large, trained army. His job was to train the new men and deploy them to the other commanders in the battlefield. He was also in charge of the security of the compound and the jail. Dak's plan was that Vulture, and his men were going to be held in reserve to support one of the forward units which were first to come under attack.

He pointed to the five on the left, "You five are going to learn how to kill the enemy today. This is not going to be easy for some of you, but to be a soldier, you must learn how to kill another man. Once you learn how to kill, the next time will be easier. Thanks to our night watch team, they have provided us with five enemy spies. They will be led out to the block, and you will administer the punishment for being a Normand spy. The sentence for being a Normand spy is death."

The five trainees looked apprehensive as they all realized they were about to take another man's life. The jailors led the five men out the door. Vulture then announced as he pointed at Michael, "He will be first."

The young man who had been asked to tell Veronica of the capture men spoke. "Captain Vulture. These men claimed to be the Queen's Guards and not soldiers or spies. Veronica is on her way to meet these men and talk with you about their treatment."

"Well hell. We do not have time to wait on her, and I am in charge."

The young man pointed behind Vulture and interrupted him, "Veronica is approaching." He turned and watched Veronica approach on foot.

***

Veronica noticed as she came out the front door of the hotel the sun was just rising over the eastern sky and the Atlantic Ocean. She knew the stable workers were on alert to have horses saddled and ready for soldiers in case of an attack, but there was no time to spare as she noticed there were no clouds in the sky, and the morning was quiet. Veronica decided to run the mile north along the road leading away from Harpers Ferry Harbor. As she approached the jail, she could see five men being led out of the jail house to the block in the middle of the compound. She increased her speed. She yelled, "Stop". She could see Vulture standing in front of the first man with his sword pulled and other men standing close to her guards. Vulture turned and waited.

Veronica was out of breath when she ran into the compound. "Stop what you are doing."
She ran past the row of men standing. Michael was on his knees with his head on the chopping block. Veronica did not hesitate, and she ran between Vulture and Michael and bent down on her knees and held him in her arms. "I am sorry Are you okay?"

"I believe my ribs are broken. Hector and Viking have been kicked in the head. They should be okay. Pretty Boy has a broken nose. Cruise is bruised from being kicked. Our scout, a man named Bebo, is dead. They all volunteered to come and protect you."

Veronica hugged Michael. Vulture smiled, "You may have a moment and say your goodbyes."

Veronica stood and turned to the man with the sword. She walked into his space and with a determined expression and said, "You will step away from these men. You will not harm these men, or I will kill you." The young soldier in training stepped backward three steps and looked at Vulture.

Veronica turned and stared at Vulture, "These men will not be harmed."

Vulture looked at Veronica. He wanted to show the new recruits and other men he was in charge. He wanted to impress Veronica by illustrating how his men followed his orders. "Listen here, Little Lady, we are not going to torture them. They will die from decapitation. We use spies as a training tool, and our new soldiers must learn how to kill. Killing men in war must be taught, and what a better method to learn to kill than to use a spy. Now, step back, so they can learn how to be soldiers." He nonchalantly motioned for the five soldiers to carry out the sentence.

Veronica turned to the five soldiers, "I will kill the soldier that harms these men. Now step back." She placed her hand on her handle of her sword. She knew these young men did not know her and were going to listen to Vulture.

Vulture looked at his twenty men plus the jailors and laughed a sinister laugh. "They do not take their orders from you. They take their orders from me, and I am in charge."

Veronica turned and walked toward Vulture. As she approached him, she shortened her last step with her left leg and without hesitating she kicked him between the legs with her right foot. As he bent forward from the kick, she hit him on the bridge of the nose with her right fist. He fell backward with blood dripping from his broken nose and running across his mouth and chin while he was hunched over in pain from the kick. She did not hesitate and went to Michael and cut his hands free. "I told you five soldiers to step backward, and I mean now." She glared at the five young men.

The large sergeant stood and walked out from the jail doorway. He looked south and saw Trey riding a horse toward them. He saw Captain Vulture trying to stand. Vulture saw Veronica cut the restraint on Cruise and Hector. Vulture ordered, "Don't just stand there. Arrest her."

The sergeant held his hand out for the men to stand still as he watched as Trey rode into the yard of the jail and jumped off his horse. Trey walked toward Veronica. He asked in a loud tone, "What is going on here?"

Vulture stood and faced Veronica as she cut the restraints on Pretty Boy and Viking. Veronica looked at a soldier, "Hook those horses to that wagon. These men need medical attention."

Vulture was leaning over as he was standing. His nose was broken and bleeding with blood drops falling to the ground in front of him. He was in obvious pain from the kick to his crotch. He screamed, "I said arrest her. Those men have been found guilty of conspiring to kill us. She is committing treason by helping them. I am your commanding officer."

Trey looked around and pulled his sword, "If anyone tries to stop my sister, I will kill them. You will do as she says." He walked to the first of the guards and looked down at the one-hundred-and-forty-pound teenager. The man looked like he was sixteen and was nervous. Trey held his sword at the man's chest. "You need to step back, or I will cut you in half."

Vulture demanded, "What gives you the right to interfere with my orders? I am a captain in the army. You have no title or rank."

Veronica turned to Vulture and answered in a commanding voice, "I am the Queen of the Normand Army. These men are my personal guards sworn to lay down their lives for me. I will not allow them to be hurt. Your men will stand down, or I will kill them. I will take my men to the doctor for treatment. They will not be staying in your jail any longer. Now hook that wagon up and bring the damn thing to me."

Trey looked surprised. He whispered to himself, "Mary, sweet mother of Jesus. You are the queen of what?"

Hulk rode into the jail compound and jumped off his horse. He was like Trey and was irritated at being woken early. He demanded, "What is going on here so damn early in the morning?" He looked mad at the young men standing with their swords pulled. They had backed up next to the wall of the jail. Vulture was bleeding from his nose and cursing every other word. Hulk saw a soldier pull a horse and wagon over to the five men who were sitting on the ground. Hulk turned to Trey, "What is going on?"

Trey did not answer but appeared to be confused as he raised his left-hand palm up and held his pulled sword to the side. He then wiped his face and ran his hand across his head and hair. He stood still and watched as Veronica helped Michael into the back of the wagon. Hulk turned and saw Zenith heading toward them on a horse at a full run. Veronica then turned and helped the next man into the wagon. Hector and Pretty Boy each walked to the wagon and climbed in the rear. Hulk noticed all the guards and the men were watching Veronica help the Normand men.

Hulk looked at the large sergeant standing in the door of the jail, "What is going on? Why are those prisoners not handcuffed?"

The large sergeant pointed to Vulture. Vulture was still bent over. He wiped the blood from his nose and spit on the ground. Veronica assisted the last of the captured men into the wagon. She climbed to the driver's seat. She looked at Hulk, "I am taking these men to the medical ward to be treated."

Zenith rode into the area and watched as Veronica turned the wagon around and headed toward the town. Vulture said, "She needs to be arrested. Those men are my prisoners."

Zenith looked at Vulture, "You were going to have those men executed and Veronica stopped you."

Hulk glanced at the five men standing along the jail wall with their swords pulled. He then looked at the chopping block in the center of the jail yard. He could see blood stains on the block and the ground around the block. He looked at Trey standing with his sword pulled and a perplexed look on his face. "Vulture, are you okay?"

"Well hell no. I am not okay. That bitch kicked me in my balls when I was not looking and broke my nose. She committed treason and freed my prisoners. She needs to be arrested and punished along with those damn Normand spies."

Hulk noticed movement to his left and saw Trey place his sword back into the sleeve on his belt and walk directly over to Vulture. He picked him up and looked him in the eyes, while holding him by his shoulders, "If you ever say anything bad about my sister or try to arrest her, I will break your back. Are we clear?" He shook Vulture until Vulture agreed. Trey then dropped Vulture to the ground. Trey walked to his horse and indicated to Zenith he was going to the medical ward to check on his sister.

Hulk stood and wondered what he had missed. He turned and walked to the large sergeant. "Come in here. I need a full report on these captured soldiers, and what just happened."

Dak rode into the jail yard and noticed Zenith was sitting on her horse watching Vulture sitting on the ground. He noticed the jailors standing around watching him ride into the front yard. He looked back over his shoulder and watched Trey heading toward the far end of the town. Zenith looked at Dak and suggested, "You might want to go in the jailhouse and get the full briefing from the segreant who is being interviewed by Hulk."

Chapter 37

Dak was more than frustrated. He knew Vulture was embarrassed with being kicked and then having his nose broken in front of his men by a female. The men under his command from the Midlander camp would not take orders from a female, and Vulture knew they wanted to go back home and not fight when they heard of Veronica and Vulture's confrontation. In addition, Vulture was forced to walk around with a white bandage on the bridge of his nose where everyone could see. His face and neck turned red when asked what happened to his nose by others and having to answer their questions. Several men who already knew the answer kept asking Vulture what happened as they all would start laughing.

During the meeting, Vulture yelled at Dak and told him Veronica needed to be arrested for treason. Dak was irate with the situation and the attitude from Vulture and told him if he did not come to terms with what had happened, he would be demoted to private and forced to fight on the southernmost front. Vulture started to storm out of the command tent, and Dak caught him by the arm and threatened him. "If you think I am going to arrest Veronica or if I am going to pick you over Veronica, then you are wrong. She has killed more Normand

soldiers in battle than any three of your men added together."
He clenched his teeth, "You need to consider that before you
really piss me off." He released Vulture and watched him walk
out of the tent.

***

Dak was a little hesitant as he reached for Zenith's hand as
they walked through the field. He felt relief when she did not
pull her hand away as they walked to the bonfire. He was tired
and hungry. He had met with all his captains over the past
several days, and they now had all been deployed. He had tried
to consider where and when the General with the Normand
Army would order the first assault. He had never fought this
general by the name of Rivers. He could not predict his
strategy or fortitude to fight. Would the Normand command be
patient and cunning or would he be bold and overconfident. At
first, he thought a cookout with his old friends would be nice
and help him relax. Now, he wondered if this was not a
mistake. The fire could be seen from half a mile away. The
attack by the Normand army was imminent. The Normand
army had been deployed along the battle front in large
numbers. Dak ordered the soldiers to be on alert. After the
fight where Veronica had kicked one of his commanders in the

family jewels, he hoped everyone would relax. He thought this was no way to start a battle. He worried about the impending battle as he walked to the fire. He saw Tommy Boy and Hulk placing additional wood on the bonfire. He could see Trey carrying some of the food to the table. "So, what did Veronica say happened to her while she was being held prisoner?"

Zenith glanced at her husband as they walked, "She has said a lot. Do you remember the little cabin by the river, when we were snowed in for four days?"

Dak was confused. Why the change of topic? "Yes, I remember all the dancing, sword fighting, wrestling which led us to making love thirty-four times in the small cabin over a four-day period. I will never forget that period in my life. We made love for the first time in that cabin and then thirty-three additional times before we left. We should have stayed in the cabin."

Zenith smiled as they walked. "Veronica has lived a lot more exciting life than we have. I do not believe she has had anyone to talk with for the past several months. She has confided in me, and I have become her friend."

Dak was surprised, "We are not boring people. What has she done? I put the stay in the cabin up against anyone. The reason that time period meant such much to both of us is we both took a chance on each other and provided our vulnerabilities to each other." Dak took a deep breath and waited. He prayed his line worked. He knew at some point they must talk about him planning to assassinate King Solman and not including Zenith in on his plans. She would not talk to him. She had created a barrier between them.

Zenith smiled again, "Did you not notice, I am wearing makeup and have a manicure?"

Dak glanced at his wife's nails and her lips. "Yes, you look very pretty."

"You did not notice until I mentioned it to you. That hurts a girl's feelings, Mr. Donahue."

Dak looked surprised. At least she was talking with him and allowing him to hold her hand. "I am not at the top of my game. It is the evening before we believe the Normand empire launches an all-out offensive on my army across a one-thousand-mile front with several more thousand men. I am also having trouble understanding why several northern districts are not agreeing to join the battle with us. I have second guessed my strategy. Should I not attack them? Should I be on the offensive instead of waiting for them to attack us and then fall back to Homestead?"

"I guess you have a reasonable excuse for not noticing." She smiled at Dak, "My girlfriend told me not to tell anyone. She made me promise, but she has been with an older man who is very experienced in love making, and he seems to know his way around the female body."

"Zenith, I am sorry for not telling you about my plan to assassinate King Solman. I am your husband. I must make decisions. You can tell me about Veronica. Besides, I have known Veronica since she was born. Our mothers would take turns nursing us at the same time and washing us when we were babies in the same tub. You can trust me."

They arrived at the fire, "You are my husband, but I cannot tell you. You never considered that I deeply love you. For you to consider you were going to leave me and most likely die trying to kill King Solman without me was selfish, misguided, and cruel. Have you ever considered I have been trained in classrooms in Merlin which focused on strategy of war. Yet you have refused to ask for my help with your strategy of war. You complain about the situation but will not ask for advice." Zenith hastily pulled her hand away and walked to the table with the food to assist Trey. Dak stood while watching her walk away wondering how he would amend his mistake and also find out what she knew about Veronica. He then glanced at Hulk watching Zenith walk away from him. Dak noticed Robin Hood rode a horse over to the tree and dropped off two turkeys he shot while hunting. He tied his horse up and started cleaning the turkeys. The group started small talk and then they sat next to the fire. In the distance they saw Veronica walking toward them. When she arrived, she smiled at everyone and sat down on a log near the fire.

Hulk walked over next to Dak and stood near the fire, "Are you and Zenith cross with each other?" Dak did not answer but grimaced at Hulk.

Hulk said, "Well hell. I wonder what that is like. Having a wife mad at you and also one that can kick your ass."

"Kiss my ass." Dak walked over and sat down on a log near the fire.

Hulk then announced, "This is like old times. All of us together, eating dinner and enjoying each other's company." He smiled and looked at Dak.

Trey smiled, "It has been a long time since we were all together. We have made a lot of memories."

Dak looked at his friends. He then glanced at Veronica, "So Veronica, what is new with you?"

Veronica was staring into the fire. "I would send a rider north to hand deliver a message to your mother. Her army needs to be ready to ride south. Matter of fact, they need to camp south three hundred miles, so they can come in support. Your farm boys are going to get steamrolled by a large, motivated army. The Normand soldiers have been promised the spoils taken in victory." She looked at Dak, "You also need to make your friends either advisors or generals in your army, so the soldiers will know to take orders from them."

Dak looked serious, "Yes, I will consider both ideas. I need to expand the administration part of this army to others. I need to delegate." He then reached up and rubbed his chin like he was thinking.

Robin Hood placed the fileted turkey meat in two large skillets. He turned around and gestured with his hands as he talked. "I believe Dak was referring to your statement this morning. The one when you told the jail guards and the new cadets, right before you kicked Captain Vulture in his family jewels and broke his nose, you were the Queen of the Normand Army, and those captured five men worked for you. He might want to know how you were taken by a Rogue Blueblood as a slave to Southern City and now have five free men willing to die for you. He might want to know about that part of your life. I know I sure as hell would like for you to fill in the missing pieces to that puzzle."

Everyone tried to hold back their laughter and smiled as Robin Hood was funny with him over emphasizing what he was saying. Veronica did not change her expression, "There really is nothing to talk about."

Hulk was smiling, "What does that mean, the Queen of the Normand Army? Does that mean you are married?"

"Yes. I am married to King Solman. I really do not want to talk about the marriage."

Hulk looked at Veronica, the same as Tommy Boy, Robin Hood, Dak, and Trey. Everyone appeared to be surprised. They realized she was no longer the skinny little tomboy they knew as they grew up together. They recognized she was very pretty, with style, with class, intelligent, and mature. Her transformation had been complete from a teenager to a woman. Hulk blurted out, "How did this happen? I mean there are several thousand females in Southern City."

Veronica looked at Hulk and paused before replying, "You mean why me?"

Hulk realized that she might interpret him to have implied she was not pretty enough to be picked. "I just mean why a wife from Cliff Tops. Why not a local female?"

Veronica glared into the fire and watched the logs burn and replied, "You may ask him when you meet him."

Dak pulled from his jacket pocket. "Here is a small amount of your Merlin gold. The rest is in Cliff Tops. He handed the bag of gold to Trey and then Trey handed the gold to Hulk who passed the bag to Veronica. She glanced in the bag and pulled out a gold coin. She looked at Robin Hood, "Merlin gold. How much does a good female cost for her services for a night?"

Robin Hood looked confused. He tried to say something and nothing would register in his mind what to say. "I know you guys have been spending your gold on women. How much does a female charge?" She turned and looked at Hulk.

Hulk looked uncomfortable. He glanced at the ground in front of him and did not answer.

Zenith said, "For heaven sakes. This is the subject all of you guys have been bragging about for days. You talked about the women you bedded since we arrived in Harpers Ferry Harbor. How much does it cost to bed one female?"

Veronica looked at Hulk, "I have five men that are in the medical tent that need to be shown a good time. I was hoping you could introduce them to the right females. Here is a gold coin. Is this not enough in payment for women for all five men?"

Tommy Boy laughed, "They thought you were wanting to buy a female for yourself." He stopped laughing when he realized no one else was laughing.

Veronica smiled at Tommy Boy. She liked his quiet nature as he was growing up. He had grown into a large strong man you did not want to fight. "I am married, remember? No thank you." She then hesitated, "Tommy Boy, you have grown four inches and gotten a lot stronger since I have seen you last. You now are bigger than your older brother by several inches and several pounds. I take it you are still doing a thousand pushups every day?"

Hulk smiled, "He wears size twenty boots. He and Trey both have gotten bigger and stronger. They have a nickname called biscuit, because they both are one biscuit away from weighing three-hundred-and-forty pounds." Hulk smiled, "No one wants to wrestle either one of them. We all do a thousand pushups every day."

Veronica nodded her head up and down understanding what Hulk had just said. "Robin Hood, you have also gotten stronger looking. You still are the smaller one in the group, but you are not a runt by any stretch of the imagination. You now are almost as tall as Hulk and Dak."

Robin Hood smiled, "I am six-foot-three and close to two-hundred-and-ten pounds. All the bow shooting has built up my shoulders." He looked at Veronica, "That gold coin is enough money for an entire week plus it will pay for Hulk also joining in with the party."

Trey announced, "Veronica, you are the one who has changed the most. I remember the little skinny girl following all us boys around. Dad would say you were too competitive to let us guys best you. Now look at you. You have turned into one of the prettiest women on the continent. Remember, big sister, I love you. I will always have your back."

Dak changed the subject. He could tell Hulk was getting angry talking about the prostitutes. He mentioned, "Speaking of which. What am I going to do with those five guards? We are at war with their King."

Veronica was direct and to the point, "You are going to stop killing the prisoners and mistreating the prisoners. I despise Vulture. He is a mean angry man full of hatred. I will take care of my men. They have sworn to protect me. You do not need to be concerned with them."

Robin Hood looked confused, "Protect you from what? You are here among people who love you."

"You have not seen what I have seen. There is a cult hidden on this continent. The cult is led by at least two Rogue Bluebloods, maybe more. They have an army of devoted soldiers and are extremely deadly. They are the force behind King Solman. Also, do not forget the Bluebloods in Merlin will be coming for you at some point." She looked at both Dak and Zenith. "They will be coming for all of us. Do not forget the assassins from the Asian Continent or the Midlanders who reside in the waste lands of our continent. We will always be at war with someone."

Dak looked at Veronica. He knew there was a hidden agenda behind what she said. He also was aware that what she said was true. Trey looked uncomfortable with the conversation, "Big sister, why are you telling us this?"

Zenith spoke, "She is suggesting we make a treaty with these groups and try to live in harmony, but we also need to be prepared for war. We need the courage to kill who needs to be killed and provide mercy to those who deserve to live, and the wisdom to be able to know the difference."

Hulk looked confused, "The Normand empire has attacked us. We are here trying to repel their brutality. We need to kill them."

Veronica looked at Hulk, "I know why we are here. You are missing the point. These soldiers on the verge of attacking you are being manipulated by an unseen cult. The real menace is the cult. They are very deadly and will be hard for you to locate and even harder to exterminate. There will be no peace until they are annihilated."

Tommy Boy announced, "The beef is done."

Robin Hood announced, "The turkey meat is also done. Let us eat."

They all filled their plates with the food and started eating. Veronica looked over at Hulk, "So, are you going to help me with the hookers and my men?"

Hulk ate another bite of food and smiled, "Yes, Queen of the Normand Army. I will finish my food, and I will contact a man who sets up this type of activity. I believe we can assist you." He took another bite of turkey.

Tommy Boy looked perplexed, "Who is this man that sets you up with these women? I thought you went into the house of ill repute and waved a gold coin in the air." The group laughed.

Hulk smiled, "The process is more complicated than that, and besides, a gentleman never does something that crude." All the guys laughed.

Zenith questioned, "So you guys are gentlemen?" The group laughed.

Tommy Boy asked, "I am serious. Who is this man that arranges for you to meet all these women?"

"You are looking at him. He is the one who also prepares turkeys for our meal."

Robin Hood faked a laugh with everyone looking at him. "Wait a minute. Hulk is pulling your leg. He does everything on his own. He does not need my help."

Veronica looked at Hulk, "I anticipate your help. Do you guys recall how we used to take the extra food to those in need?"

Dak looked at Veronica wondering why the nostalgia comment, while still admiring how she had changed her demeanor, posture, and personality. He was, however, still trying to figure out what part of her had changed the most. He could not figure out what he was missing about her persona. He said, "I do recall all the fishing trips, hunting trips, and taking the food to the old man, Taylor and his wife. We also helped the young couples with those hungry kids. We provided extra food for our village."

Veronica looked at Dak, "Three of those kids died from different viruses. I wish we could have done more. While you and Trey are cleaning this up, and Robin Hood and Hulk are setting up entertainment for my five guards, Tommy Boy and I will carry extra food to the five guards being held in the medical ward."

Everyone was quiet when Veronica suggested Dak clean up the dishes. Hulk looked over at Veronica, "What is next for you? What are you going to do?"

"I will head home with my five bodyguards and then give birth to my child in a few months."

Trey smiled, "Our parents would love to see you and love to hear you will provide them a grand baby." He then stopped smiling when he realized who the father might be. "Is King Solman the father?"

Veronica looked at her brother, "Yes. If he finds out I am with child, he will not stop until he locates me." Hulk nodded his head and glanced at Veronica with the understanding

Veronica was now special. He studied her as he sat beside her and noticed the makeup on her pretty face, the perfect smile, her well thought out wardrobe, and her long-permed hair. He turned his eyes to stare into the fire and realized the girl he grew up with was now very pretty and mature. They all stared into the fire in thought.

Tommy Boy started gathering food to take to the five guards, He looked over at his friends, "I can recall how everything used to be so simple. Our lives and our childhood were not nearly this complicated." He turned and looked at Veronica. "I hope your guards are hungry. I have plenty of food gathered."

"Thank you, Tommy Boy."

Dak stood and started cleaning the dishes and picking up the debris. The group watched with surprise. Dak turned, "Veronica is correct with everything she has said. I also realize I need to serve you. To be able to work is a blessing. It is my turn to help."

The others started leaving and Dak started the cleanup. Zenith walked next to Dak and started helping to pick up the debris. Dak noticed her next to him and whispered, "Veronica has changed. I realized she is wearing makeup, she thinks before she speaks, her wardrobe is more appealing, but I cannot place my finger on what about her has made the biggest difference."

Zenith started cleaning the skillet, "That is easy."

Dak looked over at his wife, "Oh yea. Why don't you enlighten me?"

Zenith reached for a tin plate to clean, "She now has full confidence in herself. She does not live with insecurities. She has nothing to prove to anyone. She has grace and love in her heart."

Chapter 38

The knock at the door was firm and loud. Zenith sat up in bed and immediately looked for her sword. She then remembered where she was and laid back down and pulled the covers over her. Dak rolled out of bed and opened the door. The soldiers announced, "General Dak, the war has started. The Normand army has crossed the battle lines in four locations. I am to report, our army is in full retreat."

***

Dak and Zenith walked into the command tent. "How bad are our losses?"

Hulk looked over and announced, "Our losses are not as bad as we thought. So far, we have lost twenty-five men from the forward team which still has several hundred men located south of the Waldo Bridge. The other squads are now in the process of reporting. Our men closed ranks like we planned and set up a defensive retreat." Hulk looked up from the table. "They hit us with overwhelming numbers. We are not certain about their losses. They steamrolled over our defensive wall in the desert of Zimbabwe, and once the front line was breached, they were able to capitalize on our lack of troops in reserve. The information is spotty with a full retreat being ordered, and the messengers have not reported in from the mountain region."

Dak looked at the map, "Vulture, I need you to take three squads and reinforce the Waldo Bridge. Our troops need to be on the north side of the Broad Southern River and then burn the damn thing. Anyone that does not cross the bridge before it burns will be trapped."

Hulk looked confused, "Three squads? They will hit us in our flanks. We will need those men to protect the withdrawal of the soldiers retreating through the Hando Pass. He pointed to the right section of the map."

Dak commanded, "What we know is they are attacking us here. If those men cannot cross the bridge, they will be lost. We need to make certain they are not cut off and that bridge must be burned. We do not know if their army will attack us in the Hando Pass. We need those men backing up the part of the forward team already on the north side of the river. We must get everyone across the Waldo Bridge before they are cut off." Dak pointed to the bridge. "Burning the bridge will provide us additional time to transfer resources east or west along the river. Then, we will be provided time to retreat and set up another line of defense on the Plains of Jellico."

Veronica walked into the command tent with a sense of concern. Vulture looked at her with contempt as she took additional steps toward the table with the map. The other army personnel also watched her as a few of the men stepped backward to provide her room. She smiled at Tommy Boy, Trey, and Hulk. Zenith smiled at Veronica from the opposite side of the table and then glanced at Dak. Dak acted like he did not notice her presence. Dak knew Vulture had been talking about Veronica with the other army personnel. One of the captains had told Hulk how Vulture did not trust Veronica and did not believe she should be allowed in the command tent. Hulk had repeated the concerns to his friend Dak.

Vulture asked in a concerned, harsh voice, "What about her?" He pointed toward Veronica.

Dak turned and looked at Vulture and then Veronica, "Hi Veronica. I did not realize you had arrived." He then looked at Vulture, "What about Veronica? If you have something you want to say, then say it."

"She is the Queen of the Normand Army. She should not be in our command tent. Is she or is she not a Normand soldier?"

Dak turned and slowly pulled one of his swords and walked to Veronica and handed her the handle. He turned his back to her and looked at Vulture. "I trust her with my life. She has saved me more than once. I trust her more than any man in this room." He paused. "Yes, she is married to King Solman, and given the opportunity in battle, I will end his life. Now, I have given you an order, and I expect the order to be carried out soldier."

Vulture was obviously mad and turned and walked out of the tent. Dak turned and took his sword from Veronica and said, "I trust your guards had plenty to eat last night and enjoyed themselves."

She smiled and spoke sincerely, "They did appreciate not having their heads removed. The food and the female company were also appreciated."

Chapter 39

Vulture looked at his second in command, "We will drive the Normand army back to the desert."

"Sir, If they cut us off, we will not be able to retreat across the Waldo Bridge. We will be killed or captured."

"I will leave two hundred troops to secure this bridge and then after we return, I will personally light the match to burn the damn thing. Now, I have given you an order. Saddle the horses and have the men ready to move out within the hour."

***

Vulture fired his last arrow. He pulled his sword, "We must push through their front lines."

"Sir we have lost half our men. We need to retreat to the Waldo Bridge."

"If you tell me to retreat one more time, I will kill you. Now, lead the horse platoon to the right of those archers and take them out. The rest of you men follow me."

The men rallied behind Vulture and ran from the protected ditch toward the front lines of the Normand soldiers. The arrows flying toward them were numerous with men being hit all around Vulture. He pushed forward. He and ten other men made the trip to the front lines of the foot soldiers who had long spears and swords. Once the archers were killed, and they fought through and broke the defensive line of the Normand squad, the rest of the men were able to attack from the flanks and surround the Normand soldiers, killing all. The Normand men were decimated. Vulture and his men were tired from the extended battle and from the rush of the final push on foot. Vulture sat in the shade next to his troops resting while trying to attend to the injured men. Vulture broke off an arrow sticking in the shoulder of one of his men. He then pulled the arrow out and threw it to the ground. The soldier yelped in pain. The man was covered in dirt, blood, and sweet. Vulture said, "You did your job today, Jimmy. You need to head back to the Waldo Bridge and have a doctor look at the wound. Give him a horse." He yelled at one of his men.

The sergeant in an excited voice yelled, "Here comes at least three additional squads. We must retreat."

Vulture turned his head quickly and looked into the deserted field and barren land and saw the other squads approaching on foot and by horse. He could see the archers being deployed to fire from the hillside area. He looked around as his men were cowering behind shields and trees. He realized they must retreat. "Everyone retreat to the Waldo Bridge. We must hurry."

As the men pulled back under the constant threat of the arrows, they rode double on horses, but most were on foot and ran toward the bridge.

As Vulture spurred his horse, he thought about making certain all his men crossed the Waldo Bridge and then he would burn the bridge. He wanted to make certain the men waiting at the bridge were prepared to secure the bridge until all his men were able to cross. As Vulture cleared the hill overlooking the Waldo Bridge, he rode into the open area. At first, he was thankful the bridge was still standing, and then the devastated feeling of desperation overwhelmed him when he realized they were now cut off. He saw there were over a thousand Normand soldiers crossing the bridge. He repositioned himself next to the large oak tree on his horse and noticed Normand men dressed in plain clothes like his men were wearing. The sick feeling came over Vulture. The Normand soldiers had crossed upriver dressed in camouflage as his men and then attacked the soldiers protecting the bridge from the north. They had taken the bridge and now he and his men were trapped between the thousand soldiers in front of him and the three squads of soldiers chasing them. There was no way for all of them to move across the river. Most were on foot and could not make the run far enough south to escape. He looked at his sergeant, "I will stay with my troops. We have allowed the Normand soldiers to seize both sides of the riverbanks and the fully intact bridge. We failed to burn the bridge, and we are forced to surrender. Sergeant Decker, you need to head south and cross the river and report my failure to General Dak. We have one-hundred-twenty-seven men trapped. The Normand soldiers on the north side of the river will try and cut you off. You need to ride down the river and pick your place to cross. Time is of the essence." He looked at the Sergeant with a clenched jaw, "You need to hurry. They will kill you if they catch you. You must get the message through to warn our army." The sergeant turned his horse and spurred the animal in the sides and took off south trying to beat the Normand soldiers closing the circle around them.

The Normand lookout saw Vulture and his men arrive at the edge of the field and the tree line overlooking the bridge as additional men ran from the wooded area. The Normand commander ordered four hundred horse soldiers toward Vulture's position. They were trapped, and they were limited with their choices. Most of his men had run two miles across the open country and arrived next to him. They were too tired to fight the large Normand army. He also knew there was no additional support coming from the soldiers of the north. His men were the backup, and he had ordered them to attack the squad of Normand soldiers south of the bridge. He had fallen right into their trap. The men had gathered around Vulture. He turned to his men, "We cannot make it to the riverbank with most of you being on foot. They have us cut off and control of the Waldo Bridge. If we fight, we will be killed. If we surrender, we might be killed. They might provide some of you mercy and turn you into slaves." He had known some of these men for years. Most had been with him since they had first fought with him in New Foundland. He looked in his friends' eyes as they gathered around him and could see the pain of the loss and the knowledge of the brutality they were going to face. "I am sorry. Men, I would suggest we surrender. We all knew being a soldier, we would face death at some point."

Chapter 40

The messenger rode into the camp and jumped off his horse. The dust from the road started to settle around him as he fast approached the command tent. The guard at the door announced, "Denton has arrived."

Hulk glanced at Dak, "Denton is coming from Homestead."

Dak felt sudden dread. The news could not be positive. There was only one reason a messenger would be sent from Homestead. He knew the Normand army must have sailed into the harbor north of them at Homestead in the darkness of night and fought their way inland.

Both men waited with a feeling of gloom. Denton entered the tent. "I have a report, General Dak." Dak motioned his head up and down. He had an ominous feeling the report was not going to be good. The newly formed volunteer militia stationed at Homestead were there to protect their retreat from Harpers Ferry Harbor. Denton and five other men had been sent to Homestead to convince the people of Homestead they needed to organize a local militia and fight the Normand army. Denton announced, "The Normand army has landed with three-troop carrying ships in the middle of the night. They were able to breach the main beach at Homestead."

Hulk wiped his hands through his hair. Denton then announced, "Our troops are in full retreat."

Dak was mad. He looked at Hulk. "Where did they find those ships? We blew up the three warships and a cruiser." He looked back at Denton, "Full retreat to where? There is no place to retreat. If our retreat is cut off, we will have to surrender."

Dak turned to the map. "Hulk, I need you to lead the regiment north and protect the route west in the mountains. Our army will have to be able to retreat and meet up with the two other armies from New York and Cliff Tops here at Beech Grove Village." He pointed at the map. "You cannot fail. This is the only chance we have." Dak looked at Hulk.

Hulk shook his head that he understood. "Denton, I am reassigning you to General Hulk Claiborne."

Veronica walked into the command tent. Dak noticed she was dressed in black leather with her long hair in a long wavy perm. Her sword was around her waist and her bow with arrows hung over her back. "I wished you had headed north two days ago. The main road going to Beech Grove Village has been cut off by the Normand army. They landed at Homestead and our troops were forced to retreat. We are trying to secure the route west of Homestead in the mountains. You can leave with Hulk and his regiment of men. They should be able to secure the route, and you may head north to Cliff Tops."

Dak could hear a rider coming into the front area of his command tent. The guard announced: "The messenger is Sergeant Decker. He has arrived from the Waldo Bridge and the South Broad River. He is part of Vulture's unit."

Dak commanded, "Show him in." He felt good about Sergeant Decker arriving. The news would be the Waldo Bridge was burned after all his troops had crossed.

The man walked into the command tent. Dak noticed he was covered in dirt, sweat, and blood stains on his pants and shirt. His face was sunburned and caked in dirt. "Sir, I am Sergeant Decker assigned to Captain Vulture's regiment. I regret to report the Waldo Bridge is still standing, and the Normand army has control. Vulture and his men crossed the Waldo Bridge and were supporting the left flank when the Normand army advanced in from the right flank with a regiment of soldiers. They had over one-hundred soldiers dressed in disguises cross the river north and attack us from the rear. Our troops fought hard, but we were outnumbered. The fighting was hand-to-hand with large losses on both sides."

Dak was shocked by the news. "Damn good strategy by the Normand command. How many men are trapped, and how many men crossed the bridge before it was too late?"

"Sir, I was told to report five-hundred men crossed the bridge, and they are being chased by the Normand army. We believe one-hundred-and-twenty-seven men are trapped. The rest were killed."

Dak was overcome with the bad news. "How did the Normand army get an entire regiment of soldiers to the right flank without Vulture knowing they were there? They already had us out numbered with the regiment on the left flank." Dak slammed his fist down on the table. "Sir, Vulture led his men across the bridge and attacked the Normand army on the left flank, and then we chased them two miles inland. We ran into three additional squads of Normand soldiers that were being held in reserve. Vulture walked us right into the trap."

The man looked disappointed, "Sir, Vulture and his one-hundred-twenty-seven men have surrendered. I was the lone man picked to swim the river and report this update to you. I rode straight through."

Dak clenched his jaws, and his face was red with anger, "I asked how the Normand army positioned an entire regiment of soldiers to the right flank without Vulture knowing they were there?"

Sergeant Decker was surprised with Dak's question. He paused, "Sir. I do not know how they arrived at the right flank without anyone knowing, but I was told they might have traveled in the cover of night and been doubling up in their tents. They have been camouflaging their numbers of fighting men."

Zenith said, "We have lost five-hundred-seventy-five men in this one battle."

The messenger looked at Zenith, "Yes. I would like to sleep and eat then return to the battlefield. The men who are on the north side of the river need assistance with the retreat, or they will also be lost."

Zenith looked at Dak, "This is our worst hour. If we lose all those men, we cannot protect Harpers Ferry Harbor."

Veronica spoke, "I would suggest a temporary truce and arrange to meet King Solman north of the Waldo Bridge. This will provide you additional time, so your troops all along the front can retreat to the designated battle lines."

Dak looked at Veronica. He was irate at the news, "How do you know the location of King Solman?"

"I know him. He would have left the comfort of his castle, and he would be at the command tent with General Rivers. He would want to be in the winning battle, so his men could see him kill you."

Dak looked perplexed, "This truce will provide us the needed time to move our army north. Why would he meet us? He has us on the run."

She looked with a matter-of-fact expression, "He will want to see me. I am his wife, and I am carrying his child."

Dak ordered, "Everyone except Veronica and Zenith clear the command tent. Now."

Chapter 41

Hulk stopped the troops. He pulled the map out of his pocket and stood on the crossroads. Trey walked next to him along with Robin Hood. "We will rest here tonight. We have another fifty miles before we reach the battle lines. We need to go east, and surprise attack the Normand flank."

Trey looked worried at the men and then at Hulk, "We need to rest before battle. We need to send a messenger to the men holding the line and let them know support is coming. We were ordered to secure the pass through the mountains, so our army can retreat."

Hulk looked at Trey, "We need to know where to best to attack. We need intel on the battle."

"Dak commanded us to make certain the path of retreat is open, so the troops south do not get trapped. That is our mission."

Hulk looked at Trey and then Robin Hood. He now realized why Trey was ordered to come with him and not his brother Tommy Boy. He could boss his brother around. Robin Hood normally agreed with him and would follow his orders. Trey, on the other hand, would listen to Dak. "We will adapt to the battlefield. A few of us can kill a large number of those

Normand soldiers by going east and up the shoreline. We can ambush them and hit them hard and retreat until the next ambush. We will have them surrounded and their supply lines cut off. We will have them trapped, and we will choke them to death. This is what we must do." His eyes narrowed and wrinkles appeared in his forehead as he stared at Trey.

Trey looked angry at Hulk for even suggesting they change the plan. He pointed his index finger at Hulk, "Vulture did the same thing as you. He did not follow the order to burn Waldo Bridge. Now the Normand army is in control of that region on both sides of the river. We are going to do as we were ordered, and we were ordered to protect the escape route."

Robin Hood looked at Trey, "If we kill the Normand soldiers, we have secured the escape route. They will not be expecting us to attack from the shoreline."

Trey looked very angrily at Robin Hood, "So far, the Normand army has out schemed our commanders at every opportunity in this battle. Their commanders knew they needed the Waldo Bridge intact and outsmarted Vulture. You two do not get it. They know what we are going to do before we do it. Dak said we are all overconfident after the battle of New York and Harpers Ferry Harbor. He told me to make certain you two kept to the battle plan. Our army down south will be on the run when they come this way. We need to keep the escape route open."

"Dak is not here. We need to adapt to the battlefield. I am going east and up the coast and kill all the Normand Soldiers I can. I will also cut off their supply lines. You can take the squad and secure the retreat route," declared Hulk.

Chapter 42

Dak looked at his lieutenant. "I hope this works. Remember to keep the white flag high, so they can see it. Please do not become clumsy and drop the flag." The man glanced at Dak while sitting on the horse overlooking the hill. He looked concerned and a little afraid as he secured a deep breath. He then turned his horse and rode toward the front lines.

As he rode, he was in constant fear as he kept the white flag high in the air. He looked in front of him as he rode through the high grass, small bushes, and small trees. He reached the small hill close to one mile north of the Waldo Bridge. He waved the white flag back and forth. He noticed movement from his right flank as the front guard of the Normand soldiers, hiding in the weeds and brush, stood and approached him. When they were close to fifty feet apart, he commanded, "That is close enough. My General is requesting a summit with King Solman under the terms of a white flag."

The Normand sergeant looked at his five soldiers. He thought about the man in the open with the white flag. "What is there to talk about? You can have your summit with me."

"We have something your King covets and without this proposed meeting, he will not ever see it. You need to tell King

Solman to meet us here in two hours. Tell him two hours and do not be late." The lieutenant turned and rolled north.

The sergeant turned and ordered to the rider on his left, "Ride back to the command center and tell General Rivers the rebels want to talk under the terms of a white flag. Report that they want to talk face to face with King Solman in two hours."

***

General Rivers looked at the approaching rider as he walked into the command tent. "Sir, the rebel army has sent a messenger under the terms of a white flag. They are demanding they talk with King Solman."

General Rivers was mad, "They are trying to buy time to move their forces backward to another defensive line. We need to crush them." He reached upward with his right hand and forced his fingers tightly together into a fist. He stared at the rider for a second and thought about the request. He knew King Solman was approaching the command center. He knew he would report great news about the condition of the battlefield and the winnings of his army, but still he also knew King Solman might not be as happy as he was with the results. He commanded, "We will wait for our King."

To Kill a Blueblood

***

King Solman rode a white stallion along with his six guards and the squad of horse soldiers. They were all dressed for war. He immediately dismounted and entered the command tent. General Rivers looked at King Solman as he walked by his guards with his jaws clinched. King Solman pointed is index finger at General Rivers and immediately commanded, "Why are you not pushing north? Why is my army sitting on this side of the river?"

"Your Excellency, we have secured Waldo Bridge, intact. We are moving our army across the river. We have broken through their lines all the way across the battlefield. They are in full retreat. We have one-hundred-and-twenty-seven prisoners sitting in the ditch ready to burn them alive. We trapped them here at Waldo Bridge. The plan worked better than I thought. Maybe the rebels are not as well equipped as we were informed."

He yelled, "You idiot. We must have a fast win. We must push the rebel scum all the way north and off the continent. Why have you not killed the prisoners? We do not take prisoners in war."

"Sir, they sent a messenger under the terms of a white flag. The commander of the Rebels asked to speak to you. They said they had something you desire. They request to meet you in fifteen minutes on the knoll a mile north of Waldo Bridge. We waited for you. What are your orders?"

King Solman looked at the general with ill contempt. He thought about the concession and the one thing he desired more than anything. "What is our status on the battlefield?"

"Sir, my troops are well rested. I have lost six hundred-thirty-nine men in this battle for the Waldo Bridge. I have three-thousand men across the river. The rebel scum cannot pull enough soldiers from their other regions to stop us. I can march on Harpers Ferry Harbor in two days. There are pockets of resistance; however, the rebel forces are in full retreat. Waiting for you has not set me back. My plan of attack has worked perfectly. I have total control of the battlefield." General Rivers looked at King Solman, knowing his strategy had worked better than he had estimated. He waited for the King to pat him on the back for a job well done.

"We will go meet the scum." King Salmon turned and walked out of the tent. He looked at his Captain of the guard and announced the meeting. "I, General Rivers and eighteen of my guards will meet the rebel scum on the hill."

***

Dak rode to the top of the hill in the high grass at a slow pace. He ordered his lieutenant to sit on the hill with the white flag while he watched for the Normand command to proceed to meet them. Dak was aware of the large number of Normand soldiers who had crossed the bridge and appeared to be resting. Dak looked over at Zenith as they came to a stop next to the lieutenant. Dak turned to the lieutenant, "We should never have allowed that bridge to remain standing. See how fast the current is flowing, and how wide and deep the Broad South River is at this, the narrowest point? The Normand army would have spent a half a year to a year on the other side of the river to rebuild that bridge with our army at their throats. Well, here I am. Are they coming?"

"Sir, I do not know." The lieutenant took a deep breath.

Dak noticed the lieutenant was nervous. "Make certain you do not become clumsy and drop that flag." He smiled at the lieutenant, "Looks like a good place for an ambush. All they have to do is attack us from three sides and then cut off our retreat." Dak tried to smile at the dire situation.

The lieutenant responded, "Yes sir, it is a nice place for an ambush, and my grip on this white flagpole is solid."

The sergeant next to Tommy Boy was watching through his binoculars and announced, "Here they come. There are twenty of them."

Dak looked west over the valley, "Yes, here they come. They are hard to miss riding all white horses."

King Solman rode in the middle of the column next to General Rivers. There were four guards in front of him and sixteen guards behind him. They all were dressed in the same looking gray uniforms and rode fifteen hand high white Camargue horses to the hill crest. The column stopped close to twenty-feet away in a line facing Dak and his soldiers. King Solman sat on his horse observing Dak and his men for three to four seconds as his column of soldiers aligned themselves facing Dak and his troops. King Solman then stared at Dak, "I see you scum followed the White Flag protocol with twenty men. We also followed the White Flag protocol. So, you and your warriors have elected to dress in all black. That is a fitting color for you rebel scum." He kept watching Dak, "I understand you are the scum who has been blowing up my ships, killing my men, and committing treason against my kingdom. This land is my land and you and your rebels are all trespassing. I give you three hours to get the hell off my property before I impale every last one of you."

Dak felt his anger spike with the King referring to him and his troops as scum. He stared back at King Solman, "It is you who has committed crimes against the people in the south. You need to be held accountable for your men killing innocent people and taking their land. I am here to stop the brutality caused by you and your army. You attacked my people at Cliff Tops without provocation."

"I do not have time for this. You are a common outlaw. We could kill you and your men here and now, but we are under the terms of the White Flag. What is it you want?"

Tommy Boy looked at King Solman with scorn, "Have your men try it. I dare any one of them to come forward. We will drop our White Flag, and you may drop yours."

"We have shown you scum that you are no match for my army. I might grant you the opportunity to surrender; otherwise, we will kill every one of you rebel scum and place your heads on stakes for all to see." He looked at Tommy Boy, "I had a report that two large men talked with my stable workers. I have had to punish those citizens for not coming forward with that information."

Tommy Boy thought of Denco and his manager. Could they have been tortured for talking with him and Trey? He could feel his temper starting to flare.

"You, big man, would be no match for any one of my men."

Dak knew King Solman was trying to bait Tommy Boy. He looked at King Solman and said in a commanding voice, "Why not me and you right now? The loser's men will be required to lay down their weapons and submit to the winner's army. This could save a great deal of unnecessary killing."

King Solman smiled and looked at Dak. He raised his right hand and waved his index finger at Dak, "Why would I do that? I can have my men kill all of you in time. Matter of fact, I could sit and watch as my men kill all of you right now. That sounds like a gesture of desperation."

Zenith noticed movement and glanced to her side. She noticed Dak was releasing the strap on his sword while keeping his right hand and lower arm hidden under his shield being held by his left hand. She could tell Tommy Boy was on the verge of picking a fight with King Solman and his guards. She knew she needed to intervene. Zenith reached up and pulled her hood back allowing the hood to fall over her back. King Solman was surprised to see a Blueblood warrior, and his front two guards adjusted their horses. They both glanced at King Solman with understanding that the seriousness of the people they were now facing had just changed. The Normand guards realized they were facing at least one Blueblood and maybe more.

Zenith said, "I am certain I could kill at least half your men before they could strike any blood. I would suggest you not be so arrogant and listen. We requested your appearance for a reason. Now we wait for another rider."

King Solman lifted his right arm in a gesture of surprise, "So, you two are the notorious ones with the thousand pieces of Merlin gold reward wanted dead or alive from the Merlin government. I have heard of you. You two are famous outlaws." He looked at Dak, "So, you are the drifter that beat the Blueblood in the trial by combat with the short Sai sword. I look forward to collecting the reward placed on your heads." He turned to his men, "The man who kills these two will be rich and famous."

Dak looked at the Normand guards, "That much is true. In addition, we stole three treasure chests full of Merlin gold headed for you while at sea. I will give any one of you five pounds of Merlin gold to kill this man called King Solman. I will make you my friend, famous, and rich."

King Solman saw six additional riders headed for the crest of the hill coming south toward them. He was watching them closely. He heard Dak offer his men Merlin gold to kill him, and his face turned red in anger. "Why don't you relinquish the white flag? Then, my men could kill all of you right now."

Dak unfastened his other sword and then positioned his shield in front. All the warriors prepared for battle. Veronica pulled even with the row of Dak's men and the five guards stopped in a row several feet behind her. Veronica pulled her hood back to her shoulders. King Solman seemed surprised. He smiled, "Hello wife. How are you doing?" He did not wait for her to answer. "You are going to leave with me."

Veronica looked at King Solman, "Husband, there will need to be some concessions before I agree to leave with you."

Dak looked angry and announced, "You are not leaving with him. Matter of fact he is not going to leave here alive."

Veronica commanded, "Hold your position."

King Solman looked at Veronica's guard Michael, "You five are my King's Guards. I ordered you to bring my Queen to me. I can see you have done that. You five will be well rewarded."

Veronica announced, "They are my guards, and they are here to protect me."

King Solman looked at Michael, "You have committed treason if you do not do as I say."

Veronica turned and looked at Michael, "You have permission to speak."

"The Queen saved us from being decapitated at great risk to her life. She saved all our lives. She literally pulled us away from the chopping block. We five have sworn to protect her with our lives. This is our oath taken when we were elected to the King's Guard as protector of the Queen. You know this to be true. You were present when we were sworn into the brotherhood of guards to protect our Queen."

King Solman looked at Veronica, "You rode here by yourself on a horse with the five guards. Who are they protecting you from? I want to know."

Veronica answered, "I am certain Damon, the malcontent Blueblood, will try to kill me if he sees me again. His master will order my death. You know this to be true."

"The Bluebloods in Merlin will try to kill me prior to me giving birth. They have sworn to kill or abort all pregnancies where a female is pregnant by a Blueblood."

"So. It is true. You are with my child?"

"It is true. I am with child. If you wish to ever see me again, you will need to make some concessions, or I will head north. There are two armies north of our location that are larger and stronger than this army you now face. The people in the middle of the continent will join those armies and you will be outnumbered. At some point, they will unite. You have already attacked my home at Cliff Tops. Your generals know to capture that city it would take a considerable amount of fighting men to breach that city's defenses. It would take you several years to be able to conquer Cliff Tops and by then, your child will be grown and fighting in my army."

King Solman looked at Veronica in her black leather attire and her long dark hair. He could not control his desires for her as he noticed her curved body as she sat with her back straight in the saddle. "I could kill everyone here but you and take you. Why would I need to make concessions?"

Tommy Boy raised his bow quickly with an arrow in an aggressive move. Zenith pulled her sword looking directly at the two Normand soldiers in front of her. The Normand soldiers all pulled their swords or leveled their spears.

King Solman looked at Dak and noticed his smile and the twinkle in his eyes. He realized he had just ridden into the trap. He recalled how General Cuez had been singled out and killed by these warriors he was now facing.

Veronica reacted and rode her horse between the two adversaries. She looked at Tommy Boy and demanded, "Stand down. All of you need to stand down." She looked at her husband, "You need to order your men to stand down. I assure you husband; you and your men will be killed on this hill if you elect to pursue that path. We know you are a Blueblood renegade from the old Germany country. General Cuez confessed to General Dak before his head was removed, after these two killed his six personal guards. His guards were better trained than your guards and yet they all died. You might want to consider that before you order your men to a certain death." She stared at King Solman.

King Solman considered what Veronica said and noticed she had placed herself and her horse sideways in front of Dak,

Zenith, and Tommy Boy, blocking them. He also noticed her five guards approached the front of the line watching her. He raised his right hand and commanded, "Stand down."

Veronica turned her horse and rode back to her prior position while everyone seemed to relax. The weapons were all lowered.

"What are your concessions? Tell me now. I grow tired of this conversation."

Dak announced as he looked at King Solman and then at Veronica, "I am not going to allow you to leave with him. That is not my agreement with you. You cannot trust this psychopathic maniac. He was engineered to be cruel and dishonest. That is what he does."

Veronica turned to Dak, "It is my decision, and I will make the decision." She looked back at King Solman, "Do you recall the conversation we had in your office after you returned from your four-day meeting right after we were married?" She paused.

"Yes. I recall the meeting."

She knew by his expression he remembered her telling him she did not like to be beaten, whipped, bitten, and mistreated with the baton. "That is concession number one."

King Solman started to consider not ever seeing his child or his wife. What she described of the north and the city of Cliff

Tops was accurate. The city was positioned on the top of a cliff overlooking the ocean. It would be difficult to lay siege to the city in the rough ocean waves and even more difficult to penetrate the natural defenses. His master ordered General Cuez to take the city and mine the coal. He announced, "My dear wife, I agree to this concession."

"Then, I will not repeat the concession for everyone to hear." Veronica then announced, "Concession number two is you will release all the prisoners of war (POWs)."

He looked mad, "Those rebels have burned my men. I will not release any of them."

Dak's anger spiked, "Your soldiers have done far worst to innocent farmers. We watched as your soldier rammed his sword into the belly of a pregnant women and then the squad of soldiers killed every single child, woman, and man in a small defenseless village."

Veronica interrupted, "What difference does it make if you release the men you are holding as prisoners? You have control of the battlefield. You can have your soldiers kill them in a future battle. We all need to make concessions."

King Solman looked at his wife, "What is the next concession?"

"These five guards led by Michael, assigned to protect me and fight for me, you will not interfere with my guards." King Solman shook his head yes.

Veronica announced, "The last concession is that you will take your army south of the Waldo Bridge and the Broad South River which will divide the two territories. Your armies and your spies will not be allowed to cross the river. You will sign a treaty documenting this binding agreement."

Dak could tell he was going to decline and before he spoke, "The mid area plains are great for farmland and ranches. The river will supply an endless supply of water. The farmers and ranchers will be granted a thirty-day period to be able to move across the river north if they desire. Once you sign the treaty, no one will be allowed to cross unless our governments agree."

Veronica looked at her husband trying to determine his thoughts. He was a complex man and very difficult to read. He never showed emotions except anger. King Solman glanced at Zenith who was sitting on her horse with her hand holding her pulled sword. She likewise had positioned her horse to attack his guards to the left. He knew she no doubt would kill several of his guards. He then glanced at Dak holding his shield in his left hand and with his right hand resting on his sword handle with his horse directed to charge at him. He noticed Dak's right index finger was taping back and forth on the handle of his sword. He had won a match against a trained Blueblood warrior in Merlin and killed his Blueblood general, General Cuez. The other large man was in position to attack with his bow positioned behind his shield and the arrow pulled tight. The rest of the soldiers were ready for battle. He then realized his wife had stopped the trap by riding in front of these soldiers. He announced, "You will leave with me, and I will agree to your terms. Send me the treaty to review." He turned and told his men to retreat.

General Rivers looked disappointed with the agreed compromise, but he then followed his King and the King's guards. Once they turned and were out of hearing range, General Rivers announced, "I have the army on the run. I could have killed their king and ended this war."

King Solman harshly announced, "You are overconfident and reckless. My Queen saved our lives. She positioned herself between the Blueblood, the general, and the large soldier. The Blueblood would have killed several of my guards before we could have turned our horses to run. The large man with his arrow pulled tight was going to change his aim. He was not going to shoot the guard straight across from him with the shield up. You would have been the first to die by his arrow. If you noticed, the rebels always kill our command team first." His voice got louder, "Their king killed General Cuez and six of his guards. General Cuez, in the early years, beat me in every match. He was not going to allow me to survive. You fool. This was a trap for them to kill us, and she stopped us being killed."

***

Tommy Boy rode past the other soldiers and pulled next to Dak, "Did you know that Veronica was going to leave with them?"

Dak kept the pace of the horse and his forward stare. He did not answer. "Dammit, you knew. This was all planned."

Dak blew out some air and then said, "Veronica came up with this plan. Zenith and I argued with her over the details. This is the only way our army does not get slaughtered."

Tommy Boy was mad as they rode the horses toward camp, "We could have killed those bastards." He then looked at Dak. "You cannot allow her to be sacrificed. This is not like you to allow one of your friends to be killed. You know what he will do to her. You know he is a psychopathic maniac. You know what they are capable of doing to someone."

Dak thought back to the meeting in the command tent with Veronica and Zenith. He had argued with Veronica. He had told her they rescued her to save her and not to turn around and send her back into the lion's den. Dak remembered how Veronica hesitated during the disagreement like she wanted to say something but did not know how to say it. Veronica finally looked at him and asked if he recalled the Bible story of Sampson and Delilah. After he acknowledged he did recall his mother teaching the lesson when they were age ten, Veronica then mentioned she would obtain the hidden location of the Master Rogue Blueblood, otherwise, they will not win the war. She then told him this was her decision, not his.

As soon as Veronica left the tent, Zenith asked Dak about Sampson and Delilah. He grimaced when he told her, "The theme behind the Bible story of Sampson and Delilah is that it is good to be strong physically but better to be stronger spiritually. Delilah used her looks and love making abilities on Sampson until Sampson allowed his spiritual beliefs to dissipate and then Sampson gave away his secrets. He died an ugly death after having his eyes gouged out. We must have faith in Veronica."

Dak looked at Tommy Boy, "Like I said, this was her plan, not mine. She is pregnant, and she elects to be with her husband. Now, I do not want to discuss this topic. The decision has been made. I understand your concern. I appreciate your position. Veronica will be in constant danger, and we will not be able to rescue her a second time."

Tommy Boy looked at Dak with a frustrated expression as they rode the horses toward Harpers Ferry Harbor. Tommy Boy then out of frustration punched his horse and rode faster toward the city.

Dak looked over at Zenith, "The plan is well conceived without anyone else knowing except for us three. Dammit, Veronica's plan better work."

Chapter 43

Hulk crawled to the ridge and hid behind the large granite boulders and shrubs. He counted fourteen Normand soldiers. Robin Hood crawled up next to him. Hulk whispered, "I believe they are on patrol, and they appear to be resting. They removed the saddles and bridles from their horses. They have no guards posted. A couple have taken off their chest protectors, and their swords are sitting next to the saddles. Those are nice horses tied off. The ranchers in the area must have supplied them the horses."

Hulk's face turned red with anger as he listened to the last part of the report.

Robin Hood listened. "What are they singing? Why are they making so much noise?" He hesitated, "We need to kill them for bad singing if for no other reason."

Hulk declared, "Get the men ready. Three on the left flank, three on the right, two remaining with us in the middle. Let us get this done while they have no guards."

***

The large granite rocks along the ridge and on the hillside provided excellent hiding spots. The side of the mountain was covered in small shrubs which concealed the men. The three on the left flank followed a path made by wild boars and other animals. They waited for Robin Hood to give the signal.

The men on the right flank positioned themselves a little further away, but they were all concealed behind a large granite boulder. They had a clear path to run on foot toward the unprepared Normand soldiers. Hulk's plan was for he and Robin Hood to crawl within thirty feet. He knew if they could shoot two arrows each as the other men were charging the unprepared soldiers, they could kill the rest with swords. He knew his men were experienced in fighting with swords. He had hand-picked them for this mission and left the inexperience teenagers with Trey. Hulk motioned for Robin Hood. Robin Hood motioned for the men to the left and right flanks. He and Hulk raised their bows and fired two arrows, each hitting four men. The men rushed out of their hiding places and killed or wounded the unprepared Normand soldiers. Hulk ordered, "Hold up." He looked around at the Normand soldiers lying injured or dead. The sergeant said, "They raised their hands to surrendered. They did not fight back. What is up with this?"

Hulk walked over and stood over the Normand soldier with an arrow through his back sticking out his stomach. The soldier gritted his teeth, "You damn rebel scum. You broke the treaty. We were ordered to leave the area. King Solman signed the treaty with your general. You have broken the treaty. We should have never trusted you scum."

The men looked at Hulk and the soldier. Hulk was confused, "What are you talking about?"

The soldier was in pain and knew he was going to die from the arrow. He looked around on the ground at his dead comrades, "The war is over. We were to be granted safe passage to the south side of the Waldo Bridge. The Broad South River is the negotiated line between our two armies.

***

Trey looked at the message on the paper and turned the paper over to the back to verify if there were additional information. He first felt relief and smiled. He then thought of Hulk, Robin Hood and the eight soldiers. They would not be receiving the message. He was not certain where to send a runner to contact them. He looked at his sergeant over the troops in platoon three. The man was covered in mud. His clothing was dirty and smelled. Trey's men provided the relief and reenforced the front line. All the soldiers were wet and dirty from the rain which had lasted for a solid day. When Trey had arrived five days prior, he had explained he was now a general, and he would be taking over the command. He then explained the dire situation to the four sergeants. He explained to them the importance of the mission, they could not give an inch of ground. "We must keep the road open for the army to retreat. If the army fighting along the southern front cannot retreat, then they will be forced to surrender. The armies from New York and Cliff Tops will not be expected to assist this far south." The order was given to the four sergeants and the men dug in to defend the dirt road. Trey set the schedule where the troops could rotate from the front lines daily, and he also provided them cover fire from archers.

The sergeants had explained they were farmers, ranchers, preachers, and schoolteachers. The men of the militia had not had prior training to be warriors. Trey had noted the lack of training, and his men would provide the needed relief. He also reinforced the order they would not give an inch.

Trey then glanced at the rider from the south, "You can help yourself to the water and food." The one sergeant turned to him, "General Trey, what is the message from General Dak?"

He then turned to the sergeant, "I am not certain how this has happened, but there is a ceasefire ordered. We are to hold our ground. The war is over."

He yelled the good news. "The war is over." The men all celebrated with smiles and relief. Trey said, "We will need to keep eyes on the Normand soldiers. They should also be informed of the cease fire."

The sergeant walked to the front lines and told the sergeant over platoon two and asked his men to pass the word. He mentioned the Normand soldiers might not know of the mandatory withdrawal. "Until they pull out, we will have to keep fighting them if they attack."

***

Trey looked at the four sergeants standing under the command tent out of the rain. "I do not want to lose any more men. I sent a man south to confirm the details of the cease fire." He ripped a white sheet in half and tied it to his spear. "I am going to the front line and let the Normand soldiers know the war is over."

Trey proceeded to walk from the tent into the rain along the muddy trail and to the front line where the Normand marines were thirty feet from his soldiers. The trail was a well-used path in between small trees and shrubs. Men were stationed along the path in tents and fire pits made of rocks. At the end of the trail, both forward groups were hidden behind embankments. When the Normand soldiers would charge, the first response was the northern soldiers would fire as many arrows into the charging men as possible. Then, the swords and spears would be utilized in some of the most brutal fighting of the war. There were men lying dead on the ground and men wounded after each charge. Trey waved the white flag back and forth. He waited for the Normand commander to step out from the hidden ditch. Trey yelled, "I am General Trey. We just received word the war is over. There has been an ordered ceasefire with a treaty signed by King Solman."

The Normand commander yelled, "That is bull shit."

Trey yelled, "Our orders are to defend ourselves only if attacked. You should be receiving the ordered ceasefire from your commanders in the south." Trey walked back behind the embankment. He looked at the squad of ten men who all looked tired, dirty, and scared. The men had all fought hard and killed Normand soldiers as they attacked. They had also watched as their comrades had been killed. "I really hope they do not attack. The ceasefire is real. However, we will defend this ground if necessary."

Trey walked south along the trail and talked to the soldiers as he passed their tents. The men seemed relieved with the news and appreciated Trey's personality of caring for them. Their conditions, stationed in the mud along the trail and living in tents were difficult. The hedge was so thick on the hillside no one could cross through the underbrush without first forging a trail by cutting the hedge. The small hedge-like bushes had very little open area, except the trail which had been cut back by the soldiers when they prepared to defend the route north. Trey had considered starting a fire with the wind blowing northeast and burning the Normand soldiers out, but the near constant rain kept the area too wet for a fire. Now Trey waited for the Normand soldiers to retreat. He thought of home, and how he missed his city and friends.

Chapter 44

Veronica sat on her horse on the south side of Waldo Bridge with her five guards lined up next to her as the POWs walked by them heading across the Broad South River to the waiting wagons to transport them to Harpers Ferry Harbor. The men looked weathered from not eating and being held prisoner. They appeared to have given up and accepted their fate. They knew the Normand army would not extend the needed resources to keep them alive during an extended war. She stared at Vulture as he made eye contact with her as he walked by her sitting on her horse. Vulture also made eye contact with the five guards sitting next to Veronica. She then noticed the young man that arrived at her motel door early one morning and updated her that her guards had been captured. He walked with a limp and only stared at the road in front of him. The Normand guards had their spears and swords held in a threatening position facing Vulture and his men as they walked along the road. Vulture had blood on his forehead and dirt baked into his exposed hands and arms. All the men appeared to be injured, and all had on torn, dirty clothing. Some had been beaten. The last POWs were being carried by other POWs as they crossed the Waldo Bridge.

Michael announced, "Princess, I counted one-hundred-and-twenty-seven men."

Veronica turned to her guards, "We ride south." She kicked her horse in the sides and galloped south with her five guards following her.

***

Veronica walked to the guards standing in front of the doorway to the command tent. "I request to see the King."

She then tried to walk past the two guards, and they blocked her path. "I told you I request to see the King. I am the Queen, and I will not wait a second longer."

The guard on the right walked into the tent and announced the Queen is requesting an audience with King Solman. King Solman heard Veronica outside his command tent demanding to see him. He smiled to himself as he thought of her demanding attitude. He also knew his command team inside the tent also heard her talking to the guards. He motioned for General Rivers and advisors to leave. He then motioned for the guard to allow her to pass. "What is on your mind, wife?"

"We have been riding south for two days, yet you have refused to order me to your tent to bed me." She looked at him. "Why is that?"

King Solman was surprised. "I figured you are pregnant, and I needed to wait."

She cut him off, "I have my needs. I seek enjoyment the same as you. I will be allowed to come into your tent tonight." She was stern with her statement. She then turned and walked out of the tent.

***

Veronica slowly allowed her gown to drop to the floor around her bare feet, allowing him the full view of her nude body. She walked over to her husband. She smelled of roses and many candles were burning around the area casting a soft light inside the tent. She started removing his shirt and then his pants. She looked into his eyes, "I prefer to be on top." She directed him to lie on his back on the bedroll. She kissed down his body and back up to his crotch. She looked at him, "You certainly are a good-looking man." She licked him and then sat on him rotating her hips until he moaned with gratification.

Three hours later he held her tight. "I am truly sorry for mistreating you on our wedding night."

Veronica placed her hand on his chest and looked him in the eyes. "I do not wish to be beaten or mistreated. I understand you have your vices. I would be okay if you want me to perform with Brad as you watch. I understand you enjoy this. If you set this up, I will perform for you."

King Solman considered what she had said. "Why the five guards? Do you really think they can protect you from me?"

She smiled at him. "If you want to be a good father, first you must be good to the child's mother. I hope you will be a good father. As I said before, they are to protect me from Damon. He will come to kill me and our baby. I will not allow this to happen. I will need to be permitted to train my guards on how to be better warriors."

"So, you are scared of Damon?"

Veronica rubbed her hand across his chest. "I am more concerned about the Bluebloods from Merlin. They have sworn into their law to kill any normal female that is pregnant by a male Blueblood or abort the pregnancy if the female is a Blueblood and the father is a normal male. They do not wish for the perfect code of the Blueblood DNA to be altered through pregnancies. If my tribe was able to figure out you are a Blueblood, the Blueblood council in Merlin will figure it out. They should be able to spot one of their own easier than we could. They will come for you and our baby."

"What about your tribe and the armies north? What will they do?"

Veronica looked at him. "I will protect my husband from them. I will not allow them to attack your city or you. You need to stand behind the treaty. The world is very complex, and you need to make alliances to survive with the right people. I have talked to sailors from the Asian continent. Asia has more land than our continent but less natural resources like fresh water and farmland. The living conditions are more difficult in the desert-type environment. Most of the land mass is desolate where the ocean floor rose above the sea level when the earth reshaped during the Transition Period. The Religious Sect located in the northern part of the Asian continent is trying to take over that continent and is fighting for control of the limited resources and natural ocean ports. Once they have sufficient control of the Asian continent, the Religious Sect will attack our continent. We cannot avoid war. Our history is full of wars and our destiny is to battle with others. The Persian people in the north are led by a Religious Sect and their goal is to rid the world of everyone but their Sect. They worship the old religion Islam with focus on the part of the religion that promises a fertile heaven if they die with honor in battle. They are very devoted and very deadly." She looked at him, "You were created in a lab for two reasons. One is to fight as a warrior and be a leader such as a king, and the other is to fuck me. There are a lot of wars to be fought in this world, and I am your wife, here to please you. You will be a busy man." She lifted herself on top of him, straddling his body. "While I am unable to perform my female duties due to my pregnancy and child rearing, I will arrange for you to have concubines who I will personally train to serve your needs." He smiled and pulled her down and kissed her on the lips. "One more concession. I name our children." She smiled at her husband while looking down at him.

He smiled, "You may name our children."

"By the way. What is your real name?" She kissed him on the neck and then the ear.

My given name at birth was M1204. I heard a priest's sermon once about the Holy Bible and liked how he described King Soloman and his wisdom. I selected his name."

She sat up and looked him in the eyes, "Lord have mercy. Given your birth name, M1204, I believe it would be better if I name our children. I figured you never embraced Christianity or Judaism. Did you know the correct spelling for the King of the Jews was Solomon and not how you spell your name?"

"No. I have never read the Bible, nor do I have a desire or need to read the Bible."

Chapter 45

Veronica looked at her five guards. They all were good men and great castle guards. They were adequate fighters with a sword and lived by the oath of loyalty. "I will not allow you to work out with the King's Guards. You are not allowed to enter any fighting tournaments. What you learn stays within this group. We will start working out every day at five A.M. You men will need to get stronger, faster, and more agile. I will also teach you how to be more efficient with bows and swords. We will start every morning with a five-mile run. The most important thing I will teach you is the mental aspect of combat. You must learn how to fight as a team and recognize your personal fears and then overcome those fears. When you fight for your life, you will become scared. Fear will distract you. We are going to learn to fight our insecurities. Do you men know what a Berserker is?" She waited. All five men shook their heads no.

"A Berserker warrior was the fiercest Viking warrior ever to wage war with a sword, a spear, dual-handed axes, a bow, a knife, or their hands. The men would reach an emotional state and become intoxicated with killing the opponent. During a battle, they would become animalistic in killing the adversaries. They were so fierce they were thought to have self-induced hypnosis which, based on their subconscious personalities, made them ruthless in battle." She looked at her five men. "To kill a Blueblood, you must master the use of your weapons, fight as a team, and be a Berserker."

She looked at the men, "To kill a Blueblood warrior is different from killing a normal soldier. To kill a Blueblood warrior will be an extended battle where you will need to wear him down, working as a group, and wound him a little at a time until he can be killed. There will be no quick kills fighting a Blueblood soldier. To kill a normal soldier, you are taught the faster you kill the soldier the better, so you may move on to the next soldier. That strategy will not work when killing a Blueblood warrior. Some of the Blueblood warriors are immune to pain. They do not slow down like a normal man would when they are injured. The condition is called Congenital Insensitivity to Pain or Congenital Analgesia. You will need to recognize this condition and understand his ability to keep fighting after he has been wounded. The team will be required to injure him a little at a time and take away his ability to perform until someone can provide the kill shot."

She looked at each man standing in front of her, "My goal is for you to advance quickly with the bow to shoot accurately. You will be taught to hit a target while running or while the target is moving, but first you must learn to hit the target standing still. The target area whether it is a foot, a hand, or a heart has a radius of four inches or smaller. That will be your target size. A Blueblood can anticipate the path of a spear or arrow and can block either with a sword in their hand. Their quickness is one of the things you cannot duplicate. They can also anticipate your next move. You may only have one clear shot at a Blueblood, and you must make the shot count." Veronica looked at Michael and then Hector, Cruise, Pretty Boy, and Viking. "Do you have any questions?"

Pretty Boy smiled, "Are we going to be forced to walk down the road to the nun's door in the nude and ask her for a cup of water?" The group smiled.

"Only if you want. I understand you guys got a lot of sympathy from the young ladies during those walks."

The guys all smiled when Pretty Boy said, "You can call it sympathy, but we call it something else." The guys all laughed.

Michael asked, "Why are we concentrating on killing Bluebloods?"

Veronica hesitated. She then looked at each man, "Because that is who will be trying to kill your Queen. Now, let us start our run. You guys need to learn to keep up with me and then improve to be faster than me. This will come with time."

.

***

Three weeks later, Veronica announced, "Running five miles and jumping rope has made all you quicker and more agile. You will need to keep up this workout. Rope jumping will assist you by making you a hard target. A faster soldier is a better soldier. A quicker soldier is a better soldier." The men stood in a line in the workout arena. They were hot from the run and jumping ropes. They all were standing, holding their shields. "Michael, hold your shield in front of you." Michael pulled his shield up and held it as instructed. Veronica quickly fired an arrow hitting the shield in the middle. "I need each of you to know what it feels like to have an enemy fire an arrow at you. I do not want you to panic under fire. If you panic, you will die. When you incircle a Blueblood and fire an arrow, you might miss. You must learn to keep your shield up in front of you to protect you not only from the Blueblood but from friendly fire. Now each of you bring your bows next to me and fire two arrows into Michael's shield. You will all take turns. I want you to know the sound of the arrows hitting your shields. When this happens in combat, you will not panic. The shield will not fail you. Only your fear will fail you."

***

The men all lined up in the workout area. The darkness of the night was of no concern to the men. They had become accustomed to the five A.M. workouts. Veronica looked at her five guards, "It has been three months, and now I feel the need to remind you, to kill a Blueblood warrior will be a process. You will have to use all the tools around you to win. Little things will make the difference. I hope by four months of training, you will be working better as a team and also be individually better than any of the King's guards and soldiers. Now let us begin our run."

***

King Solman looked at Veronica across his table. "You seem to be glowing. You have such a wonderful smile."

She looked at her husband, "My belly has swelled. I can feel our baby kicking from time to time. I believe the pregnancy agrees with me."

"You have now worked with your guards for five months. I also understand they are required to eat four, high protein meals daily." She looked at him closely. "I was thinking about having a tournament for the soldiers and the guards. The men all look forward to these activities. The winners are famous, and the purse winnings are very hefty. The winners are also able to advance in rank and some have chosen to be my personal bodyguards. There are always a few citizens who participate. The crowds love the fighting tournaments and the winners."

Veronica glanced away from her husband, "I do not wish for my five guards to participate in a tournament. I do not wish for them to be injured. I also do not wish them to compete against one another. Your soldiers, guards, and citizens should provide great entertainment for the crowds, and the winners will enjoy the spoils of victory." She then smiled and made eye contact with the King.

He took a bite of food. "That is a shame. I was hoping to see how good they are in combat. I understand you have made certain they have practiced more than the soldiers and my guards. I understand they run five miles every day prior to lifting weights, and after lunch, you have them shooting arrows at moving targets, while they are running and riding. You also have them shooting arrows at flying clay pigeons. You have ordered ten times the number of arrows than the entire regiment uses during their training." He took another bite and glanced up from his plate, "I even understand you have them shooting arrows into the shields of each other. It does not sound like you are concerned with their safety."

Veronica knew her husband had men watching her train her guards. She had set up an area two miles from the city where they would jog to and then work as a team on how to attack a Blueblood. These workouts were not noticed by her husband's spies. "That all is true. I miss the workouts, but since I am in my third trimester, I am unable to spar, lift weights, and run." She appeared to be nonchalant, "You know men are injured in the tournaments or even killed. My men will not participate." She then looked at her husband, "I understand you are riding out to meet your master tomorrow."

He looked at her angrily. She knew the pride he felt in himself, and he would not like the comment. He ate two additional bites of the steak. "That is true. I have a meeting. I will not discuss that with you."

"What about this man? Why is he so secret? Why not invite him to your castle? What makes him greater than you?"

He thought to himself, "The master is vicious and violent. He lives without mercy. He impales people on twelve-foot poles to teach fear to the people he commands. He looks evil with his four front upper incisor teeth. This makes his mouth look larger than the normal man. His bald head is elongated with two pointed ears. He is a strong-looking man with several tattoos." He looked at Veronica, "He is not ready to reveal his identity. I will not discuss this topic with you."

"I understand you have been providing food to the poor. Where did you obtain gold to purchase the meat and corn for the peasants?"

"Your Queen is wealthy and chooses to help the poor when she can. Who will be going with you? when will you return?"

He stared at her. "I will be traveling with my squad of guards. You ask too many questions."

She stared back at her husband. "I also understand that my sexual desires have declined with my pregnancy. I have a gift for you." He looked surprised. "Her name is Rosemary. She is a dark skin Spanish female. I believe you will enjoy her company for a few hours. I asked her to meet you in your chambers at eight-thirty tonight. I also explained to her what she should expect, and I expect you to act like a gentleman."

Chapter 46

Michael walked past Pretty Boy as he held his position in the hall at the Queen's chambers. The two men saluted as he passed. He opened the door and entered. Michael stood and waited for the Queen. "You summand me my Queen?"

Veronica looked at Michael. "Please step to the balcony. We need to talk in private."

Once on the balcony, Veronica turned to Michael, "You are my most trusted guard. I need something handle with great secrecy. I need to know if I can trust you. I need to know you will only share my request with one other person."

Michael looked at the Queen with concern. "My Queen. It is an honor to guard you, and I would die for you if needed. I am your loyal guard."

Veronica turned to the view from the balcony, "I need to know who our King is beholden. Our King has a master, and he is scheduled to ride to meet the master tomorrow. I need you to hire a rider to follow our King and report back to you. I will pay the rider one piece of Merlin gold to follow the King and one piece of Merlin gold when he returns with the information."

"You ask me to spy on the King?"

Veronica stared at Michael, "I ask you to protect your Queen. Our King, I do not believe has shared the fact with his master he has taken me as a wife. I will be given birth in weeks to come. I need to know my baby will be protected. My child is half Blueblood, and there are those that will kill the child if the news is revealed."

***

Michael dressed in plains clothes and met the man at the bar. He knew he needed someone who needed money but also was capable of carrying out the mission. The man had a reputation for being responsible for importing contraband items and also dealing with smuggling people in and out of Southern City. Michael glanced at the man, "I need something done fast and done in secret."

The man looked at Michael, "Who are you?"

"You know who I am." Michael pulled a Merlin gold coin out of his pocket and held it for the man to see.

The man looked at the gold, "Who do I need to kill?"

"No one. I will give you another Merlin gold coin when you report back to me. The mission needs to be kept between me and you." Michael explained the mission and emphasized the need for the mission to be secret.

The man looked at Michael, "Spying on the King is dangerous. Who is paying me this money?"

"You will be working for me. You are being paid more than enough for a few days work. Do you want the job or not?"

The man looked at Michael and noticed his jaws were clinched, and he needed the gold. With this much gold, he could sail to another part of the world and start a legal business. "I will take the job."

Michael handed him the gold coin. "I know where you live. I know where your wife and kids live. I know your brother and two sisters and their families. You better not disappoint me."

***

The rider stayed out of sight. He was careful as he followed the horse tracks across the wilderness. When they stopped to set up camp at the end of the day, he rode a mile north of their trail, and he camped. He slept without a fire, so no one would be alerted to his location. Following King Solman and his twenty men on horses was not difficult. His concern was riding into guards left behind on the trail to verify there was no one following. Michael told him if he was captured, he would be killed. He also explained as soon as King Solman made contact, he was to report back the location. The mission was of utmost importance, and secrecy had to be maintained. The rider felt the gold coin in his pocket. He knew he would receive another gold coin when he returned. He went to sleep and woke early in the morning. He had circled around in front of the King, and his men as they camped along the coastline. His plan was to stay hidden and allow them to pass him.

The next day he watched from the thick underbrush as the King and his men rode past him. He picked up the trail and followed them to the small inlet. When he saw the ocean in the distance, he noticed the sailing vessel anchored in the cove. He scanned the horizon for other ships, and made certain the only vessel was the one anchored in the cove. He tied his horse to the tree limb in the thick underbrush and walked closer on foot. He hid in the grove of trees in the open field, and positioned his binoculars to watch as King Solman, and two men rowed the small boat to the waiting ship. The anchored ship was close to one-hundred yards from shore and flying a red and gold flag with a dragon symbol. He did not recognize the flag. He studied the flag and forced himself to remember the design and details. The man thought the boat with the flag would be enough to locate the owner of the vessel's home port. He noticed King Solman and two guards climbing over the rail of the rear of the ship while the rowboat was tied off to the portside. A sailor met him on the ship and directed him to the interior cabin. He counted a crew of eleven men working on the large sailing vessel. He waited with anticipation with the ship possibly sailing away, but the ship never pulled up the anchor. He directed his binoculars toward the twenty Normand soldiers. They had dismounted and were waiting on the shore for King Solman to return. He made certain all the soldiers were on the shoreline and known of them had back tracked toward his position.

Close to half an hour later, he noticed King Solman walked from the cabin. He struggled crossing the rail of the ship and appeared to be holding his right arm. The rider noticed the right hand was missing as he crossed the rail and hurriedly climbed down, using only his left hand. The two sailors rowed the small boat toward shore.

The rider turned and ran to his horse. He knew he needed to beat the other riders to Southern City. He needed to provide the message to Michael and meet him at the rendezvous location.

***

King Solman noticed his master's two guards and the two men holding the rowboat. They would be paddling the rowboat out to the sailing vessel. He knew the helmets they wore hid their shaved heads. He also knew the four men had all been castrated. Being castrated was the last step for the men to show their allegiance to the master. The guard stationed at the rowboat announced, "The master has demanded to meet with you and you alone. Your men will wait here."

He stepped into the rowboat, and the men pushed the boat away from the shore. His men all dismounted and sat down on the ground and waited.

He was anxious to see the man he feared the most. He knew he had pledged his soul to serve his master. The cult had grown over the years with normal humans from the local tribes being captured and forced to serve. There were a few Bluebloods that were identified and convinced to join the cult in the early period after the Transitional Period. King Solman stared at nothing as the rowboat got closer to the waiting ship. His dread increased as the rowboat pulled next to the sailing vessel. He climbed aboard and then walked into the main level cabin. He saw his master sitting in a chair with a look of disappointment on his face. The two guards closed the door and stood watching. He bowed his head and waited. "You have disgraced me. I provided you with the means and the ability to take that entire eastern continent. Yet, you defied my orders and signed a treaty which stopped the war." He was outraged and yelled, "I do not remember giving you an order to sign a treaty. Your army had the rebel scum on the run."

"Master Drake, let me explain."

He abruptly got up from his chair and walked in front of King Solman. "There is nothing to explain other than you are a worthless, gutless prick. I thought about replacing you with another. You act like you are the master. I am forced to remind you who your master is in a way you will never forget." He pulled his knife and walked behind King Solman. The King stood still and anticipated his death.

"I do not want to hear your excuses. I am willing to provide you another opportunity. I know what the problem is, and I have undertaken steps to remedy the obstacle."

King Solman was relieved and took a breath of air. He then was confused, "Sir?"

He spoke calmly as he walked back in front, "I understand you have taken a wife, and the wife is from the northern country. She was present when you agreed to the terms of your treaty. Matter of fact, she was the one who offered the terms of the treaty to you representing the rebel scum. I also understand she is with child. I was surprised to hear she is over seven months pregnant. I do believe this woman has poisoned you, and I cannot afford for you to be under her influence. I am your master."

King Solman looked around the room for Damon. He just realized Damon was not present. His heartbeat increased. "Sir, my wife is not the problem. I can handle her. Please recall Damon. I will do better in the future. I am sorry I signed the treaty. I thought by us taking all the land north of us to the Broad South River and not losing hardly any men, you would be pleased. Master Drake, I beg you not my wife and unborn child."

Master Drake clapped his hands and in walked two additional warriors. They were dressed similarly to how Damon dressed, and they had the look of both warrior and killer. King Solman did not realize there were two additional Blueblood warriors under the control of the master. The master had kept them hidden, and their existence a secret. They were covered in tattoos, and each carried multiple weapons. "No. King Solman, I disagree with you. I have taken steps to cure you of your illness. You know I turn all my soldiers into eunuchs, so they will not be distracted by perils of the world. A female can be deceptive and persuade men to take paths even against their better judgement. A female can turn men against other men and brother against brother. Your wife will be dealt with by Damon and then we can be friends once again. That decision has already been made and, if I know Damon, he will be headed back here by now. I really hope you understand why I had to send Damon." He hesitated, "You do understand, don't you? I am freeing you of your cancer." He stared at King Solman.

King Solman was devastated. He had never imagined his wife would be killed. He always assumed he would protect her and his child. He did not realize Master Drake knew of his marriage and her pregnancy. He tried to hold back his emotions of dread. He felt the stare of his master. "Yes, Master Drake. You are so wise." He looked at the two Blueblood men standing in front of him and realized at any moment Master Drake could order the two to kill him, and there would be nothing he could do to defend himself. He also knew the two other Blueblood men standing behind him at the exit door. They all had the pointed ears and the look of cold-blooded killers. He knew he could not beat Master Drake in a battle, let alone four Blueblood soldiers. The master was too strong, fast, and vicious and the soldiers would be obedient like guard dogs to the orders of the master. No one could beat the master. He knew he would be impaled and left to die while hanging on a pole if he disagreed with Master Drake. He thought of his limited options.

Master Drake declared, "I must deal with this before returning home. You need to be motivated to do what I instruct you to do and understand there are consequences for not performing as I see fit. You will not assume to know my plans." He smiled and walked in front of King Solman. "After all, you are my number one commander," he held his left hand out, palm up.

King Solman looked at his master holding the sharp heavy long knife. The knife's curved blade sparkled in the sunlight coming through the window, "Sir?"

"You will return to Southern City, and you will carry out my future orders and force the rebel scum to succumb to you or you will order your army to execute them. The Merlin army will be ordered to cross to the east coast and wipe out those rebel scum located in the city of Cliff Tops. Now, you will be allowed to choose your punishment. Either place your right hand on the table or pull down your pants."

"Sir." King Solman looked concerned at the right hand holding the large knife. The understanding of why he was to place his right hand on the table registered in his mind. He could not fathom pulling his pants down. He placed his hand on the table and looked directly in front of him. The swing by Master Drake was swift and clean with his fourteen-inch knife cutting through the flesh and bone. His right hand fell to the floor. The four Bluebloods warriors did not flinch. Master Drake commanded for the medic to come at once.

King Solman realized the medic was on standby. He appeared within seconds and placed a bandage over his stump

and the arm in a sling. King Solman listened as the medic
further explained he needed to have the bandage replaced
every twelve hours. He sat down and was lightheaded from the
sudden blood loss and the realization he had his right hand
severed. He now knew he could never win a sword battle with
Master Drake. His master had just weakened him to remind
him how easy the task would be to kill him in the future. He
realized what he must do as he tried to gain his resolve. He
gathered his wits and walked to the boat rail. He struggled at
first without his right hand to cross the rail and climb down to
the waiting rowboat. He held his right arm as he left the boat
and the men in the rowboat started rowing the boat and headed
back to the beach. He knew he must try to make the trip to his
castle and try to save his wife if possible.

Chapter 47

Veronica woke early and rubbed her belly with the coconut lotion. She felt movement and smiled to herself as she admired her swollen midsection. She had been thankful her pregnancy had been an easy one. She then dressed. She thanked Dezie for delivering her food at four thirty A.M. She ate a healthy breakfast as she sat looking out the balcony door enjoying the warm breeze blowing through the open doors. After her meal, she walked to her balcony and looked at the beautiful view over the city. She could see the ocean in the far distance as the moon light reflected off the ocean surface. She could also look down on the city and could see the fires and streetlights throughout the city, which always created an especially pleasing view for her. She could see the silhouettes of merchants and others walking the sidewalks and streets in the darkness of the night. She knew the sun would be rising within the next hour. The sun rising was always a spectacular scene over the ocean's eastern horizon. She walked to the corner of her balcony, glanced around the corner of the castle at the rear of the castle and noticed there was no one to be seen on the street at the rear of the castle. Veronica stared over the city and had a questionable feeling arise in her mind. She tried to recall what was bothering her as she stepped away from the balcony into her quarters. The feeling was like she forgot something, but she could not place her finger on the forgotten item. She felt her baby move and smiled to herself.

She thought about her husband and his trip to meet his master. She could not gain his confidence and discover the identity of the secret cult. He would not talk to her about the cult, and she now understood he was not the type of man that could be manipulated. His personality was one of confidence and vanity with little, if any, ability to feel empathy for others. He wanted to always be in control of the situations, soldiers, citizens, and most of all her. The meals and evenings she spent with him were always controlled by his desires. He would not allow himself to be drawn into conversations of small talk or to discover interesting facts about others.

She thought about her plans for the day which consisted of her going to the arena to watch her guard's workout. She then thought about her breakfast as she retraced her steps. Dezie had not mentioned anything of interest when her breakfast was delivered. Dezie did not know when her husband would return from his trip. She also worried about the rider Michael had sent to follow her husband and his men. If the rider was captured, he would be forced to talk, and then Michael would be killed and if Michael talked, she would be killed. She bit her lower lip in concentration, "Why the sudden feeling of dread that came over her this morning while she was looking over the area in the rear of the castle? There was nothing to see. What had she forgotten?"

Her memories flashed through her mind, "That was it, nothing to see." She turned and ran back to the balcony to the corner wall and focused her view back to the rear entrance of the castle and kept her eyes fixated on the entryway. Veronica realized there was no one on guard duty. Her adrenaline elevated as she knew someone would have ordered the guards to leave their posts. An ominous feeling hit her. She reached for her belly and thought, "What are the chances with my husband being on a trip, and no one is guarding the castle for the first time? Where are the castle guards?"

She quickly walked over to her sword and knives. She placed her sword around her waist, fastening the belt and carefully hiding two knives, one in her sleeve and one in the top of her boot. She quickly picked up her bow and satchel of arrows. She eased to the door and slowly opened her door. She was relieved to see Pretty Boy standing guard. He noticed her sword and bow as she walked past him. He followed her to the stairs where she hesitated and listened while holding her hand up for him to be quiet.

"Are you alright, my Queen?" whispered Pretty Boy.

She motioned for him to be quiet a second time. He knew something was not kosher with her actions and since her belly had swelled, she had not carried her sword around her waist until now. She listened. She heard a door hinge squeaking as the door was being opened very slowly in the lower level of the castle. She knew no workers should be working at this time of the morning. Only the two castle guards at the front and two at the rear should be on duty watching the doorways. The King's guards had ridden out with the King. She motioned for Pretty Boy to hurry behind her. They descended the stairs and walked to a small hall and then down the smaller stairs used by the maids. They descended two additional flights of stairs leading to the large wooden shelf. "Hurry and pull the shelf away from the wall." Pretty Boy did not waste time. He pulled the shelf out while Veronica stood and listened. She opened the hidden wooden door, and Pretty Boy pulled the door cabinet back in place and closed the door. They walked through the arch block exterior foundation wall. Pretty Boy removed the heavy steel water grid cover, and then he assisted Veronica out the small opening. They exited the castle to the south side of the building. They walked up a small set of hidden stairs to the city street. "Why are we taking the hidden passage?"

Veronica turned to Pretty Boy, "Are you guys ready? I believe I am in danger. There were no guards posted at the rear exit to the castle. I believe the noise we heard was made by an assassin."

"Yes. We are ready to defend our Queen and each one of us will die for our Queen, if necessary."

She looked left along the sidewalk and then to the right, "I have spent all this time training you, so you would not be killed." She turned to Pretty Boy, "If I must die, it will be our Lord's decision. You five men were trained to win, not die. I believe the assassin is a Blueblood with assistance within the castle. Protecting me will not be easy."

He looked confused. "Inside the castle! We will fight for our Queen."

"Follow me." She led Pretty Boy the long way to the guard workout arena. She noticed the arena was empty as she walked into the open area. The moon light provided ample ambient light to see the main area; however, there were in the shadows, small pockets of shaded dark places. The sun was a few minutes away from cresting the eastern horizon, and she was careful to look in the dark, shady areas around the weights and the punching bags. "I will hide in the dark corner. I will be okay here by myself. We will make our stand here where we have trained. We cannot outrun the assassin. He must have help from the army. He will be allowed to find us. You need to hurry and tell my guards the perils I now face. You will need to travel to the back alley and use the rear gate. I suspect the front castle guards are already dead or ordered not to respond. There will be no one to help us. This is the reason you guards have trained, and it is now game time."

"I do not wish to leave you by yourself." Pretty Boy understood the fear and recognized what they were up against.

"I cannot run in my condition. You need to hurry. We have trained as a team. We might all die here today as a team. Please hurry."

Pretty Boy ran fast, backtracking up the steps and then turned right as he ran across the street, down a small alley to the small apartments. He opened the door and ascended the stairs two at a time to the small second apartment. He first knocked on Michael's door. Michael opened the door. "We are live. Our Queen is in danger from an assassin and is waiting for us in the arena. We will battle to the death today. This is no drill. I will tell the others."

He ran to the room of Cruise and woke him. He then knocked on the door of Hector and Viking. The men met at the door to Michael's apartment. All were carrying their shields, bows, and swords.

Michael looked at his friends, "We can do this. Remember our training." He then yelled, "For the Queen."

They all chanted, "For the Queen."

They ran toward the arena. Once they got close, Michael
motioned for them to split into two groups and quietly proceed
to the arena from the front entrance and rear door. As they
approached, they heard a man's voice which was harsh and not
an accent they previously recognized. Michael gave the signal
to be prepared to enter. He needed to allow his men enough
time to approach from the front entrance and the rear door
coming in from the street.

***

Veronica sat in the corner of the arena in the darkest
shadowed area and waited. She listened to the sounds of the
city waking up. She knew it was a matter of time before the
guards were reported missing at the rear gate. The city patrol
made rounds every six hours. However, the next round would
not be scheduled until the guard's shift was over at seven A.M.
The thought occurred to her, "Who in the castle is helping the
assassin?" She then took a deep breath, trying to relax and
considered if she had overreacted. "Maybe there was no
assassin. Maybe she should have walked to the rear entrance
and verified why the guards were not present." She was aware
of her increased emotions caused from the elevated estrogen in
her body. She sat still and thought, "Have I now allowed my

feelings to take over and cloud my judgment? My pregnancy has been so easy until now."

She glanced at the sky and the heavens. She noticed the beautiful stars in the northern sky and the half-moon in the western sky. She thought about how she missed her home and growing up with her friends, and how she made a mistake coming back to Southern City. She had underestimated her husband. She had thought she could win him over to the extent he would confide in her. She thought back to the command tent and Dak and Zenith arguing with her. It was her decision. Now, the morning sun was close to rising in the eastern horizon, and she knew her life may be over. She took a deep breath and thought about her baby living inside her. She suddenly heard the sound of someone walking on the gravel leading to the arena. The gait slowed like someone being cautious. She could tell the sound was created by only one person and not her five guards. She thought about her guards. Would they make it back in time to save her? She waited as she held her breath. The figure came around the corner of the arena. She immediately recognized the silhouette in the moonlight and knew Damon's stride as he walked around the corner leading to the arena. She remembered his strongly built-body with the outline of his cape and hood. He looked around and then stared directly at her through the darkness while she was sitting in the shaded dark corner. She slowly stood and walked to the wall of the arena in front of where the weights were located. Damon stared at her and then walked further into the arena. He then glanced around to make certain she was by herself, "I went to your chambers and hoped you would still be asleep. I am glad I located you. I understand you have five guards. Where are they? I hope they did not abandon you in your hour of need. I look forward to killing them. I understand you have trained them for six months."

"You seemed to know a lot about me and my guards. My guards are none of your concern. What is it you want from me?"

"We have some unfinished business. Do you know why the master sent me?"

Veronica stared back at him, "Because he is too frightened to come out in the open and face me himself. I now know you were sent by a psychotic, scared man to kill me. Your master waited until my husband left, so you could fight just me. Since one of us is going to die here in this arena, allow me to ask one question. What man in the castle has assisted you?"

"General Redman." He smiled, "My master knows a great deal about you. I can assure you; he is not scared of you. He fears no man." He smiled and stared at Veronica, "This is not personal. You are correct on one account. I was sent to kill you but not the baby. I was sent here to bring your baby back with me. I will kill you when I cut the baby out of your belly. I have a small satchel to carry the child. I will feed the child some of my blood and care for the child until I return to my master. The child will be raised by my master." He pulled the brown leather satchel strap over his head and off his back and laid the satchel to the side.

Veronica felt the sudden nauseating feeling of her unborn baby being removed from her body and raised by a cult, "The child cannot survive. It is too soon."

"My master disagrees. You are seven months and three weeks along with your pregnancy. The Blueblood child has matured at an accelerated rate."

"You seem to like killing people. You hung those ranchers in Tanger in a tree after you skinned them. That makes you a psychopathic maniac killer. I will not allow my child to be raised by your master or cared for by someone like you."

He raised his hands, "I wanted everyone in the Tanger to remember me. They had to be taught a lesson. I will revisit them in time. They were made aware of the consequences if they helped an outsider. The Master has a set of rules for them to follow, and they broke the rules. I had no choice but to carry out the sentence. The men had to be punished. Now, we have talked enough. The time has come for me to kill you. If you come here, I will make it fast and painless. If you make me sweat, I will skin you alive. Either way I will take the child, and you will be dead."

"Where does your Master hide? Why does he not come out?"

"What my master does is not your concern, and where he lives will not matter to you."

"You will need to break a sweat to kill me. I will fight for my unborn child." Veronica raised her bow with an arrow in one quick motion without aiming and fired the arrow directly at Damon's face. He quickly positioned his head to the side and reached up and grabbed the arrow in midair in his left hand. He held the arrow in front of him and observed the quality. "Very nicely made. It is a problem for you. Those arrows will not work against me." He then threw the arrow to the side and reached over his left shoulder and pulled his sword from the sleeve attached to his back. The sword was a thick straight steel blade. The handle was black, eight inches long, and the leather was worn from use. He started to approach her.

Veronica noticed movement from both sides as Michael ran in front of her with his shield up and sword pulled. He stood directly between her and Damon. He was followed by Pretty Boy. Hector and Cruise ran from the open area behind Damon and now had him surrounded. All had their swords out and shields raised. Viking walked out from the rear street door the same as Michael and Pretty Boy with his bow loaded and stood at the entrance.

Veronica watched as her men took their position. Her guards had been perfect in their spacing and held their positions all focused on Damon. Damon stopped and looked at the guards as he turned a circle and smiled and pointed his sword at each man, "What do we have here? I will kill all of you. You are no match for me."

Veronica commanded, "Defend your Queen." Each man took two steps closer and made the fighting area smaller. Damon lunged at Michael, and Michael jumped to the side. He rotated two steps to the side as all the men rotated the same distance. Damon turned slightly from facing north and more to the east as he considered the five guards and how best to kill them. He then lunged at Pretty Boy. Pretty Boy likewise jumped to the side and rotated two steps to the right, and the other guards did the same. Damon rotated more to the east and seemed confused why no one was attacking him. The fact was that the four guards were quick to move and then reset their position in a circle around him. He looked at Veronica and noticed Hector was now standing directly in front of her. He then tried to attack Michael a second time. This time he got close to Michael as he swung the sword, but Michael blocked his swing with his shield and was too agile to be hit by the sword. He rotated two steps to the right and the other guards did the same.

Damon quickly, in one motion, pulled a throwing knife and threw the knife at Michael. Michael kept his shield in front of him and watched the direction of the knife. He moved the shield to keep the shield in front of his body. The knife hit the middle of Michael's shield and stuck. Michael did not show fear after the impact from the knife as he peered around the shield at Damon. The four guards all held their shields in front and stepped two steps to the right. Damon turned as they turned and noticed one guard had not fired his arrow and Veronica held her bow to her side. He then quickly ran forward and swung his sword at Michael. He pulled back expecting the other guards to attack. Michael quickly rolled to the right, turning over in the sand and all four guards rotated the same distance to the right, keeping Damon in the center of the circle.

Damon looked perplexed. He started to feel something was not kosher with these guards. They were not attacking and were keeping their distance. He felt as always: his goal was to injure the adversary as quick as possible and then torture them as he pleased. He noticed they were very agile and able to dodge him. They did not show fear in the face of battle with him. He was trying to ascertain their weakness when suddenly, the sunlight cleared the east wall and beamed directly into Damon's face blocking his vision.

Veronica noticed the sunlight clearing the block wall, causing Damon's vision to be obstructed. She commanded, "Attack."

Pretty Boy, Hector, Cruise, and Michael all exploded toward Damon with their swords swinging. Viking fired two arrows. Damon rotated and blocked the sword swings, and the first arrow fired by Viking. The second arrow fired by Viking hit Damon in the bicep on the right arm. The men stepped backward into their position and waited. They realigned themselves with the same spacing and the same distance from Damon.

The men noticed Damon had not shown any signs of being hit by the one arrow as the arrow pierced deep into the arm and was wedged against the humerus bone. He did not seem to notice the arrow, but he reached over with his sword and cut the arrow off. The feathered end fell to the sand floor of the fighting pit. Veronica called out, "No Pain." The guards recalled Veronica explaining how some Bluebloods were engineered to have Congenital Analgesia.

Veronica commanded, "Attack." The four guards with the swords pushed the issue harder this time and swung three times each. Damon was incredibly quick and could block the swings from the guards and then rotate away from the guard and take on the approaching guard. Viking was forced to guess where Damon might be before he released his arrows. Hector swung his sword high trying to drive Damon backward. The attempt failed with Damon blocking the sword and then in one motion swinging down and hitting Hector's upper leg before he could move backward. He had underestimated Damon's quickness, and the mistake had cost him. He fell and then crawled out of the circle. Viking fired an arrow, and the arrow went wide, passing Damon as he moved to his left. The arrow traveled into the shield of Michael. Michael did not allow the arrow to break his concentration as he kept pushing the attack and kept his shield up. Veronica fired an arrow trying to provide cover for Hector. Damon blocked her arrow while swinging his sword and long knife at the other guards.

Viking knew they needed to injure the Blueblood. He guessed Damon might rotate to the other side of the arena after hitting Hector. He fired his next arrow low almost even with the ground. Viking hit Damon in the left lower shin. The other three guards reset themselves and waited. Damon showed no signs of being hit by the second arrow. He did not bother to pull the arrow from his leg. He looked at the guards with ill contempt. He also seemed to relax his posture and reset himself for the next assault. He now seemed to consider that with the one guard injured, he would now win the battle.

Veronica knew she had lost one guard and knew she could not afford to lose another. Damon was too gifted with his swords. She commanded, "Attack." Michael and Pretty Boy both lunged forward and swung their swords trying to push Damon backward. Damon fought back and blocked both swings. He then jumped forward toward Pretty Boy and bumped Pretty Boy as he blocked the arrow fired by Viking. The impact forced Pretty Boy to the sand covered floor of the arena. The second arrow fired by Viking was at the torso. Damon turned and blocked the arrow as he was fighting the other three guards. The sunlight was in his eyes, and Veronica released her arrow which hit Damon in the left hand holding his long knife as he was swinging to kill Pretty Boy. Pretty Boy rolled over in the sand and threw sand into Damon's face. Damon instantly swung his sword and cut the arrow in his left hand. He showed no signs of hesitating as he then blocked the two swings by Cruise as Michael rolled in the sand and stuck his small knife into the right shin of Damon. He rolled backward as Damon missed him with his swing with his long knife. Pretty Boy got back to his feet and pressed the attack from the right as Cruise pushed inward from the left. The men tried to keep Damon always fighting at least two of them. They also tried to keep their shields raised at chest level in case an arrow missed Damon. If given the opportunity, caused by hesitation or doubt, Damon would kill these men.

Veronica tried to obtain a clear shot as she moved her bow from side to side. Michael positioned himself in front of her to protect her. She was concerned if she missed, she might hit one of her guards. Cruise had worked himself in behind Damon, and Michael was standing in front of her. With Damon moving so quickly, she knew she needed to guess at where he would move next. Her and Viking fired three quick arrows. Two of her arrows either missed Damon or he blocked the arrows with his sword or long knife as he was in a constant sword fight with the other three men. Veronica was now standing behind Michael. She moved her bow from side to side trying to capture a clear shot and not hit her guard. Veronica kneeled on one knee and released the arrow from behind Michael. Michael's body blocked Damon's view of the arrow as he moved into the path of the arrow. The arrow traveled within less than an inch of Michael's ear as he was bent over trying to determine when to attack with his sword. Her arrow hit Damon in the lower stomach. Damon looked up and noticed Veronica was kneeling on her one knee behind Michael. He realized his mistake as he noticed the arrow sticking out of his lower belly.

The fighting stopped with Veronica stepping forward. Michael, Cruise, and Pretty Boy watched with their shields raised and their swords held ready to swing. All the men were tired and covered with sand and sweat. Viking pulled the string tight on his bow with the arrow leveled at Damon. She signaled her men with two fingers by her side which they understood from their training meant they should be ready for an aggressive assault. She then flashed one finger toward Michael and two toward Pretty Boy. Viking kept his bow aimed and waited as Damon considered Veronica's signals and commands to her guards.

Damon placed his long knife into the sleeve. He pulled the remainder of the arrow out of his left hand by using his teeth. He then reached behind him with his left hand and broke the sharp end of the arrow and then reached with his left hand and pulled the arrow from his stomach. He then broke the sharp end of the arrow and pulled the stub part of the arrow out of his bicep and then did the same with the arrow in his leg. He looked mad at the group watching him as he held his sword in front of him with his right hand as he now was positioned in front of the large wall with the guards and Veronica circling him. He then reached and pulled his long knife from the sleeve with his left hand and motioned for them to attack him.

Veronica announced, "The stomach wound is fatal. Your arrogance and pride have killed you. You should have waited for General Redman and his men to arrive and assist you with killing me. You now can try and run from us, but the outcome is certain. You have ten minutes tops. Your stomach acid will leak into your belly region and pollute your other organs. You are a standing dead man. I demand you tell me where your master is hiding before you die."

Damon seemed to understand his dire situation. He raised his sword in front of him, yelled, and charged at Veronica. With Pretty Boy on his right and Michael on his left, both had anticipated the move, and the two timed their swings perfectly with both swinging their swords. Michael's sword swung chin high and Pretty Boy went low for the ankles. Damon blocked Michael's swing but could not rotate fast enough to block the low swing by Pretty Boy. Michael rolled backward and stood. Pretty Boy's blade caught Damon in the right foot cutting deep into his dorsum and the talus bone. Pretty Boy then rolled in the sand with the anticipation of Damon swinging at him. Pretty Boy was quick to his feet and stood. The sword to the foot caused Damon to stumble. As Damon fell, the arrow fired by Viking from the side hit Damon in the left upper arm with the arrow traveling through his humerus bone and entering his rib cage.

Damon fell in the sand and tried to quickly stand. His left arm was pinned against his side by the arrow. He tried to raise his long knife in his left hand but realized the left arm would not move. He was confused why he could not raise his long knife. He had not felt being hit by the arrow and turned to discern what was holding his left arm in place. Veronica rushed forward and stood next to Cruise. She fired her arrow into the top of Damon's head from four feet. He slowly stood with the arrow sticking out the left side of his neck. The arrow had entered through the right part of the frontal lobe and exited his left neck region. She then dropped her bow, pulled her sword, and swung hard right to left in one continuous motion. At first, her men thought she had missed. Michael and Pretty Boy both started to rush Damon from each side as Cruise stepped closer and was prepared to attack. As Damon tried to lift his left arm to block the sword of Veronica, he realized his arm could not be lifted. Then, he started to lift his sword with his right arm, a line of blood suddenly appeared across the front of his neck. His head rolled back exposing the cut across his throat. The blood gushed from his neck with each pump of his heart and ran down his chest and robe. He looked at Veronica and then his body swayed forward and then backward as he fell in the sand. His hood fell back revealing his pointed ears and a thin layer of skin on the back of his neck which kept his head attached to his torso.

Veronica immediately rushed to Hector lying against the wall, "How bad is wound?" She could see the open cut and the blood on his hands and leg.

He grunted and appeared to be scared, "The cut went all the way to the bone. I am having trouble controlling the bleeding." He had sweat pouring from his scalp, and seemed to understand the wound might be lethal. His face was flushed and pale.

Veronica spread the wound open and inspected the area. She commanded, "I must clamp off the femoral artery." She pulled a hair pin from her hair and pulled the skin apart spreading out the muscle. She located the severed artery with her fingers and pulled it, stretching the artery toward her. She then clamped the artery tight. She tied the belt tight around the upper leg to reduce the blood flow. She then ordered Pretty Boy and Cruise to secure a tight bandage and take him to the doctor. "He must have surgery immediately." She then looked at Hector, "You should be alright. Be brave my Berserk warrior."

Pretty Boy tied the cloth around the leg and the two men picked their friend up and headed out the rear door.

She then looked at Michael, "Damon had help. General Redman has allowed him access to the castle. No doubt the general updated Damon on my morning routine. The general has no choice at this point. He will send the castle guards to finish the job. We are still in danger."

Michael turned his head toward the castle and alertly said, "Listen."

Veronica recognized the sound of multiple guards heading their way on the pavement and then the footsteps transitioned to the gravel. "Come on." The three ran to the door leading to the street. Viking gently opened the door. Michael stepped across the threshold and looked both ways. He motioned that the road was clear. Viking led the way to the old church, and he firmly knocked on the door. The three stood in the exterior main front door entrance with Veronica placing her back against the wall watching the street to see if the castle guards came through the door from the arena. Michael stood across from her with his back against the other wall watching down the street. Viking stood directly in front of the eye hole of the door hoping the elderly nun would hurry. He was prepared to knock a second time when the elder nun opened the door.

"Please, we request asylum." The elder nun looked at the three and then stepped forward to the edge of the sidewalk and looked both ways on the street. The nun could see the worry on their faces. The nun noticed no one was out this early in the morning, and the street was clear. She motioned them forward and stepped to the side. The three entered with the nun closing the door.

"Follow me." She led them along the hall and down the stairs to the basement of the church. The nun turned to Veronica, "I knew at some point you would come to me for help. You have helped these young women of our city, the poor, and I choose to help you."

Veronica looked perplexed, "How have I helped anyone?"

The nun smiled, "You have provided hope for the people of our city, and hope can lead to courage which can instigate change." The nun looked at Michael and Viking in their dirty uniforms and the blood on Michael's knife. "You may put your weapons away. This is the house of our Lord."

Veronica said, "They will have the same fate as me. We need safe passage to travel out of the city?"

The nun seemed to be reluctant to comment. "These two are my guards. There are three more. One of which is injured. All six of us will be killed if we are located. We need your help."

Viking cut her off, "My Queen. I will go to the medical ward to locate the other three before they are apprehended and bring them here before they are discovered."

Veronica nodded her head for Viking to sneak out of the church. The nun handed him a used priest's robe and suggested, "Wear this over your uniform. Make certain you are not followed. You may leave out the basement door on the rear of the building." The nun looked worriedly at Veronica. "If he is discovered, he will be made to talk, and we all will be killed. Now, we all have the same fate. Although the church is disliked by the leaders in this city, the King has ordered us to be left alone. We are not certain why we have been spared when so many others of our faith were impaled outside the city for all to see. Our King, I believe, would not hesitate to kill all of us in our church given a reason. We have very little resources, and those who choose to help stay hidden. I can assist you, but you must agree to help me."

Veronica looked worried as she watched Viking pull the robe over his head and exited the basement of the church, "What is it you require of me?"

"Follow me." The nun walked quickly through the large building. She came to a closed door. The nun turned to Veronica and Michael, "I need you to take these children with you. They need to be hidden and protected. If they are discovered, they will be killed." She opened the door, and Veronica followed her into a daycare. She saw four sleeping small kids ranging from one to three. At first Veronica wondered, "Why would these four small kids be killed?" Then, she noticed they all had pointed ears. Veronica turned to the nun, "These four children are all Bluebloods?"

The nun studied Veronica and then announced, "They all were children of girls who were slaves to our King. King Solman is the father. We had help and were able to remove the pregnant women from the soldiers' compound and saved the mothers. They each gave birth here in this room. You will take them with you."

Michael looked concerned, "Who is we? Who helped you?"

The nun looked directly at Michael and then Veronica, "I will never tell who helped us. I can arrange for you six and these four kids to be taken out on a merchant ship expected to arrive at our port in two days. You may board late at midnight on the third day. Until then, you will remain hidden and pray no one finds you. Do you agree?"

Veronica looked at the four kids sleeping, "Where are the mothers?"

Veronica noticed the nun looked older than she had first thought. She was covered in wrinkles on her neck, face, and hands. The nun looked concerned, "The four mothers had to leave the kids with us here at our church. The mothers did not have a choice. We must do what we can."

Veronica looked at the nun while holding her hand on her own belly, "If the Bluebloods in Merlin discovered these kids, they would be executed. The merchant ship will need to take us north to a remote place called Cliff Tops. Otherwise, they will never be safe."

The nun looked at Veronica, "The Normand fleet has the east coast of the continent secured with a blockade. We can place you and them on a ship heading around the horn and north toward Merlin. The captain will not sail across the ocean. His boat is not suitable for a long journey. He stays close to the shoreline."

"We cannot go to Merlin. These four children are part Blueblood and will not survive. The Merlin Senate will order their deaths. I know a port called Tanger located three days north of Southern City. We can go there, wait for spring, and then cross the mountains. But first, I need to write a letter to be given to King Solman once he returns. You will make certain he receives this letter. Now provide me with paper and pen."

Chapter 48

King Solman rode fast for eighteen straight hours and rested none. His guard detail was tired as they pushed the horses and rode into Southern City. The castle was a happy sight for the King. He handed off his horse to the stable boy and demanded his assistant to have his war council members present in the war room by three P.M. He was tired but eager to meet with his commanders. He also ordered his assistant to send the physician to his quarters immediately. He grieved at the loss of his wife the entire trip. As he rode, he had hoped his wife was unharmed, but as he got closer to Southern City, he realized Damon would not rest until she was dead, and she and her guards would be no match for Damon.

His guard knocked on his door and entered as the medic was placing a new bandage on his right arm. "Sir, you have a visitor. Dezie, the Queen's handmaid, has asked to see you. She declares her information is urgent."

King Solman motioned for the guard to allow her to pass. Dezie walked into the King's chambers. The guard closed the door as the medic walked out. King Solman was tired and irate. He was not patient. He looked at her and demanded, "What is it that is urgent?"

"I have a letter addressed to you. Someone left the letter outside my door two days ago." She handed King Solman the letter in the sealed envelope.

King Solman looked at Dezie, "Did my Queen suffer? Where is her body?"

"Your majesty, Queen Veronica, I believe is still alive."

King Solman was surprised. He turned and peered at the older lady, "How is that possible?"

Dezie hesitated, "Your majesty, I understand she and her guards have fled."

"Do you know where the Queen has gone?"

"No, I swear this to you my King, I do not know the whereabouts of Queen Veronica. I carried food to her the evening prior to her disappearing and also provided her with a breakfast at close to four A.M. that morning. She told me she had planned to watch her guard's workout later in the morning. She seemed to be enjoying being pregnant. She indicated the pregnancy agreed with her. Your majesty, I believe she would attempt to return to her birthplace and seek protection for her child."

The King was not patient. He had never liked to listen to Dezie and her drawn out answers. "You are dismissed." He recognized Veronica's handwriting on the envelope. He then motioned for Dezie to hurry. He used his teeth and jerked open the letter, *"Husband. I am not certain who I can trust and if you were part of the attempt on my life. I truly hope the attempt on my life was orchestrated by your master and not you. I want to believe you really strive to be a good husband and a great father. Damon indicated he was sent by your master to remove our baby from my body while killing me and kidnapping our child. I only hope you understand I will never be safe with you; I would ask you one thing. Please do not look for me or our child. Since your master intends to kill me and take our child, I will remain in hiding. The assassin's body, Damon, I left for you to see in the arena where I removed his head. Damon revealed he received assistance to commit my murder from General Redman."* He read the rest of the letter and walked to the candle and burned it.

***

King Solman walked into the large war room and looked at his generals and other advisers. They stood as he entered. He motioned for them to be seated. He positioned himself at the head of the table and stood looking at his seated audience. He demanded, "Where is my wife?"

General Redman looked straight ahead and responded, "She has disappeared. She has been missing for two days." King

Solman assumed she had been killed. He felt a sense of relief with the fact she escaped, and Damon was the one found dead. He had always feared Damon, who was cruel even for a psychotic killer. He tortured animals and people for enjoyment. Master Drake was able to control him and feed his sickness. He provided him opportunities to kill without mercy. General Redman then announced, "Her five guards have also gone missing. I can assure you, Sir, we will find them."

King Solman stood at the end of the table and waited for the news about Damon. King Solman allowed a few seconds to pass while he stared at the men sitting around the large table. General Redman then announced, "We had a visitor. The visitor was found dead in the guard workout arena two days ago. We can assume your wife's guards were up to the task. Sir, the visitor was the Blueblood named Damon. We located someone else's blood, but no other bodies. The castle guards arrived after the battle in the arena and found only Damon's headless body with several wounds to his person."

"What are your standing orders with regards to the Queen and her guards?"

"Sir. I have ordered the castle guards, the prison guards, and requested assistance from General Rivers to bring the five guards dead or alive to me and bring me the Queen alive."

King Solman felt the betrayal. His voice was commanding. "Why dead or alive? The guards were doing what they were sworn to do, which is protect their Queen."

General Redman could feel the anger stirring inside the King. "Sir, We felt the guards should have brought her to me."

King Solman's anger spiked. He thought, "So you could kill her." He changed the topic, "General Rivers, your orders are to plan to march our armies north. We will attack the north and push the Northern resistance all the way to the Midnight Hole. This attack needs to take place in the first of spring of next year. You need to provide me with a full briefing of your proposal of this upcoming war in two days." He started walking around the back side of the table.

General Rivers was a tall man with a long beard and a wide forehead. He looked perplexed, "Why would we stop at the Midnight Hole? Why not push all the way past Cliff Tops to the frozen tundra and glaciers?"

King Solman was tired and irritable after the long journey. He pulled the knife out of his jacket with his left hand and from behind he came up to the back of the unexpecting General Redman and sliced the neck of the general from one side to the other. The general reached for his neck and started trying to force air into his lungs by breathing heavily making a gurgling sound. Blood ran down the front of his chest and his eyes closed as he then fell dead on the floor.

General Rivers and the seven other men stared at the scene from their seats at the table. General Rivers then noticed King Solman was missing his right hand. King Solman observed General Rivers staring at his injured arm. "We all answer to someone." He held his right arm up with the missing hand. "General Redman forgot who commanded him. He assisted a Rogue Blueblood warrior to enter my castle and attempt to murder my wife. All this was done behind my back. I can only hope none of you are conspiring behind my back. His nude body will be impaled on a pole at the front wall for all to see. Guards, you need to go impale his wife and kids next to him. I better not ever find any of you guilty of treachery." With his jaws clenched tight, he walked out of the meeting.

Chapter 49

The guard walked into the army headquarters in Harpers Ferry Harbor with a man in handcuffs. "Sergeant, I have a possible spy from Southern City. He demands to talk to General Vulture."

The man in cuffs said, "I am no spy. I was paid to deliver a message to your general."

The Sergeant looked at the man in cuffs standing next to the guard. The sergeant stood from behind his desk and announced, "I will see if the General Vulture is available."

The guard and the man waited as the sergeant entered the interior office. "Sir, we have a possible spy, and he demands to speak to General Vulture."

Vulture looked at the sergeant. "I am busy. You know my policy dealing with spies. We hold them and then trade them for our spies." He then thought about the man being from Southern City. "Where did our border guards find this spy?"

"Sir, he did not come across the Waldo Bridge at our border crossing gate. He was riding in the open on the main road south about fifty miles from Harpers Ferry Harbor when our guards spotted him. He says he crossed east down river from the Waldo Bridge, so the Normand guards would not see him.

He rode through the mountains off trail. Sir, he insists to meet you. He says his request is urgent."

Vulture looked at his sergeant, "I have meeting in five minutes with our newly elected governor. I do not have time."

"Sir, the man was carrying two Merlin gold coins and several weapons. He was not hiding. He was riding in the open. He declared you would want to meet with him."

"Where is this man?"

"Sir, the guard brought him to me, and he is being held in the front office."

Vulture walked into the room. He noticed the prisoner was chained to the desk. He motioned the men out. "You have a few seconds. I am General Vulture. Now tell me what it is you need?"

The rider looked at Vulture, "I have an important message for you from Queen Veronica."

Vulture was surprised to hear her name. He knew he owed her his life and the life of one-hundred-twenty-six men. "What is the message?"

"I was told to provide you the message and you alone. The message is hidden in my boot."

Vulture ordered the sergeant to come into the office at once and uncuff the man.

Vulture looked at the message and then the messenger, "You can stay here with us, or we will escort you to the Normand front." He ordered the sergeant, "Provide this man his weapons and his gold. He may return to the south. You will escort him to the Broad South River if that is what he desires."

The man did not hesitate, "I was told to leave the message with General Vulture which I have done. I will return the same route which I came. I will return to Southern City."

Vulture thought about the new title Dak had bestowed on him. Dak announced the promotion after his return from being a prisoner, and his blunder with not burning the Waldo Bridge. He announced the promotion in the command tent in front of his men. Then, he announced his advisors, Hulk, Trey, Tommy Boy, Zenith, Robin Hood, and Veronica, which out ranked the generals. The newly formed government was to be head quartered in Harpers Ferry Harbor, and the New Republic government extended for several hundred miles in all directions. There were states established within the newly formed government, and the majority of the people of the middle of the continent agreed to the need of the established army and the newly formed government.

Vulture smiled to himself when Dak had declared he was now a general in the New Republic Army. He was responsible for the huge blunder and failed to burn the Waldo Bridge prior to the Normand army seizing control. Dak explained, "We must learn from our mistakes and that mistake will make Vulture a better soldier."

He looked in his hands and was now holding the information Dak needed. Dak explained the priority was to locate the leadership of the Rogue Blueblood Sect and destroy them. General Vulture turned to his lieutenant, "Pick three of our best men to ride north to Zenith Point. This note must be delivered to General Dak located at Zenith Point. If he is not there, they must find him. They will need to purchase additional horses on the journey. They will not stop for anyone. Make certain this message is given to only General Dak."

The lieutenant looked at Vulture, "Yes sir."

To Be Continued

ACKNOWLEDGMENTS

***

To my editor Carolyn Pegram for all the hard work.

To Chesnie Nichols for the book cover and formatting the book.

To big sister, Sherrie Rutherford, for all the loving help in writing book seven.